# Timepieces

W.A. Richards

Middle Earth

Published by Middle Earth Publications, Inc.
Copyright © 2020 by W.A. Richards

Edited by Alison Jefferson

illustrated by AveliyaDesign

ISBN: 978-0-9974512-5-2

Copyright fuels creativity, encourages diverse voices, promotes free speech, and creates a vibrant culture. Thank you for complying with the copyright laws by not reproducing or transmitting this book in any form or by any means, electronic, or mechanical, including photocopying, recording, or by any information storage and retrieval system, without permission in writing from the copyright owner. You are supporting writers everywhere and allowing Middle Earth Publications to continue to publish books for readers.

This is a work of fiction. All characters, incidents and dialogue with the exception of historical figures are products of the author's imagination and are not to be construed as real. The events during the meetings of the Continental Congress in 1776 leading up to the creation of the Declaration of Independence are historical and enhanced for the intended purpose of this work. Those situations, incidents and dialogues dealing with interactions between fictitious characters and historical figures do not depict actual events. In all other respects, any resemblance to persons living or dead is entirely coincidental.

[1. Science — Fiction, 2. Time travel — Fiction, 3. Interpersonal relations — Fiction, 4. Survival — Fiction, 5. Religious — Fiction, 6. Historical — Fiction, 7. Political – Fiction, 8. Apocalyptical — Fiction]

# Acknowledgments

This book is dedicated to my friends and family for having to endure my endless babbling about the story before writing it. To my daughter for insisting that one of the characters be given her name. And finally, I want to acknowledge my grandmother for whom the main female character is named.

# Prologue

**York, England, 1066**

The Archbishop of York lay face up on the bed, eyes closed, resting his head on the soft pillow full of duck down feathers: a gift given by Harold, Earl of Wessex, several years earlier—a singular indulgence he could not quite resign himself to sacrifice. The smell of the bedding brought back memories of his arrival here many years ago. It reminded him of a past long gone, of a place far away, well past Greenland—a place called Vinland. The Norse tried to settle the area but failed because of the harsh winters and their distrust of the natives. He was lucky to befriend the Norse leader, Leif, and get passage to Europe were his faith allowed him to rise in the church and become the archbishop.

Thoughts of his hometown came to mind. Those memories hadn't come up since the reign of King Edward the Confessor, many, many years before. A sadness washed over him, trying to remember the faces of his family—his mother, father, brothers. But they were just a blur now; mere figments of his imagination. It had been almost fifty years since he had last seen them. He missed his childhood home with its beautiful bay.

A click at the door caused the archbishop to freeze in his bed, making sure to keep his eyes closed. The door creaked open. For a few seconds he waited. *I am the archbishop, for Christ's sake!* How could someone be so audacious to enter without first knocking? Turning his head on the pillow toward the door he caught sight of the surprised look on the impudent man's face. He yelled out before the man could escape, "I am awake!"

The intruder stopped in his tracks, staring back, wide eyed. Despite the shabby grey hair which swamped his short frame, he could see the frail man was tired. He did not recognize the face of this Augustinian monk. "Who are you and what do you need of me?" the archbishop asked, as he eased himself up from the mattress to perch on the side of the bed.

The monk slowly approached, clutching papers. His hand was trembling.

"My lord, I am Folcard. I am from the Abbey at Canterbury," the monk said. His voice had more strength than his appearance predicted.

"Why is it that you entered my room without first knocking?" the archbishop demanded.

"I did knock," Folcard answered quickly, staring at the floor. "Thrice I knocked, but you did not answer."

"Yet, you entered my room knowing that I was absent, and permission was not granted! What possessed you to do such a thing?"

"I... I did not think you w... were... I thought I... I could..." Folcard stammered wiping rivulets of sweat from the side of his face. "I should have waited for you to come to the door. Forgive me, my lord." he bowed his head even lower, revealing the purposeful bald patch in the center.

Folcard stood motionless, doing nothing.

"Well?" the archbishop sighed. "Out with it. I haven't got all day."

"My lord, I have written a literary work that chronicles your life and accomplishments. I have come to show you what I have composed and to ask you some questions."

The monk spoke so fast that the archbishop could hardly understand a word. He stepped forward and held out the papers in his shaking fist.

"Let me see," he snapped, snatching the offered pages. Scanning a couple of pages of script, he was mildly surprised that this stammering man could write something so coherent. He gazed up at the man, shaking, who patiently waited for him to finish. Every sentence was understandable and accurate. The words flowed in a smooth and chronological order. "This is good," he murmured continuing to read. When finished, he looked up at Folcard in admiration. "You have done a good job. How did you gather all this information about me?"

"From church books and talking with people who have made your acquaintance," Folcard replied, seeming to regain his composure.

To scour through church books and then interview people that knew him required a special skill. Keeping everything in order was something the archbishop knew most wouldn't be able to do. "What is it that you wanted to ask me?"

Folcard shuffled his feet, the sound of his leather sandals scuffed against the stone floor. "I want to complete the beginning of your story. I have not found any records of where and when you were born. Neither have I found anyone that I have talked with who has this knowledge. If you could give me this information, I will have completed the beginning of your story." The monk's face turned red. "I met some people in the Lake District who know my lord. They say you came from across the ocean with the Vikings, from a place far away. A place called Vineland... but that is not where you were born.," Folcard said, breaking his reverie.

Silence reigned for a time, during which the archbishop grinned, reminiscing about the travels that got him to Vinland. The archbishop cleared his throat as he came to his decision. "I can't tell you the year I was born because the calendar my people use is different to the calendar we use here," he lied. "But I did come from a land far away with the Vikings. This is all true."

The monk's eyes filled with curiosity.

The archbishop couldn't tell him when or where he was born, or the places he had been and the people he had met. It would all sound like a fantasy. Validating it would be impossible and Folcard seemed the type that would want to do that. The archbishop tried to find a way to appease him. "These things you ask are not important. What you have written is clear and accurate. I am impressed."

"But, my lord—"

"You are a master scribe," he interrupted. "I want to give you a more important task. I want you to write about the life of St. John of Beverley."

"But, my lord," Folcard frowned, mopping sweat from his brow and rubbing it against his tunic. "I want to complete this work before I start another. Even if no one knows of the place you speak or the calendar your people use, at least it will be recorded. The story will be complete."

Lifting himself slowly to his feet, the archbishop approached the monk where he stood in the center of the room, and placed an arm about his shoulders, guiding him to the door. "Where I came from, the year of my birth, and who my parents are—none of this is as important as what I have done with my life. What is important is the work that we've done to keep the church here in England. We've saved so many souls." The archbishop handed the monk back his papers. "This is good. I am glad you came to visit and show me what you have compiled. Pick a place, pick a year. It is not as important as you may think. My story will be complete when you add the important things that I do before my death."

*I should tell him. Someone should know the truth of who I am*, he thought. But he brushed it aside and smiled at the bold monk. *No, not today.* "We are finished here. Good day."

The monk stood staring back agape, as the door was closed on him firmly. The archbishop exhaled heavily. He hobbled over to the stone fireplace where the disc rested atop the mantle. The rectangular piece of paper lay next to it. He reached it and held it to the candle's light, staring at the portrait at its center, before tossing the paper into the fire.

Grabbing the disc, he lifted an iron poker and sank down on his knees. Raising the heavy iron with both hands above his head, he cried out "By the will of God!" and brought the poker down on the disc as hard as he could.

The object shattered. Sparks flew from the tiny smashed pieces.

The poker clattered to the ground—metal against stone. The archbishop raised his hands and closed his eyes to block out the intense flash of white light that suddenly filled the room. In an instant, the bright light faded, leaving the room dark once more.

As the archbishop lowered his hands and his eyes adjusted to the natural light, the grey disc—the last vestige of his world—was gone.

# Chapter 1

Philadelphia, July 9, 0001

Three of them chased him, trotting a short distance behind. They prodded him, forcing him to run so he would tire trying to get away. The sorry shape of his body, all five foot nine inches, kept him from moving fast. He gulped air greedily, his heart pounded like the piston of a speeding car, ready to burst out of his chest. Sweat burned as it trickled into Tom's eyes forcing him to squint. His green striped shirt and khaki pants were drenched.

Night crept upon the forest. Trees started to fade from view. The escalating sound of growling wolves came from every direction. If only there was something he could do. Up ahead a tree was lodged against another. With a last burst of energy, Tom took a deep breath and sprinted for the fallen tree. The wolves followed and soon caught up, chomping at his heels as he climbed. A grey one managed to follow from behind. Its curled upper lip revealed sharp teeth and piercing dark eyes prompting Tom to scramble up the tree even faster.

Mustering enough strength, Tom pulled himself up on top of a thick branch. The wolves converged beneath the tree, growling, looking as if they were praying to God for a miracle that Tom would fall. A temporary sense of victory ensued as he rested, gasping for air. But when would the wolves leave? That was the real problem.

Tom watched as the full moon rose bright above the horizon and stared down unsympathetically, waiting to see what would happen next. Looking down, the wolves panted and licked up the excess saliva that dripped from their mouths. Tom pressed his stomach at the thought of them sinking their teeth into his flesh. If only he had a gun to shoot his way out. Or better yet, the disc. This wouldn't have been an issue with the disc. He hated himself for dropping it. Hopefully, by morning the wolves would have left in search of an easier meal.

The sweat-drenched clothes felt uncomfortable and the humid night air didn't help. Several branches connected with the trunk of the tree forming a vegetative chair with arm rests. There was no real comfortable position, but Tom was exhausted and even in this uncomfortable situation, he tried to make the most of it. Closing his eyes, he remembered his home, and his children.

Philadelphia, July 3, 2052

"Guys! Breakfast is ready!" Tom heard his daughter yelling upstairs.

"Breakfast is ready!" she hollered again.

Alexis was probably getting frustrated that no one responded, especially, since she had come all the way from D.C. to spend the weekend with him and Eric. She even woke up early to make breakfast.

"Dad?" Alexis called down from the top of the stairs.

How did she know he was here? He just got home last night, getting the parts he needed for her birthday present. The trip was long, but hopefully worth it. He always made something for her birthday, and every year was different. He thought about the first gift he'd ever made for her and began to chuckle remembering her remark that the doll was a demon because of its green glowing eyes and deep ugly voice. It was a girl's voice. How could that be ugly? It surprised him when she brought him to her room and waved her hand in front of the doll and it said in a slow, deep and heavy voice, 'Happy birthday, Alexis.' she wouldn't take the doll, even after changing the batteries to make things better.

"Dad?"

Tom heard her but was busy hovering over the workbench, trying to figure out why this thing he was putting together didn't work. It was a hologram projector fashioned after the one in the old *Jurassic Park* movie made at the beginning of the millennia where 3D dinosaurs appeared in the middle of the main lobby. The problem seemed to be with the quartz light-emitting crystals that encircled the top center of the disc. The QLE crystals were supposed to project images into the air. Instead they produced a heat wave. The man he bought it from told him it would work, as long as he connected the calendar display component. Well, all of that was connected and nothing displayed. So much for buying something where they only sold one thing. He should have asked the old man to put it together.

His thick fingers ran through his hair as he stared at the grey object. Why doesn't this stupid thing work? The rickety sound and soft pounding of feet against the steps on the wooden staircase caused Tom to come out of deep thought. Why does she want to come down now? He scrambled to collect the scattered pieces, trying to find anything to cover them.

"Dad?" She continued to descend the staircase. "What are you working on?"

There had to be a cover around here; a blanket or trash bag. Something! "Don't come down!"

"Why not?"

"Because I said so!"

"Fine!" she huffed.

Tom's ears registered retreating footsteps. Each foot banging hard with each step.

"What did you want anyway?"

"I cooked eggs and bacon and I just came to tell you that breakfast is ready! I won't bother next time." The door slammed hard.

Guilt swept through him. Getting eggs and bacon was a long process; they were expensive commodities these days.

Tom entered the kitchen and went toward the food. Alexis had rinsed the pans then turned around. "Dad! You smell like burned trash."

Tom hadn't smoked in over an hour. The smell couldn't have lingered around this long. He opened a drawer to get air freshener and sprayed an area of the kitchen away from the food. The lemon scent seemed to mask the smoke.

"You still smell like burned trash," she sniffed.

Tom shook the can and sprayed some more into the air. "Maybe it's not working." He sniffed then shrugged his shoulders as he put the can away.

"Dad, you need to learn how to dress." She sighed, taking in his rumpled appearance, and headed to the cupboard. "Want toast?"

Tom saw movement in the corner of his eyes and turned to see Eric walk into the kitchen in plaid pajama bottoms and no top. He sat down and laid his head across his arm on the table mumbling something unintelligible.

Tom frowned at his shirtless son. Eric's muscles were pronounced. Working out and being fit was his obsession.

"Do you want eggs and bacon?" Alexis asked.

Eric lifted up his head for a brief moment and mumbled, "Coffee!"

Alexis came over to the table and put her plate down next to one of the remaining empty spots and said, "They don't pay me enough to buy coffee."

"Where's *my* plate?" Eric sat up, frowning down at the empty table in front of him.

"You said you wanted coffee."

"Yeah! With my eggs and bacon!" Eric whined.

"The food is on the stove."

"You mean I have to go get it myself?"

Ignoring her brother, Alexis started to eat not acknowledging his whining. Amazingly, she could block him out of her head whenever she wanted.

Eric thumped down his plate heavily on the table. "Sorry, Sis. I know you had to wait a long time to get this at the store. And I know that getting Coffee is really expensive. I was hoping that maybe you brought some from work," he shrugged, as she continued to ignored him.

"So dad, where did you disappear for the last couple of days? I came Friday to visit, thinking you'd be home. It's Sunday already. I have to leave today."

"I'm sorry. I was just trying to find some things for—" He bit into the bacon. It was crunchy and salty, just the way he remembered it. "Wow! This is good. I haven't eaten bacon in a long time. You must have paid a fortune for this."

"Hmmph," Alexis scoffed, then smiled.

"Dad," Eric turned, "can I borrow the car and get some money for a haircut?"

"Why? Your hair is already short," Alexis jumped in.

"I forgot to charge the car last night. So either charge the car or, if you know someplace that's walking distance, get a haircut there." Tom grabbed his wallet and placed the cash on the table. "Here's a hundred dollars."

Eric scrutinized the bills. "This isn't even enough for the Hair Cuttery."

"They're just going to shave your head. Maybe I should keep the money and cut your hair myself," Tom started to slide the cash back.

Eric quickly grabbed the bills with a smirk. "Thanks, dad."

Tom remembered a time when a haircut cost thirty dollars. Things were so expensive these days. Rationing of fuel by the government made the cost of everything triple. Soon, food would be rationed, too, so they said. It was all over the news. Tom sighed inwardly, putting on his glasses. *The Philadelphia Inquirer* appeared on the glasses and he started accessing today's articles. "Hey, check this out," he roared excitedly.

"They're going to start implementing the bill that Senator Williamson got passed last year to get rid of illegal aliens."

Alexis' jaw dropped. "We need to wear ID tags?"

"I think that's stupid," Eric commented, lifting the brass pipe chair in front of him. "What if someone takes your ID tag and pretends to be you?"

"It says here that the ID tags are some kind of bar code. Your ID is tied to a central database that has your DNA signature. You put your finger in a device and it determines if you are you," Tom continued reading aloud. "The senator says, 'The ID tags will eliminate the criminal elements in our society and give our decent, law-abiding citizens more freedom and protection.'"

"I can't believe they're going to make us wear ID tags," Alexis muttered, shaking her head. "I'm surprised they didn't add a tracking device too."

"It seems the new system is ready to be implemented next month. You have a choice of getting the ID on your hand or your forehead," Tom read out loud. For years the government had taken away the rights of the people all in the name of safety and freedom. When was it going to end?

Eric took his plate and placed it in the sink. It was his turn to wash the dishes, but from the way he moved away Tom was sure he was hoping his sister would wash them instead.

Tom headed back down into the basement to work on the present for Alexis. It had to be something simple that he overlooked. After meticulously reading all of the schematic diagrams for the QLE, he took a break and wiped his eyes.

"Was this why you didn't want me to come down this morning?" Alexis' voice startled him.

Tom had become so engrossed with his work that he didn't hear her come down the stairs. Her long black hair, green eyes, and caramel skin were an exact copy of her mother. It made his heart ache just looking at his daughter.

"Well... um... yes. This was supposed to be a hologram that displayed happy birthday in the air with me and your brother singing."

"Oh, that's so cute!" her voice rose two octaves as she beamed with delight. Running around the workbench she hugged him tightly and kissed him on the cheek. "Maybe you can still get it to work?"

"Well, that's what I'm hoping to do!" he grinned, squeezing her hand. "You and your friends will be here for your birthday next week, right?"

"I'm ...uhm... going out with Marcus and some of our friends," Her eyes darted away toward the floor.

*Marcus?*

It felt like just yesterday, she was this little girl, standing on his shoulders, giggling, and while holding his hands, she'd flip toward the ground. His daughter had grown into a beautiful young woman. He wasn't sure where the time had gone. "Oh well." He waved his hand as if her birthday celebration didn't bother him, putting on a smile. "Enjoy yourself. I'll see you the next time. Bring Marcus with you."

Alexis hugged him and headed back up the stairs with a skip to her step.

*She doesn't need me anymore.*

As he heard the front door slam shut he went back to work. It would be great if he could finish the hologram by her birthday even if she wouldn't be here on the day.

# Timepieces

He set about disassembling the disc, then reassembling it, before crossing his fingers and holding his breath as he pressed the button to turn it back on. *Here goes!*

The display lit up with the current date.

He set it to his daughter's birthday: July 9, then pressed the blue button.

The expected hologram didn't appear.

He sighed, running a hand through thick hair. *What now?* Without warning, the display changed and showed the current date: July 1. Tom's frustration grew; he thumped the table with his fist, causing the tiny metal tools to clatter. Pressing the blue button once more changed the display back to Alexis' birth date. *What if I change the year to one? Maybe it's the date panel display.* The date was changed, and the blue button pressed.

In a split second, everything changed.

The house disappeared. Trees appeared out of nowhere. The view changed from a basement to a forest. *What the...*

He spun, looking all around, feeling his heart beating out of his chest. Behind him an incline to a hill began. Orange clouds tinted a purple sky. Night was approaching.

A small animal scurrying sounded close by. He looked down, the floor was no longer cement. His basement was gone; his house was gone! The lingering smell of bacon and eggs was gone.

This didn't make sense. *What's happening? Am I dreaming?*

The disc showed July 1, 2052 on the display. Without wasting a moment, he pressed the blue button and the basement reappeared, as if it had never left. The familiar smell of cooked breakfast hung in the air. He closed his eyes and breathed deeply, as his heart resumed its normal pace. *What the hell is going on?*

He sat, frozen in thought for a few moments. *Did the house really disappear? Was this an illusion?*

He pressed the blue button again.

The house disappeared once more to be replaced by forest. There were trees everywhere. The smell of night filled the air. A loud barking sound startled him; he turned, inadvertently loosening his grasp of the disc, and it fell to the ground. He bent down to pick it up. The growling intensified. Several wolves emerged from the trees.

Without thinking twice, he ran; leaving the disc on the ground.

---

Tom woke up to the cawing sound of a single black bird perched on another branch. The sound was deafening. He hollered back at it, hoping that it would go away. The bird stopped for a second, flew to another branch, and then continued with its cawing. Soon other birds joined in the chatter.

Tom peered down cautiously. The wolves had gone. He exhaled, swiping the sweat from his forehead. Only dirt and stirred leaves remained below.

Tom assessed the unfamiliar surroundings. A magnificent canopy of trees grew so wide that their green leaves blocked most of the rays of sunlight trying to get through to the ground. Off in the distance, the clearing where this all started, was barely visible.

He lowered himself from the branch, landing on hands and knees and headed toward the clearing where the disc had fallen. Leaves and twigs cracked underneath each step.

That's when the growling started.

A distance away a single grey wolf stood staring at Tom.

Tom ran.

The wolf chased after him.

It was last night all over again. Panting as he ran, Tom focused on his destination and ran furiously. Up ahead in the grass lay the disc.

Tom slowed and went to grab it when another wolf with large sharp teeth and hungry eyes moved into the clearing cutting off all access to his prize. More wolves popped out of nowhere, surrounding him.

He felt hopeless. His options were: get the disc or be eaten. He scanned the ground looking for something, anything, he could use as a weapon.

He reached for a branch near his feet. Tom started swinging the heavy branch wildly, yelling at the wolves to keep away. To his surprise, it seemed to be working.

Step by step, he inched toward the disc until he could bend down, grab it, and turn it on. A single moment of distraction allowed a wolf to take hold of the branch with its fangs and pull it away. Tom felt the branch being ripped out of his hand, and almost dropped the disc in shock.

The wolves moved in. Jaws snapped at Tom's leg, as he closed his eyes and pressed the blue button, waiting for the wolf's teeth to sink into his flesh.

Nothing happened.

The huffing and puffing stopped. Silence. He opened his eyes slowly. No blood, no teeth marks. Nothing was trying to bite off his leg. The wolves were gone. The timepiece displayed July 1, 0001.

He'd made it out alive.

A deep breath filled his sense with the smells of his basement. Dirty from last night's adventure, he went to his bedroom to shower. As beads of water softly pummeled his face, he felt his body relaxing, inch by inch, muscle by muscle. The chase, and the ability to escape from the thrashing jaws of wolves, had been exhilarating. He laughed with joy, as it finally dawned on him what he had done. He had inadvertently invented a way to travel through time.

Tom dressed to go into downtown, but first headed to his office. History had always been one of his favorite subjects. What better way to learn it than to experience it first hand? Books of different time periods in American history lay sprawled over his desk.

A cab brought Tom to the historic district of Philadelphia. Taking the disc, he set a new date on the display, then pressed the blue button transforming everything around him in an instant. The cars were gone; the people were gone, the ones here were wearing different clothes. The historical drawings from the history books couldn't have prepared him for what he was seeing at this moment.

# Chapter 2

Philadelphia, July 30, 1787

The modern city view vanished. Tall buildings and paved roads were replaced with structures that were no higher than two stories. The roads were made of dirt, not asphalt. Tom recognized many of the historic British colony landmarks of Philadelphia that still existed in his time. People walked along the streets in their eighteenth-century attire. An awful foul odor emanated from the street, as horses deposited their droppings, galloping and trotting through it as they passed by. Wagons rolled over it. It was everywhere. The intensity of the sun cooked the dung, causing the fumes to reek in Tom's nose. Like all the other people around him, he tried not to step in it, but his feet somehow found a way of landing on it. *No one ever mentioned this in any of the history books*, he thought, wiping his shoes against the grass. *How can these people live like this?*

Across the street stood the State House. The symmetrical Georgian architecture of the red brick building was a marvelous sight. The Constitutional Convention that would ultimately generate the U.S. Constitution was taking place at this moment. An idea struck him. He crossed the street avoiding the horses and their droppings and knocked on the door.

A man, wearing a long coat and a grey wig, opened it. "May I help you?"

Tom was at a loss for words and decided the direct approach was the best. "May I come in?"

The man looked him up and down. "Your name, sir?"

"Thomas Lynch."

The man lifted a ledger, scanned it and looked back at Tom with a shake of the head. "I'm sorry, but you're not on the list of those attending this meeting."

"I understand, but may I come in and just observe?" he asked realizing what a stupid question it was.

"I can ask the chair if he will allow it, but you won't have an answer until the morrow. Please come back then." With that, the man stepped back and closed the door.

Tom, dejected, headed back across the street and stood under a maple tree to get out of the sun.

An hour later, sweating profusely and feeling miserable, he wasn't sure whether to stick around or leave. If only it were possible to go inside and see what was going on. The history books did mention it being hot during this time; but being here now in this heat was a big surprise to how hot it really was. The shade from the tree didn't provide any relief from the sweltering hot air that sucked the energy out of his slightly overweight body. The search for a smoke only found empty pockets.

The mere act of being here aroused the attention of people on the street. A few shot him strange looks, others smiled as they passed by. Everyone stared. *Have I done something wrong?*

Looking down at what he had worn today it dawned on him. This was definitely not the correct attire for the time period; a white T-shirt, blue jeans and his favorite red Converse with the white laces. He thought about going back home and getting something more appropriate, but he was already here, it made no sense to go back and change. In any case, he didn't look all *that* different.

Tom headed over toward one of the windows—a sneak peek certainly wouldn't hurt. As Tom crossed the street the front doors of the building opened. Men swarmed out—among them were George Mason, one of three delegates who refused to sign the Constitution, and James Madison, who later became the fourth president of the United States. The two men went off to the side of the entrance continuing their discussion. The idea of getting close enough to listen to them talk was too much to ignore; but as he approached them, everyone, including Mason and Madison, turned to look at him. The men smiled, murmured something to each other, and then collectively broke into a laugh as if he'd become a clown in a circus. Tom felt himself flush to his hairline.

Four men carrying a wooden sedan emerged from the building and headed in his direction, almost dropping the sedan when they spotted him. A tapping sound came from inside the sedan as it passed, along with a muffled shout. "Put me down. I say put me down!"

The men lowered the vehicle to the ground. A feeble man sat inside, motioning for Tom to come closer.

"Thomas Lynch?" the old man yelled, popping his birdlike head into the light. His shaking hands perched a pair of spectacles on his nose as he peered at Tom. "Thomas Lynch, is that you?" Withered lips curled into a smile.

Tom studied the old man. Most of his hair was gone. He didn't recognize the man at first, but soon realized who he was. "Oh... my... god!" Tom cried as his jaw dropped. "Benjamin Franklin... You-you're Benjamin Franklin!"

The man looked nothing like any of the pictures of Benjamin Franklin he'd seen before. They had all made the man look so vibrant and alive. The years had changed him.

"I never thought we'd meet again," said Franklin, in a broken, raspy voice. Yet his intelligent eyes twinkled, as he sized Tom up. "You told me we would, but I didn't believe you. You haven't changed a bit. You look just like you did eleven years ago."

Tom was taken aback. "I told you eleven years ago that we'd meet again? Here? Today?"

"My, how time passes by so fast." Mr. Franklin extended a withered hand to Tom who clasped it gently, afraid of breaking it. "It seems like yesterday when you and I went to save Miss Audrey from her predicament. I wonder what has happened to her."

"Audrey?" Tom didn't recognize the name.

"Yes, yes," Franklin said, nodding. "You two left together the last time you were here."

"I'm sorry, but I don't know what you're talking about. Who is Audrey?" he asked, more than a little confused.

"Oh, never mind. You told me you wouldn't remember anything anyway." Franklin waved it away.

"How do you know me?"

"I know all about you, Tom." He motioned for Tom to come closer and Mr. Franklin whispered to him, telling him what year he came from and about the timepiece that he'd constructed. He looked pointedly at the pouch Tom carried.

Tom gasped. "How can you know that?"

"It is remarkable how you have not changed in the last decade. But your choice of dress is awful. You look quite the pauper."

"Maybe it is a little different," Tom looked down at his clothes, feeling the blush once again. "But it's not *that* bad."

Mr. Franklin rolled his eyes. "We definitely need to get you something more appropriate." He leaned back in the chair and told the men to continue their journey home. "Follow me to my house," he said to Tom waving his hand through the window of the sedan.

"When we get to my home," Mr. Franklin continued shouting through the opening in his sedan as Tom walked alongside it. "I will tell one of my servants to accompany you to the tailor's and get you the necessary clothes you need." A pause, then, "Are you hungry?"

"As a matter of fact, yes I am."

"Perhaps I should not have even bothered asking the question," he chuckled. "When I first met you, Tom, you told me that I bought you your clothes in the future. And here I am, about to purchase your clothes. It's so marvelous how in the grand scheme of things, everything that doesn't make sense fits so perfect and well together in the end."

"Oh, I get it now!" Tom whispered, feeling the timepiece in his pouch. Then in a louder voice said, "Oh, Mr. Franklin, this is wonderful!"

"Please, call me Ben. After all, I insisted you call me that many years ago."

Ben's Tudor home stood two stories high, a print shop and mail service off to one side. Two of his servants stood by the door and waited for the men to set him down, before helping him out of the sedan and into the house, sitting him on the couch in his cozy parlor.

Ben called out to one of his servants to accompany Tom to the tailor. The whole experience was much more efficient than Tom could have expected. Upon their return, voices could be heard emanating from the parlor. The servant, Peter, told Tom to go on ahead and join the others.

The room didn't seem large at all. A set of portraits of Ben and his wife lined one side of the room. Several wooden chairs and a brown sofa took up most of the space. Ben sat on a chair talking to two men occupying the couch in front of him. The wooden floor creaked under Tom's feet as he entered the room. The two men turned in the direction of the sound.

"Mr. Lynch!" they both exclaimed in surprise.

"Ah, Tom," Ben said waving for Tom to come closer. "You remember Roger Sherman and John Dickinson from the days of the Continental Congress?"

"Ah... yeah... How are you?" Tom said, extending his hand to greet them.

It felt strange to be recognized by these important men: John Dickinson, the one man who voted against American independence, and Roger Sherman, one of five men on the committee to write the Declaration of Independence.

"I thought you had perished out at sea on your way to the West Indies," said Mr. Sherman. He had a rugged look; more like a frontiersman than a statesman.

"No, he has come to visit me instead," Ben interjected.

"Well, this is a pleasure. I never knew that you and Franklin were such good friends," bellowed Mr. Dickinson, shaking Tom's hand.

Tom studied John Dickinson; his youthful appearance belied a man in his fifties. His tight lips, sharp nose, and glaring eyes gave him a distinguished look.

Tom sat in silence, sipping a cup of tea and listening to the men argue about issues surrounding the currently drafted constitution. This couldn't be happening. These men were only known from history books. An hour passed before the two men decided they needed to get back to their homes and bid their farewells.

"The convention is going strong," Ben said once they were alone. "There seems to be more arguments around the document than concessions."

"Perhaps I can help," Tom replied.

Ben sighed. "No, you cannot. I talked with Mr. Sherman and Mr. Dickinson before you came back and they assured me that you may not attend the constitutional convention. It is a secret convention. I am truly sorry. But please stay awhile. You are more than welcome to stay here for as long as you wish."

———————

Tom enjoyed Ben's hospitality, but by the end of the week he'd become homesick for his family. The next morning, he found Ben in the breakfast room and told him of his decision to go back home.

"Will you come back and visit me again?" Ben asked.

"I'd like to say yes, but I really don't know," Tom said. "But you could help me."

"How so?"

"Tell me how I approach you the next time I see you."

Ben told Tom what he would need to say to win over his friendship and laughed.

"One last thing," Tom added. "Where do we meet?"

"Oh, I cannot tell you that," Ben responded.

"Why not?"

"Because you told me that if I give you too much information, you might change things inadvertently and mess up the future."

"I said that?"

"Yes, you said that if I tell you about the events that will happen in the past, you may try and change things which will cause your future, our future I imagine, to be different."

"I might change something in the past that alters the future?"

"That's what you said," Ben told him.

"I might be changing the future now!"

"Then, do you want me to tell you what happens?" Ben asked, smiling as if he were ready to give up the most secret of secrets.

"No. Don't tell me," Tom said hurriedly, not wanting to get information that could make him inadvertently change his timeline. "Can you at least tell me what year I come back to?"

Ben looked at Tom as if he had been shot in the back. "I suppose I better tell you that at least." Ben paused in thought, putting his finger to his lips. "May 1776. I'm not sure which day, but I think it was near the end of the month."

"Thank you so much for letting me stay. And the clothes! My God, yes, the clothes. Thank you so much." Tom reached into the pouch and took out the grey disc.

"Oh, think nothing of it. I was destined to do it," Ben said, admiring the object Tom held with a keen gaze.

"What's wrong?" Tom asked.

"Your device brings back memories, that's all." Ben shook his head sadly. "When you and Audrey left me ten years ago, I truly believed I would never see you again."

Tom stared at Ben. "I take Audrey with me with this timepiece?" he asked, quite excited by what he heard.

"Well, no... she also had one of her own. You had mentioned before that the device only works with one person."

"Audrey leaves with one of these?" Tom pointed to the disc.

"How else would she leave?" Ben replied as if answering the most obvious question.

"Who is this Audrey person?"

"You told me not to tell you." Then he blurted out with a smile, "But I can if you want."

Tom smirked. "You're enjoying this, aren't you?"

"For the most part, yes," Ben grinned.

"Goodbye, Benjamin Franklin," Tom said, shaking Ben's fragile hand.

Tom returned to his time and walked to his house from the city. Eric still hadn't come home. Tom had a vague idea how the timepiece worked and creating another one wouldn't be easy. He went upstairs to the office and sat on the chair admiring this grey disc that could take him to any place and to any year. Meeting Benjamin Franklin, Roger Sherman and John Dickinson didn't seem real at all. What would happen the next time he went back?

One thought kept rolling over in his head: Who was Audrey?

# Chapter 3

**Milestown, January 20, 2275**

Audrey hardly slept under the three thick blankets, which barely kept her warm. The walls provided little insulation from the cold wind that seeped in. A small crack in the burlap curtain allowed a glint of sunlight to enter, in a feeble attempt to warm up the room. She wanted to put more coal in the furnace but was too cold to get out of bed. In just a few hours the sun would be higher in the sky and everything would be better.

Candlelight rolled into the room as her door creaked open. *This early?*

Shirl, one of the slave girls, peered into the room. Her rosy cheeks stood out in contrast to her jet-black hair. "Excuse me, but breakfast is being prepared for your father and I wondered if you would like to eat with him?" she asked, looking toward the floor.

"If I wanted to eat now, I would have called for you. Did I call for you?" Audrey snapped, sitting up in bed. The servant retreated closing the door quietly behind her.

"Wait!" Audrey yelled, wrapping the blankets around her body.

The door swung back open. The girl reappeared, peeking around the doorframe.

"Since you're already here, put some more coal in the furnace. I'm cold."

The girl hurried across the room, grabbed some coal from the container, then opened the rusted iron door of the furnace and threw it onto the fire, hurrying out of the room before her mistress could ask for something else. Audrey sighed, lifting the sheets against her face to filter out the awful stench of burning coal.

Getting out of bed, she flung the curtains aside, and peered toward the town center; she could make out the black, polished monument which stood in the middle of the square in honor of the founders of the city. On either side, street vendors were already setting up their wares. The ancient tower stood off to the side of the square. Many tales were told of its existence long before the city had been founded over 200 years ago. As a child, she would explore the structure, climbing the stairs from one floor to the next, throwing pebbles at people who passed close enough to be hit and getting in trouble for it. She never once went down into the levels below ground for fear of the monsters that lived there waiting for her in the dark.

To the east, past the city, the Great Bay looked out to an endless expanse of water touched by an orange sky at the horizon. Cliffs loomed toward the south. History books talked of a time when the sky was at one time blue and the Great Bay didn't exist; instead, a valley had flourished there, with just a river running through its center. She closed her eyes, trying to imagine what that must have been like. An empty expanse of grey and black rocks and dirt for as far as the eye could see, maybe a few shrubs here and there. How anyone could live in those conditions was beyond comprehension.

Coming out from under the curtain, she called out for Shirl and went over to wait on the bed. "What took you so long?" she snapped, when the servant girl finally reappeared.

The girl stared back expressionless.

Audrey tutted shaking her head. The girl was worse than useless. "I'm ready to eat my breakfast now."

Shirl nodded and hurried out of the room.

Two minutes passed before the servant finally returned with a tray of food. Audrey huffed. "Is Daddy still here?"

"He's already left." The girl placed the tray on the bed and bowed her head. "He went out with two guards."

It made no sense to her why running a city required so much of his time and effort. Everything in the city took care of itself. Nonetheless, she hardly saw him.

The slave was dismissed with a wave of a hand.

Audrey took her oatmeal and stirred in a few grapes, then crushed the cube of cornbread sprinkling it on top. It was her favorite way to eat oatmeal and for that matter the only way. She washed it all down with a cup of warm carrot juice.

With breakfast finished, Audrey got up and dressed for the day, choosing the right belt to match the light green gown she wore. *Ah yes, the grey belt will work.* Once the menial chores that required her attention were done, she started on her way to visit Logan who lived at the edge of the city. His family grew most of the food that the people of Milestown consumed. They were part of the elite; they owned one of the largest farms around.

The journey to the farm wasn't long, but she hated passing the coal miners. Huts made of clay and straw were used to house the slaves that lived and worked there, as they dug out the coal. The slaves spent most of their days working underground. Audrey felt like she was choking, grabbing her neck with her hand and coughing from the horrible smell that emanated from this area. Soldiers marched, yelling at the slaves, beating them with their batons when they fell out of line.

As Audrey looked around in disgust, she caught a tall soldier grinning her way. A sergeant, she knew only from the parties her father forced her to attend. *What's his name again?* She studied him now with renewed interest. With curly hair, brown skin, and a flaring nose, he stood out from the others. His broad shoulders and strong legs reinforced the image of how she thought a soldier should look.

"Ah, if it isn't the lovely Princess Audrey! How are you, my lady?" the sergeant greeted as he neared.

"I'm not a princess," Audrey smiled. "I'm just the mayor's daughter."

"And that makes you a princess. If something were to happen to the mayor—and I hope that never happens—then you would be the new mayor."

She rolled her eyes, started to walk away.

"Where are you off to?" he called after her.

"I'm off to have some fun!" she called back.

"If that's what you want, then you'd be better off staying here with me!" he hollered, waving his hands for her to return. "I'm off duty in an hour!"

She stopped, turned and cocked her head. "And what, make you a prince?" she laughed. "I don't think so." She turned around not waiting for a response.

The slaves weren't wearing much of anything; she didn't understand why they couldn't be kept underground. After all, that's where they worked. And it would keep the smell away from the road. Their wrinkled bodies were thick with soot, you couldn't even see the color of their skin, the whites of their eyes and teeth shining brighter because of it.

Many of the slaves stopped working as she passed, peering at her through narrowed, tired-looking eyes. She glared back at the filthy, smelly slaves and held her head high. One of them smiled.

Her eyes thinned and her lips pursed.

"What are you staring at?" a soldier growled, hitting the slave on his back with a baton. "Get back to work!"

Audrey smirked as the slave fell to the ground from the blow. He deserved it. She made a mental note to reward the soldier later, for doing a good job.

The dirty huts opened to a field with cornstalks towering high into the air. The cornfield opened up to an expanse of wheat. As she traipsed along the pathway through the field, a black stone house came into view with smoke bellowing out of its chimney.

The landscape changed to a barren field with men working, including Logan. He spotted her and waved as she walked toward him.

"Hi, Logan!" she said getting close enough for him to hear. His muscles gleamed as they bunched and moved. "Ooh, you're all sweaty."

"That's what happens when you work," he stated matter-of-factly. "It makes you sweat."

Logan stood almost two meters tall, a handsome specimen of a man in many ways. His short orange hair camouflaged against the sky. They had been friends for as long as she could remember.

"How long are you going to be?" she asked. "I thought we could go to the Ancient Tower and enjoy the day there."

Logan looked out toward the city, hand raised to shield his eyes from the glare of the sun. "I haven't been to the tower since we were kids. Why not just stay here and talk while I work? Or even better, you can help me work" he grinned.

"I... don't think so. Why don't you just sit with me while *they* work?" She pointed to the men he hired.

"Because, unlike a few people I know," he pierced her with a searing gaze, "I like doing this. Yes, it's hard work, but it is also satisfying to know that my hands did this," he said, looking around.

"Whatever." She huffed, shaking her head, hand on hips. She wasn't about to argue. Toiling in the fields was not a task she would be caught dead doing. Making plants grow and bear fruit was magic and being the recipient of that enchantment was the most work anyone would get out of her. The midday sun was hot. She took a small blanket and raised it above her head to protect her delicate skin.

"It's not that hot." Logan laughed.

"You're going to turn as red as a beet. Your skin is going to match your hair." They broke into chuckles together. "I'm going to say hi to your mom." She walked away, heading for the house, "I'll see you in a little while."

Logan's house was futuristic compared to the other houses in Milestown. This one had a relief room that didn't smell—and drained into the area where the trees grew.

The kitchen even had two counters with a sink. As she walked in, the aroma of hot spices, cilantro and onions filled the air. Logan's mother was busy chopping vegetables on the counter. Audrey knew the woman did everything herself; they had not one servant in the house! Audrey couldn't understand it. They were so wealthy—why on earth didn't they have slaves to do all this?

"Hi, Mrs. Tolbert."

"Oh my! Audrey!" the older woman gasped, grabbing her chest. "Please don't ever do that again."

"I'm sorry. I didn't mean to scare you."

Mrs. Tolbert held her chest, then took a deep breath. Gathering herself after the initial shock, she turned and went back to work. Audrey had always thought Mrs Tolbert was a great cook. As she watched her work her magic she could see where Logan got his red hair, and pale skin. Unfortunately, he hadn't acquired her beautiful green eyes.

"How are you, Audrey dear?" the woman chatted as she prepared the meal. "It's been a while. I've missed you."

Audrey could only handle talking with Mrs. Tolbert for short periods of time, her voice sounded like someone was running their fingernails down a chalkboard. "Mrs. Tolbert, how are you going to take care of things by yourself with Mr. Tolbert and Logan leaving for New Scranton?"

The woman stopped and half turned. "Oh, I'm going too my dear! We're paying Mr. Grossman to tend to our crops in our absence. When did your father tell you that Levon and Logan were going?"

"The same time he told me I was going," Audrey replied with a smile.

They laughed and chatted about Logan's father becoming the ambassador. Every once in a while, going outside to get away from the screech of Mrs. Tolbert's voice. An hour later Audrey and Mrs. Tolbert stacked the containers on a metal wagon. Mrs. Tolbert pulled the wagon as Audrey walked alongside covering herself with the blanket. As they came over to where Logan and the other men were working, shouts of joy erupted from the men. Logan shook his head, grinning at her. *What?* She knew what he was thinking, but she was royalty. Mrs. Tolbert would have been pulling the cart by herself anyway, if she hadn't come when she did. And look, several of the men came over to help pull the cart the rest of the way.

The meal was good. Everyone got their fill of Mrs. Tolbert's food and after the break Logan stood and headed toward the fields. Audrey grabbed his arm. "Where are you going?" she asked.

"Back to work?"

"Really?" Her eyes squinted in disgust. "I came all this way to visit you and you want to go back to work? Why don't you just get your slaves to finish while we go back to your house."

"They're not slaves," Logan smiled shaking his head.

"Whatever," she waved her hand. "Come on, Take a break."

Logan looked at her and exhaled, then instructed his men to finish the work they had started. They walked back to his house.

Audrey sat on the wicker sofa on the patio next to Logan

"It's a great view of the cliffs, isn't it?" she sighed. The cliffs towered off in the south, rising high into the orange sky. The picturesque dark blue water of the bay made her want to go to the shore and put her feet in the water.

"It's amazing," he said, scooting closer to Audrey on the sofa. "They say that our ancestors came from there. The cliffs helped them survive the Great Catastrophe."

"What happened? None of the books in the library talk about the actual event."

"I don't know, but supposedly the sky used to be blue."

"I can't imagine a blue sky. How weird is that?"

Logan shrugged. "I'm sure the people back then couldn't imagine an orange sky, if the stories are really true."

Something caught Logan's eye causing him to stand and walk over to the railing. Audrey came over and stood next to him. About a hundred meters away, a slave, short with straight black hair, ran attempting an escape. Two soldiers were in close pursuit and would eventually catch the runaway.

"I hope he gets away," Logan said.

"What do you mean?" She glared at him in disbelief. "He's a slave. Why would you want him to get away?"

Logan looked down and shook his head. "Slavery isn't right, Audrey. These people deserve the same life as any other person! No one deserves to serve someone against their will."

"Who would clean our houses? More importantly, who'd work the mines?"

"Pay them to work."

"Pay them?" she scoffed. "And what if they didn't want to do that work? What if no one wants to do that work? What then?" She didn't understand why Logan couldn't see why slaves were important to running the city. He was being selfish; he couldn't see the greater good the slaves provided.

As they watched in silence, soldiers caught the runaway slave and began to beat him with their sticks. They headed back to the city, making the slave run ahead of them. Every time he'd fall, they'd beat him until he got up. They watched in uneasy silence as the gang disappeared in the distance.

"I suppose you think what the soldiers are doing is necessary," Logan's voice flowed with anger. She could see his jaw clenching.

"He *did* run away," she said, not wanting to look at him any longer. "The other slaves need to see what might happen to them if they try to do the same. It's necessary."

"Slaves are no better or worse than you or me!" Logan growled.

She took in a deep breath and squeezed down on the railing. "Can we please not talk about this? It's neither here nor there. Whatever we decide won't change a thing."

What where these slaves to him? He probably thought that she was cruel and unreasonable. But this is how Milestown worked. If he couldn't accept that, well, too bad.

A moment passed and he turned to her and smiled, the argument seemingly forgotten. "Have you packed everything you'll be taking to New Scranton?"

"I'm sure Shirl has already started packing for both of us." Audrey felt more comfortable now that they were no longer talking about slaves.

"I wonder what the people there are like. Have you met any of them?" Logan asked.

"I heard my dad speaking to one of the councilmen about them. They're very rich and they have land animals. Can you believe it? I've never seen one before."

"What kind of land animals?"

"I don't know. But they raise them to eat. Dad is trying to negotiate a trade to bring some of the animals here to Milestown."

"I can't wait to see them!"

# Chapter 4

New Scranton, February 10, 2274

The morning air was cold against President Lewis' face, even penetrating his clothing, as he walked across the courtyard toward the dining room of the palace with two bodyguards. It was too early to be here, but since Kratz had returned last night from Williamsport, Lewis wanted to hear the report before anyone else could convince Kratz to change it.

A large wooden table stretched from one end of the enormous dining room to the other. It reminded Lewis of better times, when presidents lived in the nation's capital. Bright sunlight poured in from the large windows lining one side of the room, making it much warmer in here than outside. Kratz, in his officer's uniform, sat alone at the far end of the table. He appeared thinner in the face. Had he lost weight while away? As he neared the man, the smell of cologne and meat combined caused Lewis to choke and turn his head away for a moment. Lewis took a seat and continued to watch as Kratz chewed his food and played with his nappy black hair.

Kratz raised his head and his small sharp eyes focused on the president. In an instant, his eyes opened wide. The piece of meat could be seen between his teeth and lower lip. Lewis imagined the neurons in his brain firing in quick succession as he slowly realized who was sitting in front of him.

Lewis smiled. "I hope you're enjoying that steak." The words caught Kratz off guard and he gasped. His face paled. He began to cough vigorously.

Lewis watched Kratz as he choked on the meat, as if this were all part of a show.

Once the coughing had abated, Kratz—tinged with embarrassment—grabbed a glass of water, gulping audibly.

Silence reigned until Kratz understood that he was expected to speak. "Hello, Mr. President." His voice was raspy as he tried to clear his throat.

"Take your time, Kratz. I know it's been awhile since you've eaten meat."

Kratz grinned and cut another slice. He seemed to think better of taking another bite, however, with the president sitting in front of him, as he promptly put down his knife and fork. "It's not a problem, Mr. President. I'm here for a few more days and I'm sure I'll find another opportunity to enjoy another wonderful meal before I return to Williamsport." He moved the plate to the side and patted his hair.

"Speaking of which, what is the status on Williamsport?"

The president had sent Kratz to Williamsport ten years earlier to convince the mayor that he needed the Feds. The look on Kratz's face suggested the man had not succeeded.

"Mayor Frazier is still popular among his people." Kratz sighed. "The mayor wants nothing to do with us. He thinks we are evil. He says that we have a secret that once out will cause everyone to want to rid the Feds from their cities."

"Is that so?" Lewis fiddled with a spoon he found on the table. "Does he know what that secret is?"

"The meat," Kratz said. "He says that we won't trade the animals that we breed. He believes that his people will develop a taste for this meat and will continue to want it. If his people cannot produce it, he doesn't want them eating it."

President Lewis growled as he shifted in his chair and lightly tapped his fingers on the table. Williamsport provided all the coal that the Feds needed. Mayor Frazier had stopped that trade and now the Feds relied on Milestown to get their coal. Their needs were expanding and Milestown couldn't, or wouldn't, supply coal fast enough. The Feds needed coal and they were going to get it. They would probably have to use force. Williamsport was a more lucrative proposition than Milestown. In either case, a weakness needed to be found in Williamsport and if they could take advantage of this, they could attack swiftly to disable and enslave them. He liked the idea of having a city exist solely to serve the Feds.

Kratz' loyalty was to the Feds. His one skill happened to be in politics; no one better would be able to convince the mayor to deal with them.

"The mayor is building up his army. It's now about a third of his population. He knows the Feds are bigger and stronger and he wants to be prepared for an attack which he believes is inevitable," said Kratz.

"Will they attack us?" Maybe they needed to put more of their military on the border between Williamsport and New Scranton.

"No." Kratz shook his head firmly. "He's building a purely defensive army."

"But we all know that a purely defensive army eventually turns into an offensive army when they have nothing to do."

"I've been trying to advise him to engage in diplomatic communications with us. He berates me. I think he's beginning to suspect that my loyalty is with the Feds and not with Williamsport."

"And he would be right. Wouldn't he?" Lewis gave Kratz a searching look.

Kratz smirked. "The mayor of Williamsport has a polished charm and is liked by almost everyone in the city. To some he can do no wrong. The mayor rules by his gut and not by laws. The people of Williamsport like him because they believe him to be just."

Lewis kept his eyes fixed on Kratz.

"There's something else," Kratz said. The president nodded for him to continue. "There is someone that the mayor is propping up as a hero of the city. The first time I met him, I felt he could be a threat to us."

"Why is he a hero? What did he do?" Lewis didn't like it when things were not under total control.

"Three Feds wandered into Williamsport territory and tried to capture a young man and woman along the Williamsport River. This hero killed two of our men and captured the other single-handedly."

"Where is this man from?" It impressed Lewis that a man could be so cunning. Maybe this hero could be convinced to shift sides.

"Nanticoke."

"Nanticoke?" Lewis spluttered. "He lies! That city no longer exists."

"I agree. But Mayor Frazier believes him." Kratz shrugged.

The president needed Williamsport, and if he could get it without fighting, that would be preferred. "I want a solution for removing that mayor and taking the city, Kratz!" he roared, pounding his fist on the table.

"I've got a plan I've been working on."

"What is it?"

"Mayor Frazier likes to host many events. He invites many of the councilmen to these festivities." Kratz poured more water and drank. His tongue darted out to water his chapped lips. "He likes to build his ego. There are two councilmen that I've been working with." A lopsided grin appeared on Kratz' face. "Not everyone loves and supports the mayor."

"And you're going to use them to get rid of the mayor?" asked Lewis, leaning forward. "Will that work?" Using insiders had risks. They might give away Kratz' true identity to the mayor.

"Of course it will. I am Mayor Frazier's right-hand man. When he dies, I will become the mayor *pro tempore*. I will deal with him accordingly and win over the council. Then they will elect me as the new mayor."

Lewis turned away and looked out the window. *Is Kratz trying as hard as he can to get things done?*

"Everyone loves the mayor, but you've told me before that the council doesn't trust you. How will you make this all work?"

Kratz drank the last of the water and wiped his hands on a napkin, setting it down on top of his plate. "Don't worry. I have a plan in place. Soon Williamsport will be under your control, Mr. President."

# Chapter 5

March 18, 2275

The president and his staff lined the wall of the dining room, opposite large windows that looked out into the atrium, ready to greet their visitors.

The ambassador and his staff entered, staring in awe at the long wooden table. They positioned themselves to stand behind the chairs at the table. An announcer introduced the president and his wife, as they walked from the wall to the front of the table. The president greeted the ambassador and called for everyone to be seated.

Lewis stared at the man to his right. Milestown must be a poor city. Did they ration their food? He noticed how much thinner these people were compared to his own people.

The president raised his hand up to his shoulder. Doors opened and food rolled out on a long stone table. Two servants on opposite sides of the table served the guests.

When all were served the president stood with a glass of sparkling wine in hand and greeted his guest. "To the people of Milestown, Lackawana and Mayfield welcome to New Scranton." The president sat down and began to eat.

The ambassador cut into the meat for the first time, looking at it and smelling it. As he chewed, he nodded and his eyes lit up. "Mr. President. This meat is very tasty. What is this sauce you put on it? It's delicious."

"It's called béarnaise. I'm so glad you like it." The president smiled politely at the ambassador realizing now how much they looked alike. The brown balding head, oval-shaped face and flaring nose reminded him of a thinner version of himself. *Interesting.*

Once the main course concluded, the president looked over to the servers and nodded before turning to the ambassador. "I have a surprise for you and your people."

Everyone turned to watch as servers emerged from the kitchen with trays containing several bowls with three cubes of differing colors—red, green and clear. A bowl was placed in front of the ambassador, who prodded it with a spoon. It jiggled. He lifted the red cube to his nose and sniffed it. As the cube entered his mouth he smiled.

"I see that you are enjoying it, Mr. Ambassador," the president said.

"Oh yes." He laughed. "This is the only food I've ever had that is both tasty and entertaining at the same time. What is it and where does it come from?"

"It's called jello. It's a byproduct of the animals we eat."

"You must show us how to make this."

"You ask for many things, Mr. Ambassador." Lewis smiled as he looked around the room and put on his business face. "We can bottle the béarnaise sauce. We can bag the jello and show you how to make it and we can ship however much meat you desire in exchange for more shipments of coal."

It was clear what the ambassador thought: that these things the Feds provided were mere luxuries and the coal they wanted had a far greater value. The Feds would be on the losing end of negotiations, but hopefully his people wouldn't be reamed too badly.

"Yes, that is something we must discuss. We need to determine the value of this," the ambassador gestured across the table in a sweeping motion. He took the napkin from his lap and wiped his mouth. "This is all excellent. May we see the animals this meat comes from?"

As far as everyone knew, the land animals had died out long ago. Lewis knew he had the one thing that no other city had. "These animals are rare. They provide us with food and clothing."

The ambassador raised an eyebrow.

"Indeed," Lewis continued, "not only do we eat these animals, we use their skin to clothe ourselves." He motioned to a servant to bring him his jacket. The ambassador examined the garment, open-mouthed. As he stood to try it on all eyes turned to watch. The jacket fit perfectly.

The ambassador's hand glided over the material. "This is very nice. It's soft and warm." He lifted his arm bringing the sleeve closer to his nose to sniff it. "It smells nothing like the meat we've been eating."

The president grinned widely. "It's called leather. As you can see the animals are very useful. We keep them well-fed and let them roam around a fenced in area, so they don't wander off."

"When can we see these animals?" the ambassador asked again, resuming his seat and finishing the last cube of gelatin.

"It's farther than half a day outside of the city. We need time to prepare for your overnight stay once we arrive there. In a few days my assistant will make all the necessary arrangements," the president looked to his assistant who nodded. "In the meantime, rest. You've come from far away. We will begin negotiations in the morning."

---

The ambassador was brought to the president's home where they discussed numbers after breakfast: shipments of coal for meat and other products the Feds made. Several days passed as they discussed and made changes to agreements.

"C'mon Levon," Greogry said closing his eyes and arching his back while squeezing his neck. "We've been over this every day since you got here." The president grew tired of the ambassador's insistence on seeing the animals.

"I don't understand why you're making it difficult to show us these animals," Levon said. "I really don't know if I can continue these negotiations, to be honest." He stared stoic into the president's face.

Gregory straightened up. Was he serious? For the moment, making sure the ambassador focused on negotiations was the most important thing. Securing shipments of coal had a higher priority. The animals would have to wait.

"Okay, I tell you what." Gregory put his hands on the table, palms down with fingers spread. "We finish the discussions about what the Feds want and what the Feds can give Milestown and then we'll look into seeing the animals." The president smiled.

Levon returned the smiled. "Then let's finish." Levon raised his hand. "I won't mention the animals until we're done here."

Negotiations went back and forth for weeks. The Feds had many things that they produced besides meat—clothes, paper, ink and weapons. The only thing Milestown had worth trading was the coal. They were a simple people.

The ambassador negotiated with a clever awareness while the president didn't concede or reveal how desperate his people were for fuel.

"Finally!" Lewis said enthusiastically, holding up the document that took two months of negotiating. He shook the ambassador's hand. "You are a shrewd negotiator, Mr. Ambassador." He motioned to one of his assistants to come over. "We'll make copies of the document and send it to your counterpart in Milestown to give to your mayor and city council to agree to the terms. In the meantime, let's celebrate our new and lasting friendship."

---

The ambassador couldn't understand why the president was so reluctant to show their animals. He would have thought he would be excited to show something that no other city had. Every time he asked, the president would come up with some excuse. There was speculation from the embassy staff that these animals the Feds raised might be coming from another city. If so, Milestown wouldn't need to trade with the Feds after all. Why was the president delaying? Why were these animals so closely guarded? If the animals came from another city, the treaty they were working on would be worthless. The more the ambassador asked about the animals the more the president delayed. Levon had to settle on finishing discussions on a trade agreement before any animals could be seen.

The ambassador dispatched several of his men to find answers. Were the Feds raising these animals themselves, or was another city involved? Either way, they needed to smuggle a pair to Milestown.

# Chapter 6

Willack, Eloi, and Stevall traveled the countryside trying to find where the Feds kept their land animals. So far, no traces had been found. Every time they asked about the animals, they got blank stares. Inquiring at the meat shops only got them vague answers. This worried Willack. Why would they guard these animals so closely that no one has seen them?

"Ask the deliveryman. I'm sure he'd know," one of the shop owners said.

The deliveryman showed up early the next morning towing a large cart with ten containers of ice and meat on top of it. Willack befriended him and inquired about the meat.

"The place is called the Harvest," the deliveryman said.

"Where is this Harvest?" Willack asked, anticipating that the deliveryman would tell him he didn't know.

"It's in Kidder."

*Finally!* "Thank you."

"But you won't see any of the animals." The man added quickly. "The place is heavily guarded." The deliveryman described the place, telling them how to get there.

Willack thanked him again. Now they had something that got them closer to finding the animals.

The trio walked toward Kidder for most of the day. It was the farthest city northwest of New Scranton. The Feds were better at producing food than his own people. They passed farms with crops of corn that towered above their heads, and wheat that went on for as far as the eye could see.

A huge building loomed in the distance, smoke pouring out of several chimneys. It must have been as large as the Ancient Tower in Milestown, except that this structure was all-white and sat atop a hill. Squinting, he could make out two sets of fences, one within the other, with towers stationed at intervals. The towers stood about twice the height of the fences.

The smell of cooked meat filled the air; it was making him hungry. The thought of a thick juicy steak made his mouth start to water. From the growling stomachs of Stevall and Eloi, they seemed to be thinking the same thing.

They came closer to the metal fence and could see two men in each of the towers. The first fence was so high you couldn't see the one inside. What the hell kind of animals would require a fence to be so tall and impenetrable? They walked around until they got to a place where men packed boxes with meat wrapped in cloth surrounded by ice. The boxes were stacked three levels high on a metal flatbed with wheels. Two men pushed the cart to transport the meat back into the city. Guards carrying black, shiny batons walked among the packers.

Willack walked over to a man with a black and grey beard, wearing a blood-stained white smock, packing meat into a cart, and inquired about the animals. The man stopped what he was doing, wiped the blood from his hands onto his apron, then the sweat off his face with the same apron.

A tall and heavyset guard strolled over to where Willack talked with the bearded man. Anger shone from the guard's beady eyes as his lips pressed together. "What are you doing here asking questions?"

"We're from Milestown. We came to inquire about the animals. We're curious to see them."

"I'll show you what you want to see." A man's voice sounded, cutting off the guard. The man was short in a white robe and black leather boots. His face was gaunt, large eyes and paper-thin lips, which reminded Willack of a crustacean. A set of knives hung from his belt. They were much smaller than the knife concealed under Willack's own shirt. It was hard not to laugh. Didn't this man understand that size mattered?

The man gestured for Willack and the others to proceed toward the door.

"Thank you." Willack bowed his head and called for his men to follow. "I am Willack, and this is Eloi, and Stevall," he said introducing his men.

"I am Shriva," the white-robed man said, pointing to a door off to their side. "We'll enter through here."

Willack and his men followed. Two guards also came in behind them. He felt his side, making sure his own knife was in place, as they walked up the stairs to a plank that ran across the entire building. Below them were people—lots of people, forming three lines to three separate, guarded doors.

"Why are they in line?" Eloi asked.

"Who are these people?" Stevall asked. "Why are they here?"

"Shriva walked in front of them and turned around. "These people are enemies of the Feds. "They come from other cities. They form these lines so that we can process them. Some are selected for breeding and others for food preparation."

"Why do you want them to have children?" Willack asked. Milestown's treatment of slaves was much more humane than the Feds.

"So they can help with the food production," Shriva shrugged.

Willack didn't understand. How difficult could it be to take care of an animal? Not this complex. How many animals were there that would require this many people to take care of them?

They walked to the far end of the room and watched the people below. One person entered the room at a time, and it was several minutes before the next person came in. Shriva explained that it was necessary to keep order. He opened the door nearest them and motioned for his guests to pass through.

They walked to the middle of the room and looked down into what looked like a maze. The walls where tall enough that a person couldn't see anything else. The men watched someone enter the maze. It was a little girl and boy, not more than six or seven. They were forced to take off their clothes and defecate into a bowl that fed into a large vat. It was surprising that the smell of all the excrement was not noticeable in an enclosure like this.

The girl and boy entered another part of the maze where two workers put a white substance onto their bodies and scrubbed them.

"Why do you humiliate these people like this?" Stevall asked.

"They must be cleaned before they go on to the next step," Shriva answered, with another noncommittal shrug.

"But won't they get dirty helping with the food production?" Eloi asked.

Shriva didn't answer. Instead he opened the door to the next room where the plank didn't go all the way and ushered them through. The plank turned to the right and stopped at a wall with a window view outside. Willack looked out and saw people walking around the fenced area doing nothing. This place seemed more like a prison than someplace to raise animals. He went back to where the others gathered and looked down over the railing, noticing a door. The maze couldn't be seen anymore from this part of the building. The entrance was dark, two men stood by the door, waiting.

A few minutes went by before the little girl entered, the boy wasn't with her. The second she came in, one of the men grabbed her and held her tight, while the other slammed the door closed behind her. The little girl screamed as one man slashed her throat with a knife. Blood gushed from the gaping hole on her neck. Gurgling sounds emanated from the little girl as she collapsed to the ground.

Stevall's face contorted in anger. "What are they doing down there?" he whispered to his comrades.

Willack jerked, ready to go down and help her, but it was a far drop, and it was too late for the little girl. Nausea came over him. Yet, he continued to watch.

The dying girl was tied and lifted up by her legs as blood continued to gush out from her neck.

A woman burst into the room. "Where's my daughter?" she shouted hysterically to the surprised men. She looked at the little girl tied to the rope and screamed. The workers grabbed her. She struggled with the men, but managed to cry out, "Tommy, run!" before the workers slashed her throat as well.

Willack watched in horror as the girl was pushed into another well-lit room where two new men set about the task of disemboweling her.

"We need to help them!" Eloi and Stevall gathered around Willack whose eyes followed Shriva. The man wasn't paying any attention.

"We can't do a thing. They're already dead." Willack watched with growing anxiety as the woman's feet were tied and she was slung up on a rope. "We need to start thinking of a way out of here. I doubt they're going to let us leave after seeing this."

Willack and his men returned to the railing and continued to watch. The air tasted foul with the energy of violence and death.

The young boy entered the room and saw what Willack could only guess was his mother and sister, dying. The men tried to grab the boy, but he managed to escape their clutches. Willack's muscles tensed, squeezing the railing as he silently rooted for the boy to escape.

The workers slammed the door and continued with the woman, rolling her into the room where they had finished bleeding her daughter. Both bodies were disemboweled and then laid on the slab next to one another. One man wiggled his fingers into a small incision, and slowly, methodically peeled the skin off the body.

Willack sensed Stevall shivering by his side.

Two boxes were next to the bodies. The skin was placed in one, in the other, the scalps of the dead. Willack didn't know why they did this—he didn't care. The whole scene was horrifying. Yet, he couldn't stop watching.

The skinless bodies were moved into another room where three men worked fast to sever the limbs and head. With efficient precision, the meat was sliced off the bones and stacked in containers filled with ice. Bones were placed into a boiling vat of water. Other, smaller pieces of flesh were taken to another room where smoke could be seen escaping from vents that reached into the ceiling. By the time the body of the little girl and mother were fully cut up, the blood on the floor had been swept into a gutter and another victim entered through the door to the same fate.

"You eat people?" Eloi gasped as they started working on the new victim. He turned to Shriva with a broken voice. "*These* are your animals?"

Shriva smiled.

Not more than an hour ago, Willack had savored the thought of eating a steak. Now, his stomach gave out. He vomited at his own feet. Panic overcame him. He turned toward the door and yelled, "I need to get out of here!"

The two guards that faced him blocked his way. Willack pressed on. Shriva put his hand on Willack's shoulder. "I'm sorry, but I can't let you leave."

Willack turned to Shriva, but before he could speak, Stevall ran to the window and crashed through it, landing on the grassy field below. Willack and Eloi rushed to the window and watched as Stevall made his way to the first fence. A loud horn blasted through the silent air. Stevall managed to scale the first fence and ran toward the second. As he began to climb it, a guard in the nearest tower aimed his rifle.

*Bang!*

The bullet hit its mark in Stevall's torso. He fell off the fence and hit the ground. He rolled over and managed to get up.

*Bang!*

Another bullet found its way through his neck—in an instant, he was dead.

Shriva turned his gaze to Willack and Eloi, still grinning. Willack tasted bile in the back of his throat, his legs unsteady, barely holding him up. Stevall was dead. They should have fought, even knowing they would have lost, they should have fought. They were going to die, and these people were going to eat them.

As the guards closed in on them, evil sparked through Shriva's eyes. "You didn't expect *this*, did you?"

The guards grabbed Eloi and held his hands behind his back. Shriva opened his pouch and took out a small knife, the one that Willack had earlier found amusing. Not anymore. In one swift motion, Shriva slashed Eloi's jugular. Blood began to spurt out of his body in torrents. They threw him over the plank; his limp body fell twenty feet, landing next to the workers who had killed the little girl and her mother. The men hesitated and looked up as if in surprise. But it was only a split second, before they seemed to regain their composure and set about their task—preparing the body for the cutting room.

As everyone's attention was on Eloi, Willack ran across the plank pushing two guards, ramming them with his shoulders and knocking them off balance. He came out to the packing area. In a desperate attempt to escape he butted several men over like bowling pins. The guards converged. But Willack was already gone, his legs pumping, heart pounding, as he ran into the cornfields. The guards chased close behind. Willack wasn't going to let them do what they had just done to Eloi and Stevall. When they yelled for him to stop, he picked up the pace and ran even faster, his only thought to run. He didn't turn around.

Where to go? There was only one place—the embassy. Once there the ambassador would know the truth about the animals these people eat.

Several hours passed before the adrenalin rush subsided. He slowed, as a large boulder came into view. The heavy breathing continued as he repeatedly looked back over his shoulder expecting the guards to appear. The sky began to turn dark maroon, the crimson clouds hovering past, a quarter moon almost at its highest point in the sky. Standing alone and in the dark, when it finally sank in that none of the guards had continued the chase, the sense of urgency finally dissipated and so did all of Willack's energy. Getting to the embassy could wait. As he assessed his surroundings Willack noticed a small opening underneath the boulder: a perfect resting place for the night. He slept restlessly, waking up from time to time, to nightmares that the guards had finally found him.

# Chapter 7

Willack reached the embassy by midday. Music played in the distance. People stood around with plates of food in their hands talking and laughing. Fed soldiers lined up at the front of the building—something about this didn't feel right. Willack slipped around back, staying in the shadows.

The long, narrow hallway opened to a grand hall. Chandeliers holding dozens of candles lit up the room. Nothing appeared to be out of the ordinary. Everyone seemed to be having a good time. A few danced to the music the band played. Several tables were set up with a variety of foods and drinks. Willack gagged at the sight and smell of cooked flesh.

The ambassador was speaking with the commanding officer of the Feds—Commander Ramses. They both laughed as if they had been good friends for years. Willack got the ambassador's attention. The ambassador excused himself from the commander, escorting Willack into the nearest room, helping him sit on the only chair in the room.

"Take it easy, son." The ambassador went to get some water. "Here. Drink this. What happened? Where's Eloi and Stevall?"

"Dead sir." Willack breathed heavily and continued to drink. "We found the animals."

"And, what? Did they attack you?"

"No," Willack tried relaxing and catching his breath. "Lots of people."

"Were you chased away? Tell me boy! What did you find?"

"The animals... we found... the animals... They're humans. They slaughter people for food."

The ambassador's mouth and eyes opened wide in surprise. "This is sick! We've been eating... people... all this time?" The ambassador's face turned a shade of green. The plate in his hand slipped through his fingers, and clanged off the hard, ceramic tiles. He rushed over to the porcelain bowl on the sideboard and vomited.

The ambassador stood and looked over to Willack. His vein pulsed in his neck, his face was now red. The look he gave Willack was clear. He understood the intent behind his gaze, for he was thinking the same thing—they needed to get back to Milestown.

---

A soldier approached Commander Ramses and whispered into his ear. The commander's face turned in the direction of the closed door the ambassador had gone into. His cheerful expression turned stern and cold. With a snap of a finger and a wave of his hand, several soldiers were ordered to only allow Fed citizens to leave. He entered the closed door without saying a word and locked it.

"I heard some noise coming from the room and thought I should come in to see if everything was all right." He thought it best to pretend there were no problems. After all, this might not be the man who had just run all the way from the Harvest. Levon had a sick, green complexion.

"I'm feeling ill. Nothing that a few days' rest won't cure".

The man with Levon wore crumpled clothes and appeared shaken. There were bags under his eyes. He couldn't have been more than twenty. "And who is this?"

"This is one of my assistants, Willack."

"Nice to meet you, Willack." He recognized the name. So Levon knew. This *was* the running man.

"I'm sorry that you're not feeling well. Maybe it's something in the meat."

"Perhaps." Levon began to heave over the bowl.

"Shall I get you another plate?" Ramses offered, studying his friend.

"No!" he shrieked, popping his head up. "No. I'm fine. I just need to rest."

Ramses cleared his throat. Swallowed. He couldn't keep pretending—not with Levon. "I know. I know what you've been told, Levon."

Levon's face paled. He was silent for a few minutes—neither man spoke. He could feel Willack's eyes on him, but the young man also kept silent, letting it play out between two friends.

"The animals you get your meat from." Levon spoke at last. "They're not animals!"

The commander shrugged. "Well, that depends on how you define an animal. I'm sorry you had to find out about it like this."

As he reached for the door handle, calling over two soldiers, Levon pulled out a knife from under his coat. It glinted in the candlelight as he raised it and lunged for Ramses.

From the corner of his eye he saw Willack attack one of the soldiers that stepped into the small room and started screaming for help. One of the embassy staff members appeared, and as his eyes landed on the commotion she instantly started screaming.

The music died down, as embassy guards approached the screaming woman. People started to gather. A soldier held the ambassador's hands behind his back, giving Ramses a chance to take stock. Willack tried getting out of the room but the soldier grabbed him from behind and slit his throat. Blood sprayed out onto those closest to the door. Everyone started to scream and run in every direction. Chaos ruled.

Closing the door and locking it, commander Ramses went to the window and signaled his men to come in and secure the building.

No one would leave.

---

Audrey opened the door leading to the rooftop of the embassy building and searched for Logan. He didn't like parties all that much, and usually ended up somewhere quiet and alone. There he stood looking out toward the city. A warm wind blew across the roof making his short fiery red hair ruffle. She stood close, arms folded across her to brace against the breeze and looked out toward the scene that seemed to fascinate him.

"It's beautiful, isn't it?"

She cocked her head. "How did you know I was here?"

"You walk on your heels, not the balls of your feet."

"What?"

"When you walk with your heels, you make more noise than when you walk on the balls of your feet. I heard you when you walked toward me."

"But how did you know it was *me*?"

"I know your walk," he shrugged, and turned, letting his eyes travel the length of her body then back up again, until their eyes met. "You look really nice today."

She stared into his green eyes and gave him a playful shove. "Are you checking me out?"

"I was just..." Logan stammered. His cheeks turned tomato red. He cleared his throat. "Yes, I was checking you out."

Audrey grinned wider and nudged against him, not quite sure how she felt about his unexpected honesty. They were friends, for sure. And this boy was handsome, masculine, and smart; yet something was missing. Something she couldn't put her finger on.

Logan opened his mouth to speak, but frowning, he closed it again, remaining silent.

"What?"

"Doesn't this all seem... unusual to you?" he asked, gesturing with his arms out toward the city.

The question made no sense to Audrey. "What are you talking about?"

"This alliance between Milestown and the Feds." He sat down on the edge of the roof and indicated for her to sit beside him. "The treaty between our people is a good thing. But it's what they're giving us for the coal. They're giving us almost anything we want for it."

"And this is bad, how?" she asked.

"Everyone I've met here seems nice." He sighed. "The people are a bit stockier than we are but they're just like us in every other way. The longer we stay here, the more we're becoming like them. Even you've gained some weight."

"Are you saying I'm fat?" she huffed. She could feel her hackles rising. *Did I hear that right?*

"There's nothing wrong with you, Audrey. It's just that we've begun to assimilate to their ways and customs. We're becoming like them." He looked out across the building. "it's like they plan to make us part of their group."

Why did it matter? Why did he care if we became more like *them*? Wasn't it last year that he argued about freeing slaves? She liked it here. She liked these new customs. What was wrong with that? The Feds had luxuries that Milestown could never acquire without them.

Logan peered down over the edge with a frown.

"Now what's wrong?" she asked, irritated that he found fault with everything. She followed his gaze.

"There are more soldiers today than on other days."

"There's a celebration going on," she huffed, hands on hips. "Maybe they wanted to provide extra security?"

"We have our own embassy guards. Why would we need Fed soldiers? And if you hadn't noticed, why are the soldiers facing toward the embassy?"

He had a point, but she didn't have time to mull it over. The calm was broken by screaming and shouting coming from inside the building. They watched on from their perch above the fracas, as Fed soldiers fought with embassy guards and gave chase to Milestownians as they ran out of the building and down the street.

Logan tugged on her dress. "Hurry!" he whispered, pointing toward the water tower at the back of the roof. Without hesitation, she jumped up and ran with him. They hurried up the ladder to the top of the water tower.

Several soldiers barged through the door, bursting onto the roof only moments after they had reached their hiding spot above them. Logan and Audrey ducked, barely escaped being noticed. She peered over the top of the water tower and saw the embassy staff being marched onto the rooftop, including the ambassador and his wife.

"You decided to go looking for our animals!" Ramses said in a clipped tone which was directed at the ambassador. "The president told you he would show you all in good time. But you were in a hurry to see them. So now you've seen them. Well, we can't let you go home with that information, can we?"

The commander walked back and forth in front of the ambassador.

"Do you really think we'd continue to eat *that*?" said the ambassador, "I demand to see the president."

"He's busy."

"You'll imprison us here?"

"If we had prisoners," the commander scoffed.

Audrey felt defenseless watching her people being held against their will. Her aunt was among those lined up on the rooftop. The woman's eyes drifted and spotted them hiding. A soldier turned around to follow her gaze. Logan and Audrey slid deeper into the shadows, barely escaping the soldier's scan. They moved to another side of the tower to position themselves for a better view of what was happening.

The commander looked at the ambassador with disdain. Sliding out his fighting knife, he plunged it into the ambassador's chest and then quickly removed it. The ambassador's lifeless body fell to the ground.

Logan watched as his father died right in front of him. Audrey could hear his breathing increase. His jaw tightened—he was ready to jump down and fight. "You can't help him now, Logan!" she whispered vehemently, holding on to his arm as tightly as she could. "You'll only be getting yourself killed."

She needed him now. Avenging his father meant suicide. There was no way she would allow that. Eventually, Logan sat back down, staring at his father's lifeless body lying on the rooftop. Logan's mother appeared to be on the verge of collapse herself, swaying as though her legs would give out. There was screaming and yelling, people ran in all directions trying to get away. Some managed to jump only to find their fate waiting for them on the hard surface below.

In less than ten minutes, twenty-three people lay dead on the embassy rooftop.

Soldiers brought up tables and boxes with ice to the roof, stacking the bodies to one side. Men in white lab coats and gloves rushed through the roof door, each carrying square pouches made of leather. More bodies of men and women were brought up and laid next to their dead comrades. They must have been the ones who had jumped. Dead bodies were placed on the tables one at a time and in a matter of moments, what was once a person became a stack of meat and hide.

Tears fell down Audrey's face as she held on to Logan's arm tightly. For some reason she couldn't pull her eyes from the carnage. As a slow, burning fury raged inside her, tears continued to stream down her face. Escape would be difficult with so many soldiers milling around. The human slices of meat went into the boxes. When they were done, the soldiers took the boxes of meat and the tables downstairs.

"Clean up the excess debris," an officer ordered a soldier.

"Shall I wash the rooftop down?"

The officer shrugged. "I don't care, just clean up this mess."

The soldier swept entrails and small pieces of cut-up human flesh. Afterwards he grabbed a rolled-up water hose and began washing down the rooftop.

Audrey rested against the slanted roof of the water tower, her head spinning. The smell of blood filled the air. The conflicting horror of what had just happened clashed in her mind with the sweet smell of cooked flesh from the celebration. She gagged. The tears started again. Her aunt, Logan's mom and dad, all dead. Everyone was dead. How were they going to get out? Home seemed so far away.

# Chapter 8

The sun had already fallen below the horizon as the lone soldier swept the excess water and remaining debris off the rooftop. He approached the water tower, stopped for a moment, then began to climb up the ladder. Logan seemed to have already heard the noise when Audrey looked at him; they switched sides. Logan clutched the knife that was strapped to his leg. As the soldier's head popped up over the tower roof his gaze fell first on Audrey, then on Logan. Logan moved in, slashing the soldier's face.

The soldier fell, screaming on the way down, landing hard on the rooftop with a dull thud. Logan quickly climbed down the ladder; she followed right behind. The soldier put up his hands as Logan slashed at the young man in a blind rage, blood splattering on his shirt and face.

The soldier lay lifeless, yet Logan continued his violent rampage tearing at his opponent's face and chest. When he finally stopped Audrey approached, hesitantly. Kneeling down beside him, she gently put her hand on his back. He didn't flinch; she wasn't even sure he noticed. Eventually Logan's muscles relaxed under her touch.

"What do we do now?" she asked.

"We move him against the wall, over there," he said pointing to the far side of the rooftop.

Together, they carried him, positioning the body to make it look like the soldier was taking a nap, the bloodied, mangled face turned away, so it wouldn't be noticed from a distance.

With the sun having set over an hour earlier, Audrey looked up into the dark red sky and watched the last remnants of daylight disappear over the horizon. The moon hadn't yet started its ascent. She looked over the roof and spotted soldiers still standing guard at the entrance of the building.

She felt a firm hand on her shoulder, pulling her back.

Logan put his finger to his lip and motioned for her to sit down. She obeyed.

"We're going to have to wait until a few hours before the sun comes up before we make our move," he said.

"Logan, how are we going to get home?"

"I'm sure if we follow the river north, we'll get home."

They rested on the opposite side of the roof, away from the tower and the dead soldier. It wasn't long before she felt her eyes get heavy and start to close.

"Wake up! Audrey, wake up!" Her eyes unglued. Her body ached as she lifted her head from Logan's lap.

"Get to the river," said the voice.

Who was talking? She looked around and found no one. Logan's eyes were closed, his breathing even and steady. She risked a quick glance toward the water tower—the soldier was still dead.

The air was cold, the moon was not in the sky. Audrey shook Logan awake. His eyes focused on her then looked up to the night sky. He stood quickly.

"What's wrong?" she asked. Her senses on edge.

"We have less than an hour before the sun comes up," he said. "You didn't sleep?"

"I did. I woke up to the sound of someone talking to me. I thought it was you."

They went to the edge of the roof and saw no soldiers on the streets. Logan took the hose and tied it around the water tower and dropped the other end over the side. The hose hung two meters off the ground. Audrey went first. She was not even halfway down when she heard voices coming toward her. She let go of the hose and fell to the ground and rolled against the wall, trying to hide. The voices continued on. When all was clear she could hear Logan begin his descent.

Logan landed on the ground softly and came over to Audrey putting his hand over her back. "Hey, are you okay?"

Audrey turned around and embraced him, crying. "Logan, I'm so afraid. What's going to happen to us?"

"Shh," he whispered. "You're too loud." He turned looking around.

"I don't want to die."

"You're not going to die." He stood and pulled her up. "We need to get to the river. Come on," he said grabbing her hand and leading her away from the building.

They started walking toward the river, making sure to keep away from any houses that still had fires burning. They were approaching the farmlands. A battered sign read 'Leaving Scranton.' The word new was haphazardly painted above the word Scranton. She remembered this area when they arrived. They were close to the river. Night was turning into day, even though the sun hadn't come up yet. As they came to the last house on this side of the city, Audrey spotted Shirl.

"You still live!" the servant cried.

"You must help us!" Audrey ordered. "They've killed everyone. We must get home and tell my father."

Shirl's slanted eyes darted between Audrey and Logan, before her mouth curved into a sly grin. "Guards!"

"What are you doing?" Audrey hissed.

"Guards, there are still two from Milestown that live!"

She couldn't believe her own servant would betray her like this! Stepping closer to the slave, she slapped her across the face. The woman responded by connecting a fist with Audrey's mouth, causing her to fall back. Logan caught her fall.

Audrey didn't understand this betrayal. She was still reeling when Logan grabbed her hand and pulled her in the opposite direction. With a last look at Shirl and her self-satisfied smile, Audrey let Logan lead her away.

They reached the river with Audrey trailing behind Logan, her breath now coming in gasps as her feet slipped in the dewy grass, but it muffled the sound of their pounding footsteps as they ran. They blindly ran north along the riverbank in their haste to get away. They ran for what must have been hours before Audrey collapsed breathing heavily. Logan stopped, tried coaxing her up, to get closer to the river's edge to drink. Logan cupped some water in his hands and brought it to Audrey's mouth. She began to drink.

"Are they following us?" Audrey asked.

"I don't see anyone," he said, looking back the way they had come.

"Maybe they've stopped chasing us," she mumbled.

"Why would they stop chasing us? I'm the ambassador's son and you're the mayor's daughter. I'm sure there will be more soldiers following us soon." Logan looked her over. "Can we continue? We don't have time to rest right now."

Audrey continued breathing heavily while Logan seemed to not be tired at all. *How was he doing this? He must still be traveling high on the tide of his bloodlust*, she thought.

"I can't run anymore," she forced out between gasps of labored breaths.

"We'll walk then."

She nodded. He stood and helped her up by the shoulders. At first, he tried getting her to walk at a fast pace, but the more he tried the more she wasn't cooperating.

Logan scoped the area. Audrey was sure the soldiers had stopped chasing them. She just wanted to rest. The landscape had changed. The area was littered with boulders that hid them well. It also hid any soldiers that might be following them. Small, dead shrubs and thin vines grew around the boulders in patches. Grooves on the land had been caused by the erosion of water during the rainy season. The river itself was like an oasis passing through a desert.

He tripped over a branch that had been sticking out of the ground and fell to his knees. Audrey came down with him.

"Please, let's just sit here... just for a while," she pleaded.

---

Logan turned around to investigate the protruding branch. It was an exposed ancient tree sticking out of the ground. A majority of it was lodged in mud the rest stretched into the river. Moving swiftly, he found a large rock and started digging, loosening the dirt to expose the dead tree. He lifted the tree and dragged it into the river. It fell in, with a loud splash. He held his breath, stood still. There was no movement along the river or up by the hills. If the soldiers were still following them, they wouldn't be too far behind.

"Audrey," Logan said as loud as he dared, "we can use this to float down the river." Audrey was barely awake and just sighed, closing her eyes. "Audrey, wake up. I need your help," he coaxed. "Help me move the tree."

She opened her eyes, looking, but not focusing. The river was shallow. The ancient tree sank into the mud at the bottom of the river. She could hear Logan lifting the tree and dragging it down the river. "Help me!" he screamed.

Startled, Audrey lifted her body with what little strength she had left and went over to the tree. The water and mud enveloped her feet. She lifted one of the branches and pulled on it, dragging it through the water. The river deepened enough for the tree to float and she lay over it to rest. It sank a little under her weight, but not enough to drag along the river floor.

Logan walked alongside the tree, holding on to one of the larger branches for balance. The water was too shallow to hold them both. The tree made ripples through the water as it was pushed. His eyes never stopped scanning their surroundings. All was clear—for now. A sense of relief ensued, even though it may be short-lived.

Logan tested the ancient tree, by climbing onto it, to see if it would support them both without sinking into the mud, now that the river became deeper and the current stronger. It didn't drag. He lay back resting against one of the branches and fell asleep.

The sound of rushing water woke him. The current had picked up a little. By midday, the clouds had disappeared, and Logan started to feel the scorching rays of the sun hitting him like hail. He scooped up some water with his hands and poured it over his face and any exposed skin that was already turning red. Audrey still slept, wrapped in her dress with only one leg exposed to the sun. She wouldn't get burned too badly.

The river's mood changed, and they started to speed up. Audrey woke up to a fast current. They both tried holding on tighter to the branches as the tree went through some rapids. The water splashed violently around them and Audrey screamed as a sudden dip caused them to fall into the angry current below. Audrey managed to hang on. Logan was not so fortunate. He fell off and splashed about in the water while Audrey floated away.

A fork in the river and the strong current caused the tree to go in a different direction. Logan swam toward the tree. Audrey helped him get back on and they managed to balance themselves without rolling over.

"Are you all right?" Audrey yelled over the sound of the loud rumbling water.

Logan nodded his head in the affirmative. "Very tired," he said breathing in gulps of air.

"We were supposed to go down the other way, weren't we?"

"Yeah."

"We can always swim to shore and backtrack."

He shook his head and said, "The river is going too fast. Let's just continue on this course to wherever it may lead." Logan inhaled deeply. "The Feds won't think we came down this way."

Backtracking wasn't a good idea. They needed to get to the ocean, and from there, the Great Bay and home.

By the afternoon, the river had changed from rapids, to calm, and back to rapids, never allowing them to rest. The faint smell of the ocean let them know they must be nearing the end of their journey. They floated under a rickety bridge. It had to have been one of the ancient structures built long ago. Its rusted metal beams stretched across the river. From this vantage point, the bridge didn't lead toward any passage on either side. The river showed no clear passage into the bay that lay ahead. The entire landscape seemed to just stop.

"We need to swim to shore!" Logan shouted, moving closer to Audrey. "Now!"

"Why, what's going on?"

"No time to explain. Just do what I say!" he shouted and jumped into the water, kicking against the current which was desperately trying to rip him away.

Audrey followed and swam to shore.

The tree floated downstream for a distance, tilted up and disappeared. Logan took the lead and walked toward the edge. Off to their right, a magnificent waterfall flowed into the sea as the ocean splashed against rock formations.

With several hours of sunlight left, Logan scouted for an area littered with stones to construct shelter. As he worked, his stomach began to rumble. It had been over a day since they had eaten. Thoughts of eating meat entered his mind. In repugnance, he tried blocking out those visions.

Audrey also needed to rest. The running and heat from the sun bearing down on her had been too much. Logan began piling stones together. The energy left stemming from his anger and pain seemed to keep him going. She mustered up whatever strength she could and went over to help.

"What are you doing?"

"Building a hut."

"I can help. I'll find some stones." She walked away searching for stones among the large boulders.

Something next to a large rock caught her attention—a vine. The plant had a black fruit growing out of it where the green leaves were attached. The taste was sour. With nothing else to consume she continued to eat until there was no more fruit.

Climbing over the boulder revealed a small oasis of vines spread out and growing in several directions. She bent down and collected the fruit. For every three collected she would eat one. After a while, it became too exhausting to pick any more and she sat on a rock to rest.

"So, this is where you've been all this time." Logan stood behind her.

Startled, she turned around to see him framed by the orange sky.

"I found some fruit." She held it up in her hand so he could see it.

"I can see that. Why didn't you call me over?"

"I was going to bring some to you. See?" She stood showing him what she had collected in her lap.

Logan didn't wait for an invitation and ran over, grabbed some of the fruit, and shoved it in his mouth. The sour taste made him grimace. Audrey laughed at the dark purple color that formed around his lips.

With the hut completed, they went to the river and washed up for the night. Logan dug into the ground to find some dead tree branches he could use to make a fire. It was dark before the fire started and the cold winds were already blowing in from the east. Audrey was beyond exhausted. Logan had pushed her beyond her limits. Her stomach rumbled from the fruits eaten yet they weren't enough to kill the hunger pangs. They curled up next to each other and fell fast asleep.

That night she had a dream. She was thirteen years old. A child about the same age stood a distance away—a slave attempting an escape. A soldier chased him and out of nowhere a man appeared. She couldn't make out his face. He grabbed the boy's arm and ran. The soldiers shot at them hitting the child. The man stopped and helped the boy up when a woman came running toward her son. She cried out for the soldiers to stop shooting. Someone in the crowd knocked her to the ground. The soldiers reached the man and the boy and tied the child's hands behind his back.

"No!" the man shouted, trying to pull the soldiers off the boy. The soldiers struck him with the butt of their guns, and he fell to the ground. An unusual object fell out of his hand. The soldiers went over and smashed it to pieces. Sparks flew and a bright light flashed, blinding everyone for a few moments.

The child started to run with his hands tied. The soldiers spotted him and shot him in the back, killing him. Then they turned their attention to the man on the ground and beat him.

# Timepieces

Audrey now saw everything through his eyes as he lay on the ground. The man recognized her. Or maybe it was that she recognized herself. Her point of view then changed back. The man tried to get up, screaming, "Audrey!" Who was he? How did he know her? He crawled toward her trying to smile at her. She backed up in fear. One of the soldiers shot him in the back. As death approached, his eyes were fixed on her. He moved his lips, yet no sounds came out. Like a gust of wind blowing against her face she could hear him say, "You kept your promise."

A promise? What promise? How could she keep a promise she didn't make?

"You kept your promise," he said again.

Logan's voice pierced her consciousness. "Audrey, wake up. Audrey?"

Audrey jerked and focused on her surroundings.

"Are you okay?" he asked. "You were shaking."

"Yeah, I'm fine." She sat up.

"Had a bad dream?"

"It felt so real. I dreamt about a slave. The one we saw running away in your fields last year."

"Want to talk about it?"

"No. It's not important."

It was unusual for her to dream about slaves. What were they to her, except someone to order around? Somehow her dream was related to Shirl's betrayal. The Feds had likely rewarded her for what she did. The actions of slaves were so insignificant and any thoughts of them needed to cease. There were other more important things to think about, such as where they were and how they were going to get home.

The winds calmed down as it got warmer. Logan scoped the area once more to make sure there were no traces of their enemy. The area was an empty expanse. A few vines with the dark fruit grew in places. She picked and ate the fruit with Logan.

The cliffs were flat in some places and had deep ravines and fissures in others. Both of them had gone climbing along the cliffs near Milestown and had mastered jumping from one stone to another.

By midday they started trekking along the cliffs heading west. The scorching sun beat down on their backs. It wasn't long before they took a break and sat on one of the rocks overlooking the water. Audrey sat swinging her legs slowly back and forth.

"I must look like the slaves in the coal mines," she said giggling. Her dress looked like a piece of black charcoal from the dirt it had collected during their escape from New Scranton.

"You're so beautiful," Logan told her after a bout of silence.

It caught her off guard. "What?"

"I was just remembering when we were on the embassy roof and I told you how nice you looked. I should have told you how beautiful you are."

Audrey wasn't ready for this. Not now. Logan was like a brother. A best friend.

"Oh, Logan," she said, "we've been through so much together... I—" she paused and looked into his eyes. "Maybe you want to be with me because we're in the middle of nowhere all alone."

"Maybe being in the middle of nowhere all alone has made me realize what you mean to me," Logan said and leaned over to kiss her.

She pulled back. Logan's face turned red. Before being able to explain fear gripped her and she jumped to her feet. Logan frowned and then turned around.

Three men stood a few meters away from them, eating the same type of berries Audrey and Logan had found in the area. Two of the men had long blond hair. The third had tight curls and very dark skin. They all wore leather jackets.

All this time they thought they had escaped. Instead, they'd been followed. Would they kill them here, or wait to slaughter them in New Scranton? Audrey didn't want to die. Not yet. Not like this.

The way these men looked at her didn't make her feel like they wanted to kill her, but the way they looked at Logan, it would be a miracle if he'd survive the next minute. She wasn't about to let them have their way with her. They both jumped up. Logan grabbed her by the hand and ran, pulling her at a rapid pace along the treacherous cliffs. They jumped from one rock to another. The drop to the ocean menaced off to one side of them. As they reached the edge of a cliff, Audrey looked back, got distracted, and forgot to jump. She floated on air before gravity pulled her down. She fell a long way, scraping arms and fingers trying to stop her descent. Finally, she clutched at the edge with one hand, while the other hand tried to find something firm to grab onto. After several failed attempts that got only loose rock, she found something solid and dangled high above the water, holding on for dear life. Tiny pieces of rock and dirt rained down on her head. Logan crashed on the ledge hitting it hard.

"Logan!" she cried. His face twisted as he tried fixing his eyes on her. He was weak, but she needed him now. "Help! I can't hold on much longer," she begged.

Logan grabbed both of her hands in a viselike grip. His neck veins bulged as he tried pulling her up. His feet slipped on the uneven surface littered with debris. A couple of times he slid but managed to regain control by inching backward. On the third attempt, he skidded, and several rocks fell from above landing on his back. He grunted something unintelligible and tumbled over the edge, taking Audrey with him.

They hit the water sinking into the icy cold. She rose to the surface, gasping and looking up to where the soldiers stood on the ledge from where they'd just fallen, looking down at them, and then they too jumped into the water!

In a panic, Audrey swam farther out away from the cliffs, trailing Logan. The freezing water paralyzed her senses, making it difficult to move. "Will they reach us?" she stammered.

"It doesn't look like they know how to swim." He shuddered.

The men hung onto one another in an attempt to stay afloat. One of them tried to use the others as a buoy. Soon there were two and then only one. The man called out for help. Audrey and Logan watched as the cold water pulled him down.

Getting out of the water and scaling the solid vertical surfaces of the cliffs would be impossible. She didn't know how much longer she could bear it. She closed her eyes trying to send her mind somewhere else. The freezing water started to shut her body down. It was difficult to move.

"I f- found s- something," Logan stammered. "Follow m- me."

They swam to a bend in the cliff. With all the strength she could muster, Audrey swam for the beach, passing Logan. She crawled out onto the sand, gratefully basking in the warm rays of the sun. After a few minutes of glorious warmth, she was still alone. *Logan?* She lifted her head and looked out; there was Logan, still in the water, having trouble reaching the shore. Without a second thought, she jumped up and dove back into the frigid water.

Eventually, they managed to swim together, as she helped pull Logan along. Looking battered, Logan slumped on the wet sand, breathing heavily. Audrey collapsed down next to him, wrapping her body around his to keep them both warm. Here was her hero; he had saved her from certain death. She kissed him on the cheek.

# Chapter 9

Cannibalism: when one person eats another. The Feds ate people. They were cannibals. Audrey couldn't comprehend it. Why did they begin trading with her people? Was this all a ruse to befriend them and then cannibalize them?

Audrey combed her fingers through Logan's hair and noticed the bruises on his neck. She couldn't do anything to help him other than watch, and wait, as he moaned softly. A few rocks littered the beach. Not enough to make any kind of shelter to protect them from the elements. The cliffs stood tall with no noticeable way out. Nothing grew here. The water was too cold and too far from any safe landing to swim anywhere.

Audrey lay on the sand next to Logan and looked up into the bright orange sky. *What do we do now?* She thought and then closed her eyes.

When she opened her eyes again, the sun had started its evening descent in the east. Logan still slept. Looking off into the distance, there was only blue water until it met the orange sky at the horizon. She turned peering up at the cliffs which surrounded them; they were too high to climb, but a little over to the left there seemed to be some loose rocks, rising as high as the cliffs. Maybe this would allow them to escape to higher ground? As she scanned her surroundings, something grabbed her attention at the far end of the cove. It looked like it might be another type of rock in the cliffs, but upon closer inspection it was definitely man-made. The middle of the strange cliff-face had an outline like a door with no knob.

Logan moaned and opened his eyes, looking up at her. "We got away," he croaked, cracking a faint smile.

"We got away," she nodded, grinning back. "How are you feeling?"

"Like the cliffs fell on me." He closed his eyes.

She ran her fingers through his hair once more, bent over and kissed him on the lips. He let out a groan of approval.

"Where are we?" he asked, carefully propping himself up on an elbow.

"I don't know. But there is no way out, except back out through the bay. We might be able to climb the loose rock over there," she said pointing.

Logan looked around the cove.

"But I found something Can you get up?"

"Show me." He lifted his upper torso with his arms, then slipped his feet underneath and stood up.

"Over here." She walked toward the man-made cliff-face, holding Logan's hand. The right side exposed some of the brownish-grey metal that made part of a wall. It was impossible to tell how far into the cliff the wall went. To the left next to the door was a panel.

"Hey, check out these squares," said Logan.

## Timepieces

Twelve silver squares made up the panel. In each square was a carving of what looked like short pieces of rope etched in the metal. Some of the carvings were vertical, others had etchings that crossed over each other, and on a few squares the rope met at a single point at the bottom.

Logan knelt down and touched the squares. "I'm surprised that the metal hasn't rusted from the salty air."

"What do the symbols mean?"

"I don't know," he shook his head, inspecting the impressions. He touched one, pushing it in. He tried the others, it seemed as if all the squares could be pushed inwards.

"What are you doing?"

"I'm not sure. Maybe pressing these in a particular order might open the door." When he finished pushing in all the squares, nothing happened. He tried again starting from the bottom right. The door still didn't budge. Sighing, he started again, this time pressing squares in no particular order. After a few minutes without success, he gave up. "Maybe it's a solid piece of metal," he shrugged.

"Why would someone set a solid metal object into a cliff?" she asked, coming over to the squares. They felt smooth. She didn't know exactly why, but she had an instinctive feeling that these blocks were the way to get the door open. She pushed in one at random, then another, but after a few minutes gave up, just as Logan had.

"There's something we're missing," Logan said.

"Maybe if we just push this one," she said fighting back the frustration, as she pushed in another square. Nothing happened.

Logan came over and sat next to her.

"Maybe if we just push this one," she shrugged, touching another square. Again, nothing happened. She couldn't help it; the tears spilled over and down her cheeks.

"We'll figure something out," he said softly, putting his hand on her shoulder.

"Logan, if we can't get into this thing, there is no way out of this cove. It will be night soon and we will be caught in the cold. There is not enough of anything here to make a hut and nothing to eat. The only thing that might help is this stupid thing!" She jammed her fingers in another square at random, and exhaled.

"And you think pressing the squares will help?" Logan asked.

"It makes me feel better," she snapped, pressing another one. When she lifted her fingers off the square, a dull clunking sound of metal on metal could be heard coming from inside the cave.

"What was that?" She looked at the door then at Logan.

Logan stood, putting both hands on the door, leaning on it with all his weight. As if by magic, the door pivoted and opened. They looked at each other with surprise and shouted in excitement.

The empty chamber smelled of stale air. The white walls were smooth to the touch. They felt around for some kind of opening but found nothing. At the bottom of one wall was a series of horizontal and vertical lines with *X*s and *O*s scattered about. Some had lines going through the *X*s or *O*s. To her left was a panel with three green bulbs. Next to it, a knob with numbers that went from fifty-five to ninety-five and a lever that moved between the words: Heat, Off, and Cold. She tried setting the switch to Heat. Nothing happened.

As they entered a passage leading further into the cave, she noticed a red square object on the wall with the word Emergency written above it and a button at its center. Thinking that it might be like the squares outside, she pressed it. A soft click could be heard, and then dim lights shone inside the chamber.

The passage was long with openings that led into other chambers that were also empty. At the end of the passageway there was a door with big red letters that read: *It's a matter of time before you find the key*. They tried opening it, but it was locked.

"What could that mean?" Audrey asked.

"It's some kind of riddle. Maybe it means that in time we'll find the answer."

"How long will we have to wait?"

Logan shrugged his shoulders. "Let's go back and figure out what we're going to do for tonight."

When they reached the entrance, the wind started to blow hard from outside. Logan closed the door against the cold.

"I wonder how long the light will stay on?"

"I don't know," she said, curious that the light did not give off any heat.

They huddled next to each other, getting whatever warmth they could.

Logan noticed a clock on the wall. "Hey, look there's a clock." Audrey turned to view it. "Was that clock working before we got here?" he asked.

"Maybe it started when I hit the emergency thing?"

He shrugged. "I wonder if there's any food in here." Logan got up and headed down one of the passages to explore, to see what they might have missed earlier.

"There isn't anything in the other rooms!" Audrey yelled. She lay on the floor trying to make herself comfortable. A few soft blankets would have been nice right now.

Logan came back empty handed and stretched out behind Audrey, getting close enough to keep each other warm. He put his arms around her, moving his hand toward her middle. Burying his face into her hair, he squeezed her stomach and his erection poked her lower back. His warm breath landed on the back of her neck and the way he positioned himself aroused her. It surprised Audrey that he could be this way, playing the innocent little boy who was just trying to get comfortable and sleep. *Oh, Logan, you sly little boy. I know what you're trying to do, but I'm not going to make it easy for you. You're going to have to wait until we get home, if we ever get home.* She turned to face him and kissed him. "Not now."

"When?" he asked kissing her again.

"When we get home."

"We may never get home." He rubbed her arm and squeezed her hand. "We may never get a chance again." He kissed her again.

Deciphering the riddle seemed more important than making out. It didn't make sense that they would have to wait a certain amount of time before the key would appear. It was impossible for the statement to ever come true. It was ridiculous. Unless the time started when they entered the cave or when they pressed the button that said Emergency and the rooms lit up. Maybe the clock started at that moment.

Logan's hands were caressing her body. Her breathing became shallow and intense as her hands felt his strong arms and firm chest. Was this really Logan? He kissed her neck and rolled her on her back. She stared at the clock and watched as the second hand made its way around the large numbers and thought about the riddle and how the clock might help them find the key. After all, it did keep time.

"I found the key!" she cried out, pushing Logan off her and getting up.

"Where is it?" he asked, sitting up annoyed.

"I've been looking at that clock. Watching the seconds go by and I thought about the riddle. 'It's a matter of time before you find the key.' Don't you get it?"

"I'm not getting anything right now," Logan said in frustration. "If you know where the key is, then go get it," he grumbled.

"The clock keeps time. It could also keep a key!" she said, ignoring his grumpiness. Standing under the clock, she reached up. "It's too high for me to reach. Help me."

"Aren't you excited?" she asked as he handed her the clock.

"I was!" he said sullen and downcast.

Audrey wanted to hug him at that moment and tell him that he just needed a little more patience but decided against it. If she told him that, he would try even harder and spoil everything. Playing innocent would work for now.

Turning the clock over revealed a small box that turned the dials. Next to it was an object wrapped in a piece of cloth. Unwrapping the cloth exposed a key. Holding it up, she raced for the door. Logan followed. She tried putting the key into the small slit. It wouldn't go in. *Damn it.*

"Try putting it in the other way," Logan offered, now getting caught up in her excitement.

Nothing happened.

"No, here—" Logan said impatiently, "give me that thing!" He took the key and fit it into the opening, turning it to the right.

"Try turning it to the left!" she screamed.

Logan turned around and gave Audrey a stern look, but he did what she said, all the same. There was a small click, and the door unlocked, opening to a small space, not even big enough for a person to fit in. It was filled with shelves and on one was a box.

As he snatched the box from the shelf, Logan's eyes grew twice in size. "Someone knows you're here," he said, handing her the object.

She shook her head, not understanding what he meant and reached for the box—that was when she saw her name written on it. Her heart skipped a beat. Who would know she'd be here? The box contained an old, weathered letter, and a circular object.

She turned her attention to the letter.

*Dear Audrey,*

*I know you've never been here before and I know that you would never expect to find something addressed to you. I cannot explain anything to you at this time. But soon all your questions will be answered. Inside the box you will find a timepiece. The display on the timepiece can be set to take you anywhere in time. More importantly, it cannot take you to any place except where you are standing. The reason I'm leaving you with this timepiece is because you must go back in time to a place called Philadelphia and find Thomas Lynch. I've already fixed the settings on the timepiece to send you back to May 4, 1776. When you're ready, go outside and press the black button on top to turn it on and then the blue button to transport you back in time.*

*Your friend*

She handed the letter to Logan and walked back to the larger chamber. He caught up with her sitting on the floor. "Do you really believe this thing?" he asked.

"How does it know who I am?" She inspected the disc. "It must be true. We need to try it."

"You can't go outside now!" Logan argued. "I don't even understand why he wants you to go outside."

"How do you know it was written by a man?"

"I don't."

"It said I can go to any time, but I can't go to any location. This place is inside a mountain," she said, looking around the room. "If we go to the time in the letter, maybe this chamber won't exist and we'll be inside the mountain, solid rock."

She studied the timepiece and pressed the black button. Lights appeared on the side displaying May 4, 1776.

"Are you going to do it?" Logan asked.

"Let's test it in the morning," she said, pressing the black button again. The lights on the disc went out.

---

Audrey couldn't sleep all night. The lights in the room were still lit. Logan had decided to curl up by himself after several failed attempts at getting Audrey's attention. She turned over the clock that sat on the floor and checked the face. 8:17. There were no windows to determine day or night or if the clock even kept the right time. She got up quietly, so as not to wake Logan. Finding a metal lever next to the door, she pulled it down, then tried pushing on the door. It wouldn't budge. She started to panic. Logan had never tried opening the door after he closed it last night. They were stuck inside. She franticly pounded on the door.

Logan came up next to her and pushed the door. "Try pushing it on this side," he said as the door swung open.

The light from outside was so bright they both had to squint.

"Thanks." She walked outside and sat on the sandy beach, motioning for Logan to come sit next to her. Her thumb hovered over the blue button. *Should I do it?*

Taking a deep breath, she turned to Logan, and pressed it. Before she could even blink an eye, Logan, the beach, the bay, and the metal cave all disappeared.

A different landscape came into view, abundant in trees with big green leaves. Behind her, the metal cave was gone. In front of her was a valley where the ocean had been moments before. The sky was blue. Yellow and orange leaves littered the ground. She could feel the damp brown dirt she sat on and noticed the grey rocks scattered here and there. Nothing like the dull grey desolate valley she had imagined it to be. This image was breathtaking.

Logan was nowhere to be seen.

There were rustling sounds coming from the leaves on the ground. Once in a while green balls would fall from the trees. Off in the distance were sounds of someone yelling, yet it didn't sound like a yell a person would make. A few meters away, a huge animal with a fluffy tail, beige pelt, and long legs that made it appear tall, stared at her with its huge eyes and a shiny nose. Her heart started beating rapidly. Basic instincts told her that standing still was the best action to take without knowing what this creature would do. After a moment she decided that the animal was harmless.

The timepiece was still lit, bit now, it displayed something totally different. She pressed the blue button again and was back on the beach with Logan sitting beside her.

"How long have I been gone?" she asked.

"You haven't gone anywhere!" Logan answered.

It was odd that the timepiece transported her alone, and nothing else around her.

"Give me your hand." She grabbed Logan's hand as she spoke.

She pressed the blue button and the scenery changed again. The huge creature saw her and darted off. Logan wasn't with her. Pushing the same button once more brought her back to the beach.

"Why did you let go of my hand so fast?" Logan said annoyed.

She studied the timepiece and whispered, "It only works for me."

"What?"

It did work. The device *really* sent her back in time! But who put it in this metal cave for her to find? How did they know she would solve the riddle? And why would they want her to find someone in another time? There were so many questions and no immediate answers.

At first fear gripped her that someone could even have such knowledge. Yet the adventure of being someplace new and the excitement of finding someone she had never met before made her decision easier to make.

"Logan, this thing," she said, holding up the timepiece, "can take me to a different place and time. Well, not a different place, but a different time. It's here, and it's so pretty, Logan. The sky *is* blue!"

He put his hand to her forehead and said, "Are you all right? The sky is orange. Not blue."

"Logan! This thing works and I'm going to find that person named..."

"Thomas Lynch," Logan finished.

"Yes. Thomas Lynch," she said. "You stay here. I'll be back. If it's like you said when I first tried it, you won't know that I'm gone."

"Give it to me. I want to try it," Logan said, his curiosity getting the better of him. "I want to see a blue sky."

"No!" she said. "It's for me. They made this thing work for me alone. The box had my name on it. That would explain why you didn't come with me."

"Maybe it just allows one person to go back in time," he said as he tried to grab it out of her hands. She moved away so he couldn't reach it.

"Logan! How did it know I was going to be here? There wasn't one left for you!"

"Let me take a look at it!"

"No!"

"Let me just try it and see if it works for me," he begged.

"It's mine, Logan!" She held the timepiece close to her body.

"Give it to me, Audrey," he ordered.

Never before had she seen him behave like this. His eyes were focused on getting what she was holding. He had always been the calm one and now he was acting like a child.

"Okay," she conceded, slowly handing it to him.

As he reached for the object, Audrey yanked it back, turned, got up and ran.

"What the—" Logan got up and ran after her.

"Logan, stop!" She ran along the beach, having fun at his expense.

Logan ran faster than Audrey. Even with his injuries, he closed the distance between them. She sprinted faster, trying to get away. With the timepiece held out in front of her, she pressed the blue button and disappeared, reappearing in the forest and before she knew what was happening, ran straight into a tree.

# Chapter 10

Philadelphia, July 2, 2052

Tom was in his office with the Declaration of Independence sprawled over the desk. Thoughts of meeting Benjamin Franklin flooded his mind. Knowing about events before they happened was an unusual concept for him—or anyone, for that matter. What were the ramifications on the current timeline knowing what was going to happen before it occurred? Could the events of the past be changed with this knowledge? What would happen to the current timeline if he decided not to go to 1776 and meet Ben? It was simple, Ben would never have known who he was in 1787. His head spun at the thought that he would meet Benjamin Franklin and this time Ben wouldn't know him.

He turned to his monitor and pulled up the browser, searching for anything on the Declaration of Independence. The front door slammed shut interrupting his thoughts. Footsteps ascended the stairs.

"Hello. Whatcha doing?" Eric said, popping his head into the office.

"Eric. You're home." Tom glanced up at his son, and back at the monitor. "I'm looking for anything that might be unusual in the Declaration of Independence."

"You mean like your signature?

"What!?" Tom said, looking at Eric.

"I would have thought that you of all people would already know," Eric said, grinning. "I didn't know you were *that* old."

"Well, I'm not that old, thank you," Tom frowned, his eyes now scanning the document on his monitor. "Where's my signature?"

"Wow! You don't know, do you?" Eric emitted a slow whistle. "I know something you don't!" Tom gave him a stern, fatherly look and waited for an answer. "Dad, Thomas Lynch Jr. was the representative for South Carolina in the signing of the Declaration of Independence." Eric leaned over the desk and pointed at the signature. "See? Right here. It's awesome that both of you have the same name."

On the bottom half of the second column of names in plain sight was the signature of Thomas Lynch Jr. Something *was* unusual in the document, after all. In all the times he had gazed over it, he'd never once looked in detail at the signatures.

"Cool, huh?" Eric said. "I used to tell my friends in history class that you signed the Declaration of Independence."

"I did sign it," Tom mumbled imagining the events that must have unfolded.

"What?" Eric snorted.

Tom, still in shock from the discovery, repeated, "This is *my* signature."

Eric scoffed. "Whatever you say, Dad. Did you eat yet?"

"No, and I'm hungry," Tom said and then stood up. They went downstairs to the kitchen looking for something to munch on.

"We have fruits and vegetables from the garden. Did you manage to get any meat from the store?" Eric asked.

"They were out when I got there. I stood in line for two hours just to find out they were out of everything." Tom opened the refrigerator and moved some containers around in his search. "Hey look! There are still some eggs your sister brought over the weekend."

"We'll make omelets."

Tom and Eric spent dinner talking about school and the day's events. Eric was already in his second year at Temple University with plans for the navy. Time moved so fast. It seemed as if it were just yesterday that Eric was learning how to walk.

"This summer is turning out nice. We should take your sister and her boyfriend out camping," Tom mused.

"Okay." Eric shrugged, gobbling down his food.

"We can go camping at the vault that Uncle Miles has up in the hills."

"Vault?"

"What else do you call a metal box with a door lodged inside a mountain?"

"Yeah, I guess. How did Uncle Miles get that place? And all the equipment. What's up with that?"

"Your uncle is an inventor like..."

"Like you, dad."

"Well he works for the government, so he actually makes real inventions and not little things like me. But anyway, he bought the vault..." Eric gave his dad a stern look. "... the cabin from the government. He then started acquiring the old equipment from the government as they started upgrading with new equipment. Supposedly, it all works. The last time we were there he didn't show us anything."

"I liked the view." Eric finished drinking his ice water and got a little more serious. "Remember what Uncle Miles told us?"

Tom looked up at Eric. "Which of your uncle's theories are we talking about now?" Miles had conspiracy theories for almost everything, especially about the world ending. It was supposed to end at the start of the new millennia and when that didn't happen, it was the end of the Mayan calendar in 2012. People always came up with reasons to prove the world was coming to an end and to his surprise, his brother had believed them even when they didn't come true.

"The comet; the one that they just named Tonatiuh?"

Tom shook his head. "They're just stories to get you scared. Nothing weird is going to happen."

"But, Dad, it's getting harder and more expensive to buy food. Almost everyone works for the government in one form or another. Laws are being passed to restrict our freedoms. Every country in the Middle East is determined to wipe out Israel and they are blaming the U.S. for allowing Israel to survive."

"And what does that have to do with an asteroid?"

"Maybe it's not an asteroid that ends civilization. Maybe it's us."

"So, you think that we are going to blow ourselves up?"

They finished their food and argued about Uncle Miles and his predictions.

Tom worked the rest of the day collecting the pieces he would need to make a timepiece for Audrey. Screws, bolts, computer chips, microchips, QLEs and wire were scattered across his workbench. Safety goggles on, a hot soldering iron in one hand and solder in another, he started connecting the pieces to the microchips. It was time-consuming, especially with the smaller parts that required three hands.

The cool air around his eyes was welcome as he lifted the goggles and reached over for a glass of water, savoring its taste. One component was done.

Maybe Eric was right. Current events were getting worse. With the war in the Middle East that had been going on for almost a century and the food shortages across the country, something unexpected was going to happen. Even though he didn't believe Earth would be hit by an asteroid, something was about to happen to change everything. Call it intuition, but it was there. The more he dwelled on the future, the more his stomach began to cramp.

After a cursory look through the remaining parts around his workstation, he realized he needed more material to make additional timepieces for Eric and Alexis. And even more if he was going to make pieces for his brother's family.

Could he be getting caught up in these conspiracies that his brother had implanted in his children's mind? A feeling of urgency overcame him.

———————

Several weeks went by before Tom had even completed one of the new timepieces. The device turned on, and he set it to an arbitrary date ten years into the future. He pressed the blue button and found himself surrounded by freezing cold water.

He hadn't thought he would need to hold his breath! As he resisted the urge to take a deep breath, he now realized he had exhaled when he arrived in this time. The timepiece began to flicker. It was going to short out!

As fast as his fingers could, he pressed the blue button, and the basement reappeared. Water splashed on the ground as he gasped for air. The lights on the disc flickered and then went out. Water trickled out of the casing as he opened it. Turning it on did nothing—all the electrical components had shorted.

Something was wrong. Something was terribly wrong. This place, his home, was going to be under water. Sometime between now and ten years in the future there would be a major flood... or worse.

# Chapter 11

**Somewhere in Lehigh County, Pennsylvania, May 4, 1776**

Audrey opened her eyes to a large tree looming above. She had no idea how long she'd been lying unconscious on the ground, and for that matter, no idea where, or even who, she was. The sky was blue—she remembered it being orange. A memory flashed—the bay was gone. Trees now replaced the cove, and the metal cave was no longer there. The display on the timepiece had changed—August 29, 2276.

As she studied her surroundings in more detail, her memories began to return. This place was still the cove. What had made this all go away in her time? Off to one side far down in the beautiful valley was an area with no trees and a few houses. In some ways it reminded her of the farm that Logan lived on. If these people could help her get to Philadelphia, she would be that much closer to finding Thomas Lynch. The cove had the same problem as it had in her time. There was no visible way out.

Everywhere she looked, everything about this place was beautiful. Off to the side, a creature popped its head out from behind a tree. It was the same animal she had seen the first time. The animal ignored her and went back to chewing the flowers. Audrey kept her distance, all the same.

Out of nowhere, a dark black thing darted down from out of the sky and swooped over the animal, cawing loudly. Audrey yelped as the creature startled her. She jumped back as it sprinted past her, racing up the small split in the rock formations, leaving her alone in the cove. The flying thing was in perfect control of its motion, turning from side to side, before flying up out of the cove. Her world only had the fish and crustaceans in the bay, no animals existed on land and definitely none that flew through the air.

She followed the path the animal had taken and ascended out of the cove. The view was better at the top. Off to the left, a river flowed. Trees were everywhere, as far as the eye could see. Were these the ones they'd been digging up out of the ground in her world?

"Hello there, little girl," came a voice from behind.

She turned, clutching her chest with both hands. There, sitting on a rock, was a pale man with straight black hair. His arm muscles bulging under the thin shirt, despite this thin frame. She'd have put him around thirty-five, maybe forty—an old man by her standards. "You scared me!"

He smiled, parting his lips. She smiled back.

"You seem lost."

"I am, actually." She nodded. "I'm trying to get to Philadelphia. Would you know how to get there?"

"You're far away from Philadelphia." He chuckled. "Why are you going there?"

"I'm supposed to find someone named Thomas Lynch."

He frowned and said, "Who is he?"

"I don't know. I was just told to find him." Why would he need to know who Thomas Lynch was? He was either going to help her or not?

The man's eyes peer down at her hand. "What's that thing you're carrying?"

"Oh… It's a plaything." She held the object tighter, bringing it closer to her body. If this man were a thief and took it, there'd be no way to get back home! Coming to find Thomas Lynch might have been a bad idea.

"You should put that away. Something like that must be very valuable. Someone's bound to steal it."

This old man knew more than he was saying. She took a step back.

He looked out to the valley below, nodded. "I'm sure those people in the valley can help you get to Philadelphia."

"Do you know them?" she asked. If he knew that she was far away from Philadelphia, then he knew how to get there; but he kept stalling.

"Afraid not." He shook his head. "What's your name?"

"Why do you look at me that way?" she questioned.

"What way is that?"

The look on his face told her everything; he was too old to be hitting on a young woman. The stare reminded her of the way Logan stared at her. It was time to go. Who knew what this old man would do next? "Nice meeting you," she said hurriedly, and walked away.

"You know…"

She hadn't walked more than a few meters. Stopping, she turned around to hear what was coming next, despite herself.

"If you want to get to the valley, it's an easier walk this way." He pointed behind him. "Be careful. I know you're not from around here and this place is not easy to navigate."

Audrey's stomach tightened. Something was wrong with this picture. Had he said her name? It felt like he had been expecting her, or he knew her, somehow. He didn't know how to get to Philadelphia, but now he was telling her where to go? What a creepy old man.

"Thank you for the suggestion, but I'm going to go the other way," she told him and turned away, heading in her original direction.

"It's your choice. You're going to find that there is no way down from there."

"I'm sure I'll manage," she muttered, not caring if he heard or not.

The cliffs were covered with trees, a few shrubs sprouting here and there. The green vegetation and unusual blue sky felt surreal. The roots tripped her, and the trees blocked the way, as she tried to move between them. There seemed to be no way down. The old man had been right after all. A few more minutes went by before she gave up and went back the way she had come.

She was relieved that the old man was gone. It would have been embarrassing to see him again and acknowledge that he had been right. The path down into the valley was an easy walk. At the bottom, where the cliff met the valley, she came upon a piece of paper lying on the ground. Some sort of certificate. An identification card of some kind, with her name on it. Who knew she would be here? The person who gave her the timepiece, that's who. More riddles and no answers. She folded the paper in half, putting it in her pocket with her timepiece, and continued walking toward the houses.

Several people were working the land as she approached. That feeling came back. Someone was watching her. She turned around and looked up toward the cliffs, but no one was there.

Five people worked the land. Two of them were white, the other three black. The blacks did the bidding of the white men even though all of the men were dressed in similar clothing. The blacks must be their slaves. Logan was so mistaken in his belief that slavery was wrong. How wrong could it be? Even in this time period they had slaves.

The men watched as she walked toward them. Even the slaves stopped and stared as she walked by. How dare they look at her this way! She glared back, holding her head high, and continued toward the white men.

"Hello!" she said, smiling. "I'm lost and I was hoping you could help me."

The two men cocked their heads and looked at each other.

*How odd.* Did these people speak the same language? The old man at the cove did. The letter she found was written in her language too. The men didn't say a word but continued to stare.

"Do you speak English?" she said slower and louder.

"You talking to me?" the heavy-set man with black hair asked, pointing at his chest. The dirt on his face was almost indistinguishable from his hair stubs.

What could be offensive in being cordial? "I'm trying to get to Philadelphia. Can you help me?"

The man's face turned red. Even the dirt on it changed color. Her smile faded. What could it be that offended them so much?

"Nigger, don't you look at me like that!" the man snarled. "Who you think you are?"

The word *nigger* meant nothing to her, yet it was obviously an insult. Their hostility made no sense. The blond man looked at her the same way she looked at the slaves in her world. The three slaves had their heads bent, averting their gaze. These men thought she was a slave, but why?

"Oh, I'm not a nigger," she told them, pointing to the slaves.

The men started to laugh. "She's not a nigger," they said to each other between gasps of breath. When they recovered themselves, the blond one said, "She said 'I'm not a nigger,'" in a high-pitched tone, mocking her. They laughed harder.

Audrey stared at them, not sure what to make of it all. They quieted down and regained their composure. "Nigger, you don't talk to me like that. Who do you think you are?" The blond man locked eyes with her. His hair was so thick with oil, it stuck to his head.

*What's going on here? Did I do something wrong?* She didn't feel comfortable staying any longer. It made no sense why these men would react so angrily.

"Thank you for your help," she muttered, ignoring his question. She got out of there as fast as she could. "I'm going now."

"Bitch, where you think you going?" one of them said.

Bitch? What did that word mean? These people were hostile and very strange. She walked a little faster, deciding not to run so as not to provoke them. The men soon caught up and grabbed her. Yanking her arm free, she ran, but they gave chase and tackled her to the ground. Audrey struggled to get free and got up to run again. One of the men grabbed her by the hair.

"Nigger, you don't leave till I tell ya you can leave." He grabbed her arm, turned her around and slapped her hard across the cheek.

Audrey put her hand to her face feeling the spot pulsating. No one had ever treated her this way. No one had the right. She saw red. As hard as she could, she kicked him in the groin. The man started to scream. His friend grabbed her, but she managed to get out of his grip and twisted around to face her new assailant. She swung and he ducked moving out of the way. The black-haired man came in and tackled her to the ground. She turned and swung her legs up far enough to grab his head and knock him over, then got up and ran. The blond man reached out and grabbed her. She turned around and swung at him. He ducked, then pounded his fist into her stomach, knocking the wind out of her and causing her to fall to the ground. The blond lifted her up and the black-haired man coiled his fist to punch her in the face.

"Stop!" a man from behind them yelled as he made his way to them. "What the hell is going on here?"

"We got us a runaway, sir!" the fair-haired man said. "She tried to get away."

"Is that so?" The new man looked at her, grinning seductively.

"Yes, sir!" her captors said together.

"Bring her here."

The man had very fine clothes, like nothing she had ever seen before. He looked important, possibly an official of some sort? Right now, he was her only hope of getting out of this situation.

The men dragged her closer, holding her arms so she couldn't run away. This new man who was clearly in charge roved his eyes over her body slowly. She knew what was going on. He wouldn't help her unless she bribed him with her body, and she wasn't about to do that.

"What's your name, girl?"

Even though he had a deep accent, Audrey understood what he was saying. "My name is Audrey and I'm lost," she started sobbing, still trying to catch her breath. "I'm trying to find my way to Philadelphia."

"You sound different," the man said. "Where are you from?"

Audrey didn't fully understand the question and said nothing.

"I am the owner of this here plantation," he said. "Do you have any papers to show that you are a free nigger?"

She remembered the paper that she had found on the path. She yanked her hand away from the blond man, reached in her pocket, and took out the paper. She unfolded it and read it again.

*Audrey Bushnell, a black woman, aged 18 years, 5 ft. 3 in. high, who was born free on August 11, 1758, is registered in Fredericksburg—/s/ J.J. Chew, clerk, Fredericksburg, 22 Feb. 1776.*

She handed the plantation owner the paper and said, "I got here this morning." She tried getting her other arm free. "I don't know why you're treating me like this. I'm not a nigger!"

The plantation owner smiled at her comment and continued to read the slip of paper. "This paper has no seal on it," he said, waving it in her face. "This is a forgery."

Of course it was a forgery. Someone knew she would be here and made it. Whoever it was, they didn't do it right. "I'm Audrey Bushnell. I'm eighteen years old," she said in a panic.

"I believe you," the plantation owner said. "But I also know by the way you speak that you can read and write, and you wrote this, didn't you?"

"No, I didn't!" she hissed.

"Of course not," he said, grinning. "So, tell me, where do you come from?"

Audrey wasn't going to tell them what just happened. These people were violent, and if they got hold of the timepiece, there'd be no way to get back home. On impulse, she struggled and freed her other hand. The man with black hair wouldn't budge. She turned and scratched his face. He screamed in pain and let go of her. The blond tried to grab her. Kicking him in the shin caused the man to buckle. The men ran and tackled her to the ground. She struggled, but the men were too big for her.

"Put her in the shack for now," the owner of the plantation hollered at them. He took the slip of paper and ripped it into several small pieces and then threw it on the ground. The men lifted her up.

"Who are you? Why are you doing this to me? I didn't do anything to you!" she cried out in desperation. "I'm not a nigger!"

They ignored her pleas. One of them stopped and turned her around and hit her square in the face. "Shut up!" he screamed. "Ya say one more thing and I'll hit ya so hard you won't have a mouth to shout out of!"

The men put rusted shackles on her hands and feet. She kept struggling and yelling, making it hard for them. They slapped her several times to get her quiet and dragged her to a shed. Its age made it look like it would soon fall apart. She tried one last-ditch effort to run away with the shackles on her feet, but the men grabbed her. They lifted her up, threw her in the shack, secured her to a wood beam and locked the door.

These people in this world were so strange and violent. *I'm not a slave. Why do they think that I am? I'm not even from this world. If I hadn't listened to that old man, I wouldn't be here now. Why would he send me here? It was a trap. The man must have known I wouldn't know how things worked in this world, and he made sure I'd get caught. I wish I were back home right now. I'd rather deal with the Feds than these people.*

The dirt floor was cold and damp. The only fragment of light filtered through the outline of the door. Tears trickled down her face mixing with the blood from her cut lip. The shackles made sitting uncomfortable. She sat in her dark cell trying to figure a way out of this mess.

*The timepiece!*

But she couldn't reach it. The shackles limited her movement. It was her way home. She'd have to wait for them to come and let her out. They'd have to take the shackles off. A small ray of hope began to lift her spirits. The timepiece was her way of getting back home and away from this forsaken place. Soon they'd take these shackles off her and then she'd make her escape.

# Timepieces

Food came once a day, and if the water spilled, she had to wait until the next day for a drink. How stupid was it to do what someone wrote in a letter? And then to listen to a man she didn't even know tell her where to go? *I'm such an idiot!*

A small animal crawled between her legs as it sniffed the ground. It startled her and she tried moving out of its way but realized that her motion was limited. She screamed. The animal wasn't afraid of her at all. It stood on its hind legs sniffing at her and then continued to scurry around the dirt floor.

Someone was at the door trying to unlock it. Her eyes closed as the door opened and bright light flooded the space. She turned her face away to avoid its intensity. The small animal escaped out the door.

A man stood at the door, but she couldn't make out who he was. "I'mma let you get cleaned up in da house. Massa wanna talk witcha," he said.

He bent over and took the shackles off her hands, then grabbed her arm leading her outside. One of the slaves standing nearby was called over and he let go of Audrey's arm.

*This is it.* Audrey took the opportunity and ran toward the fields. The shackles on her feet made it hard to run and her feet weren't going fast enough to get her away.

"Nigger on the loose!" he yelled.

Audrey kept running. She didn't dare look back to see what was happening. The two men who had captured her earlier appeared in front of her. She turned and ran into the field. A slave stood in her way and she bumped into him, knocking them both to the ground. Before she could get up, the man who had opened the shack was on top of her. Audrey fell back to the ground screaming.

"Ya thinks ya can get away from me?" he sneered. "Ya needs a lesson in following orders."

"Let me go!" she shouted.

He dragged her to a nearby tree. Someone brought rope. They threw it over one of the overhanging branches and tied her hands, pulling on the rope until her feet were barely touching the ground. They ripped her dress, exposing her back.

He turned her around and asked her, "Is ya gonna run away again?"

Audrey didn't say anything.

"I aks you a question," he said.

Audrey looked at him. He had a round face and a scruffy beard and was about the same height as she. His breath smelled like the outhouses in Milestown. Looking into his monstrous eyes, she spat into his face.

He wiped it off on his sleeve, moved back a couple of paces and took out a long whip. He snapped it at her with amazing precision and power; Audrey screamed in agony as it connected with her back.

"Is ya gonna run away again?" he repeated.

Audrey still didn't say anything. He snapped the whip again. She screamed out and began panting from the pain.

"Answer the question!"

"I want to go home!" she cried out, trying to get loose. "I want to go home."

He laughed. "Nigger, this is home." He snapped the whip again. She screamed and kept trying to get herself free from the rope that held her up.

"Is ya gonna run away again?" he yelled.

She kept silent. Again, he snapped his whip.

"Stop!" she begged. "Please! Stop!"

He snapped his whip again, Audrey screamed out even louder.

"Is ya gonna run away again?"

She was in too much shock to answer. Again. he snapped his whip.

"No! Please stop! Please!"

"Is ya gonna run away again?"

Audrey could barely concentrate. The stinging sensation was unbearable. There was only one way to stop the pain.

"No," she said.

"No what?" the man asked.

"No... I won't run away."

# Chapter 12

Her shackles adorned her hands like macabre jewelry. The small creature came visiting again. She barely noticed it. Her strength had diminished and her will to escape was all but gone. Days blended into nights, the passage of time becoming unrecognizable as she sat for what felt like an eternity in the dark cell.

Audrey closed her eyes as the door opened and the light flooded the room. A slender silhouette stood in front of her. It was impossible to tell who it was. Not the man who had whipped her. She'd remember him anywhere. It was a man though. One of the other slaves, perhaps? He brought her some water. She was parched. The shackles made it somewhat difficult to drink, but she managed.

"You is fine," the slave said, putting his hand on her knee.

The slave looked old to Audrey. He had very dark skin and smelled like he had never taken a bath his whole life. From what she'd experienced in the days she'd been here, more likely than not, most of his life had been hard. The slave looked at Audrey, sniffed her and touched her hair. He started smacking his lips as she drank the water. Audrey paid little attention to him.

"You's not liken any udder girl here," he said. "I'm funna ax Massa if'n I can haves ya fa myself." His hand moved from her knee up to her thigh, squeezing her soft skin as he glided upward. A grin appeared on his face, as he began to lick his lips and breathe erratically. Aware of his motives, she quickly moved her legs out of the way.

"I's knows what I gonna do witcha," he said as if he was already having his way with her.

The shackles made it almost impossible to defend herself. The feeling of being trapped was overwhelming. He came closer, but she managed to push him away. He leaned in trying to kiss her, but she moved her face from side to side. "Stop!" she cried out. *There must be a way out of this!*

He grabbed her face and forced his lips on hers. She thrust her head back as far as she could and spat on him. The old, creepy man responded with an eerie laugh as his hands found their way between her legs. He squeezed, closing his eyes in excitement. The shackles kept him from spreading her legs even farther, but he was more than satisfied with the use of his hands and started to quiver as he felt her up. She screamed and he covered her mouth with a dirty palm, still pressing his body on top of hers. He began to pull up his shirt and slowly removed his hand from her mouth. She screamed again and he slapped her hard.

"Ya yell again 'n' I's gonna hurt ya mo," he threatened, lifting his hand up as if he was going to slap her again. She looked at his hand and then at him and hit him hard with her shackles and screamed for help at the top of her lungs.

He screeched from the pain and slapped her even harder. "I's telling ya ta shud up!"

He raised his hand as if to slap her again. She flinched to block the blow. Instead of hitting her, he grabbed her dress and lifted it. "Ahh... If'n I tells ya ta do somtin, ya does it," he said. "I ain't gonna hurt ya. I promise."

Her dress came up even higher as his eyes sparkled with excitement. Saliva started dripping down one side of his mouth. He fumbled to pull down his pants and ended up ripping them open. Now fully erect and ready to have his way with her, he came down on her as she continued to squirm frantically beneath him and push him away. He slapped her again and again, each time his penis rubbed up against her leg, and each time, she felt like she would vomit.

The door to the shack opened. "Tobi!! What da—Dis here bitch isn't for you. Git ya damn hands off a her." The man moved over to Tobi and kicked him off of Audrey.

Tobi fell back. Despite the blow, his face was awash in the glow of ecstasy.

"Get your damn clothes back on and get back out in da field," he said, kicking him one more time. "Massa wants dis bitch fo his self. Now git back to da field to help pick the crop!"

Tobi grabbed his pants and shirt and left the shack. Audrey's dress was stained with the thick, white ejaculated fluid of the slave. The man called out for one of the other slave girls to come over. "Take her and gets her cleaned up. Massa wants to be wit her tonight," he said, pointing to Audrey.

The slave girl tried to get Audrey to sit up, but Audrey shrank back into the corner of the shack; she didn't want anyone touching her.

"Go wit her," the man said. "She'll git ya fixed up. She won't hurt ya."

Audrey didn't understand what any of them were saying. The slave girl bent down and straightened out Audrey's dress. Audrey looked at the girl and then at the man who had whipped her earlier and then at the girl again. What could she do? The slave girl helped her up and they walked to the main house, the shackles bore down on her.

Tobi watched on from a distance, smiling and dancing a victory dance of sorts.

She heard the overseer yelling. "Tobi! I dun told ya to git out and work da field. Do ya want me to whip you, boy?"

"Tobi a crazy nigga," the slave girl said to Audrey, who wasn't the least bit interested in anything she had to say. "He tinks he can have any nigga he want. The overseer sure did give him a lickin' though."

When they got to the door, a short and heavy-set slave walked them to one of the rooms next to the kitchen. The room was small, not that much better looking than the shack outside. It smelled of sweat and dirt. The new slave told Audrey to sit on the bed.

"She done need her shackles off" said the first slave girl who had accompanied her to the house.

"Massa'll take dem off when he comes to her tonight," the house slave muttered. "You can go. I takes care of her now."

The slave girl left, closing the door. The house slave brought a pitcher of water and a towel, sitting it on a table next to the bed. Soaking the towel in the water she wiped Audrey's face gently. The towel wasn't all that soft.

"When Massa comes, he gonna have his way wit ya. Do whats he wants and ya's won't gets hurt," she told Audrey. "You's born cursed with beauty, child."

Once she was done washing Audrey's face, she began to pat it dry. "When he be wit ya, just pretends you be someplace else. It go quickly. I'm telling ya, it go quickly."

# Timepieces

As the house slave stepped out, Audrey wept, unable to keep it in any longer. She understood perfectly well what was going to happen to her. Now more than ever, she wished that she'd given in to Logan's advances, but it was too late. Everything was all wrong.

It felt like forever as Audrey sat alone in the small room with a tiny window, not even big enough for her to escape. A bed had been slept in and took up most of the space. Her stomach roiled. The slave came back into the room with some food and water. By the time she got back to the door, Audrey had already finished eating.

"Can I have more?" she asked. "Please."

The house slave turned around with a raised brow then stepped out and brought her some more food and water.

This slave was not like the others. She was not as dark. The clothes she wore were different. The slaves outside wore flimsy clothes while hers appeared to be made of a better material. "Thank you," she said as the woman was leaving.

The slave turned to look at Audrey, again with raised brow. "Ya welcome." She walked out the room, closing the door behind her.

Audrey was alone in the room. The timepiece! She pulled up her dress. Trying to reach for the pocket with the device. Her grip slipped and the pocket fell away. The shackles were not helping. She tried again, slowly, pulling up her dress until she could fish out the disc. *Got it!* She turned it on. The date on the display showed August 29, 2276. She got up and stepped over to the tiny window, looked down at the object in her hand and pressed the blue button. She found herself underwater, and it was like a thousand needles pricking her skin at the same time. *Oh, my!* She forgot that in her time this was the ocean floor. With shackles on her hands and legs, there was no way she could swim to the surface. She pressed the blue button again and came back to the small room. Water splashed onto the floor. She tried squeezing as much water as she could out of the dress, then put the machine back into her pocket and went over to the bed and laid on it, crying.

She woke up to a wet bed, sweating. *Bad dream.* The air in the room was stale. She sat up to a dark room, and quickly realized that it hadn't been a dream at all.

The rusted shackles reminded her of a lost freedom. She had come on a quest, hoping to find someone, and now that hope seemed to be fading. Would she ever find this person named Thomas Lynch? Did he even exist? Being trapped here, she would never know.

Someone fidgeted at the door. The doorknob turned and the door swung open with a creak. Audrey moved to the side of the bed, trying to get away from the door. It was the man from the day she had come to the plantation. He was short—shorter than she remembered. A sly grin spread across his face as he walked in with a candle that dimly lit the room.

# Chapter 13

Henry closed the door and placed the candle on the nightstand. He stared, admiring her beauty. He enjoyed the company of negro women. Their dark skin excited him. But this girl was more than that. Her long, wavy black hair was unusual for a negro. Her sultry lips and hourglass body made him lust after her more than any other woman he had ever known. He was more than excited. He had found the perfect girl to keep him company when he tired of his wife.

"Hello there," he said. "I am Master Henry. What's your name, honey?" The girl was afraid, he could see it in her wide, almond-shaped eyes. She needed to feel comfortable if this were going to work for both of them. He didn't want her to struggle and then have to beat her to get her to stop. How enjoyable would that be? Maybe a little.

"What's your name?" he asked again, sitting on the bed next to her. The sheets were damp.

"Audrey," she said. She sniffed and backed away.

"That's a very pretty name. You're a stunningly beautiful woman."

His hand found her shaking knee. She tensed as he touched her warm skin.

"I am Master Henry."

"Why do I have to be chained up like this?" She showed him the shackles. "I didn't do anything to you."

"Well, you did try to run away," he said, caressing her soft arm. "But I can fix that." He got a key out of his pocket. "As long as you behave, you will not have to wear these."

He told her to lie down on the bed and glided his hands over her soft legs, squeezing her firm muscles until they reached her ankles. He removed the shackles and dropped them at the foot of the bed. Seeing her lying there on the bed almost drove him to his limits.

*Oh God! Thank you for this gift.*

Tears flowed down Audrey's cheeks.

"Ah, there is nothing to cry about, honey," he said as he crouched over her body, putting his hand on her stomach. "I won't hurt you. I promise." Rubbing her belly in a gentle back-and-forth motion felt good. His other hand cupped a soft breast. The more he touched her, the more he tried to stay calm, the more excited he became. Her dark skin glowed and he was all too ready to have her. He pulled on her dress, exposing her shoulders and began to kiss them. She pulled away as his lips moved to her neck. Standing, he stood and took off his pants, looking down at his erect penis.

"I think we need to take off that dress of yours and get a little bit more comfortable." He lifted her dress and saw his prize, but the shackles kept him from pulling it over her head.

"It appears that we need to take the shackles off your hands too, to get that dress off." Fetching the key out of his pants once more, he sat on the bed next to her and laid her hands on his lap, purposefully letting them fall on his penis. The second the shackles were unlocked she quickly took her hands off him.

He threw the shackles at the foot of the bed, and took off her dress, throwing it on the floor as well. The dress fell with a loud thud on the wooden floorboards.

"What is it you got there in your dress?" he bent down.

"It's nothing!" she said eyes wide, bending over the side of the bed trying to get the dress, but he managed to get the dress before she did. He rummaged through it, finding something in a hidden pocket—a small wheel of sorts. "What's this?" He fished out the object and let the garment drop to the floor. He was no longer excited. Now he was mad that this thing he got out of her pocket, whatever it was, was intruding on the real purpose of why he came down here. *What is this thing?* He thought to himself as he turned the object around in his hands.

She came at him clawing and screaming trying to get the thing back. He moved out of the way and grabbed her long black hair and pulled her head back. "Stop!" he said, trying to keep his composure. "Now, we are going to behave ourselves, are we not?"

Audrey looked at him, panting. "Yes" She tried to nod her head, but his grip was too tight.

He let go of her hair, letting her fall to the bed. "What is this thing?" he asked, sliding his hands over the disc. He pressed the black button—the display lit up. "Why is this thing showing these dates? And, how do they glow the way they do?"

"It's nothing. Just something..." she hesitated, swallowed. "Just something I found."

"Is it?" He looked deep into her eyes. "Is that why you ran at me like a crazy nigger, trying to get it?"

"It's just a keepsake. It means a lot to me."

She seemed desperate to get the object back. If it was nothing, he would return it. A token of his appreciation for what they were about to do. He turned his gaze to the strange buttons on the disc.

"What does this date mean? August 29, 2276." He slid his finger across the display, changing the numbers. "Now, it shows July 13, 2259."

"Let me show you how it works," she said, getting up from the bed.

He didn't trust her. She seemed too anxious to help. "I think not." He moved away and stepped over her dress as he studied the object in his hand. "What does this blue button—"

Henry was underwater. It was dark. The pressure of the water pushed down on him. The illuminating numbers on the object started to flicker and then disappeared. He swam up toward the surface, not knowing whether he could hold his breath long enough before reaching the top. The climb was difficult, and the water was freezing cold. It seemed like forever to get to the surface. He gasped for air when his head came up out of the water. Nothing could be seen except for the stars in the night sky. Not knowing where the shore might be, he swam in no particular direction. Each stroke required a tremendous amount of effort. He didn't want to die, not like this. His head was underwater more than it was out and his body started sinking as it ran out of strength. At last, he found footing on some ragged pebbles that made up the sea floor and could stand with his head above water. The more he walked, the higher his body came out of the water until he managed to climb a few feet up on dry land. Only the shirt on his back protected him from the hard, cold wind that blew against his body. He was lucky he hadn't drowned, but the wind kept whispering to him that drowning might have been the better option. He curled up to keep himself as warm as possible.

Henry woke up to the rays of sunlight warming his body. God showed his mercy by letting him live. He opened his eyes, sat up, and looked around. *Oh my god! I'm in hell!* The warming air and orange sky provided no doubt as to where he was. A vast expanse of water stretched for as far as the eye could see. Behind him, the earth was just rubble, as if it had been blasted with cannon fire and this was all that remained. No signs of life surrounded him. No trees or vegetation of any kind. No animals, no people.

The rocky beach inclined up toward a cave. The rocks were sharp, it hurt to walk on them. The cave went on into the darkness. Going farther inside the cave or venturing around the shore frightened him. The best course of action would be to stay near the entrance.

As the day wore on, it got hotter. The sun baked the rocks. The disc had no display. Shaking it wouldn't make the date reappear. It was a one-way trip.

All his life he had been a good Christian. He committed no sin that could have brought him here. The slave girl came to mind, but it was *she* who had seduced him. After all, had she not been so pretty, he would have left her alone.

"I'm sorry!" he cried out as loud as he could. "I'm so sorry!"

The cave was damp and cold. All he could do was wait, wait for Satan and his demons to come and welcome him home.

# Chapter 14

Audrey's mouth dropped open in shock when master Henry disappeared. She wanted to leave, but there were several problems. The man not only had the timepiece, but her dress had gone with him as well. Her head sank into her hands. With no clothes and no sense of direction, how would she get away from this place? Running away might lead her to another plantation; there were bound to be other places like this.

The candle was more than halfway gone. Taking a deep breath she made her decision and wrapped the bed sheets around her body and stepped out of the room climbing up the short flight of stairs to the kitchen.

The room was small, a stove in one corner and a table in the middle. The house slave slept hunched over the table.

"Psst," Audrey called out, not knowing if anyone else was near.

The house slave raised her head and looked around with tired eyes, before putting her head back down on the table.

"Psst," she tried again.

This time the house slave snapped her head up, more alert now, and scanned the room through suspicious, narrowed eyes. The woman looked over to where the sound had come from. "Child, what ya doin' there?" she asked. "Where Massa be at?"

"He's gone away."

The house slave's eyes opened wide. "How he be gone? He'd awoke me up if he'd a passed by me. Is you a witch or somtin?"

"I don't know what a witch or a somtin is. So, I guess I'm neither," Audrey shrugged. "Can you help me?"

"What you needs my help for? How I know you not make me disappear?"

"I can't make anyone disappear," Audrey said. "Right now, I have no clothes."

"You what? Where your clothes be at?"

"Massa took them."

"He took 'em?" She cocked her head back. "Why he do dat?"

Audrey didn't want to spend the whole night explaining every little detail to this slave, especially, while covered in a bed sheet. "Can you please just help me?" she hissed.

The house slave got up and walked over. She eyed Audrey and, after some hesitation, walked down the stairs opening the door to the room. There was nothing inside. The room was empty. "No one be here! Where Massa Henry gone to?"

Audrey gave her a blank stare.

The slave called out, "Massa Henry!"

Silence.

"Massa Henry gone!" she said, looking at Audrey.

"I already told you that."

"Where he go?"

"Some place far away, I hope."

"What we gonna do?"

"Can you get me something to wear?" Audrey wrapped the sheet tighter around her body.

Seeming to make up her mind finally, the house slave disappeared, and a few minutes later returned with a slave's garment. Audrey took what looked like a rag used to clean up spills. The smell of it turned her stomach. "What are these?"

"Them's was all I could find, child."

The garment was disgusting, but it was better than being naked. She put on her new clothes and asked the house slave her name.

"My name be Lilly," she said, watching Audrey dress. "And what be yo name?"

"My name is Audrey. Thanks for the clothes," she said, trying not to inhale too deeply.

"Where's you from? You talks almost like Massa Henry, but you's got a heavy aksent."

"I don't know how to explain it," Audrey started. "I'm from a few miles away from here. But not from this time."

It took a while to explain how she ended up here and how everything in her world was different. How the sky was no longer blue but orange, and how the plantation was now part of an ocean. She even explained how she escaped from the most horrible people in her world and ended up finding the metal cave and the letter with the timepiece. How the old man at the top of the cliffs tricked her to come down here to ask for help. How Massa Henry said the slip of paper she'd found was a forgery and locked her up, until today when he was going to have his way with her.

"And that's how Massa, whatever his name is, disappeared. He took the timepiece I had in my dress," she finished.

Lilly looked at her with wide eyes and open mouth. "Don't goes tellin' nobody what you's just told me," she said shaking her head. "They think you's crazy and they shoot you on da spot."

"Why would they do that?" Audrey frowned.

"'Cause that be crazy talk, child."

"But it's the truth!"

"Crazy people always thinkin' they talks the troof, but they be crazy. Massa Henry got no time fuh no crazy niggas." Lilly shook her head.

It was still dark outside, and Audrey needed to get as far away from the plantation as possible. Could this slave be trusted to help her escape?

"I's be here alls my life, child. Lilly don't knows nut'ing else."

"But don't you want to be free?" Audrey asked, confused. "Do you like being a slave?"

"I's be alive, child. I see new niggas trying to be free niggas only to be dead niggas. I's be alive."

Audrey watched Lilly's sad face. If she could only get her to want to escape, to be free from this horrible bondage. Lilly's hands were calloused and rough— slaves' hands. Fear made her too afraid to run away—too afraid to want to be free. They had broken her.

Audrey needed Lilly to help her escape. And if they were to do that, she needed to convince Lilly to *want* to be free. Audrey had always favored the beating of a slave trying to run away in her world, but now, it was her life that was in jeopardy.

"I can't stay here, Lilly. If you won't come with me then just tell me which direction I need to go to get to Philadelphia."

Lilly thought about it for a moment. A look of fear was on her face as tears slid down her cheeks. "If'n I helps you escape, they gonna know I's did it and whip me!"

"You can tell them that I hit you on the head and knocked you out."

"I can'ts lie. I be a bad liar. They's won't believe me."

"Then come with me!"

They stared at each other. Was she getting through? She needed Lilly's help and even though she was putting her life at risk, it was worth it. Audrey needed to escape.

"Where we go?" Lilly asked. "We got nowheres to go!"

"I need to get to Philadelphia. I need to find a man named Thomas Lynch. I need your help to do that."

"And if'n we finds that fella you's looking for, what happens to me?"

"I'm sure he'll help us both," Audrey said, not knowing what to expect from this Thomas Lynch. She had never met him. Hopefully he could help her. Hopefully he could help both of them.

"But the letter tells you to find him," Lilly said. "It not say nothin 'bout me."

Audrey could see how worried Lilly was. It would be impossible for her to promise that everything would be all right. This world, this time, was not her world. Anything could happen. A promise like that couldn't be made. The letter was addressed to Audrey. Maybe the person who wrote the letter didn't know about Lilly, or Logan, for that matter. What if Thomas Lynch was black? He would surely help her then. Would he help her if he was white? With this kind of reasoning, she shouldn't be friends with Logan in her world because of the color of his skin. It was more than ridiculous it was insane. "I don't believe for a second that he would turn you away."

"But I be a slave," Lilly said.

Those words hit Audrey hard. In all her life, how her servants felt had never crossed her mind. They were needed, especially the coal miners, to keep Milestown running. Now, here, a slave needed to be convinced to help her run away and be free. But this place was twisted. Only blacks were slaves here.

"Maybe Thomas Lynch is a free slave!" Audrey said. "But in this world, I am a slave, too."

The letter told her to find Thomas Lynch. That was the reason for being here. Finding him would hopefully help her get back home. If he didn't have a timepiece, there would be no hope for her. He was her only salvation.

Lilly sat on the bed and seemed to be warming up to Audrey. It was Lilly who had made Audrey see what being a slave meant. Lilly was broken.

Lilly sat on the bed rubbing the sheets, that had covered Audrey, with her fingers. "These is much softer than da ones I be sleeping on. I be sleeping in da kitchen. They don't be giving me no room of my own," she said to Audrey. "But why would I needs one? Most of my work be done in da kitchen." She looked forlorn. "Every night after I cleans everything, I take out my cot and lie it on da floor and sleep on it. Some nights, like tonight, I just be falling asleep on da table."

Guilt swept through Audrey. All those years she had mistreated her servants. Now she understood why Shirl was so happy to give her up to the Feds. Freedom. Tears filled Audrey's eyes.

"They be slaves in your world?" Lilly asked, looking into Audrey's eyes. "Why you's crying?"

"Yes," Audrey choked, not able to meet Lilly's eye, as the tears spilled down her cheeks. She changed the subject, wiping her nose on the smelly sleeve, she cleared her throat. "We need to come up with a plan and get out of this place!"

"You be a slave where yous from, too?"

"No, I wasn't," Audrey said, wiping her eyes. After gaining her composure, she added, "What do we need to take when we leave?"

"Why you not wants to talk about slaves in your world?"

"It's just something I really don't want to talk about." Audrey offered a half-smile as she wiped her eyes again.

Lilly smiled. "You owned slaves, did ya not, Massa Audrey?"

Being called 'Massa' made her grin. Her hesitation would leave little doubt about who she was.

"Yes, we have slaves in my world."

"And you was they massa?"

Audrey didn't answer. It was like being on trial for committing the most horrible crime. They would find her guilty and now she was going to pay for it with her life. The fear of being stuck here was overwhelming.

"Did you treat dem wit respect?"

That would be a hard question to answer. "I never hit a slave."

Lilly clamped her mouth shut and stood. "I can't help you," she said curtly. "Me and you, we's different." She walked out the door and up the stairs.

Panicked, Audrey ran after her. "Please, don't do this!" she begged. "Maybe... maybe I was brought here for a reason."

"Go on," Lilly said.

Audrey squirmed and fidgeted. Her anxiety was making her lose focus. *What can I do? What can I say?* She took several deep breaths. "Maybe I was brought here to see how wrong slavery is and to change it in my world."

"And how you's gonna do dat?" Lilly asked. "Tells all da massas that it be wrong to have slaves? And they say 'Okay, Massa Audrey say we not gonna have no slaves' and they free 'em all and let dem go to day homes they not see fo'ever?" Lilly yelled. She started up the stairs again. "You can't do nut'in, child. You's just a crazy nigga."

Lilly was right. She was just a crazy nigger. But she didn't want to stay here as a slave all her life. She wanted to get back home to her world.

"Please!" Audrey cried out.

Lilly turned and looked at her. Silence reigned for a moment. They stared at each other.

"I be a slave all my life," Lilly finally said. "My mum tell me stories 'bout the world where she grows up. She belong to the Ovibunu. I liked her stories 'bout the mans and womans and they ways. When I be seven, they takes my mum aways from me. She be sold to another massa. I never see my mum again after that. I be sold many times too before I come here. I meet other slaves that be from Ovibunu and they knows my mum. They tells me dat da stories my mum be tellin' me be true. But that be long ago, child. I not tink of my mum for many years now. I not even remember her name or even da name she gives me when I was born. The massas names me Lilly and dat be my name till I die."

Audrey had opened up a wound that Lilly had for so many years tried to keep closed. It was similar to the way Shirl was a slave in Milestown. Yet, Milestown didn't have slaves based only on the color of their skin. Shirl had a flat face and slanted eyes. Others were black or white. A war had brought Shirl to her household. What were her people supposed to do, just let her go? Shirl's people had fought, they lost, and her mother became a slave. In many ways, it was justifiable. Shirl was born to a slave and that made her a slave, too. It was wrong, but Audrey didn't make the rules. Somehow, they needed to be undone. Things needed to be made right in her world. But nothing could be done being stuck here.

"Where I come from, my father is mayor," Audrey said. "When I get back, I will tell him what I went through as a slave and how wrong this is."

"Ma'or?" Lilly said, surprised. "What da ma'or gonna do? Tell da king?"

"We don't have a king," Audrey answered. "My father is the leader of all the people where I live. I will convince my father to free the slaves."

"You's do dat, Massa Audrey?"

"I'll do that," she said. "I'll convince my father that this is wrong and convince him to let our slaves go home to their people."

Lilly stood by the door for a moment starring at Audrey. "You's promise it?"

"I promise."

"You promise it to God?"

Audrey frowned. "Who's God?"

Lilly stepped back with a surprised look on her face. "You not know who God be?"

Audrey shook her head.

"God be da maker of everyt'ing. He makes me and he makes you."

"Where is he?" Audrey asked.

"My Lord! Child, God be everywhere."

"Is he here now?" Audrey said, looking around the room. Maybe she wasn't the only crazy nigger.

"He be here now."

"What can he do?"

"He do anything and everything."

"Can he get me out of here?"

"If'n you aks him."

"God, please get me out of here."

Nothing happened. Audrey looked at Lilly.

"You needs to promise God you free da slaves." Lilly explained.

Only the two of them stood in the room. Where was this God? She wanted to tell Lilly the story about the mayor who had no clothes. But, that would take too long. To make Lilly happy, she made the promise.

"God, I promise to free the slaves. Please get me out of here."

Lilly grabbed her hand and embraced her. "An if'n ya don't keep dat promise, the Lord he gonna strike you dead the moment you break it."

It didn't make any sense. Even if God could strike her dead, how would he know when she broke her promise? And could he travel through time to see if that promise was kept? Her questions would have to wait. The night was almost over and they needed to get moving.

Lilly had no idea what they should take. They packed food, enough to last for several days and ran out the back door. Audrey made sure it was shut properly so as not to arouse suspicion. The forest was two hundred meters away. They sprinted from the house and into the dense vegetation. They were free.

# Chapter 15

Two days passed; they didn't sleep much and didn't travel as far as Audrey would have liked. Having worked as a house slave with little physical activity, Lilly tired easily, and they found themselves making more and more stops as they fled. The trees hid them well, their leaves shading them from the sun's harsh rays.

This was now their third rest of the day, the sun not even at its midpoint in the sky. Lilly went off in search of food. Audrey could hear her rustling the bushes as she traipsed around just out of sight.

"These be edible," she reappeared, handing a dozen or so tiny berries to Audrey.

"I've eaten these before," she said, taking them gratefully. "Thank you, Miss Lilly."

Lilly's eyes opened wider.

"Did I say something wrong?"

"It's just... no one call me miss befo'," Lilly blushed. "It sounded nice. Miss Lilly." She quietly repeated it, over and over, testing the words on her lips, as if savoring the sound. "Miss Lilly."

Audrey smiled in amazement at how the simplest gestures could make a person feel so much better. The berries were sweeter than the ones she had eaten in her time; they felt furry on her tongue as she rolled them around in her mouth. Unlike the ones she was familiar with, these berries had tiny, prickly hairs growing out of them. They stuck to the tips of her fingers and hurt after a while. But the taste was well worth the pain.

A faint but persistent noise could be heard in the distance. Audrey decided they were just the sounds of this world and continued eating the berries. The sound got louder.

Lilly jumped up staring toward the sound. "If'n dem dogs catch us, we's be dead!"

"What dogs?" Audrey asked, heart racing.

"Dem's da ones barkin, child."

"What do we do?"

"We run!" Lilly shouted.

Lilly headed off in a direction opposite the sound of the barking dogs; Audrey turned on her heel and followed. It was like being in New Scranton all over again, escaping from the Feds. The area was denser and their ability to move through the trees was much slower. As they ran, the sound of the dogs got closer. Lilly picked up the pace. The fear of getting caught overtook any previous tiredness.

Audrey was afraid. She had never seen a dog before and could only imagine what kind of creature would make that kind of sound—one that wandered around finding and eating slaves, apparently. Or worse, they would hold her captive until the overseer got to her and whipped her for running away again. Her imagination ran wild; the fear made her run even faster.

The forest sloped downward at a steep angle. Audrey couldn't adjust and lost her footing, falling on her butt. She slid down the slope, feeling every bump and stone underneath her. Lilly was not so lucky; her foot got snagged by the root of a tree, causing her to fall headlong, tumbling past Audrey, who could do nothing but watch in horror. Arms outstretched, knees bent, Lilly crash landed, screaming out in pain and holding her knee as blood splattered in every direction.

On hands and knees, Audrey managed to move her way across to Lilly and set about tearing pieces of cloth from her garment.

"Keeps runnin'!" Lilly gasped, managing to groan a few comprehensible words between spasms of pain.

"You're hurt. I can't leave you!"

"I's can't walk. If'n they catches you, they's gonna kill you. Now gets!" she stammered, shooing her away.

"I won't leave you Lilly!"

"Listen, child. You made a promise. The Lord, he help you keep dat promise. Go!" She pointed in the direction she wanted Audrey to take, grimacing at the pain. Blood seeped through the fingers, which still held her knee.

Audrey slowly rose to her feet and began to walk away. She turned around and looked back at Lilly one more time, guilt and terror pulling her in two directions.

"Remember yo' promise." Lilly gasped, nodding solemnly. "Put yo' trust in God, Massa Audrey. He helps ya find your way outta here."

"I will," Audrey whispered, before she turned and ran.

Without Lilly, Audrey didn't know where she was going, stumbling blindly through dense brush. The sound of the dogs was all around her. Every tree looked the same. For all she knew, she could be headed back toward the plantation! Despite the direction, she made better progress without Lilly running beside her.

Audrey didn't know how long she'd been running, spurred on purely by fear. After some distance, her feet splashed in a small creek and she stopped. For a few moments her mind went blank. Thirsty, she bent down and sipped some water.

*Bang!*

The sound rang through Audrey's head, startling her back to her senses. *Why did I stop?* She popped her head up, then stood. The forest was quiet, and then she thought she heard Lilly screaming. The sound was faint but clear. It had to be her. Who else?

*Bang!*

She ran. Following the flow of the water, Audrey ran faster than ever before. Lilly was dead—she had no doubt about it. They were coming to do the same to her. Lilly had said to put her trust in God and at this moment, she needed all the help she could get.

"God, if you are a friend of Lilly's, I hope you will be my friend too," Audrey gasped as she ran. "Please help me get out of this. Please help me get to Philadelphia."

She kept running. She didn't dare stop. Shallow, muddy water splashed under her feet. There was a bend in the creek and as she turned, she came to a complete stop. A huge tree stood in front of the creek, causing it to fork and split into two streams.

"Which way?" she screamed, jumping up and down.

The sound startled a flock of birds out of the tree, flying off to her right. A single bird flew away from the flock to the left. The dogs were behind her. They were getting closer, their barks and growls getting louder. Audrey followed the bird travelling alone, just like her. She shadowed the stream, keeping it on her left, running as fast as possible. It wasn't long before the trees thinned, and the stream flowed into a wide river.

Audrey stopped at the riverbank. Farther downstream, the river bent; nothing could be seen past that point. Across the river were two log cabins. Audrey could see a man by the river watching her.

The barking got louder. The man turned and ran toward one of the cabins.

*Friend or foe?*

There was no time to find out. Audrey didn't cross but continued running. Minutes later, another house appeared in front of her. There was no other choice but to cross the river.

The current was strong, constantly tugging at her. As she passed the middle of the river, water came up to her shoulders, but she managed to get to the other side. The man she had seen earlier waited as she waded closer to the bank. He stood above her, holding a rifle in one hand and a basket in the other. His oblong face and sharp nose made Audrey want to turn around and swim back. She wasn't going to make it after all.

The man put a basket on the rocks in front of her. "Take off your clothes and put them in the basket."

Audrey couldn't believe what she was hearing. What kind of world was this where every man had only one thing on their mind? She looked at the man and then the rifle. She started to get out of the water.

"No!" the man barked. "Do it in the water."

The clothes came off. Shivering and naked, she placed them into the basket, and the man pushed the basket out into the river and let it flow downstream.

"There are clothes here," the man pointed to the pile at his feet. "When I leave, get out of the river and put 'em on and run into the bahn."

The man started to walk away. What was going on? Why was he leaving? Where did he want her to go?

"Where's the bahn?" she shouted after him.

Without turning, the man held out his right arm, and pointed. "It be the one with the livestock. The one on your right."

The word 'livestock' meant nothing to her, but 'the one on the right' did. She still wasn't sure what to do. Running away and getting someplace safe seemed like the better option, but she couldn't keep running blindly deeper into the unknown. Surely, if he were going to give her to those chasing her, he'd have shackled her already.

The land sloped. One of the cabins had smoke coming out of it. The man was nowhere to be seen. A decision needed to be made. Should she stay, or should she go?

"You'll be safe here," a voice behind her said, making her jump.

She turned to the sound of the voice. But there was no one around. *I must be tired.*

The woods were her only way to escape; she headed straight for them.

"Where are you going?" the voice said again.

Audrey stopped dead in her tracks. She turned to see who was talking but saw no one. "Who's there?" she commanded, hearing the shake in her own voice. Fear seized her. *Have I lost my mind?*

A light breeze ruffled her hair. She felt different now, more relaxed.

The fear had subsided. The sound of the barking dogs had disappeared. She opened the door to the building the man had said to go inside. There were animals everywhere. Creatures she had never seen before. The smell was awful, like sweat and pee and dried grass. Hay was all over the floor. Piles of it were in a corner and more rising above her in a loft. The animals came closer, making her raise her hands, not wanting to touch them. Would they harm her? The feeling came back again, like at the river, relaxed and calm.

Climbing up to the loft, the sunlight streamed in through gaps in the barn door, which opened up to provide a view of the farm below. Off in the distance was the river she had crossed. The sky was an amazing blue and the sun was getting closer to the horizon. Finding a spot away from the opening, Audrey collapsed on the hay, exhausted. The smells of the barn had a calming effect; she lay there and let her brain mull over the events that had happened. How she managed to get away from that terrible place; how Lilly sacrificed herself to help her escape; how a single bird showed her the way out; how a stranger decided to help her.

At one point, she thought she heard the dogs off in the distance, but she knew they were gone. Her eyes began to close, and she let herself drift to sleep, knowing that her mind would be filled with dreams and nightmares. She was too tired to worry about it.

Her eyes cracked open as she felt the presence of something, or someone. She was alone, yet that sensation of having company remained. The thought of Lilly's god entered her mind. *Thank you, God*, she thought as her heavy eyelids closed shut once more. *Thank you for helping me. But why didn't you help Lilly?*

# Chapter 16

Philadelphia, July 29, 2052

Tom woke up to his son calling out to him. "Dad, wake up. Time to eat," Eric said. Groggy, Tom sat at the dining table and poured some of Eric's freshly made soup into a bowl. He winced but took another spoonful—he'd had worse.

"Dad, I'm worried. I'm not so sure I'm going to be able to find a job. There's almost forty percent unemployment." Eric whined. "Why are there so many people out of work?"

Eric was always anxious about the economy; the boy had little faith that things would get better. Who could blame him? Unemployment was out of control and the steps the government was taking—giving corporate America less environmental restrictions—wasn't quite working out as planned. Companies were going out of business left and right. The dollar had fallen sharply against other currencies. Almost everything, even food, was imported, therefore expensive and hard to come by. The depression was lasting longer than anyone expected; so many people had been forced onto the streets. Luckily, Tom's family hadn't quite got to that stage just yet—but it wouldn't be long. The newspapers were projecting that the entire U.S. economy would collapse in five years.

"You don't have to worry about that, Eric," Tom said, putting down his spoon. His appetite had vanished. "When you graduate, you're going to join the navy. By the time you get out, this won't be a problem."

"I went to the Department of Homeland Security today after school and got the mandatory barcode on my arm," Eric nodded, changing the subject. He extended his arm to his father, revealing the barcode with the letters and numbers: PA 420 312 114 PH.

It wasn't right that everyone was presumed guilty until proven innocent. Why should people need to prove their citizenship? The country had changed. It was no longer the America that everyone around the world wanted to live in. It hadn't been that country for a long time.

"Hey, I'm going next door to Chris' house," Eric said suddenly, placing the dished in the sink, not bothering to wash them. "If you need me, I'll be there."

"Go ahead. I'll finish cleaning up." Tom shouted after his son, as he dashed out the door.

Tom sighed. Four plates, a handful of cups, some silverware, and a few pots. *It'll keep for later.* With another deep sigh, he threw the towel back onto the counter, and headed back downstairs to continue his work.

He grabbed the object he had been fiddling with and screwed on the case. Now fully modified and hopefully waterproof, the date was set far into the future. Would his house even be standing?

As a last thought he grabbed the waterproof flashlight from the wall above his workbench, he took a deep breath, then pressed the blue button.

Again, Tom immediately found himself immersed in freezing cold water, but to his amazement, the timepiece was still working. *Yes!* It hadn't shorted out. In the beam of light Tom could make out his basement. It was in complete disarray, but it was definitely his basement. The workbench was right where it was supposed to be. It crumbled to the touch.

Instinctively, his lungs wanted air. Pressing the blue button, he instantly reappeared in the present. Water splashed on the ground, going everywhere. The light—still shining its white glow—shook in his trembling hand. What happened that put his house underwater for over two hundred years?

The doorbell rang. He wasn't expecting anyone, or was he? Eric had a key. Trudging up from the basement, Tom spotted Eric's backpack. On impulse, he quickly hid the timepiece in one of the pockets for safekeeping.

The doorbell rang again. *Yes, yes, I'm coming, I'm coming.* "Alexis!"

Tom's daughter smiled back at him, holding a rather large box. "Are you going to let me in?"

"Let me get that," he said, taking the box. It wasn't as heavy as he thought it would be.

"I forgot to bring my key." She shrugged, before her smile turned into a frown. "Why are you all wet?"

"Ah... doing some experiments in the workshop," he said, walking into the living room with the box. Water footprints trailed behind him on the hardwood floor. He put the box on the coffee table

"Always trying to invent something, aren't you, Daddy?" She gave him a hug before quickly backing away from his wet body.

"Always," he grinned.

"Daddy, you need to clean the house up more often!" Alexis scolded her father. "Why don't you hire someone?"

Tom looked around the room. She had a point. There were papers and empty wrappers all over the table. He followed her into the kitchen and watched his daughter begin organizing. She had her mother's obsessive-compulsive disorder; she couldn't keep from cleaning when things were in disarray, even if she wanted to. "It would cost too much to hire someone."

"You and Eric are both slobs."

As she cleaned, Alexis told Tom about her promotion at work. She had just come back from visiting her mom in Los Angeles, which explained the box.

"That must've cost a fortune!"

"It was expensive, Dad. And the plane was packed with all kinds of produce. I almost didn't get back. They couldn't find fuel. But somehow... at the last minute they found a truck with fuel."

The door creaked, and both of them turned to the sound.

"Hey, Sis!"

Slamming the door behind him, Eric hugged his sister.

"I just got back from Mom's," she said. "She sent some stuff back for you. It's in the living room."

"Great!"

Eric rushed out to the living room, Tom and Alexis trailed behind. Eric opened the box with a knife from the kitchen and pulled out some clothes, books, and his favorite cookies. Eric took the box of cookies, plucked one out, and sank his teeth into it with a sigh.

Tom and Alexis instantly broke into laughter.

"Wha?" Eric said, through a mouthful of crumbs.

"Nothing." Tom shook his head, sighing. "Just watching you eat. Anyway, can I have one of those? Oh, and while I've got you here, do either of you have a friend or know anyone named Audrey?" He'd almost forgotten.

Eric and Alexis looked at each other.

"I don't have any friends named Audrey," Alexis shook her head.

"Me neither," Eric added. "Who would name their kid Audrey, anyway?" he laughed.

"Who would name their kid Eric?" Alexis teased.

Eric ignored her. "Why do you ask?"

"Someone told me about a girl named Audrey and I just thought that you might know her," Tom said, clearing his throat, opening another pack of cookies, hoping they wouldn't notice.

"Dad, things are getting pretty bad around here." Alexis said after Eric left them. She resumed the cleaning, taking his box of goodies to his room, then coming back. "I mean, everywhere. When I was with Mom, there were so many homeless people. There's hardly any food in the stores. I even have a hard time driving around with all the cars left abandoned in the streets. Maybe we should get ready to go to Uncle Miles' cabin."

"Wow!" Tom said. "Your brother said the same thing at dinner." He didn't know why he was so reluctant. Maybe because, if things got worse, Tom knew he had something that would save his family—the timepieces. "Maybe you should move back up here and stay with us."

"Dad! My job is in D.C. My boyfriend is in D.C."

Tom shrugged. "Eric wanted to go camping again. The vault is—"

"The cabin," she corrected.

"Okay, the metal cabin, whatever you want to call it. It's an hour away from here. We could go camping this weekend."

Alexis fixed him with an intent look, hands on her hips. "So, you *are* worried."

"Why would I be worried? I just think that spending a weekend there might be fun," Tom flashed her a smile, trying not to show his concern.

"If that's the case, then this weekend is no good for me. Let's do it in two weeks," Alexis finished, wiping the counter.

---

It took longer than Tom had anticipated completing another timepiece. Getting the parts and shipping them was extremely expensive. He went upstairs and put on his network glasses. A few looks at different pages got him to a popular news site. Chicago was having problems finding the funding to finish construction for the upcoming Summer Olympics.

Tom brought up the electronics store on the screen, navigated to the parts section, ordered four sets of the original components he had used to construct the first timepiece.

The desk drawer contained his personal papers. Thinking that his passport might be useful to show Ben, Tom put it in the pocket of the coat that Ben bought him. He brought up the Declaration of Independence on his monitor. His imagination took him to 1776 where he found himself beside all the delegates from the thirteen colonies waiting to sign the document. But how was he supposed to do that? Was he just going to walk in and claim he was Thomas Lynch Jr.?

# Chapter 17

Audrey woke to the sight of a blond-haired little girl, staring at her with bright green eyes. Freckles dotted her face and she had the cutest puffy cheeks Audrey had ever seen. The girl couldn't have been more than six years old.

"She's awake!" the little girl whispered to someone over the ledge who Audrey couldn't see.

"Leave her be, Elsie," said the voice of a man from below.

Audrey sat up, walked over to the ledge to look down, accidentally spilling some of the hay over the side. Audrey knew, even from this angle, with his light brown hair and thin frame, that it was the man that helped her yesterday. Wearing a loose, beige shirt and brown pants, the man sat on a stool next to a huge animal that was two to three times his size. She couldn't quite make out why he sat reaching under it.

Some pieces of hay fell in front of the man who then stopped what he was doing and looked up at Audrey and his daughter with their heads poking over the loft. "I hope you ain't thinking ya gonna sleep all day," he said.

The gaze in the man's eyes was very much like Master Henry's. Very much like that of the man she'd met on the cliff top before being captured, and like the way Logan looked at her sometimes.

"I see why they was looking for you," he said with a grin. "They was here last night asking about you."

Fear shot through her, freezing her in place. Master Henry. But no, he was gone. She saw him disappear. Maybe he figured out how the device worked and came back. "I'm trying to get to Philadelphia." She shouted down. "I don't know what direction to go. Please, just tell me how to get there!"

The man's mouth gaped open. "You sure don't talk the way I was expecting."

At first she was stunned by his comment; but then, she thought about it a little more. Lilly hadn't spoken very well, and she probably couldn't read or write either. It made sense that he would expect her to speak the same way. Every slave in this world most likely spoke the way Lilly did.

"There's no need to worry. I told them there be no slave girls here," he reassured her. "They left soon after." He grinned at Audrey and his daughter. "My name is Nathan, and that pretty little troublemaker next to you is Elsie."

Elsie was too young to be aware of anything. Her innocent grin won Audrey over. Audrey couldn't hold back her smile and grinned back at the little girl.

Nathan was still staring up at them, watching silently. He gave off a friendly air.

"I'm Audrey," she said cautiously, still uncertain if she could trust this stranger.

"Glad to meet you, Audrey." He transferred his attention to his daughter. "Elsie, take Audrey down to the house. Your momma should be finishing up the food. I'll be done here soon."

Elsie ran to the ladder and started to climb down. She waved for Audrey to follow her. Audrey trailed Elsie and now had a better view of what Nathan was doing. The animal had a big round sack with several tubes hanging out from under it. One hand pushed up, then yanked down and squeezed out a white liquid into a bucket. He did this with two hands, each hand alternating the motions of the other.

*Yuk! What are they going to do with that?*

Elsie grabbed Audrey's hand and led her out of the barn. Before they could leave, another four-legged creature approached Audrey and sniffed her. She stiffened in fear, but Elsie quickly hopped over and began to pet the animal, a wide grin spread across her face. "Don't be afraid," she said, giggling with pure joy. "It's only a sheep. It won't hurt you. See?"

Elsie seemed quite comfortable handling the animal; what harm could it do. Hesitantly, Audrey reached out a hand, and nervously touched the animal Elsie had called a sheep. The animal nuzzled her hand, and she gasped, yanking her hand back in surprise.

"She be looking for food. You can touch her. See?" Elsie put her hand out for the animal to sniff, then pet it.

Mimicking Elsie, Audrey took a deep breath and stretched out her hand once more. The sheep pressed its nose into her hand; it was wet and warm. Nothing like she had ever experienced. She smiled and laughed out loud. Feeling a little braver, she stroked its back. The animal's hair was unexpectedly both rough and soft at the same time. It was remarkable.

"When I first got here," Audrey said, continuing to pet the sheep, "I saw an animal eating some flowers. It had long skinny legs and a puffy thing on its back side. Do you have any of those here?"

"Sounds like a deer. Most of the time they'll run away from you."

Now she had a name for the first creature she had seen in this world—deer. The animals in the barn weren't as vicious as she had originally imagined.

Elsie grabbed Audrey's hand again and pulled her along, out of the barn. "How old are ya, Audrey?" Elsie asked as they walked toward the house. "I'm six. Next month, I'll be seven."

"I'm eighteen."

"Where are you from?"

"I'm from very far away." Thoughts of Logan popped into her head. She wondered what he was doing.

"I figured," Elsie said, "'cause you don't talk like any of the other slaves I know."

"I'm not a slave," Audrey said, irritated.

"You're free? Then why was you running?"

"They didn't believe me when I told them I wasn't a slave. I had no choice. I had to run."

"Well, you don't sound like a slave," Elsie said, shaking her head. "I'd a believed you."

The aroma of something cooking filled the air. It reminded Audrey of New Scranton. The smell of burning flesh caused her to stop in her tracks.

Elsie pulled on Audrey's hand to get her moving again. "Come on. We are almost to the house. Come on... What's wrong? Audrey?"

"Does everyone here eat meat?"

"We all eat meat." Elsie shrugged. "My dad especially."

Shocked, Audrey turned on her heel and headed away from the house. It was New Scranton all over again. The Feds had survived all this time. Long before Milestown was ever a city. Audrey started to run.

"Momma!" Elsie yelled. "Momma, she's leaving!"

Nathan came out of the barn, looking around. Elsie started yelling at the top of her lungs, "Look! She's running away."

Audrey ran past the barn, ignoring Nathan; her only focus was to get as far away as possible. Yet, she still hadn't recovered from yesterday's marathon sprint, and her body quickly slowed. It wasn't long before Nathan caught up with her.

"What's the matter?" he said grabbing her arm, panting.

She yanked her arm away and glared at him. "I have to go!" she yelled, gasping for air. Her body was about to give out. Breathless, she bent over and began to heave, but there was nothing there to come out.

A woman she could only assume was Elsie's mother had caught up to Nathan, looking at him with opened hands. Nathan shrugged and shook his head. Audrey fell on her knees, panic-stricken and shaking.

"You all right?" Nathan asked.

"No, I'm not all right!" she said, not wanting to look at him. "You seemed like decent people, but now I find out that you're Feds!"

"What are you talking about Audrey?"

"You're Feds!" she screamed.

"We be good Christian folk. We ain't Feds. Who are these Feds, anyway?"

"You eat meat, don't you?"

"Well, yeah."

"Then you're Feds! Feds eat meat. You eat people!"

"What! Now hold on!" Nathan said, glancing at his wife with mouth opened, eyes wide. "Meat ain't people. Meat is from animals: the ones in the barn. Nobody here eats people!"

Audrey's stomach roiled. "Is that why I'm in the barn?" she asked. "You think I'm an animal?"

Nathan scratched his head and looked over to his wife again, with a frown. "You are in the bahn 'cause there ain't no room for you in the house, is all," he shrugged.

Elsie's mother bent down, brushing her blond hair away from her face, hooking it behind one ear. She was older. Audrey could see the flaking, dry skin, the faint wrinkles around the woman's eyes.

"We don't eat people, dear," said the older woman, softly. "Like Nathan said, we eat animals. The animals in the barn. Nobody eats people."

"So, why am I in the barn?" Audrey cried. "So you can eat me, too?"

"Not at all. We don't know you, is all. We not gonna let you stay in the house without knowing who you is. And we not keeping you here. So, if we was planning on killing you for food, we would have tied you up. You can go any time you want."

Audrey felt the woman rubbing small circles on her back, in a soothing motion.

"I'm Elsie's momma. My name is Ruth," she smiled at Audrey. "I prepared some good food for you to eat. You don't have to eat the meat if you don't want to."

Audrey calmed down. These people seemed nice. Ruth was right, they hadn't tied her up. Hadn't yelled at her. She'd been safe. In fact, Nathan had saved her from the dogs. Perhaps nothing was wrong. Maybe they weren't Feds, after all. Audrey sat quietly, thinking it over, and took a few deep breaths. It took a moment before she stood up and followed Ruth back into the house.

"What happened?" Elsie asked, as they approached the house where she had clearly been waiting, anxiously.

"Never you mind. Go inside and put the chairs around the table."

"But, Ma—"

"Do I have to ask you again?" Ruth interrupted her daughter before she could finish complaining.

Elsie darted into the house and was pushing the last chair against the table when the three of them finally walked inside. Nathan took a seat and motioned for Audrey to sit next to him. Elsie and her mother put out the table settings and brought food over. Audrey's stomach gave a loud grumble; she hadn't eaten in two days, everything looked good. It was embarrassing that these people had gone out of their way to help her and here she was accusing them of eating people. She felt her cheeks flush hot in embarrassment.

Once everyone had sat down at the table, Audrey cleared her throat. "I'm sorry for what happened earlier," she said. "When I smelled the meat, I thought…"

"It's all right, dear," Ruth said with knitted brows and tilted head. "I can't imagine how there could be a group of people that could eat other people. But we don't do that here. I can promise you that. This all comes from the plants and animals we grow and raise on the farm." She waved her hand over the food she had prepared. "I have been up most of the morning preparing it in the hopes that you would eat with us."

Ruth smiled. "Let me re-introduce myself." She put her hand to her chest. "I am Ruth. This is my husband Nathan and my daughter Elsie. Welcome to our home."

"She's Audrey!" Elsie yelled, joining in. "She slept in the barn. I watched her wake up."

"Thank you." Audrey nodded, looking between Nathan and Ruth in turn, offering Elsie a brief smile. "Thank you for letting me stay with you."

Still on her guard, Audrey still couldn't trust these people one hundred percent. It was understandable that they probably didn't trust her, either. It was a gracious gesture that they had taken her in.

The house was small; just a single large room with three sections to it. On one side was a fireplace made out of stone. There was a single cot off to the side. The kitchen was simply appointed: a stove in the corner, a cupboard, and a bench in the middle where they sat.

Audrey waited for them to start eating. But instead, they all bowed their heads and clasped their hands. Nathan spoke. "Thank you, Father, for the meal you have blessed us with. Amen." He took the bowl with the yellow substance and put some on his plate. "Put as much as you like on your plate." He handed the bowl to Audrey.

The bowl was warm. The yellow substance reminded her of gelatin, but they told her they didn't eat people, so the food was safe to eat. She put half as much as Nathan spooned for himself on her plate, just in case she didn't like it. For each of the plates on the table, Nathan was always the first one to be served. Elsie the last.

Audrey grabbed her fork and was about to eat the yellow substance when she was stopped by Ruth. "No one may begin to eat before the head of the house."

It was almost an eternity before Nathan took his fork and began to eat. Had he taken a second longer, she would have passed out on the floor.

The debris falling into Nathan's unkempt beard made Audrey want to gag, especially when he picked off the pieces and put them into his mouth.

Tearing her gaze off the man's disgusting eating habits, she concentrated on tasting her food. As much as watching Nathan turned her stomach, she was still acutely aware that her own stomach was very, very empty. "This tastes very good," she nodded to Ruth through bites, genuinely impressed.

"Thank you," Ruth said, warmly. "Do you eat this kind of food in your home?"

"We have corn and a similar type of bread. And I don't know what this yellow thing is. We don't have this where I'm from."

"Well, the yellow stuff is eggs," Ruth said. "They come from the chickens."

Audrey grimaced at the thought of eating something that came out of an animal but realized she had already eaten some now anyway—it was pretty good.

"And this is milk." Elsie raised her cup in the air.

"Milk?"

"It comes from Betsy."

Audrey paused in confusion.

"It's the cow in the barn," Ruth clarified.

Audrey thought about it for a moment, then remembered what Nathan was doing in the barn. She smiled at Elsie, gritting her teeth.

"Oh my!" Ruth suddenly exclaimed, looking at Nathan with wide eyes, then quickly getting up. "I forgot all about the meat!"

Just the word alone made Audrey cringe. Her hands shook. Everyone stared at her.

"It's all right," Ruth said in a comforting tone and then got up to get the meat off the stove and bring it back to the table. Audrey's memory tugged at images of her aunt and Logan's parents, and what the Feds had done to them. Silent tears started to fall down her cheeks.

"Maybe we should not eat meat today," Ruth suggested, looking at Nathan.

"And just let it spoil?" Nathan's eyes narrowed as he let out a growl.

"I'll salt it and make jerky out of it." Ruth put the meat back on top of the stove.

In a very short while, the rest of the food was gone. No one said a word. Silence reigned.

Audrey swallowed. "I want to apologize to you, again. You seem like good people. I should have asked about the meat instead of reacting the way I did. It's just that I saw my Aunt Joyce killed by the Feds and her body..." She choked. The tears wouldn't stop. Finally, she got a grip on herself. "I want to thank you for your hospitality, and if I can repay you for your kindness, please tell me what I can do."

Nathan leaned in, mouth open, jaw dropped. "I'm sorry for staring, but you speak really good for a nigger. Where are you from?" he asked. "And tell me more about these Feds."

Audrey sighed and took a deep breath. "I'm from a different place. I'm not sure where exactly," she said. Lilly told her not to tell anyone her story or they'd think she was crazy. She decided to follow that advice and not tell them everything. Not just yet, at least. "The Feds are a group of people we thought were our friends, but it turned out they are absolutely not."

Audrey told them the story of how she and Logan escaped from the Feds and ended up on the cliff top.

"So, these Feds are close by. Are they Indians?" Nathan asked.

"I don't know any Indians," Audrey said. "When I got to the cliffs, I saw a few houses in the valley below and a man told me to ask the people there for directions." She told them what happened and how she was just asking where to go when they bound her and put her in a shack. "That man tricked me into going down into the valley to ask for help. If Lilly hadn't helped me, I would still be there."

"Lilly?" Ruth asked.

"Lilly was the slave girl who helped me escape." Audrey's voice broke. "We ran and she smashed her knee against a rock. She told me to keep running without her and I did. They caught up to her and I heard them shoot her."

"Well, thank God you were able to escape," Nathan said.

"Lilly said that if I put my trust in God, he would help me," she sniffled. "I haven't seen her god, but I felt his presence."

Nathan looked at Ruth and then back to Audrey. "We are Christians," he said.

"I'm Milestownian," Audrey offered, not sure why he changed the subject. She continued on with that line of thought. "How far is Christ from Philadelphia?"

They seemed caught off guard with her comment, no one spoke for a few second. "No, no. This place is Lehigh County."

"Our religion is Christianity," Nathan explained. "That makes us Christians. We believe that Jesus Christ is our savior. That's how we worship God."

"A savior?" Audrey asked confused.

"It's someone who helps you when you're lost, to find the right path."

"So, then Lilly would be my savior."

"Ah!" Nathan wiped his hand across his forehead. "This isn't going to be easy."

---

The days went by fast. Audrey was more than happy to help around the farm. It didn't take long to get used to the animals and soon they weren't as mysterious as before. Even the neighbor's dog who frequently wandered over wasn't anything like the vicious monster she'd imagined had been chasing her in the forest.

The food was good, and Audrey always ate everything on her plate, yet never once took a serving of meat. Every now and then Ruth tried to get her to eat some. "Don't you want to at least try some of the meat?" she would ask. "I cooked it just right."

"No thank you. I don't want to eat something that I took care of," Audrey replied, feeling a little nauseous.

"But that is the life of this animal. To feed us," Nathan explained, matter of fact, as if that would make her feel better.

"If you say so," Audrey replied flatly. "I'm fine with the fruits and vegetables and the bread and eggs."

They stopped trying to convince her after a while. They talked about the day's events and things they would have to get done the next day. Never once did they leave any food to throw away. Ruth always knew just how much to cook for their meals.

"Tomorrow we don't work," Nathan said to Audrey. "Tomorrow is the Lord's Day: Sunday."

"We don't have that where I'm from," Audrey said. "Sunday is simply the last day of the week, but every day of the week there is something to do. There are some days where we have big celebrations. Like the Founding Fathers' Day, the birthday of the city, and New Year's."

"The Lord's Day is a day when every Christian goes to church. We must dress in our best clothes and celebrate the reason we are Christians."

"But I am not a Christian and I don't have any nice clothes."

Ruth got up and went toward the big room. "I'll give you one of my dresses," she offered, pulling a dress from the clothes she had folded on the floor next to the cot. "You're about my size, so these should fit you."

Audrey stood and came over to Ruth. She was noticeably taller.

"Try this on. Let's see what it looks like," Ruth said handing her the dress. She turned to the others. "Everyone turn around, don't look this way."

Audrey took off her clothes and tried on the dress. It was a really tight fit.

Elsie started laughing really hard.

"Sh! Elsie that's rude." Her mother eyed her with a frown. She got the scissors and cut the dress where the blouse and skirt came together.

Adurey was able to pull the dress down to where it came just under her knees.

"She looks like a giant," Nathan said. Elsie laughed out loud again.

"Nothing else is going to fit her!" Ruth gasped.

Nathan shrugged. "So much for her being your size."

Ruth stomped her foot staring hard at Nathan, then smiled. "I'll make it work."

# Chapter 18

It was a long ride through a narrow trail to reach the church. From the outside, the building looked like a regular house, except one part of the roof extended up much higher than any other part of the building. This extension could be seen from miles away, which was probably its purpose. Audrey admired the simplicity of the construction.

People came in their wagons and a few walked. Everyone wore their best clothes. The air crackled with positive energy. This was a very important day for these people.

"Hey there, Nathan," said a man, approaching. He was the same height as Nathan and looked to be about the same age. Without a doubt these two were brothers. If not for the color of his sandy blonde hair, it would be easy to get the two confused.

"Hey there, Joseph." Nathan grabbed his brother's hand, and they hugged.

"Hello, Ruth." Joseph gave her a kiss on the cheek.

"And who is this?" he said, smiling at Elsie. "My, you've grown so much since last week!"

"Hello, Uncle Joe." Elsie rushed to him and hugged his leg. Everyone laughed.

Joseph turned his gaze to Audrey. The lusty perusal in his blue eyes made her want to vomit. Why did every man she met stare at her as though she was an object they had to possess?

"Ahem!" Nathan said. "This is Audrey. She's visiting with us for a while." He turned to Audrey. "This is my brother Joseph."

Joseph couldn't stop staring at her. Nathan grabbed his shoulder and shook him to get his attention. "Oh, yea," Joseph blurted out. "Glad to meet you." Nathan nudged Joseph and they began talking and walking into the church a few meters ahead of the women.

"I guess we should be going in too," Ruth said, directing Audrey and Elsie to follow the men.

They all entered the building. Benches lined either side of the church and formed rows facing a large table, and a podium stood off to the side. The table stood on an elevated floor, draped with a bright, white cloth; cups and bowls made of brass lay upon it. On the back wall was a large plus sign, stretched at the bottom.

A man, Ruth mentioned was the minister of the church, stood at the podium and greeted everyone as they took their seats. They found an empty bench and sat. A few moments later the church service began. The minister read from a thick book, and songs were sung by the entire congregation. This place had a feeling of community, reminding her of Milestown.

The minister, a small, thin man with oily black hair, stood up at the podium after the last song was sung and began to speak with a bellowing voice. "What is it that we must do every day in our lives to be good in the eyes of God, besides pray? I say to you, brothers and sisters, that it is not just our thoughts but our actions that make us good people. The Ten Commandments need not complicate our thinking because each is a part of one whole: duty to, and love for, God and our fellow human beings. Our Lord Jesus Christ reminds us of this when he says: 'Thou shalt love the Lord thy God with all thy heart, and with all thy soul, and with all thy mind.' This is the first great commandment. And the second is like unto it: 'Thou shalt love thy neighbor as thyself. On these two commandments hang all the Laws and the Prophets.'"

These words struck a chord for Audrey: to love thy neighbor as thyself. She thought about the slave escaping through Logan's fields and how the soldiers had chased him. She was that slave in this world, trying to run away; trying to be free. Logan had been right all along. Everyone had the same right to be free.

The minister continued, "We take for granted the role of Jesus in our lives. Why is he here? What is his purpose? We find that purpose when we read from the book of John: 'For God loves the world so much that he gave his only son, that everyone who believes in him should not die, but have eternal life. God did not send his son into the world to be its judge, but to be its savior.'"

Audrey was intrigued about the love these people had for this man they called Jesus. She wanted to learn more about his relationship with God. Why did God send his only son? How could he do this? What kind of powers did Jesus have? Audrey couldn't wait to meet him. She looked around the congregation, trying to spot who he may be. Surely, he would come up to the podium to speak.

The minister raised a plate and held a cup up in the air. "Now let us remember the sacrifice that Jesus made for us and let us celebrate his death by eating from his body and drinking from his blood, so that our sins may be forgiven, and we may have everlasting life."

Audrey's heart stopped. *What did that man just say?* They needed to eat his body and drink his blood to live forever? Nathan and Ruth lied! Even after she had gotten to know this family, she still lived in the barn with the other animals. She didn't want to be a sacrifice like Jesus so they could live forever. These people were crazy!

She jumped off the bench in a panic and tried to make her way toward the aisle to get out. Nathan grabbed her by the arm. "Where are you going?" he whispered, trying not to attract any attention.

She swung her hand free and screamed, "You lied to me!"

The entire congregation stared in their direction. Nathan's face turned red.

"You said you don't eat people! You lied! You lied! You lied!" She kept scrambling to make her way out of the church.

Two men blocked her exit. She began to hit them in a vain attempt to get out. Joseph grabbed her from behind to quiet her down.

"Calm down," he said as he struggled with her. "You won't get hurt, I promise."

"Lies!" They were all lying! She turned to face Joseph and dug her fingernails into his face. He screamed and pushed her off. The men blocking her path wasted no time and moved out of her way when she raised her hands, ready to claw at them as well. She hissed at them then ran out of the church.

Joseph sat and watched as Audrey left. No one in the church moved, everyone seemed to be in shock, not knowing how to respond to what had just happened. Ruth ran to Joseph to attend to his wounds, ripping a part of her dress to wipe the blood from Joseph's cheeks. Nathan came toward Joseph, Elsie followed her dad. The minister also made his way up to them.

"What's going on here?"

Nathan turned from Joseph to face the minister. "She thinks we eat people."

There was a collective gasp. People started to talk among themselves.

"Why would she think we eat people?"

"She's a crazy nigger," someone said.

"I think," Nathan began, looking toward the person who made the comment, "that it was when you said, 'let us eat from his body and drink from his blood,'"

Joseph winced, as Ruth dabbed his face with the cloth.

The minister shook his head. "Nathan, why did you bring a non-Christian into the church? Now she is afraid of us."

"Where will she go?" someone in the congregation asked.

"She's trying to get to Philadelphia," Nathan said. "She's looking for someone named Thomas Lynch."

The minister raised an eyebrow in a silent question.

"I don't know," Nathan said. "Perhaps another slave?"

"Let me go find her," Joseph finally put in.

Nathan stopped him. "But you don't know her. I will go."

"She doesn't trust you anymore, brother."

Joseph knew his brother had thought he had done the right thing by introducing her to their ways. But the thing everyone took for granted, she had blown out of proportion. The girl wouldn't trust Nathan now. As far as she was concerned, he was the enemy.

"Go!" he agreed, bowing his head in resignation.

---

Joseph did not know Audrey. Nathan had been right about that. But that was about to change. One thing he did know was that she was extraordinarily smart; it was obvious from the way she held herself in a crowd. Now, the problem would be finding which way she went. Being negro and alone would keep her off the roads. This left only two ways to go: the river or the forest. But if it was Philadelphia she was trying to get to, this river would take her farther away from her destination. Did she even know which way Philadelphia was?

The forest was dense, and it didn't take long to find the conspicuous traces Audrey had left behind. From the time she left the church to the time he left to follow her, Audrey had a good ten minute head start. Joseph knew there were wolves living in this forest; this was no good. If he wanted to find her before they did, he would need to pick up his pace.

It surprised him that she had gotten this far. It had to be her fear that kept her going. Never in all his years had he seen any girl run this far without resting! Half an hour went by, and he still hadn't caught up with her. Another Fifteen minutes passed before the path grew cold. No signs of her were anywhere on the ground. The trees showed no signs of anyone being in them either.

"Audrey!" he shouted. "It's me, Nathan's brother, Joseph!"

No response. Turning around a thick tree, he noticed the trampling of some green foliage. *This has to be Audrey!* He continued on the path, then felt a sharp pain on the back of his head and fell to the ground.

# Chapter 19

Audrey pulled vines from the ground and tied Joseph to a tree, making sure that she fastened his hands, feet, and body tight and secure so he couldn't get away. On the opposite side she sat at a tree and stared, waiting for him to wake up. They would never take her back. She wasn't about to become lunchmeat for those Feds. They hid what they did so well. They killed the animals to make her lose sight of the fact that they also ate people. Poor Jesus, he said so many nice things and this was their gratitude.

Joseph woke up with glazed eyes and looked around, confused. Then his eyes met hers. "Audrey," he winced, "what are you doing? Untie me!"

"Why? So you can take me back to the others and do to me what you did to Jesus?" Audrey said. "No, thank you! I don't want anyone celebrating my death that way."

"What we did to Jesus? Audrey... I cannot comprehend your reasoning. We don't eat people."

She kept silent. His words fell on deaf ears.

"Untie me, please!" he pleaded. "Let me explain. I won't harm you. I promise."

Audrey was tired of hearing shallow promises and tired of obeying people who meant her harm. Standing up with the tree branch in her hand she marched toward him. "You *promise*?" Hatred started boiling inside of her. "You mean like the slave who gave me water to drink and started doing things to me to please himself?" She paced back and forth. "You *promise*? You mean like Massa Henry who promised he wouldn't hurt me if I did what he wanted to do to me?" She paused and looked into his eyes. "You *PROMISE*?" she screamed at the top of her lungs.

Joseph's eyes widened in fear, which is what she wanted to see. He tried to wriggle his hands free, but she had tied him down well. Coming close to him, she bent down at a level with his face, and continued to speak. "You mean like your brother who said he didn't eat people, yet he kept me in a barn with all the other animals and then took me to your gathering place where you were about to eat the body and blood of Jesus? You *promise*?" She stood and backed away. *"I promise* I won't hurt *you* if you just shut up!"

Audrey sat down and kept her eyes trained on Joseph, hoping that he would say something and give her a reason to take the tree branch and hurt him. Joseph didn't say a word. He just stared at her. She stared back at him; she was at a loss at what to do. They were deep in the forest now, no food, no shelter. If she left him there, it would be a day or two before they would find him. That was what she needed to do, leave him here and continue on her journey to Philadelphia.

But a deep voice gave her pause. "Untie him," the voice behind her said.

Audrey turned around and looked at where the voice came from. But there was no one there. Joseph stared back in silence.

"Untie him," the voice said again.

She stood up and looked around again. Someone else was here, but she couldn't see anyone.

"What is it?" Joseph asked.

"Shut up!" She looked around. "Someone is here. One of your friends." The voice sounded familiar, but she couldn't remember who it belonged to. The man from the cliffs?

"I came alone," Joseph said. "There is no one else here."

"Shut up, I said!"

"Audrey, if you will let me explain." Joseph tried to talk with her, but she was not paying attention. "Audrey! Can you stop and listen to me?"

She came up to him, ready to rip his head off with her teeth. "You are like your brother. You even look like him. He lied to me! He's a liar! And so are you!"

"Audrey, we don't eat people!"

Audrey stood back up. She didn't know what she would do with someone else hiding in the forest.

"Listen to him!" the voice said. But this time it came from above.

Audrey looked up, but from where the voice emanated all that was there were tree branches. Someone had to be hiding in them. "Who are you?" she called, looking up into the trees.

Joseph was now staring at her, his forehead crinkled. "Who are you talking with?"

Audrey ignored him. "Who are you?" she asked again, her gaze darting back and forth from branch to branch.

"I am Lilly's friend," the voice said.

"I don't believe you," Audrey said. "If you come near me, I will hurt him. I swear!" She lifted the tree branch into the air ready to hit Joseph.

She could feel the quiet. The noises that she had not paid much attention to before were now gone. A bright light exploded in front of her in the midst of the trees, as if the sun had burst in her face.

"Agh!" Joseph screamed, turning his head and closing his eyes.

Audrey dropped the branch and used her hands to block out the light, but it was too bright. As quickly as the light flashed, it disappeared.

Several minutes passed before she realized she was blind. "I can't see!"

She stretched out her hands, feeling for anything she might bump into. The root of a tree caused her to stumble on the ground.

She tried to walk again with arms outstretched but kept stumbling, until she found a tree to lean against. She stood, afraid, trying to assess her situation. *Why is this happening to me?* With Joseph tied up, she could make an escape. But where could she go being blind? They would come looking for him.

"Audrey," Joseph said, "you need to untie me."

"No!" She wasn't going to help him. Hopefully, her sight would come back.

"Listen to me," Joseph persisted. "It'll be dark soon. You're blind and I'm bound to this tree. If you don't untie me, we'll be dead by the morrow. I know other people have hurt you, but my brother didn't lie to you. We don't eat people."

*Why can't he just shut up and let me think. I am so done with this place. I want to go home!*

"Listen to me. Jesus is our savior. He died for us over seventeen hundred years ago. The body and blood are *symbols* we use to celebrate him. we don't *actually* eat him."

"Liar!"

"We use bread to symbolize his body, and wine to symbolize his blood."

"Liar!"

He sighed. "Audrey, listen." He took a deep breath. "There are wolves in this forest. I know you don't know what they are. My brother told me that you have never seen animals before. They are like dogs. I don't even know if you know what those are, but these wolves hunt other animals. They always hunt in packs. If we don't build a fire soon, they'll come and eat us."

Audrey slid down the tree to a seated position, dropped her face in her hands.

"Audrey, I don't want to die like this, tied to a tree. Audrey, please untie me," Joseph said.

Moments passed and she did nothing. She lifted her head and looked from side to side, trying to see anything. "I can't see," she responded, calmer now. "I don't know where you are, so I can't untie you."

"Walk toward the sound of my voice," he urged, his voice an octave higher.

She stood up and started to inch toward him.

"I'm over here," he said, repeating it over and over as she got closer.

She bumped her foot on the root of a tree and fell. It happened more than once, but each time she got up and continued toward Joseph's voice. Still, it was taking so long that she groaned in frustration. At one point, she stopped and threw her fists in the air. Tears streaked down her cheeks.

"Audrey! Listen to me."

"I can't see!"

"Listen to me," he said, more firmly. She sensed a slight irritation in his voice.

She sniffed.

"Just crawl. That way you won't fall."

She got down on all fours and began to crawl toward the sound of his voice. When she found a root on the ground, she crawled over it.

"That's it. Just come to my voice."

Finally, she found his leg. He didn't move. She untied his legs and then slid up to free his hands, before backing away cautiously.

Audrey heard a rustling sound. "What are you doing?" she asked.

"I'm pushing away some leaves to build a fire."

It wasn't long before he had a strong fire going; Audrey could feel the heat against her face. She heard him stand up and could swear he'd pulled out a knife. She felt the air change, as he got close to her and she gasped.

"Audrey," he said. "I am going to fetch us some food."

She could hear him as his feet stepped on the leaves of the forest floor around her. Straining her eyes revealed only pitch-black. She began to cry. Almost the instant she had come to this world she had encountered problems. *The people in this world are evil.*

A noise gave her pause. She snapped her head in the direction of the sound, instinctively. "Joseph?" she called out. Leaves rustled as if someone were walking through them. "Who's there?" she repeated, growing more anxious.

No response. Her heart thudded in her chest.

A scurrying sound came from nearby. Something or someone was there. What could she do to protect herself? This blindness was driving her mad. Had Joseph gone to fetch food, or was *she* the food? Had he left her to go fetch the others? It was stupid to believe him. *Stupid, stupid, stupid!* She hated this place now more than ever.

The sounds were frightening at first, but then it was obvious that it was just the sound of the animals that scurried through the leaves and climbed up the trees. Being blind allowed her to notice with her ears what she hadn't noticed before using her eyes. If there were any danger, it would have already happened. She put her hands on the ground and felt around, eventually finding a pile of leaves; the ones that Joseph had moved to make the fire. Next to them was the bare ground, and heat. It grew more intense as she got closer. A light breeze blew through the forest, causing the fire to flare, heating up her face.

"Audrey."

"You're back," she said, startled. "You've been gone a long time."

No response, only the sounds of the animals and the fire crackling. Her imagination was playing tricks. The voice was so real. It was just like the first day at Nathan's field. She was hallucinating again. *Joseph, where are you?*

"Audrey." The voice came again.

It wasn't Joseph and she wasn't imagining it. She started to panic. "Who's there?" she said, straining her eyes to try to catch a glimpse of something. She straightened up against the tree, pressing into the bark with her palms. The feel of something tangible, something real, was comforting. Someone was here and whoever it was knew her. She could hear footsteps. "Whose there?!"

"I'm here." It was Joseph's voice.

"Why didn't you say anything earlier?" she asked, embarrassed.

"I just got here."

"Someone was here. They called me by my name."

"There's no one here, Audrey."

The thought that she might be talking to herself again made her feel uneasy. She pushed it away—there were more important things to worry about right now.

"I was able to find us something to eat," Joseph said.

"I'm not hungry." She sat and put her head between her knees. The smell of death filled the air as she listened to Joseph skinning the animal and cleaning it. She had visions of her aunt on the rooftop back in New Scranton being butchered by those men; the ones who claimed to be their friends. She covered her ears and tried to think of something else.

# Chapter 20

Audrey and Joseph didn't say much to each other. He ate the rabbit smacking his lips in the process. Joseph tried getting her to eat by putting the food up to her mouth. She slapped it away, hearing it land on the leaves. Laying on the ground, her tears flowed over, dripping onto the ground. The occasional sniffle betrayed the quiet that was around her.

"Audrey."

"What?" she snapped.

"Why do you feel sorry for yourself?"

"I'm stuck in a world I don't understand. I've been touched by..." She shuddered. "And I chose to come here. No one forced me. I'm so stupid! And now I'm blind."

"Then why did you run away from the people I sent to you?"

Audrey sat up in a swift motion. "You sent people to me? Who did you send to me?"

"When you yelled 'which way?' I told you which way."

"How did you do that?" she asked, hearing her own voice when what she had said was repeated. The moment she asked the question she could see in her mind a flock of birds flying in the air and the one bird that went flying off by itself.

"Nathan was waiting on the other side of the river. You ran away," the voice said. "When you crossed the river, Nathan was there again, and helped you. But you tried to run away again."

Everything was true. Someone *was* helping her. She asked for help and it was given. "And now you're running away again. You need to stop running."

She was so caught up in the conversation that it took until this moment to realize it wasn't Joseph talking to her. "Who are you?" she asked.

"I am Lilly's friend," the voice said.

"Lilly's friend?" she said in contempt. "You mean God? Why did you save me and not her?"

"I did save Lilly. She's with me."

"Where is she?"

"She's with me."

Audrey didn't know what that meant. How could he have saved her when she was dead?

Something around her was changing. The conversation stopped faster than it started.

# Timepieces

**Five minutes earlier**

Joseph watched Audrey in confusion. She stared at him mumbling some gibberish that made no sense.

"Audrey?" Joseph spoke. "What are you saying?"

The mumbling continued. Whatever she was saying couldn't be understood. She stood up and looked straight at him.

"Who are you talking with?" he asked turning to see who might be out in the forest and seeing no one. *Is she crazy?*

Every now and then she would move her hands in agitation. Her eyes focused on something nearby and the gibberish continued. An unholy thought washed over him; he backed away and constructed a small cross from the twigs on the ground. She was fully animated now, still mumbling incomprehensible words and making no sense. A spirit must be possessing her body, trying to communicate with its master! He held the cross in front of Audrey's face. "By the power of the Father, the Son, and the Holy Spirit, I command the demon in Audrey to come out!"

He tied her up to a tree using the vines Audrey had used on him; she didn't resist. This should prevent the demon from using her body in immoral ways.

The mumbling stopped, as she became aware of her surroundings. Joseph checked the vines to make sure they were secure.

"What's going on?" she screamed.

"You are not Audrey!" Joseph screamed back, holding his cross to her face. "Demon be gone!"

"I am Audrey!" She tried to free her hands. "I don't even know what a demon is. Untie me."

"I will not untie her until you leave her body," he said, paying no attention to her.

She argued with Joseph, but to no avail. "How long will I be tied like this?"

"For as long as it takes for you to leave Audrey's body," he said determined.

"But I am Audrey," she begged.

Joseph ignored her pleas.

---

Audrey tired reasoning with Joseph. The fire crackled as Joseph tended to it. A rustling of leaves followed. Joseph was making his forest bed for the night. The vines prevented her from lying down. Audrey's head drooped and she soon fell into a fitful sleep.

A voice entered her dreams. "Audrey, wake up! Audrey, wake up!" it kept repeating. The voice pierced through Audrey's haze and brought her out of sleep.

"I'm awake!" she yawned.

"The fire is almost out. The wolves are near. Wake up Joseph and tell him to tend to the fire."

Wolves? Audrey didn't have to be told twice. "Joseph!" she yelled. She kept shouting at him until he stirred.

"The fire!" she said. "It's almost out. The wolves are near!"

She could hear Joseph scurrying about, picking up branches here and there, throwing them into the fire. Soon, she could feel the heat—much stronger than before.

"The fire feels good, doesn't it?" she sighed.

Joseph didn't respond. It wasn't long before his even breathing could be heard. After a while, she also closed her eyes and fell asleep.

By morning, the cawing and twittering of birds woke her up. She sensed that Joseph was also awake. "Is there anything to eat?"

"I will not feed one of Satan's minions," he snapped.

Something like a stick poked at her forehead. "Demon, be gone!" Joseph ordered.

"Joseph, I am not possessed." She reasoned with him. "I don't have a demon, or a Satan, or a minion. I don't even know what those things are. Please untie me."

"You are a demon. I saw you last night talking in tongues so that no one can understand. Now you're trying to use deceit to get your way."

"I was talking with God," she said.

"You expect me to believe that?" She could hear the anger in his voice.

"I expect you to untie me." She squirmed. "Last night I told you that the fire was out, and you tended to it."

"You did nothing of the kind."

"Joseph, I woke you up and you added more wood to the fire."

"I slept all night. No such thing happened."

"Then explain how the fire burned all night," she snapped, frustrated. A shiver ran down her spine. She saw a vision. "Joseph," she said, as images unfolded in her mind, "you had a sister. You were playing in the barn and you hid from her in the loft. She came up and tried to find you. You ran to the ladder and started to climb down. You passed her and startled her, causing her to lose her footing. She stumbled and hung over the edge screaming for you to help. But you thought she was tricking you. You continued down the ladder. She did need your help. When you reached the bottom, she fell from the loft at your feet and broke her neck. You told everyone that you heard her screaming and came into the barn where you found her on the ground. You lied because you didn't want anyone to know that you ignored your sister's pleas. You didn't help her when she needed you."

"How do you know that?" he whispered, barely audible.

She could hear the panic in his voice, which wavered as he spoke. "She died and you never told anyone the truth about what happened."

"Who's telling you these things?" he screamed.

"I can see these things in my mind."

Joseph didn't respond. Silence ruled for a while. The leaves cracked under the weight of Joseph's feet as he paced back and forth. The occasional sound of twigs breaking thrummed in her ears. Eventually, the footsteps stopped, and she heard him exhale loudly. She could feel his eyes boring into her. "Joseph?"

"I... I believe you," he said. "God talks through you."

"Really?" she said sarcastically. "Is that why I'm blind?"

"There's a reason for it," he said.

"I can't imagine what that might be," she said. "Now can you please untie me?"

He rushed over and untied her. Free of the vines, Audrey stood up and stretched her arms and legs. "Can I ask you to do something for me?"

"Ask."

She turned in the direction of Joseph's voice. "Teach me about your God."

"I wouldn't know where to start—"

"Just start at the beginning."

Joseph talked about God, stopping to answer her many questions as he worked his way through the Old Testament. He took a break to hunt for food before it got too late. When he returned, he started to explain the life of Jesus Christ.

"I don't understand," Audrey said, hearing Joseph put wood on the fire. "Why would God come to the world in human form and then let himself be killed?"

"He did it to fulfill the prophecies, to sacrifice himself for the forgiveness of our sins so we can enter into the kingdom of heaven."

"But why go through this elaborate game just to get into heaven?"

"I assure you, it's not a game."

Audrey questioned Joseph about original sin; she couldn't understand why God punished Adam and Eve for not following an order. And why did God punish the snake when the snake had no control over what it was doing while Satan possessed it?

"I cannot answer why God made such decisions. It's not for me to question. Nor should you."

"But God never told me not to question him. And I'm not questioning God. I'm questioning *you*."

"When we get back, you can always ask the minister."

"I can't go back there," she said. "I'm so ashamed for what I did and how I acted."

"It was a misunderstanding. They'll let it pass." he said squeezing her hand. "I'm fascinated that God speaks with you. I've never heard of anyone talking with God the way you have, except for the prophets. I still don't understand why God talks with you when you don't even know who he is."

"I don't know why he speaks to me and not to you, either. I don't know why he blinded me and not you. He was the voice I heard telling me to untie you."

"Really?" he said. "Did God mention anything about not scratching people?"

"I am so sorry about that, but I thought I was brought to the church for..."

"Yes." Joseph said. "How did you ever come up with such a ridiculous idea?"

Audrey told Joseph about her world, her city, the Feds. Lilly would have had her keep quiet about it, but she trusted Joseph a little more.

"Your story is rather hard to believe," he said. "But it does explain a lot about you, especially the way you speak."

"The way I speak?" she said touching her mouth.

"You have an accent."

"I don't have an accent," she said indignantly, "you do."

"I guess we both have accents." He chuckled.

The evening came and they talked about their lives and the things they did most of the time. She smiled inwardly as he fumbled to find out if she was seeing someone. She wasn't interested in him that way and avoided answering the question for fear that he might leave her, knowing the truth.

That night they slept well. Joseph woke up several times to keep the fire going. In the morning, they ate what was left of the rabbit. She ate hesitantly, mechanically, trying not to think too much about the past. Even though the meat was from an animal, it still reminded her of the Feds. But hunger and desperation won out over fear.

"We need to get out of the forest," he said. She heard him wiping his hands. "We've been out here two days. My farm is close to where we are. If we walk today, we can get there by tomorrow in the afternoon."

"But I'm blind," she said. "I'll trip over the roots and branches."

"I'll lead you."

She agreed. The next stop would be his farm. They walked for a long time talking more about God and themselves. But eventually, her feet began to drag. "Can we take a break?" she begged. "It feels like we've been walking for days."

"We've walked through most of the night," he said. "It will be dawn soon."

"Why'd you do that? Why didn't we stop to rest when it got dark?"

"You cannot see. The moon was out. I could make out where we were going." He directed her to sit on a log, and she sat and listened to him rustling about as he started a fire. He told her he would fetch firewood, and she listened to his steps recede into the forest.

As she sat alone, she meditated on how beautiful the forest was without being able to see it. She could hear the wind blowing through the trees, birds singing, animals scurrying about diving in and out of leaves. How she wished her world was like this—so alive!

"Are you okay?" Joseph's voice sounded close by. She heard him drop a pile of branches on the ground near her feet. She smiled, focusing on figuring out what he was doing.

"Are you okay?" he repeated when she didn't respond.

"Yeah, I'm fine," she said, snapping out of her reverie. "I was just thinking how I wished my world were more like yours. Something terrible happened to change it."

"Maybe this Thomas Lynch knows. It seems odd that someone in your time would send you here to find him. Perhaps he's the one that made the device."

"I hope so. I can't get home without it and I'll be stuck here in this world."

"Is that so bad?"

"In this world the color of my skin prevents me from being free. People can make me their slave claiming I don't have the proper papers."

He paused. "Yes, I can see how that would be a problem. But when one gets to know you, your manner of speaking would cause many people to forget that you are indeed a negro. To me, you are just a beautiful woman, and a fascinating one at that."

She felt his warm hand engulf hers.

"I'll take you to Philadelphia and help you find this Thomas Lynch fellow."

She smiled, despite herself. She was both excited and nervous in equal measure. "When can we do this?" she asked impatiently.

"My farm is another five miles from here. We can take the wagon into town." He let go of her hand. "Let me prepare the rabbit now."

She watched Joseph skin the rabbit. The scars on his face had healed quite a bit since she last saw them. Several small animals scurried about and ran inside a hole in the ground next to a tree. *Oh my!* Audrey jumped up and looked around her, spinning in a full circle. "Oh my, I can see! Joseph!"

She pinched herself and rubbed her eyes to make sure it wasn't a dream. The green leaves on the trees were beautiful. The blue sky above was marvelous with its white fluffy clouds. The brown dirt on the ground was the most wonderful thing she'd ever seen. She hugged a nearby tree.

Joseph stared at her in utter shock. She rushed over to him and hugged him. He dropped the rabbit and returned her embrace, struggling to keep balance. He moved back from her, gazing into her eyes. "Understand, Audrey. God has done all this."

Her mood changed from cheerful to discontent. "God has done all this to me?"

"You told me that God asked you why you kept running even after he told you to stop." Joseph leaned down and picked up the rabbit. He started to skin it. "When you were about to hit me, a bright light blinded you. But it didn't blind me. Why? Somehow God needs me to help you." He paused, letting his words sink in. "Now, for the last three days, what have we been talking about?"

"God," she said.

"Correct. And you have learned as much as I can tell you about God. So, after three days of understanding God, he has restored your sight. This in itself is a sign that God has plans for you."

Audrey thought about what Joseph said. She closed her eyes. "Why did I have to go through all this just to learn about you?"

"It's not for you to question God's will," Joseph stated.

"I just don't like being used like a plaything."

"Why are you so negative?"

"Why do you think everything has a purpose?" she retorted, annoyed with Joseph's insistence everything is because of God.

---

The horse trotted along pulling the wagon behind it, as they made their way to Philadelphia. They had passed many farms and patches of grassland. Joseph called them meadows. The towering trees of the forest looked so different to Audrey from afar than when she was in the thick of them. The smells called out to her to come back and stay longer. Everything was so new and beautiful. In her world this was all underwater, its beauty hidden. This was to become the sea floor of the ocean beyond the Great Bay. As she sat contemplating the scenery, a black-and-white-striped creature with a tinge of red on the tips of its wings landed on her finger. Its wings opened and then closed.

"What's this?" she asked, lifting her hand so that Joseph could see. The animal flew away.

"That was a butterfly," Joseph said. "They are caterpillars first before they become butterflies."

"Caterpillars?"

"Yes. They're like hairy worms."

"Worms?"

"The caterpillars make cocoons and sleep in them. After a while, they become butterflies." Joseph eyed her and smiled. "I guess you have to see them to understand."

"Oh."

"You have no idea what I am talking about, do you?" he chuckled.

"I understand you perfectly well," she pouted and turned to look out at the road. "So, tell me," she said. "What's a worm?"

They both laughed.

# Chapter 21

Isaac had come out of the house and noticed Joseph riding up to the house in his wagon. What a surprise. It was more surprising to see a negro woman sitting in front with him. *To what honor am I granted this horrific sight?*

"Hello, Isaac," Joseph greeted, as the horse and carriage came to a complete stop.

"Afternoon, Joseph. How are my sister and her family?" His gaze fell on Audrey. She was beautiful. *A runaway?*

"They're doing well," Joseph smiled, and made the introductions. "This is Audrey. She is with me."

He smiled at her. So, he has a fondness for this negro. No doubt his daughter, Sarah, would be able to break this spell she had on Joseph. Her posture was unlike any other slave he had met. *Who does this woman think she is?* His heart began beating faster. There was something about this slave; something evil. She needed to be gone, sooner rather than later.

"Hello," Audrey said.

*An unusual accent.* He stared at her as if she were the cause of all his problems, which for the moment, she was. She fidgeted on the bench averting his gaze.

"We hoped to stay with you for a day or two. We have business to tend to in town."

*We?* This negress was a big disappointment. "Oh, of course. Sarah will set another plate on the table."

He smiled, yet inside he fretted. This girl might be an obstacle to his plans for Joseph to marry Sarah. The proposal had already been discussed with Ruth and Nathan. Joseph and Sarah had gotten along fine since they were children. It was the only proper thing to do. Joseph was smart and would do what was right. Isaac would indeed help him do just that.

Isaac called out to his wife and daughter, who came out to greet Joseph.

"What happened to your face?" Sarah exclaimed, looking horrified.

"I... ran." He looked over to Audrey. "Into... some bushes. I was walking with Audrey and slipped over some roots and fell headlong into some bushes."

"Oh my, that does look bad," Mary remarked, inspecting his bruises.

"It happened several days ago. I'm all right. It'll heal."

That evening, they gathered around the square wooden table and ate a simple meal. Audrey ate on the kitchen table, alone. Isaac kept turning to look at her. She smiled at him. He stared back not smiling. But she continued to stare at him as if she were the one in control. Was that a smirk on her face? *Who do you think you are? You're lucky I'm allowing you to be inside my house.*

He suppressed a wave of anger and smiled.

"So, why are you traveling with Audrey, Joseph?" Mary asked.

## Timepieces

"She was staying with Nathan and Ruth," Joseph answered. "We met when they came to the church. She's trying to meet with someone here in town, so I volunteered to bring her."

"Oh, that was a nice place to meet. Did you—"

"So, is Audrey a free negro?" Isaac asked, interrupting his wife, continuing to look at Audrey as he spoke.

Mary pressed her lips.

"She is," Joseph replied, looking back into the kitchen at Audrey.

Isaac tried hard not to show his anger at Joseph's obvious, foolish crush on this negro girl. "Does she have papers?"

"We—we left them at Nathan's house.".

*How disappointing that he couldn't just tell me what was really going on.*

"Sarah here is glad to see you, too. Aren't you, Sarah?" He patted his daughter on the back. *This negress is just a passing fancy, boy. Sarah is the one you want.*

"Yes, I am so glad to see you, Joseph," she said lowering her head.

If only he could tell her what to say in a situation like this. Isaac looked over to Audrey and she continued to stare back at him as if *he* needed to be careful. *What? Did she think Joseph would protect her here?* He suppressed another wave of anger.

Sarah went into the kitchen. Audrey stood as she came in. "Is there anything I can do to help?" Audrey asked.

Sarah shook her head but never looked at Audrey. "No," she said, not looking at her and grabbing the cake, then walking back into the dining room.

Isaac was ecstatic that his daughter did know the place of negroes in this world.

"Joseph," Sarah said, putting the dish on the table, flashing him a huge grin "I made your favorite dessert."

Joseph's eyes grew, as he salivated over the carrot cake. "You didn't know I was coming. How'd you prepare it so fast?"

She smiled and started cutting into the cake. "Mr. Post wanted me to prepare one for him. I promised I would." She shrugged her shoulders. "I'll prepare another one for him on the morrow."

Everyone got a piece of cake. Mary took one of the remaining slices and gave it to Audrey.

"Thank you." Audrey smiled.

"You're most welcome," Mary said, smiling back at her. "Your accent is unusual. Where are you from?"

He couldn't believe that his wife was conversing with this insignificant creature! Couldn't she see that this girl was causing Joseph to have improper thoughts? Didn't she see that it was this negress witch that was taking Joseph away from their daughter?

"I'm from... a place called Milestown. It's far away from here," Audrey hesitated.

"I've never heard of that place. You speak very well."

"Thank you." Audrey cut into the cake and put a piece into her mouth. "This is good!" Audrey called to Sarah, "How do you make it? I hope there's no meat in this."

Everyone except Joseph, stopped eating and looked at Audrey in confusion.

"What sort of question is that?" Isaac asked. *Stupid woman.* "Of course, there's no meat in carrot cake."

"Excuse her, sir," Joseph said, apologetically. "Audrey has a preference for not eating meat."

Isaac looked at the girl's plate. It was clean except for the meat still on it.

Mary frowned at him. "What is it, Isaac? Why do you get so upset?"

"I don't want trouble. Someone may find out we have a runaway in our home!"

"She's not a runaway!" Joseph shouted a little too loud.

"And even if she is," Mary chided, "we've helped runaways before, Isaac. What makes her different?"

"I don't know. I feel that someone is after her. I'm afraid for you, dear," he lied, looking over to Audrey and forcing a smile on his face. He hoped no one sensed the veiled sarcasm in his tone. He wanted her out of his house. The sooner they took care of their business in town, the better.

---

The moon was full that night. She could clearly see everything in the kitchen without the need of a candle. This is where she would sleep tonight. Memories of Lilly came back. She recalled finding her sleeping on the kitchen table in Master Henry's home.

"Audrey, wake up!" Her eyes flew open and she sat up from the kitchen table. It was as if she was coming out of a bad dream. Her mouth was dry, her stomach cramped. Something was wrong.

"Audrey, you must leave now!" God was talking with her again.

She went into the bedroom and saw Mary and Sarah asleep in a small bed. Their long black hair looked like a blanket. On the opposite side, Joseph slept in another larger bed, the other side of it was empty. She didn't see Isaac anywhere.

"Joseph," she whispered, shaking him, "wake up!"

Joseph came to. Drowsy, he lifted himself up on his elbow and murmured something unintelligible.

"Joseph, God spoke with me and told me to leave!" Audrey looked to the other end of the room, Mary and Sarah were still asleep. She turned back to Joseph. "Where is Isaac?"

"I don't know," he whispered. "He most likely went outside to relieve himself." Joseph was now fully alert. "Can we at least wait and tell him we need to leave?"

"I think he's the reason I need to leave. He doesn't like me."

"I think you're wrong, Audrey."

"Are you blind?" She tried not to be too loud so she wouldn't wake up the others. "I'll explain later. Let's go!"

"Maybe we should wake up Mary and Sarah and tell them we're leaving."

"No. Joseph, you're wasting time. Let's go!" she urged, trying not to panic. She pulled at his shirt and he got on his feet.

Joseph and Audrey gathered their few belongings and headed toward the front room. He opened the door and looked out. She poked her head out so she could see too. No one was outside. No sign of Isaac.

**One hour earlier**

Isaac couldn't sleep. Joseph was blindly attracted to Audrey. Yes, she was beautiful.

# Timepieces

Isaac knew women, and he was sure that she was using her beauty and charms to bewitch Joseph into falling in love with her. *Satan works his evil with all negro women!*

He had experienced this type of lust. Many years ago, before getting married, his father had helped some negroes escape bondage. One of the women in the group had become friendly with him. Her glowing black skin and soft quiet voice had a mesmerizing effect on him. Isaac would finish his chores as fast as he could and then slip out to the barn and talk with her. They would stay up almost every night until dawn. The attraction he had for that girl was so strong it became painful to stay away.

The day before the group was to leave, he told his father that he wanted to help them get to Canada. His father denied the request. Isaac had made a decision to leave with them, with her, regardless of what his father commanded. But that night when he got to the barn, they were gone. His father was there in their place. A man who knew his son better than his son knew himself. Isaac received a beating that night, one that removed the spell that Satan had put on him through her. He was a better man for it. He never felt that way with any other woman since, not even his wife. He was grateful to his father for releasing him from the demon that Satan had sent.

Just then, he knew what he needed to do to help Joseph. He got up out of the bed while everyone slept. Without a sound, he made his way outside the house and, with the light of the moon, found his way to Tun Alley and found the business he was looking for. The sign read: James Simmons Auctions and Negro Sales.

Isaac knocked on the door several times, and after a few moments, James appeared.

"What the hell you doing knocking on my door at this time of night?" James huffed, his eyes weary from sleep.

"I must speak with you," Isaac said. "It's important."

"Can't this wait until morning?" James' long, bushy mustache covered his lips and moved in a peculiar way when he spoke. His thick eyebrows sagged over his eyelids, giving him the countenance of a shaggy dog.

"It might be too late by then. Please!"

"Very well," James sighed and opened the door wider. "Come in."

James limped toward the counter, setting the lamp on top of it. Ghostly shadows danced on the walls. "Tell me what ya want that cannot wait till morning," James said, irritated.

"I have a runaway in my house."

James' eyes narrowed. "Why are you telling me this?" he asked. "You of all people have contempt for the work that I do. As a matter of fact, I can remember several times when you've helped slaves get away from me. Why are ya telling me about this one?"

"This one is evil," Isaac said. "She casts spells on innocent young men. She has gotten Joseph under her spell. He follows her everywhere. He doesn't even notice my Sarah anymore."

"What it sounds like you're tellin' me is that Joseph has taken a fancy to this nigger and has forgotten all about your daughter," James sneered.

Isaac didn't respond.

"How do you know she's a runaway?"

"She has no papers."

"And you don't have a problem just handing her over to me?"

"Of course not."

"Of course not," James repeated slowly, studying Isaac.

"It's not a trick. Why would I come in the middle of the night to fool you?"

James said nothing for a while and then, "how am I supposed to get her?"

"I'll tell her that I have come across the runaway she's supposed to meet and send her outside where you'll wait in ambush to capture her."

"Oh, this is too good to be true, Isaac." James shook his head in disbelief. "If only ya was like this all the time, I could make a decent living with just the slaves that run through your farm." He paused. "When do you want to do this?"

Isaac gritted his teeth, trying not to lose his patience. "Now!"

"Now? I can't do this now. Everyone's asleep."

"My family cannot know that I did this," Isaac pleaded. "During the day she'll be with Joseph and he'll not leave her alone."

James thought about it and finally nodded. He went into the back room to wake up his two brothers. The trio collected their shackles and chains, putting them in a sack, and followed Isaac back to his house.

Isaac instructed the men to wait in hiding while he went inside and got Audrey to come out. But as he approached the door, he could see it begin to open. Thinking fast, he ran into the outhouse at the side of the house.

---

Audrey stepped out as Joseph held the door open for her. He followed behind her as they walked away from the house and walked through the gate. Several men appeared from behind a bush and stopped them. One of them grabbed Audrey by the hands while the other began to shackle her. Joseph tried to fight them but was no match for three men.

"What are you doing?" Audrey cried.

"Let her go!" Joseph screamed.

At this point, Isaac came out of the outhouse. "What's going on here?" he asked. "James, why are you here at my house with your brothers?"

James stared for a moment, then with a sly smile said, "This here slave is a runaway. We taking her to be sold at auction."

"No! She's not a slave," Joseph shouted, holding onto Audrey's hand.

"Do you have papers?" James asked.

"No. I don't. Not with me."

Isaac stepped up. "This is the sort of thing I was worried might happen, Joseph."

"He did this!" Audrey shouted, trying to get away. Her anger was directed at Isaac. He smiled a smile of jubilance. No one noticed because they were all staring at her! "He did this, Joseph. How else would they know I was here?"

Joseph turned to Isaac. The smile quickly changed.

"I... I just came out of the outhouse. How could I have done this?" he said putting his hand to his chest.

"I'm not getting into any family quarrels," James said, grabbing Audrey. "If ya bring the papers, I'll have no choice but to give possession to ya. For now, she'll be at the pen with the other slaves. If ya cannot get me the papers, I'll put her up for auction." With that James and his brothers left with Audrey in tow. Joseph stood by and let the men pass. He did nothing to help her as they took her away.

## Timepieces

Audrey followed her captors as they yanked and pulled her chains. She saw a couple arguing as they watched the scene. "How can you say that?" the woman said.

"The only difference between us and them is the color of our skin. We are no better than they are," the man said.

"You just don't understand," the woman scoffed. "We *are* better than them."

Audrey remembered a similar conversation she had with Logan. He'd been right all along. She knew that now. Her arrogance left her feeling ashamed. Maybe she deserved this as punishment. Her heart sank at the thought that she would never see him again. The overseer, from the plantation, was right. This was her home now. She'd never get back to Milestown. She'd never see her family again.

The group made their way back to the auction house. They pushed her down to the floor and removed the chains letting them drop next to her. Tears rolled down Audrey's face.

"This one be very pretty," said one of the men, kneeling down and sliding his hands through her hair.

"Maybe we keep her fo' ourselves," the other man leered as he squatted on the opposite side and pulled at her tresses.

Audrey closed her eyes and stayed perfectly still, trying not to provoke them.

"We is running a business. We do nuttin' to her. We sell her and make money," James admonished. The man turned behind a cabinet and opened a book. He then told her to stand up. She turned on her knees and shuffled up. The chains rattled as she stood.

"I need to ask you some questions and inspect you. I'm not going to hurt you unless you give me trouble. I'm not trying to do anything to you except get some information to get you ready for sale. So, don't think I'm trying to do something wrong. Everything will be all right. Do you understand?"

Audrey gave him an affirmative nod. James looked her over. He opened her mouth and inspected her teeth then grabbed her hands and felt her skin.

"Was you a house slave?" he asked her.

"I'm not a slave."

"Where you from?"

"Milestown."

"Where that be? I never heard of it."

"My father is mayor where I come from," Audrey said proudly. "And his soldiers would kill you if they saw what you were doing to me right now."

James stopped his inspection. "So, you're the mayor's daughter?" Suddenly, he broke into laughter. The other men followed suit.

"You speak like you been educated. Who taught you to speak this way?"

"My parents did. And I went to school to learn to read and write if that's what you're getting at."

"Since when did they have a school for niggers? You been taught to write and that is illegal."

Audrey didn't care what this man thought. She was going to be sold as a slave and at the moment had no way of escaping.

He went over to the book, dipped a pointed stick into a small glass jar with black liquid, and then wrote some things on a clean sheet of paper. He turned to one of the men. "Gordon, put the *mayor's* daughter in the yard out back with the other slaves," he snickered.

Gordon took her to the back. Two brown dogs with large ears that sagged to the sides of their heads patrolled along fences next to the yard where they kept the other slaves. Their incessant barking rang in her ears. It was the same sound she'd heard when she was running away with Lilly. Gordon put a chain around her waist and linked it with another slave.

Audrey sat and wallowed in her misery. Nothing could be done to get out of this situation. Here she was in Philadelphia, and yet the possibility of escaping and going home or even finding Thomas Lynch was too small to even fathom.

The sun perched up over the horizon. There were about a dozen slaves out here and all of them were linked together by a single chain that went through a hook around their waist. How could they escape? The yard was fenced in so that people on the outside couldn't see in. Spikes all along the top of the walls further prevented slaves from getting out. In one corner of the yard she could see a pile of dirt where the slaves went to relieve themselves.

A slave sat in front of her wearing a dirty raggedy dress that at one time could have been white. The woman spoke, "Day gonna git good mon'y for ya. You's pretty. All dem massas gonna wants ya for day selves. Ya won't haves to work no more in da fields." She looked her up and down. "Ya runs away from ya massa, didn't ya?"

Angry, Audrey turned and stared at her. "I'm not a slave!" she hissed and looked away. "They just think I am."

The slave moved her head back and stared in shock. "No, you's not a slave. Everyone who be listening to you can tell dat. I knows 'cause ya talks better than some massas I used to belongs to."

Who cared that she wasn't a slave? She was no more important than the others tied by this chain. How was she going to get out of this? And where was Joseph? He had done nothing as these men took her away. What kind of man was he?

---

Joseph did not know what to do. He needed Isaac's help to get her back. "We need to get her out of that place," Joseph said to Isaac.

"Joseph, I'll help you in any way I can. But right now we cannot do a thing. Let's get some sleep. In the morning, we will figure out what to do."

Joseph conceded that going to the auction house would not prove worthwhile. He went inside and sat on the bed feeling miserable and worthless.

"What happened? I heard shouting and you weren't here," Mary whispered. Mary got out of her bed and came over to Joseph, putting her hand on his arm. Mary had always been the one who'd go out of her way to give comfort and reassurances. He was grateful for her warm touch.

"Slave traders came and took Audrey to the auction house!" Joseph told her.

"Oh my! What can we do?" she looked to her husband as she pulled her long black hair to the side and brushed it with nervous fingers.

"Nothing at this moment." Isaac took off his shoes. "It's night. Let's get some sleep and in the morning we'll come up with a plan." He got in bed, pulled the sheets up and turned away from them to sleep, as if Audrey was not important at all. Why was he acting this way? Audrey had said that Isaac didn't like her, but that made no sense. Isaac had no problems with negroes. He had even helped several escape.

Sarah woke up and Joseph repeated the story of what had happened.

"Joseph! Sarah!" Isaac yelled, popping his head out from under the blanket. "Go to sleep!"

"But aren't you worried they might do harm to her?" Mary asked in a worried tone.

"They won't harm her. They're in it for the money," Isaac growled, turning toward the wall.

Mary, Sarah, and Joseph got up and headed into the dining room to talk some more and leave Isaac to sleep. As soon as they sat down on the wooden chairs at the table, Isaac walked to the door to go out.

Joseph noticed Isaac walking toward the door. To relieve himself? That seemed odd. What seemed odder was that Isaac was outside when the slave traders came to the house. Did Isaac plan this? "Where are you going, Isaac?" Joseph asked.

"I'm going to the outhouse, if that's all right with you." He mumbled it as he walked to the door.

Joseph felt as if someone took an ax to him. He suddenly felt nauseous. Isaac had just come from the outhouse, just a quarter of an hour ago. Why did he need to go back? How stupid was he not to have noticed! Audrey had been right all along! Isaac didn't like her, but why?

A few minutes went by before Isaac came back into the house. Joseph kept his gaze on him, never letting up, but Isaac never returned his stare. *Guilt.* "Why did you do it?" Joseph said, loud enough so that everyone could hear.

Isaac's eyes opened wide.

Mary leaned forward. "What do you mean, Joseph?"

"Yes, Joseph, what do you mean?" Isaac said, getting a little bolder now that the initial shock wore off. He walked to the dining room and sat in the chair next to his wife. Sarah took Joseph's hand, yet he didn't spare her a glance.

"Since I arrived here yesterday, you've been different. You're upset that I brought Audrey here," Joseph said.

Isaac raised his hands in the air. "I told you already that I thought this could be trouble and see what's happened!"

"How did they know she was at your house? They waited outside."

"I don't know why they were out there." Perspiration beaded on Isaac's forehead. "In the morning we'll ask how they came to be here."

"It's convenient that you happened to be in the outhouse when they came," Joseph insisted.

"I had to relieve myself. What's wrong with that?" Isaac said, becoming defensive. "This is my house! I can do as I please in my house."

"Of course," Joseph said. "But why did you want to go back out to the outhouse not just a quarter of an hour after they took her away?"

Isaac's mouth fell open. Finally, he uttered, "I needed to go again!"

Mary clasped Isaac's hands and said, "Isaac, what have you done?"

Isaac's face went white. "She's bewitched the boy!" he blurted out. "He thinks he's in love with her. The Devil's in that woman and I wasn't going to let her charms manipulate him. What if he were to marry her? No white man marries a negro woman and maintains his respect in this community! No one! Nathan, Ruth, and I had it all planned out. He's to marry Sarah!" He turned to Joseph and said, "I was helping you, Joseph."

Sarah let go of Joseph's hand and kept her eyes to the floor. Tears slid down her cheeks. Joseph wasn't about to deal with Sarah at the moment. He shot straight up, knocking down the chair. Mary started to sob. It took all of Joseph's will to contain his anger. He pointed a finger at Isaac. "If anything happens to her..."

He walked toward the door.

"Wait!" Mary jumped up and went to Joseph, wiping the tears from her eyes with a handkerchief. She gave him a warm and inviting hug.

"I won't blame you if you never want to see us again," she said in a low voice. "Go to the house on the 300 block of Market Street and ask for Mr. Franklin. He may be able to help. He's the most respected person in Philadelphia." She held him close, then kissed him on the cheek, "And please don't forget that we love you."

# Chapter 22

Philadelphia, May 29, 1776

Horses grazed along a sloped pasture. It was early morning and it already felt like a furnace. The period clothes Tom had on made the heat unbearable. A pair of jeans and a T-shirt would be welcomed right now. The landscape hadn't changed much since he was last here in 1787. There were fewer houses in this part of the city than he remembered. The streets still smelled of horse manure, and as luck would have it, no matter how much he tried to avoid it, he eventually stepped in it.

He stood a distance away from Benjamin Franklin's home. The house was smaller than the last time he was here. He couldn't pinpoint exactly what it was except that something was different. As he gathered up his nerve to walk up and knock on the door, a man with the most awful scars on his face, wearing farm clothes walked past staring at him. The farmer approached the door of Mr. Franklin's home and knocked several times before a servant came to answer. Tom looked on and waited for the farmer to conduct his business and leave.

The servant closed the door on the man as he stood waiting. The man turned and looked at Tom, who lingered around. Tom turned away and debated whether to leave when the door opened. Mr. Franklin appeared wearing a simple white shirt and brown pants. Tom stepped in a little closer to hear the conversation.

"Yes? What is it?" It was clear that Mr. Franklin didn't recognize the man.

"Good morning, Mr. Franklin. I'm here to ask for your help in a matter that is of the utmost urgency."

Mr. Franklin noticed Tom, who smiled and nodded, then returned his attention to the farmer. "What is this urgent matter that requires my assistance?"

"My name is Joseph, I have been traveling with my companion from Lehigh and last night we arrived at my brother-in-law's house. She happens to be a negro woman. Slave traders arrived and took her away, claiming that she is a runaway slave. They intend to sell her if I do not show them proof that she is a free negro. She is free and I can attest to that, but I do not have any papers with me."

"What makes you think I can do anything?"

"You are a respected member of Philadelphia society. People look up to you."

"I think what you need, sir, is a lawyer," Franklin said as he turned his gaze to Tom. "Are you with that man?"

The farmer turned and stared at Tom. "I thought he might have business with you. We approached the house at the same time and he decided to... stand there."

"Excuse me," Franklin said to the farmer and then addressed Tom. "Excuse me, sir. Can I help you?"

Tom should have known this was going to happen. It was his fault for conspicuously standing in front of the house, watching a conversation. He walked over to the front door. "I believe you can help me." He nodded to the farmer, acknowledging him, then spoke to Mr. Franklin who stared at him oddly. "You may think this is out of the ordinary, but do you know someone named Audrey?"

"Audrey? I know several women named Audrey. What is her surname?"

"I don't know. That's all the information I have."

"Audrey is the woman who was with me," the farmer said to Tom with a puzzled look. "By any chance, are you Thomas Lynch?"

"Yes, I am," Tom said surprised.

"Very well," Mr. Franklin said. "You two have matters to take care of. Good day, sirs." He moved to go back into his house and close the door.

"No!" Tom pushed his hand against the door, preventing it from closing. "You need to help."

"Why must I do that?"

"It's difficult to explain. I just know there's a connection between you and Audrey."

"Sir, I don't know you and right now I have other things that need attending. So if you don't mind, I must leave you," he said stepping back.

"Sir!" Tom said. "I meet Audrey through you. This is hard to explain. I wouldn't believe it if someone told it to me, but you... you bought me these clothes."

"I bought you those clothes? What kind of joke is this? What are you two trying to do? Please move away from my property."

If Benjamin Franklin went inside without helping them, who knew what would happen to the current timeline. There must be something he could say that would convince him to help. Thinking fast, he said, "I know you are part of the Second Continental Congress and I know that you, Thomas Jefferson, Robert Livingston, Roger Sherman and Samuel Adams are in a committee to write the Declaration of Independence."

"How do you know this?" he asked, becoming agitated. "There is no such congress and there is no such committee."

Tom hesitated. Telling him that he was from the future would make him sound like he was an idiot. The fact that Mr. Franklin bought the clothes he was wearing had already been disclosed. It was a stupid thing to have said. Right now, the man probably thought he was crazy or a spy for the British, or worse, a spy for the British pretending to be crazy.

"There is a Continental Congress and in several days you'll be on that committee," Tom hedged.

"Tell me how you know this, or I'll close this door and we'll never speak again!"

This was not the way he imagined things would be going. Telling him the truth seemed to be the only option. "Sir, the first time we meet... I mean, the first time I meet you will be in 1787. You buy me these clothes at that time." It sounded stupid once it came out of his mouth.

Mr. Franklin bent over and inspected Tom's clothes, then straightened up. "I buy these clothes for you?"

"Yes, in 1787. That's when you tell me about Audrey. I ask you how I could befriend you and you tell me to just ask about her and the rest will happen naturally."

"You really expect me to believe that you are from some future time?"

"I know it's hard to believe, but you asked for the truth." Tom shrugged.

"Audrey told me that she is from some other time as well," Joseph interjected, moving his gaze from one man to the other. "And I did not believe her either. She said in her world the sky is orange."

"Orange?" Both Tom and Mr. Franklin spoke at the same time.

"I thought you would be from the same place as she," Joseph said to Tom.

"The sky is still blue in my world," Tom said. "Mr. Franklin, if we help this man get Audrey, then maybe we can solve the mystery of what is going on."

"You mean you don't know this man?" Mr. Franklin said to Tom.

"This is the first time I've seen him," Tom said, looking at the farmer. "I'm Tom by the way." He put out his hand to the farmer. "But you already knew that."

Mr. Franklin stared at Tom as if he wasn't quite sure what to make of him. Tom reached in his pocket and pulled out his passport. He opened it and showed it to Mr. Franklin who in turn inspected it. Mr. Franklin looked at Tom and then back at the document, turning the blue pages.

"You've sparked my curiosity," he said returning the document back to Tom. "Let me get some things. Wait for me here." He went inside and returned a few minutes later. "Where are we going?" he asked them both.

Tom turned to Joseph.

"To James Simmons, at his store in Tun Alley," said Joseph, then turned, one hand raised. "Follow me."

---

Audrey sat on the dirt floor, wallowing in self-pity.

"God," she said, "I feel your presence everywhere. You talk with me and you tell me what to do, but is that all you can do, just talk?" She raised her hands with the handcuffs. "Can't you get these things off of me and set me free?"

Sitting on the floor and staring at the other slaves was the only thing she could do in this place. Time was going extremely slow.

"Where will you go?"

A smile came over her at hearing God's voice. He hadn't left her.

"I'll go home," she said sullenly.

"You're far away from home."

"Then to find Thomas Lynch," she said in desperation. "Isn't that why I'm here, to find him? Didn't you send me here for that reason?"

At that moment Gordon came into the yard and approached Audrey. "Sit up," he said. He unlocked the chain that connected her to the other slaves. "Hold out ya hands." The handcuffs were unlocked. "Stick out ya feet." The shackles came off. "Seems ya master has come to collect ya."

Frowning, Audrey followed Gordon into the building and to the office. Joseph stood with two other men close to him. Relieved, she ran to him and hugged him. *He came back!*

Holding onto Audrey, James pointed at a heavy-set man and asked gruffly, "Do you know this man?"

She could only guess. "That's Thomas Lynch."

"And what is he to you?" James asked.

She stared at Thomas Lynch for a second. If she told the truth, she would stay here and be sold to someone else. "He is my master."

Both of the men with Joseph perked up and looked at her as if she had said something they didn't understand. The fat one grinned. "And where you from?" James asked her.

The question made no sense. The man was an idiot. "How should I know?" she said defiantly. "I'm just a slave!"

James raised the back of his hand to her.

"Stop!" Thomas Lynch cried out, then paused. "Don't you damage my property!"

It was doubtful that this overweight man had ever owned a slave. By the look on everyone's face they thought the same thing. She would be found out and be stuck in this place and sold to some awful slave owner.

"This ain't your slave," James sneered. "What, you think you can fool me?"

One of the other men stepped forward and said, "Mr. Lynch here is new to owning slaves. He doesn't know how to handle them, as you can see, since this one ran away." He took out his purse. "He's from out of town and is very willing to compensate you for capturing his property."

James looked at them unconvinced, but finally sighed. "I'm not gonna argue, especially with you Mr. Franklin. The cost for holding your slave be twenty dollars."

Mr. Lynch stared at Mr. Franklin and told him he had no money. Joseph offered three shillings. Mr. Franklin shook his head and took out twenty Spanish silver dollars and placed them in James' outstretched palm. "Mr. Lynch, I'm beginning to believe your outrageous tale more as time progresses."

James gave them a receipt of sale and they all walked out of the building.

When they got outside, Joseph turned to Audrey and said, "You were right, Audrey. Isaac did this to you. He brought the slave traders to the house."

"Don't ever mention his name to me again."

"Who is Isaac?" Mr. Franklin asked.

"He is my brother-in-law," Joseph said. "We stayed at his house while we tried to find... him." He pointed to Mr. Lynch.

"He's a big, heavy-set man," Audrey said staring at Mr. Lynch, noticing that he was also heavy-set like Isaac. She continued, "With blue eyes that burn through your skin when he stares at you. And when he talks, he talks down to you. I hate him and never want to see him again. I hate this place and want to go home!"

Mr. Franklin listened. "Interesting," he said. "Let's go back to the house where you can explain everything."

They walked along the street. Audrey stepped into a pile of brown gunk. "What is this stuff?" she asked. "I stepped in some last night and it stinks."

"It's from the horses," Mr. Lynch said. His accent was different from the others. "Just try and avoid it if you can."

"Why don't they clean it up?"

"They try, but there are too many horses," Mr. Franklin explained.

Audrey didn't understand how people could live like this. She desperately wanted to be home where the streets were clean.

# Chapter 23

Audrey followed Joseph and Thomas Lynch as Mr. Franklin led them to his house and directed them into a room. As she entered, Joseph led her to a brown sofa sitting against the far wall. Two wooden chairs faced it, along with what looked like an eating table. Audrey and Joseph sat together on the sofa. It was much better than the wicker sofas she was so used to in her world. Depictions lined the walls. She turned to look behind the sofa and saw a depiction of Mr. Franklin when he was much younger than now. She didn't recognize any of the faces on the other drawings. They were probably his family or friends? Her world didn't have anything like this. If she ever got home this would be something she would mention to her dad, depictions of the mayors of Milestown in the library they had.

Mr. Franklin called for someone. It took a while, but then a black man entered the room. Audrey took note of the color of his skin and determined that this was his slave.

"Peter, hi! How are you doing?" Tom exclaimed. He grabbed Peter's hand and shook it.

The man shot a wide-eyed and confused look at Mr. Franklin.

"Peter, do not bother with him," Mr. Franklin sighed, took his arm and directed him away from the parlor. "Just get us tea."

"Is that his slave?" Audrey asked Joseph.

Mr. Franklin turned to her. "I don't have any slaves. Peter works for me, as do the other servants in my house."

This impressed Audrey. It would've been something Logan would have done, if he had servants.

She was supposed to find Thomas Lynch, but instead he found her. He was taller and heavier than anyone else in the room. She couldn't figure out where he was from by his accent. Definitely not from her world and he didn't sound anything like these people. He sat on the lone chair against the back wall and kept looking at it as if he expected to find something there.

Mr. Franklin sat, commanding a presence of royalty in the only remaining chair, and looked over at her. She smiled. He lowered his gaze to where she was holding hands with Joseph—he didn't seem happy.

"Can someone please tell me what has brought us together today?" Mr. Franklin said, his legs crossed, looking to Tom.

No one said a word.

Thomas Lynch cleared his throat. "I believe, Mr. Franklin, that we're all here because of her." He gestured toward Audrey.

Everyone looked to her, and then turned back and stared at Tom, waiting for him to elaborate.

"I am here because you told me to make one of these for her." He held up the timepiece at Mr. Franklin and with his other hand gestured toward Audrey.

"May I see that?" Mr. Franklin sat up and stretched out his hand reaching for the timepiece.

"That's what I had when I got here!" Audrey whispered to Joseph.

"Please don't press any of the buttons on that," Tom warned.

"Very well." Mr. Franklin turned the object over in his hands. "Continue with your explanation, Mr. Lynch."

"All right. In 1787, I meet—"

"I told you to make one of these for *her*?" he interrupted and looked at Audrey as he said it, then continued to look at the timepiece.

"Yes." Tom nodded. "In 1787, we meet and you tell me that I need to make a timepiece for Audrey."

"In 1787?" Mr. Franklin glanced at Audrey again, looking at her as if he couldn't fathom why she was so important. As if this was some sort of mistake.

"I know it's hard to believe, but this device allows a person to move through time. I made another one for Audrey and left it on my desk. She must have taken it and come here."

"No," Audrey said turning to face Tom. "I found it in the cave made of metal. There was a note that told me to find you. The note was addressed to me."

Tom stared at her with a blank expression on his face.

"Someone left me a note. It told me to find Thomas Lynch. They said they were a friend."

"What cave?" Tom asked, frowning, before his face suddenly lit up. He jumped out of his seat. "That's it! You added an extension to this room. This has been bugging me since I got here, and I didn't know what it was." Tom put a hand to his head. "Whew! I feel so much better. This whole section is opened up." Tom waved his hands around the wall as if by doing so it would magically appear. He turned to look at Mr. Franklin. "Oh, sir! It's going to look so much better."

Mr. Franklin cleared his throat, giving Tom an odd look. "Is that so?" Their host pressed his lips together and did not look the slightest bit amused.

"Okay, let's see..." Thomas turned back to Audrey. "What cave?" he asked again.

They all stared at Audrey.

"There is a beach by the cliffs that we found by accident that looks out to the ocean. Inside the cliff a metal cave with a door has a panel with squares you can push in. The blocks have lines carved in. Some were parallel or meet at the bottom or crossed over each other. We kept trying to push the squares until the door opened."

"I know that cave." Tom stared into space. "My brother bought it because he thought that something terrible was going to happen on earth. From the sound of it, something terrible did happen!"

"What happened?" Mr. Franklin asked, intrigued.

"From what Audrey is describing, I would say that the ocean levels have risen and most of Pennsylvania is underwater."

"And what would cause this to happen?" Mr. Franklin asked leaning forward.

"Oh, all sorts of things—global warming, glaciers melting, earthquakes causing some areas to sink below sea level."

"Is that possible?"

"Anything is possible. The real question is, is it probable? And to be honest, I don't know." Thomas put his hand into his pocket and waved the other as he spoke. "Yes, global warming could have occurred, but even if all the ice melted, it wouldn't have risen enough to make the location where the cave is to become a beach. But it *is* a beach, and something had to happen to make that a reality."

Audrey couldn't grasp what he was saying. Her world was as it always had been. Joseph and Mr. Franklin continued looking at Thomas. She offered, "It was late afternoon when we finally got in. The sun was setting in the east."

Tom's eyes narrowed. "The east? If it was late afternoon, the sun would be setting in the west."

"The sun rises in the west and sets in the east," Audrey said. "It's the same here."

Mr. Franklin shook his head. "That's impossible. The sun rises in the east and sets in the west."

"I think that we are all thinking the same thing," Tom said.

"How so?" Mr. Franklin asked, his hands on his knee and head cocked back.

"Because," Tom said, walking in circles, "the way we determine north is with a compass. The magnetic tip always points north. Am I right?" Everyone stared at him. He continued. "Maybe in Audrey's world, north and south are opposite to what they are here right now. Something happened that caused the magnetic poles to reverse." He turned to Audrey. "What year are you from?"

"In my world, the year is two hundred and sixteen."

"You're from the past?" Mr. Franklin asked. "How could the earth have been moving in the opposite direction back then?"

Audrey didn't know how to answer the question and looked, as did everyone else, to Tom for an answer.

"No, she is not from the past." Tom turned inspecting the wall he said the extension would be in 1787. "If she were from the past," he softened his tone, "the metal cave wouldn't have been there." He suddenly turned in her direction. "What was the date on the timepiece?"

Audrey closed her eyes and tried to think. "May 4, 1776."

"That was the date here in this time. Did you look at the date afterwards?"

"Yes." She closed her eyes again. "August 29, 2276."

Tom and Mr. Franklin looked at each other. Joseph let go of her hand and moved ever so slightly away from her.

"What's wrong?" She asked reaching for his hand.

Joseph kept his face averted and scooted farther away. "Nothing is wrong."

"And what year are you from, Mr. Lynch?" Mr. Franklin asked.

"For me, it's two thousand fifty-two," he said.

"Yet your time doesn't have the sun rising in the west and setting in the east."

"No, it doesn't. My world is the same as this one, with a few technological advances." He looked at them all. "Come on, her world is almost the same."

Both men gave Tom a blank look.

"Okay, so the sun comes up in the west. No big deal. And the water levels have risen a bit. Okay maybe it's a bit strange that the sky is orange, but there are still trees and animals." He turned to Audrey. "Am I right?"

"We only have trees that we plant. There are plants and bushes in very few places. Some of the other cities have different kinds of plants that we trade for. There are small fish in the water, but no animals on land. Our sky is a beautiful orange, even though I've come to like the blue sky here."

"Sounds like hell if you ask me," Thomas said quietly.

"Is that the same hell that you talked about, Joseph?" Audrey asked as Joseph stood up. "What's wrong?"

Joseph was visibly shaken. "What's happened to change this world?"

"Maybe God has abandoned it," Mr. Franklin suggested, matter of fact.

"Tell me more about your world," Tom asked Audrey, ignoring Mr. Franklin's statement.

Audrey told them about her city, that her father was mayor, how she was part of the ambassador's staff in New Scranton. She told them of how they found out that the Feds ate people, and how she barely escaped with Logan. She told them about the Feds entering the southeastern border of her father's territory. She talked about the cliffs and how she and Logan found the metal cave and the timepiece addressed to her.

"It sounds like your community is in trouble, or soon will be," Tom said.

"What in God's name is going on?" Mr. Franklin bellowed. "Why would people eat other people?"

"Well," Tom said, "if there was a catastrophe, maybe some of the people found that eating other people was their solution to staying alive."

"I originally came here to find you," Audrey said to Mr. Lynch. "But I think I was sent here to find God."

Mr. Franklin clasped his hands and laid them on his lap. "Why would God send *you* to find him and what would be the purpose of it?"

He didn't believe that she was important enough for God to send her here. Why? Because she wasn't white? But it was the truth. She didn't plan it. It just happened. The purpose was simple—she needed to know God and free the slaves in her world. But she couldn't free the slaves without first understanding what being a slave meant.

"Did you find him?" Thomas asked her, a smirk on his face.

"Yes. God has helped me since I escaped from Master Henry."

Mr. Franklin sneered in disbelief. "*You* have spoken with God?"

"I have," she said. "When I got here, the feeling of this place was different. I couldn't figure it out." She summed up her learning experience up to the communion incident at the church.

"What happened at the church?" Tom asked.

"I didn't know Jesus lived over seventeen hundred years ago. I thought they were Feds! I thought—"

"They were going to eat Jesus?" Thomas finished her sentence and chuckled.

"Is there something funny?" Mr. Franklin asked sitting crossed legged, holding the timepiece.

"I was just thinking about how they might have a pit... with smoke..."

Mr. Franklin stared at Thomas Lynch as if he were an idiot. Thomas sputtered and swallowed, then turned serious. "No, nothing funny."

"So, I ran away and heard God talking to me." Audrey continued. "But I think he started talking to me when I was in my world with the Feds."

"Enough!" Mr. Franklin interrupted and sat up in the chair. "You really expect me to believe that you both come from the future? And different ones at that?"

Tom nodded as he thought about it. "Yes."

"This is preposterous. So, you're telling me that if I press this blue button, I will travel to your time..." Mr. Franklin looked at the timepiece and pressed the blue button. Nothing happened. He pressed the black button, and lights came on, showing him a date. "Oh, how convenient. Is this a trick you're playing on me?" He stood and moved away from Tom who pursed his lips and shook his head.

"What will happen if I touch this display? Oh look, the year has changed."

"Please, don't—"

Mr. Franklin pressed the blue button and vanished.

Audrey's jaw dropped. Mr. Franklin had just disappeared with the last timepiece.

# Chapter 24

Ben fell to the floor that was made of a stone he had not seen before. He looked around at what were parts of what used to be his house. *Oh my God!* He began to breathe quickly and felt faint. There were people everywhere. A large group of children sat eating a few yards in front of him on some steps. "Look!" cried one of them when they saw him. "There's Benjamin Franklin."

He stood quickly as the children swarmed around him.

"Are you Benjamin Franklin?" some of them asked.

"As a matter of fact, I am he. Where might this place be?" he asked. This couldn't be his home.

"Wow! He even talks like Benjamin Franklin!"

"How is it that you recognize my form of speech?" he asked them.

"You have to be Benjamin Franklin. You're speaking ancient."

A woman came over to see what the fuss was all about and stood next to him. "Hey, they really did a good job on you," she said. "You do look like Benjamin Franklin. Where did they find you?"

"Madam, I do not know what you're talking about. I assure you, I am Benjamin Franklin."

"Yeah. Whatever." She moved over to the children. "Hey, kids, let's line up here so we can go see a movie about the life of Benjamin Franklin." She raised her hand. "Follow me."

The kids formed a line in front of a brick building with a blue metal door that opened outward. Ben followed. There were no windows or candles in this room, yet it was very bright. All the children found seats to sit on. Ben approached the last seat and fumbled with it, not quite sure what to do. The child next to him unfolded the seat.

"Thank you, young man. That was very kind of you."

The lights dimmed and moving images appeared on a tarp draped in front of the wall. Music could be heard even though no band was in the room. The moving images were impressive and contained factual information about him. Many of the events mentioned he had forgotten. He was amazed at how much these people valued him. But, how did they know about events which he had forgotten?

Ben squinted as the lights came back on, and followed the children, who talked loudly, as they walked out of the building. On the wall, next to the door, was a mural showing his accomplishments during his lifetime. Fear gripped him as his eyes read the last line on the mural, the date of his death. *I surely did not want to see that.* Could he use the timepiece and go back in time so as not to see that date? But he already saw it. It was imprinted in his mind. There was no way to change what he had already seen.

He made his way back to the open area where he had started his journey, turned on the device, and pressed the blue button. The servants looked at him with surprise as he appeared before them in the kitchen.

He walked into the parlor room., to find his new friends waiting for him. "This timepiece," he said to the surprised faces, "with its ability to transport one to anywhere in history, should not be used to find out the day and year of one's own demise."

Sitting down in his chair, he stared at the timepiece, thinking about what he had just seen. "I believe you now, Mr. Lynch. It's a very powerful tool. In the wrong hands, this can be used to do harm." He handed back the device.

"So, what do we do now?" Joseph asked.

"I think somehow I need to help Audrey in her world. Something is about to happen there, and I need to get you there quickly." Thomas Lynch looked at Audrey. "The problem is that I've left the other timepiece on my desk at home. If I give you mine, I'm stuck here in this world." Mr. Lynch turned to Mr. Franklin. "Not to be offensive, but I'd prefer to be in my own time."

Mr. Franklin waved Mr. Lynch off. "None taken. So how do you propose we get her the other timepiece?"

"I go home and get it. But can we eat first? I'm starving."

---

It was afternoon before Tom, Audrey, Joseph, and Mr. Franklin arrived at what would eventually become Tom's walkout basement. Tom admired the scenic beauty. Horses roamed a fenced in area that stopped at the incline to a hill. The contrast between the present and the past was remarkable. This was grazing land for horses, but in Tom's time it was a housing complex. He noticed Audrey looking around, probably thinking the same thing he was—the differences between this and her world where this was nothing but water.

Audrey spoke up after watching Tom turn on the timepiece and set a new date. "What if you don't come back?"

"I don't see why I wouldn't. I just need to change the timepiece to two thousand and fifty-two and I should arrive back to the exact time I left."

"That's not altogether true," Mr. Franklin admitted. "When I came back, I had fumbled with the day and month as well as the year."

"What? Why did you do that?"

"I didn't think that it would matter. What's the harm?"

"I don't know what will happen. There could be a shock wave that distorts the entire space-time continuum," Tom uttered.

"There's only one way to find out." Mr. Franklin shrugged.

"But if there is a problem, then I wouldn't get back home," Audrey said. "I don't think it's worth the risk. Let me go instead."

He held a ball of air in his mouth and swooshed it around as he engaged his mind in thought. Tom saw no issues and set the date on his timepiece, then pressed the timepiece into her palm. "Okay, it's set. When you arrive, you'll probably find me in my office. Just tell me you need my help, tell me your name, and show me the timepiece. I'll understand. I'll give you the timepiece I made and then you come back with both timepieces. Understood?"

"Yes," Audrey said nodding.

"How long will it take?" Mr. Franklin asked her.

"You won't even notice I left."

"Then how will you know it worked?" Joseph asked.

"I'll have two timepieces with me," Audrey answered. She leaned over and kissed Joseph on the cheek. "I'll be back." Audrey pressed the blue button and disappeared.

For a few seconds, Mr. Franklin and Joseph looked at each other in awe as if some miracle had occurred. Tom looked around. *Where is she?*

"Something went wrong," Tom said.

"What do you mean? It hasn't been more than a minute," Joseph said, beginning to breathe erratically. "Where is she?"

"It means that I don't know what happened. She went to my time and something must have happened to her there."

Joseph pursed his lips. "Could she be hurt? Why did you let her go if something could happen to her?" he asked in a tense voice.

Tom ran his hand through his hair. "I didn't think anything could happen to her. Maybe she didn't find me, or I didn't believe her. It could be a million other reasons," he postulated, staring at the spot where Audrey disappeared.

"What are you talking about, Mr. Lynch?" Mr. Franklin asked with concern.

"It's a timepiece. From our perspective, we wouldn't know she left except that when she comes back, she would be carrying two timepieces. The timepiece would bring her back to the moment just after she left. She's not here right now, which means something has happened to her!" Tom said. "I don't know what to do!"

Joseph and Mr. Franklin looked around, waiting for her to pop out of thin air.

Tom waved his hand. "I'm sure we'll see her again."

"How can you know that for certain?" Mr. Franklin asked.

"Because when I meet you in 1787, there is only one of me and not two."

Mr. Franklin stared at Tom. "I don't quite follow you."

"If we never see Audrey again, the me from 1776 will exist in 1787. The first time I use the timepiece to travel back in time is to 1787. So, the me from 1776 and the me from 1787 will exist at the same time: two Tom Lynches. In 1787, you didn't mention anything about me not leaving."

Joseph seemed to have a hard time following the conversation, his brow furrowed. But Mr. Franklin's eyes shone with comprehension. He seemed to think for a moment and then said, "But what if you die before 1787?"

"But I haven't told you to tell me about Audrey and how we really meet yet!"

"You just did."

"So much for that thought," Tom said, looking around, hoping that Audrey would be walking toward them. "Look, I'm sure I don't die because when I talk with you in your future, you don't appear sad about the events that are going to happen. So, I can only guess that I'm alive and well. At least, that's what I want to believe."

Tom put his hands to his head not knowing what to do. He needed to be optimistic and believe she was coming back. He sat down on the grass, feeling nauseous.

"So, what do we do now?" Joseph asked Tom, who wasn't listening.

"Is Audrey dead?" Joseph asked Mr. Franklin.

"I don't think so," Mr. Franklin said. "I think that Mr. Lynch is going to be staying in this world much longer than he anticipated."

# Chapter 25

Philadelphia, August 2, 2052

Audrey found herself in an enclosed space with walls that were the color of green peppers. The sweet smell in the air made her feel relaxed. The room was unnaturally bright, everything here looked so clean and new. The depictions on the walls didn't look like someone had painted them, these looked real. One of the pictures drew her attention. It was a skinnier female version of Tom, perhaps his daughter. The girl stood in the rain, smiling, with the sun shining behind her.

She took off her shoes and sank her feet into a soft fabric that covered the entire floor. Was Tom from some royal family? No way did average people live like this. The large bed in the middle of the room looked inviting, much more comfortable than the beds in her world or even the ones in 1776. She wanted to lie on it—she was exhausted. But what would Tom do if he found some stranger lying on his bed? She shrugged. *There's no one in the room.*

Laying down, she felt the soft red blanket against her cheek. She turned on her back to a firm bed, inviting her to sleep, and discovered why it was so bright in here. Two openings in the ceiling let light flood in, revealing the sky. But as comfortable as she was, she had things to do and people to see.

Two different doors led out of the room. The room on the left was like a closet, there was no other way out. The floor was made of stone that was cold on her feet. Clothing draped over some type of glass door. Her hands touched her face as she looked into a mirror, poking at the bags under her eyes. *I look so tired.* Maybe she should have stayed on the bed.

She stepped back into the main room making a creaking sound on the floor. She stopped in her tracks. This may be Tom's house, but she didn't want to scare him by appearing out of nowhere.

"Dad?" A muffled voice came from somewhere outside the room. "Is that you?" It was a man's voice, but it didn't sound anything like Tom. She looked under the bed. Could she hide there?

"Dad?" the voice yelled out again.

This was the place Tom sent her. But what if he sent her to the wrong time? Taking a deep breath and gaining control of her fears, she prayed to God that this person would be able to help. She walked toward the door and opened it, stepping into the stairwell.

"Hello."

**60 minutes earlier**

Eric came into the house from his first day of summer classes.

"Dad!" Eric shouted, closing the door behind him. The house was quiet. Laying the keys on the counter in the kitchen, he yelled, "Dad!"

No response.

Eric went upstairs to get some Magic cards out of his bedroom and snuck a glance into his father's office, noticing something peculiar on his desk. It was the disc—the one he'd seen in the basement. He peered at the paper note attached, which read, "For Audrey." Wasn't that the girl dad asked him about last week? The name still didn't ring a bell.

The disc turned on and displayed August 2, 2052. On a whim, he changed the date to September 5, 2051 and pressed the blue button. The object lit up.

"Oh, come on, Dad," Eric mumbled, "this is so sci-fi."

He kept pressing the blue button and the date continued to change between August 2, 2052 and September 5, 2051. The fake look and feel of it made him shake his head and grin. "What a piece of crap. It doesn't even keep the right time."

Down in the kitchen he foraged for something to eat, making a sandwich. He decided to watch some TV. The only thing worth watching was a very old show called *Continuum* which soon had him dozing on the recliner.

Footsteps from the ceiling roused him. "Dad?" Eric shouted. "Is that you?" No answer. There were more footsteps. "Dad?" he shouted from the bottom of the stairs. Again, no answer.

He started up the stairs when a shadow appeared out of the master bedroom.

"Hello," said a girl staring down at him. Eric lost his footing and grabbed the railing.

"Who the hell are you?" he bellowed, clutching the railing, trying to keep from tumbling down. "What are you doing in my house?"

The girl stood there not responding at first. "I'm looking for Thomas Lynch," she said with an unusual accent, taking a step forward.

"How did you get up there?"

"I don't understand." Her brows knitted. "I was sent here to find Thomas Lynch. Can you help me? It's important."

Was she for real? How could this homeless girl wearing these rags know dad? And why would she just come inside the house without knocking first? "Why are you looking for Thomas Lynch?"

"I need him to make one of these for me," she held out her hand, slowly descending the stairs. Eric backed up, trying not to trip, as he peered at the object she held. "Do you know where he is?"

He grinned, recognizing what she held and sighed in relief. Just one of dad's crazy customers wanting one of his inventions. "You want to buy another one of those from him?"

"Buy?" She propped her head back. Her eyes knitted. "I want him to give me one."

"Well, he's not here right now. You should have knocked before coming into the house."

She stared at him as if he were the intruder.

"You must have seen me in the living room?" he looked to his right—a clear path from the stairs to the sofa.

"I didn't come in through the front door," she said a little louder, her tone annoyed.

"Oh, so you just popped into the room upstairs?" he said raising his hand in a fist, then expanding his fingers.

"Pretty much, yes."

"Seriously, how did you get into the house?"

She rolled her eyes, then smiled at him waving the timepiece in her hand.

"Where do you live?" he asked, eyeing her.

She stared at him for a moment and then said, "I'm from Philadelphia."

"This *is* Philadelphia. Tell me the truth, or I won't get my father for you."

She looked him over, checking him out. "Let's sit somewhere and I'll tell you."

It was amusing the way she kept her gaze on him as they headed toward the dining room. "I'm Eric by the way." He held his hand out to her as she took a seat.

She looked at him, then at his hand, and then back at him, with a blank stare. "I'm Audrey."

So, *this* was Audrey. He grinned, understanding now why his dad thought he might know her. She was about his age and pretty.

"Do you want something to drink?" he asked. "Water?"

She nodded.

He came out of the kitchen with a glass filled with ice and water.

"Wow! This is cold." She looked into the glass. "What's this?" she said pushing down on the ice and watching it float back to the top. She smiled and did it again.

"You've never seen ice in water before?" he asked, eyeing this girl in tattered clothes.

"No, I haven't." She pushed down on the ice again. It floated back to the top. She did this several more times, giggling each time.

"So, you were telling me where you're from," he prompted, taking a seat.

She took a sip of water and recounted all the things that happened to her from when she found the timepiece to finding his dad. "Tom, your dad, sent me here to get another one of these so I can go home."

"You're telling me that this thing is a time machine?" Eric asked chuckling. "I tried one. It didn't work for me."

"Did you press the blue button?" she said smirking and pointing to the button.

Eric shook his head. "I don't know if I believe you," he said, recounting the story in his mind. "It does explain your clothes," Eric mused, looking her up and down.

She looked at her clothes and gave him a blank stare. "Can I have more water?"

Eric brought Audrey into the kitchen and filled her glass. She played with the ice again.

As they stood there, Eric couldn't find a reason not to believe her. Her accent was so strange, like a combination of Asian and Swedish and New Yorker mixed up. Was this the Audrey dad was asking about the other day? The way she described dad and the vault in such detail, how could she make this up and why would she? Her story had to be true. But traveling through time? No way! That was something he did want to see—watching her disappear from thin air.

She was pretty. Maybe that was making him want to believe her story. Or maybe the way she smelled; it was worse than the city dump. "Do you want to take a bath?"

he asked, figuring he'd let her clean up before returning to wherever she came from.

"Sure. You'll take me to the river?"

"What? No." Eric shook his head. "You can take a bath here."

"In this house?" Audrey's left eyebrow went up. "This place is amazing," she giggled

"Everyone's house is like this," Eric shrugged as they headed to the bathroom. "This is the shower," he explained. "If you turn the knob this way, the water gets hotter. This way for cold." Setting the water to a comfortable temperature, he even explained the soap and shampoo.

---

Audrey was in awe. Here, one could bathe at a moment's notice. Closing the curtain behind her, she ducked under the stream; the water was wonderfully warm. The bubbly soap kept slipping out of her grip, but after a while she got the hang of it. The bottle Eric had told her was shampoo had an image of strawberries on it. *Who would ever have thought to use strawberries to wash their hair?* she wondered in amazement, as she rubbed the sweet-smelling liquid into her hair. Eric told her that if there were no suds, she'd need to wash it again. *What do suds look like?* It took three goes, but this time the bubbles were big and covered her hands—this had to be what he meant! It was like magic. Rubbing some of the soft bubbles on her face she immediately felt the stinging in her eyes and screamed.

The bathroom door opened causing the curtain to ruffle. "What's going on?" came Eric's urgent voice.

"My eyes! They're burning."

"Put water on them and let the soap wash out."

"It wasn't soap," she cried. "It was shampoo."

"Okay. Let the water wash out the shampoo."

It worked. The stinging sensation went away.

"Better?" he asked.

"Yes, I'm better now."

She turned the water off then dried herself with the towel Eric gave her. She quickly got dressed in the clothes Eric had laid out for her. He'd said they belonged to his sister—a pair of something he called jeans for her legs, and a white top, just the right size. They felt and smelled so much better than the clothes she had been wearing.

Heading downstairs, she hovered by the door to the kitchen. Eric hummed a tune as he moved a container with long, yellow sticks on his side of the counter. He stood tall, almost as tall as Logan. She hadn't notice this before, but his clothes hugged his body, showing a muscular frame that looked nothing like his father. She coughed to alert him of her presence. Eric turned to see her. Audrey smiled. It didn't bother her the way he stared at her. His eyes followed the curves of her body all the way down to her feet and then he brought his gaze back up to lock with hers.

"Wow! Alexis never looked like that," he rasped.

They stood looking at each other for a few moments, as if hypnotized. She flushed under his scrutiny, boldly returning his gaze.

The water in the pot behind him started to boil over and sizzled on the stove.

"What are you making?" she asked, relieved by the distraction, as he turned a knob and cleaned up the spilled water on the stove.

"It's called spaghetti," he answered.

*Spaghetti?* Feeling brave, she wandered over for a better look. She felt his eyes on her the whole time. Something smelled good—could it be the spaghetti? No, it wasn't food. Only boiling water was in the pot. She took in the smell of wood and spices and... Sniffed again. Was that a lime scent? *Ooh.* It was coming from him. She swallowed, suddenly feeling extremely self-conscious, and flushed. *Stop! Focus on the food.*

Eric took a bunch of the yellow sticks from the container and slid them into the pot.

"Why are you putting those in water?" she asked.

"This will make the noodles soft."

"So, it's not supposed to be hard?"

Eric smiled. "Not spaghetti."

She liked how he kept his composure even though she knew exactly what he was thinking. Or did she? Maybe she just wanted him to think that. If he were Logan or any other boy, they would be a nervous wreck. She had all the control. The way they looked at her, hoping that she would pick them. It didn't seem to be going that way at the moment. There was something about Eric that attracted her, but she didn't know what it was. Yet, there was something that made her want him to like her. But why? He wouldn't be going to the future with her and she wasn't going to stay here with him.

Audrey ate with Eric in the dining room. The red sauce and noodles were delicious. "What's this called again?" She held the long strand in her hands and then slurped it into her mouth. "How do you make the noodles?"

"It's spaghetti. And the noodles are just water and flour really."

The noodles were good. She didn't know why they didn't make this in her time. The sauce didn't seem too difficult either. She smacked her lips and could taste tomatoes, garlic and onions, some pepper, basil and oregano.

She watched Eric eat and a piece of spaghetti dangled from his mouth. He sucked it up. That looked like so much fun. She tried doing it. *Ha!* She put her hand to her mouth then sucked on another noodle. When she got back to her world, she would make this every night.

"What's it like in your world? What's the food like?" Eric asked.

"Well the food in my world is spicy, even though I do like this sweet spaghetti sauce. We usually eat everything with rice. Except for breakfast then it's just oatmeal."

"Oatmeal for breakfast every day? Doesn't that get boring?" Eric stuck out his tongue.

"Not at all. You can mix other things into your oatmeal. Like cornbread and grapes, rasins, which are kind of the same thing. Strawberries, or cucumbers."

"Cornbread and Cucumbers in oatmeal?"

"Yeah. Why not?"

"I don't know. It doesn't sound right. We do eat oatmeal with raisins. We also sometimes put in strawberries or bananas or honey."

"Bananas? Honey?" Audrey shook her head.

"Banana is a fruit and honey is bee spit."

Audrey gasped. "Why in the world would you eat something's spit?"

"If you try some you'll want more. Unfortunately, I don't have any to give you."

Audrey shrugged. "Shouldn't your father be home right now?"

Eric waved his hand. "Sometimes he takes off for a few days and disappears. He'll probably be back tomorrow. So, what do you do in your world?"

Audrey dabbled her fork in her food. "I do lots of things. Visit friends. Buy things from the quad."

"The quad?"

"It's an area in the city where people come to buy and sell or trade for things they made or have. For instance, if I made a food stand and sold this spaghetti, I would probably make a lot of money. Then I could buy things like clothes or other food."

"Interesting. What about the weather? Do you still get four seasons?"

"Seasons? It gets hot most of the time during the day and cold at night. There are parts of the year where it rains a lot. Those days are much cooler."

"Wow. So, it doesn't snow anymore. Here we have four seasons in a year: winter, spring, summer and fall. Winter is cold and all the leaves on the trees are gone. Spring comes and the leaves on the trees come back to life. Summer is really hot and the flowers start to blossom and fall is when the leaves start falling off the trees so they can get ready for the winter. It's a lot cooler than summer. And then it goes back to winter when it's cold and there's snow on the ground."

"Snow?"

"It's frozen rain. It's white and floats through the air as it comes down."

"That would be so fantastic to see."

Audrey was impressed with how easy it was to talk with Eric about things. This attracted her even more than his looks.

"So, what do you do in your world?" she asked.

"We wash the dishes," he said gathering his plate and cup and standing up. "Come on. You can help me."

"You want me to do what?" she said following him into the kitchen.

*He even does the things that servants do. I don't know if I like that in a man.*

He put his plate into the sink and then turned to her. "What?" Eric said looking at her as if there was something wrong. "Where's your plate and cup. Why did you leave it at the table?"

"I have people that would do this."

Eric came back with her plate. "Oh, excuse me! I didn't know I was in the presence of royalty. Had I known I would have bowed before you."

"You still can," she teased trying hard not to laugh.

Eric turned with wide eyes. "Oh my god! You're serious aren't you?"

She just stared at him. She loved his smile.

He turned facing the sink again. "I don't think I can marry a woman that doesn't know how to wash dishes."

*What was he thinking?* She smiled despite herself, realizing *he* was now teasing her.

"Marriage? You need to be my boyfriend first before we can even talk about that."

"Well then, I don't think I can be your boyfriend if you don't know how to wash dishes."

She scoffed. "So, you think that because you're cute and handsome that I would want to be your girlfriend?"

Eric turned completely around and faced her, wiping his hands with a towel. "Well, now that I know you think I'm cute and handsome." He shrugged his lips then nodded his head. "I do think you want to be my girlfriend."

She looked at her nails then looked at him. "I don't think I said you were cute and handsome."

"Yes, you did."

"I think what I said was 'because you're cute and handsome'. It's not the same."

"It's exactly the same."

She huffed, hands on hips. "Well, maybe I want a man who knows how to be with a woman and not someone who thinks he can impress her by doing these menial chores."

He shrugged. "Maybe *I* want a woman who knows how to be with a man and impresses him by doing these menial chores." He crossed his arms over his chest as if waiting for her response.

"Move!" she stormed over to the sink and elbowed him out of the way.

"Ouch!" he said after she jabbed him. Hopefully it wasn't too hard. He clasped his hands and laughed. "Okay, so it looks like someone wants to be my girlfriend."

She just smiled and saw him opening a door and slide out some wire framed drawers. "What is that?"

"It's a dishwasher."

"A machine that washes dishes? That's amaz… Wait, so you wanted me to wash the dishes when you have some thing that does it for you?"

"Well, you still have to rinse the crud off the plate before you put it into the dishwasher. And you're helping me, remember?"

"I think you want a wife just to wash your dishes and clean your clothes." She said, putting the last of the dishes into the machine.

"What! I'm shocked that you would say that," he exclaimed in mock horror, hand on his chest. "Where did cleaning the clothes come from anyway? I have no problems with you washing the dishes or me watching you wash the dishes. Either way is fine by me."

He was toying with her and she fell right in. Revenge is what was needed now. But what? She turned the faucet on, cupped some water in her hand, and splashed it on him.

"In some places, that would be considered an act of war!" He wiped his face with his hands, a smile played at the corners of his mouth.

He grabbed a bottle of water from the countertop and squeezed. She retaliated. They laughed as they threw water at each other. Soon, water was all over the floor and they were both soaking wet.

"Maybe we should get out of these and dry off. The clothes you have on are the only set my sister left over here."

Did he think it would be that easy? "Oh," she said, touching the soaking white blouse and wet jeans, "you were expecting me to walk around the house naked while I waited for the clothes to dry?"

"Expecting? Definitely not! Hoping? Yes!"

He winked again, and she laughed hard. He seemed to enjoy it because he started laughing with her. A few moments went by before the laughter subsided and they both stared at each other. She wanted to come over and grab his hand, but instead, she hesitated, waiting to see what he would do.

"I have something else for you to put on. Don't worry."

She wasn't worried. He fetched a large shirt and some socks, then led her to a bedroom and told her to change. She came out and found him leaning against the wall outside of the bedroom, waiting. He grinned when he saw her. Standing straight, he looked her up and down, seemingly pleased. The shirt came down to just above her knees.

She went back into the room and sat on the bed, running her hands over the covers, hoping that he would follow her. Instead of sitting down next to her, he instead gave her a quick tour of the room, showing her how to turn the lights on and off.

"Good night," he said and then closed the door.

Audrey played with the light, turning it on and off. It was like the metal cave when she pressed the emergency button. The room had enormous pictures scattered here and there across the pink walls with names on them in big letters. There was a writing table with a mirror. She adjusted it and saw how different she looked—so clean. The chair at the table swiveled. She sat and spun herself around, occasionally bumping her knee against the table top. After a while, she got bored and stood up and went over to turn off the light and lay in the dark and quiet of the night. She was happy here in this world. Happy she had met Eric. But why wasn't Tom home? Could it be that he hadn't come back from 1776? Just a thought. All she wanted to do now was sleep on this amazing bed.

As for Tom, she'd just have to wait and see what tomorrow would bring.

# Chapter 26

Philadelphia, June 1, 1776

Joseph tried his best to stay away from magic, yet he had just witnessed Audrey vanish right in front of him. The story of a future world where the sky was orange and no animals existed was hard to imagine—it couldn't be true. But after seeing her vanish, it was hard denying it. Maybe this was all just a dream of a beautiful girl he'd met at a church and chased into a forest. Maybe he would wake up in his bed.

No, this wasn't a dream, this was real. *She* was real.

He trembled from the stress of waiting for her to reappear. When would she return, if ever? This was unbearable. It was time to go home; with Audrey gone there was nothing here to keep him any longer. He bade both men farewell and walked through the city, spotting a butterfly which reminded him of Audrey. She never got the chance to see many of the different animals and flowers of this world.

*I hope you're happy, Audrey, wherever you've gone.*

The streets had people going about their business, bustling about with purpose. And then it hit him. His horse and wagon were at Isaac's house. He clenched his fists at the thought of having to see him again. Going back was not something he looked forward to, yet it was unavoidable. Isaac's decision to have Audrey captured ruined anything that he and Sarah may have had. Isaac wanted to control everything, especially his daughter's future. Why couldn't he have let things work out on their own? *You are such a fool, Isaac.*

Joseph was a block away from his brother-in-law's house, when he came to a stop at the corner of Church and 3rd. Isaac and Sarah were coming straight toward him. His fists clenched and his breathing became erratic at the sight of that man. He fought hard to control his anger at Isaac. He didn't want Sarah seeing him this way; but it was too late. He had already been noticed; she was pointing directly at him.

"Joseph! Where is Audrey?" asked Sarah as she approached. "We just came from Mr. Simmon's—he said that you came with two other men and got her?"

Joseph glared at Isaac. He wasn't sure what he would have told them. Surely, he wouldn't have told them the truth about what he did, what happened after? They would think he was a madman.

"Where did she go?" Isaac asked, bracing Sarah, showing a little remorse.

"As your mother suggested, I went to find Mr. Franklin to help get Audrey back, and Thomas Lynch was there." Joseph was careful with his words. "After we managed to get her released, she explained to everyone where she was from. We went to a hill on one of the farms and then she just... she just..." Joseph began to cry. "She's gone!" He wiped his nose. "It happened so fast. She was talking to us one moment, and then the next she was gone."

Isaac Paled. He looked at Sarah and then to Joseph. "I am so sorry, Joseph. This is my fault entirely."

Joseph hid his smile; this was what he wanted, to make Isaac feel utterly worthless for what he had done. More likely than not, it wouldn't make him feel anything. Isaac *had* no feelings, except what he felt for himself.

"I am so sorry." Sarah reached out to take Joseph's hand, her palm small and warm in his. "I am so sorry."

"Is there anything I can do? Where is her body? May we see her one last time?" asked Isaac.

Joseph tensed. He didn't think Isaac of all people would want to see Audrey. Or did he want proof that she was dead and no longer a problem? But he had no body to show them. "Mr. Franklin and Mr. Lynch are attending to that and I don't want any part of it."

Would that work? Would that be enough for them not to insist on seeing her?

"What will you do now?" Isaac asked.

Joseph let out a breath of relief. "I came to get my things and go back to the farm. Mother is probably worried about me."

"That is the best thing. Perhaps... Sarah... could come with you and stay for a while... to help you and your mother," Isaac said, half-smiling. His eyes gleamed.

"That would be nice." Joseph nodded, his gaze on Sarah. He knew what Isaac was trying to do. If he ended up marrying Sarah, it was because he chose to do it, not because Isaac wanted it.

He looked into Isaac's beady round eyes. Were things still going the way he had planned? More likely than not, they were.

---

Mary saw them entering through the fence and came out to greet them. Joseph explained what had happened to Audrey. Even only having known the poor girl a day, she was heartbroken. She and her husband had sworn to help runaways from being captured by the slave traders. Why would Isaac bring those men to the house? With a finger she wiped her eyes. She knew that Joseph had feelings for Audrey. She could tell by the way Joseph always smiled at her when he looked her way. But Joseph also had feelings for Sarah. Eventually, he would have made a choice. Why was Isaac so obsessed with making sure Joseph would pick Sarah? She would have found a suitor, if not Joseph, then someone else. She was intelligent and pretty. It was wrong to have done what he did to that poor child. Looking at her husband, she barely recognized him now. When had he become so heartless? And how had she not noticed?

Isaac and Mary agreed to let Joseph take Sarah with him to his farm and bring her back the first week of August. Mary helped her daughter prepare for the journey. When they came to the wagon, she gave Sarah one last hug. Sarah hugged her father and then went to the wagon were Joseph helped her get in. Joseph climbed up on the other side and took the reins of the horses.

The sun was still high in the sky. The air was warm. Mary and Isaac waved goodbye as Joseph and Sarah headed away from the house; away from Philadelphia. They continued waving to Sarah and Joseph until they got out of sight around the bend.

# Chapter 27

Philadelphia, August 3, 2052

Audrey woke sprawled across the soft bed with her head buried under the pillow. The sunlight reminded her that it was a new day as it shined through the half open curtains. She crawled out of bed and opened the door, to find the clothes she had been wearing last night, neatly folded.

She found Eric in the kitchen. A red cylindrical container with a picture of a man's face sat on the countertop next to the stove where he stood stirring a large pot. "What's for breakfast?"

Eric turned to her with a half-smile. "Oatmeal and toast." He pointed to the cupboard to his right. "Get two bowls out of there for me, please."

Setting the bowls on top of the stove, she watched as he poured oatmeal into them. His shirt fit tightly to his chest and back, showcasing ripped muscles. Her heart skipped a beat. She couldn't help lowering her gaze over his backside and sculpted thighs.

Eric chuckled.

"What?" She averted her gaze.

"Oh, nothing." He put the pot down. "Toast?"

"I'll just have some bread, not toasted," she said, feeling herself blush and wanting to just go into the dining room.

The oatmeal was far too sweet. She took a bite of bread to offset the taste, it didn't help.

"Why is this so sweet?" she asked, not wanting to finish the food in front of her.

"It's the same as mine," He shrugged, leaning over and tasting a spoonful from her bowl. "It's not sweet at all."

Her eyes opened wide. "That's so rude!"

"What's rude?" he frowned.

"You don't put your spoon in someone else's bowl without asking them first." She reached over to put her spoon in his bowl only to find that he had finished eating it all.

"I didn't think you would mind." He scooped up some more and ate it.

"You did it again! Why do you think I won't mind?"

"Because you think I'm cute," he grinned, "and because of that, you'll let me get away with it."

"You think I think you're cute?" She forced herself not to smile.

"You don't think I'm cute?" He licked the spoon, winked.

She didn't expect this level of self-assurance. He was playing with her. If she admitted he was cute, he'd win. "Do you think *I'm* cute?" She smiled and batted her eyelashes. The ball was back in his court.

"Oh, you're not cute," he said shaking his head. He paused, looked her in the eye, turning serious. "You're beautiful."

It was unexpected. His penetrating grey eyes fixed on hers. It was more than she could bear. Completely flustered, she got up and left the table.

"Where are you going?"

"I'll be back."

Audrey ran into the bathroom upstairs, closed the door and sat on the toilet. She didn't expect this. *Oh my! What did he mean by that? Of course, I'm beautiful. Everyone knows that. So, why am I in here freaking out, talking to myself?* This was all happening so fast. Her palms were sweating. She stood and looked into the mirror. Her hair was all over the place. How could he like this? She washed her hands and splashed water on her face. Looking in the mirror as she dried herself with a towel, she smiled. *He likes me!*

Returning to the dining room, Audrey chanced a glance at him as she sat back down.

"Are you all right?" He placed a gentle hand on her arm, she tensed, struggling to control her emotions.

"I'm fine," she said straightening in the chair as if nothing had happened, then changed to a safer subject. "Your father said I would find him when I got here. Instead I found you. He said he wouldn't recognize me." She bit her bottom lip and leaned back on the chair, trying to think. "He already made the timepiece and he knows where it is. He didn't mention anything about meeting you. I know you said he leaves for a few days, but is there any way to find out when he'll be back?"

"Usually he's home now," Eric said, a worried expression crossed his face. "Let's call him and find out where he's at."

Eric pulled an object out from his pants pocket.

"What's that?" she asked.

"It's a phone. Shh." Eric placed the phone on the table between them; she could hear it ringing. Tom's voice sounded, coming from the device. "Hi, Dad, it's me. I'm here with Audrey. Can you call me when you get this?" He pressed a button and the device made a sound like someone tapping a metal pole.

"How will he know it's you, you didn't say your name?" she asked.

"Because he knows my voice, and because his phone has my number." He turned the phone so she could see the screen and showed her a list of names and numbers.

"See? This shows me everyone who has called me. The ones I know come up as names. The ones I don't know only show numbers. It also tells me how many times a person called."

Fascinated, she looked at the list of names and numbers. "Who is Freddie? She called you four times."

"Freddie is my best friend and *he* called me four times," Eric said with a grin.

"Is that right?"

The phone started to ring and vibrate. The name Freddie appeared on the phone. Eric answered. "Hey dude."

"Hi Eric, how are you doing?" The voice on the phone was a woman.

"Hey, I'm kind of busy right now. Let me call you back," Eric said. He seemed to be waiting for a reply, which Audrey didn't catch, before ending the call and putting the phone back down.

# Timepieces

"I knew Freddie was a woman after all," she said, pushing the phone away, fighting to hide her annoyance. She tried for nonchalance but was too upset for allowing herself to feel this way.

"Oh my god! You're jealous!"

"No, I'm not." She huffed, turning toward the window. She didn't want to look at him at the moment; especially because he was right.

"Yes, you are."

"Whatever," she pouted.

Eric couldn't help but laugh. "That was Freddie's girlfriend."

"Really?"

"You're so jealous. I love it!" he beamed.

"I don't know what it is, but I like being around you," she blurted, before she could stop herself. When had she become so bold? She didn't know why this was happening. It wasn't as if they would be together. They were from two different worlds.

"Stay with me. Let's get to know each other. Don't go back just yet." Eric clasped her hand.

She sat back in her chair, staring at him. "I... I have promises I have to keep."

Eric brushed his fingers against her arm and clasped her hand. "Break them."

"I can't break a promise."

"Then stay with me until my father comes home."

"I don't have a choice, do I? Only *he* knows where the timepiece is. I came here looking for him, instead I find you…, and I'm so glad I did." She put her other hand on top of his.

Eric took a deep breath and blew it out. "I have something to show you." He sat up and waited for her to stand. "Follow me."

"What is it?" She followed him upstairs.

"I think this is for you." He took a box from the desk and handed it to her.

It had her name on it. Opening the box, heart hammering, relief flooded her as the familiar object glinted. "This is it!"

"You said you find this in the cabin, right?"

"You mean the metal cave?" she corrected him. "Yes, I did find it there." She stared at the timepiece and then hugged him and kissed him on the cheek. "You could have said nothing to me about this and I would have stayed with you, waiting for your father. I'm so glad you told me."

"Stay with me the weekend, before you go."

"The Weekend? How long is that?"

"Saturday and Sunday. Just two days."

Why did she have to meet Eric here, now? It was the worst timing. Yes, the timepiece could return her back anytime, but looking at him now, she knew he was the one. She didn't just like him, he was more than that to her already. But what was she to him? Did he feel the same way for her? Did he genuinely want to be with her? What if he just wanted to use her? *Oh God! Why does this have to be so difficult?* "Just two days then. No more," she finally said. *Am I making the right choice?*

# Chapter 28

Philadelphia, June 1, 1776

Mr. Franklin watched Tom wander into the study as he gave instructions to his servant to prepare the guest bedroom. He turned his attention to Tom. "So tell me, Mr. Lynch, do you have any idea how you're going to get out of this mess?"

"Sir, if you could address me as Tom, I'd feel so much better."

"Very well. And you may call me Ben." He sighed, smiled. "Tom, do you have any idea how you're going to get out of this predicament?"

"I don't know how it's going to happen… but I know that Audrey will return. I also know that I sign a document that you, John Adams, Roger Sherman, Robert Livingston, and Thomas Jefferson are on a committee to write."

"What is this document you are talking about?" Ben asked.

"Oh! Today is June first. I forgot. It hasn't happened yet."

Ben came in closer to Tom. "What hasn't happened yet?"

"In a few days, you will begin to help write one of the most important documents in the history of this part of the world." Tom smirked while pushing down on Ben's shoulders with his fingers. It was an unusual gesture, to say the least.

"And you and I sign this document?"

Tom pointed to himself. "Yes, you do! And I sign it, Thomas Lynch Jr."

"Thomas Lynch Jr.?" Ben said, rubbing his chin, then looked at Tom. "I still know nothing about the document you're describing, but I do know something about Thomas Lynch Jr. It seems that Thomas Lynch Sr. suffered a stroke and his son was elected into the Continental Congress by the South Carolina assembly. He's supposed to arrive here in Philadelphia soon. He is to begin attending Congress once he arrives." Ben looked to Tom. "How do you plan to take his place, if that is what you intend to do?"

"Well, I think it will be a very simple thing, really." Tom grinned at Ben. "*You* must tell the real Thomas Lynch Jr. that he is better off taking his father back to South Carolina, seeing that he's very ill and all. Let's hope that he agrees to it and goes home."

"You want *me* to lie to him?" Ben asked not wanting to be a part of some scheme to trick Thomas Lynch Jr.

"Of course not! I want you to encourage him to go home." Tom stopped as if he could find nothing more to say. Why did he need to switch places with this person? Ben had no idea what was going through Tom's mind. Tom continued, "All I know is that I sign the document. There must be some reason why I did it and the real Thomas Lynch Jr. did not."

Today was a trying day for Ben, being asked to lie to someone was not something he wanted to be a party of. So far, nothing had gone the way Tom said it would. This didn't seem to be the correct course of action to take. But having seen the future, he couldn't deny what the man said was true; he decided to go along with Tom's plan and pay the real Thomas Lynch a visit.

A house slave answered the door and let Ben inside to that waiting room which had a magnificently large window facing the street. Within minutes, Mr. Lynch walked slowly into the room. He was very thin and frail, with eyes that were sunken in, probably due to the stress concerning his father's cerebral apoplexy.

"Mr. Franklin." Mr. Lynch extended his hand out. "it's an honor."

"Mr. Lynch. How is your father?" Ben stood to greet Mr. Lynch and shook his hand.

"The physicians tell me he has not improved since the cerebral apoplexy," Mr. Lynch answered, a nervous tension in his voice. "But we have the finest physicians we could find in Philadelphia helping him."

"Yes, I'm sure they will do their best." Ben paused a bit and looked into Mr. Lynch's eyes, seeing the worried look of a son knowing that his father might die any day now. Was this Mr. Lynch ready to take on the task that was required of a delegate? "Mr. Lynch, I want to talk with you about the other reason you are here."

"Of course. Shall we?" Mr. Lynch motioned for Ben to enter the parlor room and sit down on one of the chairs. "Would you like some tea?" he offered.

"Yes, that would be nice. Thank you."

A slave girl was told to fetch some tea. Mr. Lynch sat down, sinking into a chair, closing his eyes for a moment and taking a deep breath. "I just got in. I am excited about attending the next session of Congress. I plan on being there first thing Monday morning. Is it possible for you to bring me up to date?"

Ben took off his spectacles. "My concern here is for you and your father."

"I assure you, Mr. Franklin, I can perform my duties in Congress and take care of my father as well. I believe that the civil war that is transpiring between America and Great Britain is of vital importance to us all."

"Yes, these things are important. Your family is just as important. I want to suggest that you prepare your father for the long journey back home. I know his condition. I talked with the physicians while you were on your way here from South Carolina. I fear that he will not survive the year."

Lynch sighed, shook his head in dismay. "I believe you're right, Mr. Franklin. My father will probably not last the year. Yet I have a duty here; I was elected to take my father's place. I must finish what he came here to... what all of us came here to accomplish." Tears welled up in Mr. Lynch's eyes.

The slave busied herself adding three teaspoons of sugar to Mr. Lynch's tea, the tinkling of metal on porcelain the only noise to break the uncomfortable silence. She scooped some tea and looked to Ben who shook his hand and grabbed the saucer from her small, delicate hands before she could ruin it.

"Mr. Lynch, take your father home," Ben said, before taking a sip. "There are other delegates from South Carolina here already. Have you met them yet?"

"I just arrived yesterday. You're the first to visit me." Mr. Lynch took a sip of his tea and softly moaned.

"I see." Ben turned his head toward the hallway it was dark. "May I see your father?"

"Of course." Mr. Lynch put down his cup and led Ben into a room down the hallway.

Thomas Lynch Sr. lay in bed. His frame was more skeleton than flesh. The entire left side of his face was sunken in and lifeless. When his eyes met Ben's, the half of his face that could move lit with a smile.

"How are you, Mr. Franklin?" The slur made it difficult for Ben to understand what Tom Senior was saying.

"I am doing well," Ben said louder than normal, gently taking Tom Senior's hand. "I was telling your son here that he should take you back home, to South Carolina."

"No!" His voice was small, weak; the only trace of emotion came from his eyes. "We have work to do here!"

"Yes, there is work to do. And as I told your son, there are other delegates from South Carolina already here."

"The South Carolina assembly elected him. He must stay."

"I assure you, Sir, that history will take note of the contributions that you and your son have made here." Ben leaned in closer. "Now, you must enjoy your remaining days with your family, with your son. But not here in Philadelphia. It's time to go home, my friend. It's time to go back to South Carolina." Ben squeezed Tom's hand. He could see that he had struck a chord with the elder Lynch; the man would rather die in his home in South Carolina than here in Philadelphia.

"I'll make the necessary arrangements in the morning," Thomas Jr. said, looking at his father. "I'll meet with the other delegates from South Carolina and tell them of my plans."

This was unexpected; yet, he should have anticipated it. It would be something any elected official would do. "I will arrange for you to meet with them before you leave tomorrow."

"Thank you, Mr. Franklin. My father and I appreciate all that you are doing for us."

---

Ben entered the house and found Tom in the library. Tom looked up at him with anticipating eyes. "How did it go?"

"How did it go? I feel like a thief. I've convinced two good men to leave so that you can take the place of the younger one."

"I don't know how else we could have handled it."

"*We?*" Ben squawked. "*You* are the one telling me that this needs to be done. What if I'm conspiring to change the course of history by blindly following you?"

"I swear to you that my signature is on that document. If he attends those meetings and he signs the document instead of me that *will* change history."

"And right now, you're the only one who knows this." Ben stared into Tom's eyes. *Who was this man?* Someone from the future to come here to do what? To change the outcome of the past?

Tom went to the desk and pulled out a piece of paper. Taking a pen, he dipped it into the inkwell and signed the paper several times before turning and handing over the paper.

"What is this?" Ben asked.

"Those are my signatures."

"And?"

"I'll send you to my time so you can see that the signature in that document is mine."

"And how do you propose I go to your time, Tom? Audrey has your timepiece and she has disappeared."

"Damn it!" Tom growled, darting his eyes away from Ben.

"I will not have you swear in my house, Mr. Lynch."

Tom held the paper in his hand in silence.

"A very curious inconvenience, isn't it?"

Tom pushed back his hair with one hand and put the other into his pocket, pulling out an object and thrusting it toward him. It was the passport. "You showed me this when we first met." Ben shrugged, trying to keep his anger in check. "So what?"

"Listen to me," Tom insisted. "You went and saw your own history. The things that you have done, the things you will do in your lifetime. Do you think, now that you've seen those things, you would change anything?"

"I don't know."

"Well, I do." Tom walked around the desk, putting it between him and Ben. "I went to 1787 and you recognized me but I did not know you. Not the way I do now. What that tells me is that wherever anyone goes in time, they are supposed to be there. In other words, if you continue with this line of reasoning and believe that I am here to change the future, then you will have contempt for me and you won't greet me in 1787. Instead, you will just pass me by. Or worse, you will assume I'm there to try and change history after failing to do it in 1776. And if you think that, then you will never befriend me and you will never tell me about Audrey. This means I won't be here right now." Tom kept his gaze on Ben. "Because the only reason I am here, right now, is because you told me I needed to be here to help Audrey. And you told me in 1787."

"That argument is very circular."

"Yes, it is, isn't it?" Tom pressed his lips together. "If you had not told me to come here, I wouldn't have looked at the document and I wouldn't have seen my signature on it. If the real Thomas Lynch signs that document, then history *will* change in the future. But then again, maybe he doesn't sign the document. Maybe he had already been thinking of leaving and you going there tonight only reaffirmed what he had already decided."

"Perhaps," Ben said. He placed his hands on the desk. "But there is still a problem. He wants to meet with the other delegates from South Carolina to tell them of his plans to go back home."

"If he meets with them, then there is no way I can attend the sessions."

"I thought the same."

Tom paced. "We need to send the real Thomas Lynch a note indicating that they cannot meet with him. I need you to write a letter to Mr. Lynch."

"I will not write a letter that is a lie!" Ben pounded his fist on the desk. "I will not allow anyone in this household to deliver it."

"You're not going to send him anything. I'm going to write it and deliver it to him myself. I just need you to tell me how to write it." Tom looked at him sheepishly. "I don't know how to write the way you people do in this century."

Ben smirked. "What do you mean 'you people?'" He grabbed a sheaf of papers and sat behind his desk. "Mr. Lynch, you are surely trying my patience. And I haven't decided, yet, who is the bigger fool; you or me." He dipped his pen in the inkwell and leaned in above the paper ready to write, then looked up at Tom and said, "what do you want it to say?"

---

Tom walked along the street, breathing in the sweet scent of flowers that grew in front of the townhouses along the road. The night was clear with so many stars shining brightly. In his time, because of light pollution, only a few stars were visible. As Tom climbed the steps up to Thomas Lynch's townhouse, he felt his stomach tightening. He was about to meet the man he would replace at the convention. With letter in hand he knocked on the door. It wasn't long before a house slave answered, peering out at him through narrowed eyes.

"I have a letter for Thomas Lynch Jr." Tom held out the paper. The house slave closed the door, and in a few minutes the door opened again this time, it was Thomas Lynch Jr. standing before him.

"You have a letter for me?" he asked, his face pale with dark circles under his eyes. Tom handed over the letter.

*Dear Sir,*

*Mr. Franklin has informed us that you wish to meet to appraise us of your plans concerning your father. Regrettably, we will be in a special session all day and will not be able to oblige you. We wish to make it known that we understand your decision in this trying time for your family. We wish you and your father a successful journey back home. May God show his mercy on you both.*

*Your most obedient and humble servants,*

*Edward Rutledge*
*Arthur Middleton*
*Thomas Heyward Jr.*

Mr. Lynch's face showed no emotion. He folded the letter and took out a shilling from his pocket with a slight tremble in his hand, handed the coin to Tom and said, "Thank you." He stepped back and closed the door.

Tom inspected the coin, turned around, and headed back to Benjamin Franklin's house.

# Chapter 29

June 3, 1776

Today would be an exciting day to say the least. Participating in the Continental Congress was the furthest thing Tom ever imagined doing. Yet here he was about to take part in one of the most important events in the history of the United States. Tom finished dressing, grabbed his hat, and headed downstairs. Ben was already in the kitchen, drinking a cup of tea and reading the morning paper.

"Good morning, Ben," Tom said, sitting at the table.

"Good morning, Tom. And how are you this morning? Are you ready to impersonate the real Thomas Lynch?"

"You make it sound like I'm committing a crime." Tom grumbled.

"And I am an accessory to the fact." Ben smiled as he continued to read the paper.

"Would you like breakfast, Mr. Lynch?" a servant asked.

"Yes, please."

"The hardest challenge you're going to have today is sounding like you are from South Carolina," Ben interrupted, turning a page of the paper.

"You're right." He hadn't thought of that. "Maybe I can get away with saying I was schooled abroad."

"You don't sound like anyone I've ever met in this world," Ben chuckled.

"I hope it won't be too obvious."

"I hope no one will care," Ben shot back.

As they walked, Ben told Tom how things would go and what to expect during the session. Tom could see the state house up ahead. It had a steeple that wasn't there in 1787, during the creation of the U.S. Constitution. Upon further scrutiny he realized that two connected buildings from his time were also missing—City Hall and Congress Hall. They entered the building and Tom's heart began to beat faster with excitement. There were so many faces that he recognized from history books: Samuel Adams, Benjamin Harrison, and Robert Livingston. There were other faces he didn't recognize, but every one of them must have had something written about them in American history books, he was sure. Ben pointed to where the South Carolina delegates sat before walking off abruptly to go sit with the Pennsylvania delegates.

There were two other delegates here, but he wasn't quite sure if they were part of the South Carolina delegation. They nodded at him and he nodded back. There were several chairs only one had the best view in his section.

He started to sit when a voice with a hint of Southern accent and a touch of British flare said, "That would be my seat," It was Edward Rutledge. His grey hair matched the long, grey jacket; the white shirt ruffling out at the neck and sleeves was exactly as he'd seen in a portrait of the man.

Tom stood to move, but Mr. Rutledge took his hand and patted him on the shoulder as he made his way to another seat. "How is your father?" he asked.

Tom hoped not to be called out so quickly. Considering that this was where all the other delegates from South Carolina sat, it made sense that Mr. Rutledge would ask about his father. "He is doing as well as can be expected. Thank you for asking," Tom responded. "I have made arrangements to have him sent back home."

Mr. Rutledge stared at him curiously, looking up and down his face. Tom smiled, hoping that he didn't realize that he wasn't the real Thomas Lynch, Jr.

Charles Thompson—the secretary of the Congress—banged the gavel and the room stood, as a clergy of the Presbyterians recited a prayer to the resounding chorus of 'Amen'. The secretary read the minutes from the last meeting and unresolved issues were debated among the other delegates. Most of the issues had to do with payment to the militias. A resolution was suggested that allowed the army to employ Indians for its fight in Canada. Quotas for militias were established in the different colonies and they decided that three major generals and two brigadier generals be added to the Continental Army. Delegates rose to express their thoughts; it reminded Tom of Parliament in England. Bored, Tom soon stopped paying attention and let his mind wander. At some point the secretary stood and declared that Congress was postponed until the next day.

After the session in Congress came to a close, some delegates stayed and chatted. Ben had joined John Adams, Benjamin Harrison, and John Hancock in a discussion.

A hand settled on Tom's shoulder. To his surprise it was Mr. Rutledge.

"We need to talk," the man whispered in Tom's ear. "Alone!" Rutledge led Tom into one of the rooms in the back.

Something was wrong. Did Mr. Rutledge know Thomas Lynch Jr. personally? The history books never mentioned any discourse between them prior to being in Congress.

"Mr. Lynch," Mr. Rutledge said, closing the door behind them. "Why did you send your father home? Why didn't you have him stay here with you?"

"My father is very ill and I decided that he would be better off being at home with family."

"But *you* are his family."

Tom was caught off guard. Did Thomas Lynch even *have* any other family? Thinking off the top of his head he mentally crossed his fingers and blurted, "I felt that being home in South Carolina with other family members would be better for him."

"I can understand that." Mr. Rutledge stared into Tom's eyes. "But it is a long way to Hillsborough. How long do you imagine it will take for him to get there?"

Tom didn't expect to be asked these kinds of questions. Mr. Rutledge's gaze never wavered. Tom's insides coiled. He had no idea how long it would take to get to Hillsborough. Tom shrugged his shoulders and said, "I have no clue."

Mr. Rutledge stared at him with an intense gaze. "Hillsborough is in North Carolina, not South Carolina. Who are you? And where is Thomas Lynch Jr.?"

Tom could feel the blood leaving his face. "I... I am Thomas Lynch!"

"I know Thomas Lynch Sr. and I know his wife and you look like neither of them. You don't even talk like a South Carolinian. Who are you? Are you a spy for the Crown?" Mr. Rutledge moved to the door to open it. "I don't know what's going on here, but I'm about to find out!" He turned to walk out of the room and bumped into Ben. "Mr. Franklin. Pardon me," Mr. Rutledge said and then pointed to Tom. "I don't know why, but I believe this man is not Thomas Lynch, Jr.! He's an impostor! He may have even murdered the real Thomas Lynch Jr. and his father!"

"Mr. Rutledge, please step inside. There is something you must know," Ben sighed, gesturing for Mr. Rutledge to step back.

Mr. Rutledge's jaw dropped in surprise, but he retreated into the room, nonetheless. "You *know* about this?" The man couldn't, or wouldn't, close his mouth.

Ben put his right hand up to silence the man. "The real Thomas Lynch is on his way home with his father. Nothing has happened to them. I can assure you."

"What is the purpose of this impersonation? Of all people, I would not have expected *you* to betray us to the Crown. All the work you have done. Is it your son? Has he won you over? What will you do with me?" Mr. Rutledge's eyes were wide in panic.

"I have betrayed no one," Ben said, firmly. "It will be much easier if I show you, than it will be to explain it to you." Ben turned to Tom. "Show him."

Tom had no idea what was being asked. He stared back, dumbfounded, still in shock from being found out.

Ben made an outline of a square with his fingers. "The document."

"Oh yeah, the document." Tom nodded, catching on. He fished in his pocket for his passport and handed it straight to Mr. Rutledge, who skimmed over it with a frown.

"What kind of trickery is this?"

"I know this is hard to believe," Ben took a deep breath and continued. "But this Thomas Lynch is not from our time. This is why he sounds misplaced. But look where it says he's from on that page." Ben nodded to the passport in Rutledge's hands.

Mr. Rutledge looked down at the front cover and read aloud, "Passport. United States of America."

"We did it, Mr. Rutledge! In the future, we shall no longer remain part of the Crown," Ben said.

"You really expect me to believe this? Anyone could put something like this together," Mr. Rutledge said, on the verge of tossing the document.

"Feel the texture of the paper," Tom interjected. "Look, there's a picture of me. And if you're still not convinced, look at the date of issuance."

The man looked at Tom with distain, as though he was about to refuse, but opened the document and looked at the date as directed.

"It would defeat the purpose for a spy to use a date like that," Ben said. "If this were a forgery or even a trick, it would still serve no purpose to use a date so far into the future as this one."

Mr. Rutledge scoffed and looked at Tom, handing him back the document. "When do these things happen?"

"On Friday, June seventh, there will be a resolution for the colonies to be free and independent states," Tom explained slowly, in as calm a voice as he could muster. "Several colonies will ask for a postponement of three weeks as they haven't fully agreed to it. On July second, all the colonies are in favor of independence. New York abstains, and on July fifteenth, they join the fight for independence."

"All this will begin on June seventh?" Mr. Rutledge asked. "That's in—"

"four days," Ben confirmed, nodding.

"So, you know everything that is going to happen?" Mr. Rutledge asked Tom.

"Only the major events. I don't know the details."

"We cannot tell anyone about this," Ben stressed.

Mr. Rutledge shook his head, still staring at the passport in wonderment "I will not say anything, for now."

Tom let out a breath he'd been holding for a while. "Now that that's settled, how about we find something to eat?"

---

Tom, Ben, Mr. Rutledge, Arthur Middleton, along with James Wilson, another delegate from Pennsylvania, made their way to Merchants' Coffee House. The pub was quaint; Tom had read that it had been a favorite of Ben's. They gathered around, everyone discussed the different committees they were on or assigned.

Tom had been quiet throughout most of the discussions. The food was so delicious, he couldn't get enough of it.

"What do you think, Mr. Lynch?" Mr. Wilson asked.

"Huh?" Tom looked up wiping his mouth. "I'm sorry, I wasn't listening."

"It seems to me like you're making love to that steak."

Everyone laughed.

"What's your opinion on the separation of the colonies from Great Britain?" Mr. Wilson repeated.

"Oh." Tom drank some ale. He wiped his mouth, then put the mug down and said, "I think that the King of England and Prime Minister North can diffuse this debacle, but the Prime Minister's pride and King George's illness is keeping this from happening. I think that something will be done in a few short days that will turn the tide toward independence."

"And why do you speculate this?" Arthur asked.

Tom had barely started chewing the huge bite of steak when the question was asked. Arthur stared at him, waiting for an answer.

"I don't know," Tom swallowed hard, then added, "I just have a gut feeling."

Mr. Rutledge shook his head and smiled at Tom.

---

On June 5, Tom was assigned to participate in a committee along with Ben. They were tasked with figuring out a way in which several Continental posts could send communications between themselves without the British intercepting them. Despite already knowing the outcome, he felt good participating in these committees. It was as though, in some strange way, he was supposed to be here, to make sure things turned out the way they did?

# Timepieces

Two days later, June 7, as he had predicted, Richard Henry Lee stood and motioned for the colonies to become independent states. John Adams, a few seats behind Lee, seconded the motion. John Hancock called for a debate of the resolution. John Dickinson rose and waited for the delegates to calm down before speaking. "I motion that the issue of independence be postponed indefinitely. We are British gentlemen and we shall remain British."

George Read of Delaware stood. "I second the motion to postpone independence."

The congressmen started talking on top of one another. Mr. Rutledge shot Tom a glance, then stood and waited for the delegates to quiet down. All eyes were on him. "I think we are all in agreement that it is impossible that we should ever again be united with Great Britain."

Some of the delegates started shouting. "Treason!"

Mr. Rutledge held up his hand. "Yet I am not in favor of adopting this resolution at this time."

The other congressmen began to speak among themselves. John Adams and Mr. Dickinson got into a heated argument.

Robert Livingston stood and addressed the Congress, "I am in agreement with Mr. Rutledge. The middle colonies are not yet ripe to bid adieu to the British, but that connection is ripening as each day passes. I am not in favor of adopting this resolution at this time."

Dickinson motioned for the vote to be postponed until the next day, insisting that the colonies should not separate from England.

John Hancock addressed the congress. "Gentlemen, I do not think we will resolve this issue today. Let us postpone it until ten o'clock tomorrow. All members of Congress should be punctual." With that congress was adjourned.

On Saturday, Tom and Ben arrived at the State House. Tom greeted Mr. Rutledge and other members of Congress as he moved through the floor to take his seat. A prayer was said by the Quakers, which a few congressmen protested because of their pacifist beliefs. Congress resolved into a committee to take into consideration independence from England. The committee debated for some time, then John Hancock resumed the chair and asked, "Mr. Harrison, what is the resolution on the matter of independence?"

Mr. Harrison stood. "The committee has taken into consideration the matter but has not come to any resolution and desires that the resolution be postponed until the next session of Congress."

Monday morning, Tom, Mr. Rutledge, and the other South Carolina delegates got together for breakfast to talk about the upcoming session. The all agreed that whatever the outcome, South Carolina should be in agreement with separation from England.

"The only problem I see is that the northern colonies abhor slavery. But slavery is vital to the economic well-being of the southern colonies," Mr. Middleton said.

"Actually, it is not," Tom argued. "If you think about the cost of housing, feeding, and taking care of the basic needs of slaves and the number you need to maintain a plantation, you will see that in the long run, you are spending much more money having slaves than if you just paid people to work the fields."

"But no one would work for such low wages," argued Mr. Heyward. "You would have to pay someone twice the going rate of the street sweeper. Paying that much to have someone work the fields then becomes more expensive than having the slaves."

"A free person would work more efficiently than a slave who has nothing to look forward to at the end of the day," Tom said.

"This may be so," Mr. Rutledge said, "but the way of life in South Carolina is deeply ingrained with slavery. There is no quick solution for this." He paused for a few moments, deep in thought. "You are right about one thing, Tom, a free man is happier. If this Congress were to force the issue, I would not oppose it."

Tom Heyward and Arthur Middleton looked at each other as if surprise that he would allow slaves to be free. Tom took another drink and then said, "I'm sure one day there will not be slaves, and not because you want to free them, but because it will not be profitable to keep them."

"If we let them go free, where would we send them?" Tom Heyward asked. "There's no way a nigger is equal to a white man."

"Yes, where would we send them?" Arthur asked.

"Possibly to the west with the Indians," Mr. Rutledge said, chuckling. "We can let *them* deal with each other."

"You need to stop looking at people in terms of being white, or black, or red," Tom said to the group. "You all think that anyone who is not white is inferior to you, but there is no difference between you and them. All men are created equal. You have met stupid white men in your travels. Not every negro and Indian is as stupid as you may think. What you discriminate against is what you can noticeably see. In the case of the negro and the Indian, it is the color of their skin and not what is in their minds and hearts. And because of the color of their skin you look at them as dogs and not men."

The group went quiet, some faces flushed confirming to Tom that this was indeed how they looked at these people. To them, if the black man and indian were animals, how could putting a leash on an animal be wrong? *Because they're not animals*, Tom thought. *They're no different than you.* They finished their meal and walked back to the State House.

Tom was glad that today was not as hot as the previous week, albeit not that much cooler. Today he decided not to wear the jacket or the cravat; it was way too hot for that. What he wouldn't have given for a couple of electric fans. A desire to be in his home world swelled inside him.

After everyone had sat down, John Hancock asked for a vote on independence. A roll call vote counted the yeas and nays, which resulted in a tie. John Adams nearly jumped out of his seat. "Mr. Hancock! May I remind you that as president, you must break the tie."

Mr. Dickinson immediately stood. "Any acceptance on the issue of independence must be unanimous." He sat back down as did John Adams.

Mr. Hancock stood. "On the issue of independence, I agree this must be unanimous. For any colony that was not for independence would likely be forced to fight on the side of the English."

The room fell silent. Mr. Hancock called for another vote for independence. After much discussion, Benjamin Harrison stood before Congress and read the decision.

# Timepieces

"That the consideration of the first resolution be postponed to this day, three weeks, and in the meanwhile, that no time be lost, in case the Congress agree thereto, that a committee declaration to the effect of the said first resolution, which was in these words: 'That these United Colonies are, and of right ought to be, free and independent states; that they are absolved from all allegiance to the British Crown, and that all political connection between them and the state of Great Britain was, and ought to be, totally dissolved.'"

"I accept this resolution," John Hancock said and then banged the gavel. "We are adjourned."

Mr. Rutledge leaned toward Tom, speaking quietly into his head. "So, things are going as you say. I still find it hard to believe that in just three weeks we will be declaring our independence from Great Britain."

"Things happen fast when you least expect them."

On Tuesday, a committee was formed to prepare the Declaration of Independence. Tom sat in awe as the names of Thomas Jefferson, John Adams, Roger Sherman, Robert Livingston, and his friend Benjamin Franklin were called out.

Tom stayed with Mr. Rutledge to continue a more in-depth discussion of slavery. Mr. Heyward and Mr. Middleton decided not to join them. Tom noticed that the men did not even excuse themselves as they left.

After the discussions Tom went back to Ben's home. Ben sat in his office behind his desk, reading his mail. Tom knocked on the door. Ben looked up and motioned for him to come in.

"You've been elected to write the declaration for independence," Tom smiled.

"Yes, it seems I have been elected to that service," Ben nodded. "Unfortunately, I don't see myself with much time to devote to it. Mr. Adams and I have agreed to let Thomas Jefferson make the first efforts. I've given him my document on the Dutch Declaration of Independence from Spain. I'm sure he'll find many insightful ideas there."

Tom had thought the Declaration of Independence was an original idea. It didn't occur to him that parts of it may have been borrowed from other documents. He looked around at the books on Ben's shelves and asked, "You only had one copy of the Dutch declaration?"

Ben looked up from the letter he was reading, at Tom. "Why would I have two?"

"I was hoping to have a look at it," Tom said sheepishly

"You may look at it when he returns it." Ben continued reading his letter.

---

Several weeks passed when Tom spotted Jefferson hurrying into the building with several documents, handing one to each member of the committee. Cutting his morning walk short, he hurried back to Ben's to wait for his return, eager to see what they'd come up with in the first iteration of the declaration of Independence.

Ben sat in his office, the document sprawled over his desk, crossing out sentences here and there and adding pieces.

"You're changing it?" Tom asked.

"It's good, but it could be better," Ben mused, as he continued marking up the document.

It was June 28 when the committee presented the first draft of the Declaration of Independence to Congress. Ben had made enough copies for everyone to read the document over the weekend.

Tom was smoking outside when Ben got back to the house. "Seems there are going to be a lot of changes to the document come next session," Ben said.

"Why is that?"

"Oh, people have opinions," Ben said joining Tom in a smoke. "Oh, by the way, Mr. Rutledge has agreed to keep the part about slavery in the document."

"What? No!" Tom said surprised. "We can't leave that in the document."

"Why not?" Ben asked. "Slavery is abhorrent. If we can start a new government where slavery is nonexistent, then by God, let's do it."

"The document in my time doesn't have those words in it."

"I don't understand what the ramifications will be in allowing this to remain."

"Nor do I," Tom said. "But if that section remains, my world may no longer be the way I left it."

"Are you suggesting that the future I saw may not exist the way I saw it?"

"That's exactly what I'm suggesting!" Tom exclaimed.

"How will you stop him?" Mr. Franklin asked.

"In Congress I'll have to publicly disagree with him and hopefully the other southern states will back me."

"And if that doesn't work?" Ben asked.

"Then I don't know what effect this will have on the future."

Tom and Ben entered the statehouse on Monday with apprehension and went to their seats, as the rest of the congressmen filed in. Mr. Rutledge came in with a big smile and patted Tom on the shoulder. "Good morning, Mr. Lynch."

Tom didn't smile; he felt sick, knowing what he may have to do. "Good morning."

Everyone stood for the prayer, this time by the Presbyterians, with which no one seemed to have any objections. When the issue of the Declaration of Independence document came up, there were objections to the language on individual persons, and it was agreed to take those out. No other disagreement with the document was voiced.

Tom slowly stood up. "As a delegate from South Carolina, I cannot call the King of England a tyrant because of slavery. South Carolina depends on slaves. For without them, there would be no way to maintain the plantations we own. I don't believe that we should keep the part about slavery in this document." Mr. Rutledge opened his eyes in surprise. Tom continued, "I feel that if this piece stays, South Carolina must withdraw its vote for independence." Everyone was taken aback by this. Tom knew from his history that the northern delegates wanted nothing to do with slavery. The southern delegates knew it was wrong and could go either way. Tom continued to speak. "It is true that the northern colonies do not have as many slaves as the southern colonies, but they do participate in the slave trade and profit from the cargo of slaves to the southern colonies."

One of the delegates from New Jersey spoke. "But this makes the entire second paragraph hypocritical."

"I truly believe that when we are referring to men, any learned individual will make the correct assumption that we are talking about white men only. In that regard we can take out the word *inherent* in the sentence that reads: We hold these truths to be self-evident, that all men are created equal, that they are endowed by their Creator with certain inherent and unalienable Rights..."

All the delegates looked to Mr. Rutledge who stared at Tom. "May we have a ten minute recess?" Mr. Rutledge said, pushing Tom toward the aisle. They excused themselves and went into the next room, Ben trailing not too far behind.

"What's going on here?" Mr. Rutledge said through clenched teeth, his angry eyes burning into Tom. "You convinced me that slavery is wrong and should be abolished. Now you say you want to keep it?"

"I know that I told you that slavery is wrong," Tom said, "and it *is* wrong. But in my time, this document doesn't have anything about slavery in it. If I let it stand, I don't know what will happen to the future; to my family. This is why I need to object to the wording. I do apologize for this surprise."

Mr. Rutledge's face contorted in a mixture of confusion and anger. "If you truly are from the future as you say you are, then I don't understand why we cannot change it for the better. It doesn't matter what has happened from what you say, but rather what we, as individuals being given the knowledge of what wrongdoing is being done, that allows us to choose to do the right thing. I'm not in favor of your current argument."

"In my time, the wording is not there. This is the only reason I need to take it out."

As they returned to the session, Mr. Rutledge announced his disagreement with Tom. As Tom had hoped, Mr. Heyward and Mr. Middleton stood up and announced their agreement with Tom, to which Tom gave an inward sigh of relief.

One of the delegates from Georgia stood. "Georgia also concurs with Mr. Lynch and will not commit to independence with the wording in the document as it stands."

Mr. Rutledge stood up once more, looked at Tom, and shook his head. "I will not oppose my colleagues. South Carolina will not vote in favor of independence until this wording is removed from the document."

Tom knew that Mr. Rutledge had no problems with slavery. He had slaves himself. But the fact that he was willing to give it up made Tom feel miserable that the wording couldn't be kept. Change would not happen in South Carolina right now. Tom had just made sure of that. In the future, Fort Sumter in South Carolina would start the civil war. Were the decisions he was making now the cause of the civil war in the future? Or would it have happened anyway? Tom wasn't so sure he should have said anything about the wording at all.

After debating the issue for almost an hour, Congress agreed to remove the part about slavery from the document.

It wasn't until July 2nd that Congress voted for independence from Great Britain, with New York abstaining.

Mr. Rutledge turned to Tom and shook his hand. "It seems that we are now closer to becoming an independent nation, Mr. Lynch," Mr. Rutledge said cheerfully. "But we are not there yet, are we?"

"We still have to wait on New York," Tom said.

"And they will agree to this?"

"Yes. On July fifteenth, they join the fight for independence."

On the fourth of July Tom sat excitedly, already knowing the outcome, as the votes were taken about the wording in regard to the document that was the Declaration of Independence. It was agreed to by all the delegates in attendance.

Tom was excited at what was happening and even though he knew how things would work out, it was still fascinating to see it all unfold.

A month later, on August 2, 1776, Tom found himself standing above a desk signing the Declaration of Independence. He was the third of the four South Carolina delegates to sign the document. It was surreal for him to be standing in this building not just observing but also participating in one of the most daring adventures of the eighteenth century. No other colony outside these thirteen had dared declare independence from England.

# Chapter 30

Philadelphia, August 27, 2052

Audrey curled up on the black leather sofa in the study and peered out the window, prying open the blinds with her fingers. She'd been with Eric for over three weeks; so much for just staying a weekend. But she was happy. She pushed thoughts of his father and her mission out of her mind. For now, she was content with their new routine. Eric would head off to school every morning and upon his return he would teach her more about his world.

Eric showed her how to access the Internet, allowing her to access thousands of pictures, just by pressing a couple of buttons. Some even moved and had sounds of people and places that Audrey never dreamed existed. She watched the life of Benjamin Franklin and admired all the things he'd done.

Audrey and Eric had become like a married couple in many ways, arguing about ideas and events, collaborating on what they would eat and working together on household chores. She was grateful for all the things Eric showed her, and despite her early resistance on many occasions, she found herself washing his dishes and cleaning his clothes. The strange thing was, she didn't mind.

Life in this world was exciting and yet she felt sad. Her people would never know about these luxuries and achievements. If only there were a way to retain some of this knowledge and take it back home.

She woke up with a sense of listlessness and boredom. Another week had gone by and Eric still had another five days of summer school left. The fun of research and discovery had faded. Being home alone gave her nothing to do except watch shows or surf the Web, as Eric called it. There had to be more to this world, to this life. Like seeing how the city had changed from 1776. But Eric didn't want to take her outside, telling her that the Department of Homeland Security would be looking for people who didn't have a bar code on their hand or forehead. She pleaded, but the answer was always no.

"You don't understand," he said, "the bar code knows if you are you. If I put a fake bar code on you, they would find out that it was fake, and they would deport you for being an illegal."

"Where would they send me?"

Eric laughed. "Immigration wouldn't know where to send you." His smile faded as he became more serious. "But that wouldn't keep them from putting you in jail."

"But you said it's used for buying food and going into stores. I just want to walk around. We don't have to get food or go into stores. I only want to get out of this house and see what else there is in this world."

"There are agents that walk the streets. They choose people at random and scan their bar codes."

"Please!" she begged.

Without a word, Eric headed into the kitchen and grabbed the keys, before calling her over—it was apparent that he didn't want to stay in the house either. A button on the wall made the garage doors roll up, letting sunlight rush in. Excitement ran through her, finally able to ride in the shiny, black machine.

"A Honda, right?" she asked approaching it and running her hand along the surface. It was smooth and cool to the touch.

Eric nodded, as he unlocked the car, and as she got in, Eric reached over and strapped the belt around her. "This is for your protection."

She smiled, leaving her hands on her sides, surrendering to him. *Click!*

"Now you're my slave." He laughed, then kissed her.

For a moment, Audrey forgot where she was. The garage disappeared. She was back at the plantation, back in the shack. Tobi was trying to kiss her. She closed her eyes and turned her face away. His heavy breathing was overpowered with a stench of early morning breath. The cold chains restricted her movement as Tobi came down on her with that hideous smile. She opened her eyes.

*This isn't happening!*

"Get away from me!" she shrieked, pushing Tobi's head hard against the wall. He bounced landing on her lap and grabbing her legs for support. Feeling trapped, she hit and kicked him to free herself.

"Get away from me!" she cried. He mumbled something unintelligible.

Yanking on the chains did nothing. They were on too tight.

"Get this off me!" she shouted hysterically.

Tobi reached over. She wasn't going to let him do anything to her. Pounding his head with her fists and knees, he tried to get away, but it was too late. She grabbed his ear and squeezed it with all her might. He screamed and yanked her hand off him and pulled back, managing to get away. The chains weren't coming off.

"Get these things off me!" she cried out. "Get me out of here!"

She tried grabbing Tobi's hair. But rather than long, slimy locks, it felt more like a short crop close to the head. A nagging doubt crept in her mind. A hand appeared on her left side. It kept trying to grab her. She dug her fingernails into warm flesh and heard a howl of pain.

"Let me go!" she yelled again and again. "Let me go!" After pulling and tugging several times, she freed herself from the top chain that crossed her body from shoulder to hip. The other chain was still securely strapped around her waist.

*Click!*

The chain flew off setting her free. She jumped out of the shack and was back—in the garage.

Disoriented, she focused on her surroundings. Eric stood on the opposite side of the car, his eyes wide. She ran over to him. "Oh, Eric, it was awful!" He backed away, but she held on to him fast. "They couldn't keep me locked up," she said with her arms around his waist. "I got away from Tobi!"

*What just happened?* Aching from the pain of the blows inflicted on him, Eric pulled away. "You need to explain what just happened."

Her eyes showed fear, then she noticed the scratches. "Oh my, what happened to your ear and your hand?" She made to touch him, but he flinched.

"You're kidding, right?" he said, raising his voice, getting upset.

She stared back at him, expressionless, mouth open.

"*You* did this to me." He pointed to his cuts. "You pretty much kicked my ass in that car."

"I'm sorry," she said quietly, voice quivering.

"You're sorry? What the... what's the matter with you?" he yelled, feeling his heart racing.

Her lips trembled. "I thought he..." she stammered, "in the shack."

"What the hell are you talking about?"

Tears streamed down her beautiful face. She went to hug him, but he backed away. What was going on with this girl? She'd flipped from calm to crazy in an instant, and then back again. He simply stood and watched her cry silently. He wasn't even sure he wanted to comfort her.

It took a few minutes before she composed herself and told the story of how the most awful people captured and made her a slave. The tribulations she had gone through in 1776.

# Chapter 31

Audrey was happy that summer school was finally over for Eric. She slowly became accustomed to the seatbelt; Eric suggested she just sit in the car, hold it, and lock it into place. There were a few times when she would have an anxiety attack and couldn't get the belt out of the locking mechanism. Not wanting to repeat what happened last weekend, Eric always unbuckled it from the driver's side.

When she woke Saturday morning, she was excited; today was finally the day she'd get to go outside the house. As they entered the garage, the light from outside glinted off the shiny, black car. He opened the passenger door and Audrey stepped inside eagerly and strapped on the seatbelt without trepidation. As Eric strapped on his seatbelt, he gave verbal orders for the car to drive and the car slowly cruised forward out of the garage and into the street.

They hadn't driven far when she noticed things didn't feel right. People stood in the street wearing dirty clothes, and though they were alive, they seemed disillusioned. Like they had lost hope. People sat in chairs, many on the floor, motionless. As if they were dead. Cars were abandoned in the middle of the street. When they had to stop behind one of the abandoned cars, Eric said something to the car quietly, and then used the big round wheel to maneuver the car around the other vehicle.

"Is this normal?" she asked as the car continued along the street.

"Unfortunately, yes. Some people can't afford to charge their cars. When people run out of power, they just abandon their cars where they stop."

"When do they come back and get them?" she asked as they turned a corner.

"Most of the time they don't. The city tries to move the cars. See, over there? A tow truck—it's taking those cars." A block ahead of them a large vehicle with a car on top of it pulled another one from behind.

Their car slowed at the intersection of two streets unexpectedly. "Why are we stopping?" No other moving cars were around.

"It's a red light." He pointed to the three lights that dangled from the pole in front of them. "Red means stop and green means go."

"What does the yellow light mean?"

"If the car is not driving itself then depending on how far you are from the corner, it could mean that you should slow down because the light is going to turn red or that you should speed up to cross the street because the light is going to turn red."

"Huh?"

"It just means that the light is going to turn red," he said squeezing the wheel and not saying more. Was he upset with her for not fully understanding what the colors of the lights meant? "Are you mad at me?"

"No," he said looking at her. "More at myself for not being able to explain it better."

The light turned green and Eric made a left turn on a street that had no street signals nor buildings along either side, for as far as she could see. The car lurched forward and picked up speed. White lines on the road flew by on either side of the car as other cars moved at about the same speed. On occasion, a car would fly right past them, causing her to jump in her seat.

Eric pressed an image on the display panel and music started playing all around the car. He swiped the image which changed to a different image on the panel and also the music. When he stopped, she began swiping the images to listen to different music. Sometimes it wasn't music but people talking. After listening for a while she'd press another image doing it again and then again.

"Wait!" Eric tried to go back to a song that had been playing. "Don't you like that song?"

"Yes, but there are so many different things to hear, I want to hear them all."

Eric laughed, then found the song he wanted to hear while Audrey sat back in her chair and looked out her window, staring at people as they passed in their cars.

Off to the right an island of buildings clustered in one area, towering larger than any structure she had ever seen. "What's that over there?" she said, pointing in front of them.

"That's downtown Philadelphia," he said.

It wasn't the Philadelphia she knew. Here the structures were so tall and reached so high into the sky. They looked so much bigger than the Ancient Tower back home.

"We don't have anything like this where I'm from. The Ancient Tower is the tallest." It was sad to note that this was her past and the knowledge of creating tall buildings and many other marvels like it were lost to her people.

Eric slowed the car down and turned onto a road where he had to dodge the abandoned cars and the people on the road. It didn't seem easy driving here. People walked on the streets and several times he had to honk the horn to get by and most of the time the people just ignored him.

Trash littered the streets and signs had been torn off some of the businesses and their windows broken. Cars with smashed windows blocked the road. There were police here, many of them on horseback.

"Where are we?" Audrey asked, looking at the desolation and destruction.

"We're about three blocks from Benjamin Franklin's home." Eric said looking around. "Something must have happened here recently. I've never seen this many police."

A few doors down, a police officer was beating a looter who had just come out of a store. Eric took them down another street, and then another, until he found a part of the city that looked quieter. The car stopped between two white lines in an open area between two buildings.

"I know a place where we can eat," he said, getting out of the car. He went around and opened the door for Audrey. "I don't know if the place is still open with the food shortages and all."

When they reached the building, the doors were boarded up and the windows smashed. Everything inside was gone except for tables and benches that were bolted to the ground.

"It looks like we'll have to eat at the house."

"I'm fine with that. I don't feel safe here."

Eric took a different route to the car. They got to a place with a sign that said Pathmark grocery store. A long line of people stood out front.

"Why is there a line here?" she asked.

"Only a few people can shop in the store at a time. And then you can only buy a few items. Because we live in a city, all of our food has to be shipped in and the fuel shortage has made that difficult."

"When will it end?"

"I don't know," he shrugged. "Most of the oil-producing countries hoard their supplies for themselves."

"Oil?" Audrey frowned.

"It's what the machines that bring the food from other places use. Let's get in line. It's not too long," Eric took Audrey's hand and together they walked toward the end of the line.

"Not long? It goes all the way to the corner!"

"I've seen lines that are twice as long. This one is short, trust me," he said, squeezing her hand and kissing it. As they got to the end of the line, other people started lining up behind them.

It took most of the day to get near the front of the line. This wasn't Audrey's idea of fun when she had imagined going out. Two women argued just ahead of them.

"You weren't in front of me!" one woman shouted.

"Yes, I was. I've been here all day," the other woman screamed back.

A fight broke out, punches were thrown, and soon one of the women was bleeding from her nose. The woman screamed and grabbed the former by the hair, pulling as hard as she could. They moved in circles grasping on to one another's heads, shrieking and yelling.

The police soon came over and broke it up. Audrey watched with interest as they scanned each woman's hand with some type of device, before sending them both away.

"You did this!" the woman who was bleeding said, throwing a punch that almost connected.

The police held the woman back and told the other to go, but just moments later the second woman was released, and she ran after the first, disappearing around the corner.

"Why was she so mad?" Audrey asked Eric in a whisper, so as not to draw attention.

"Because once the police come and break up a fight, neither can buy food for the rest of the day."

"That's awful. Why don't they just send them to the end of the line?"

Eric shrugged his shoulders. "I guess this way it'll make you think twice before getting into a fight."

Six people were still in front of them. The guard scanned the mark on the person's forehead and the light turned green. The lights on the device were the same colors as the street sign.

"So does that thing tell them if you've been in a fight?" she remarked.

"Oh shit!" Eric looked toward the front of the line. "I totally forgot that you don't have a mark. They won't sell us food if you're with me." They were so close to the entrance of the store. "I'm sorry, let's go home."

"You want to leave now after we've been in line all this time?"

"Not so loud," Eric said, holding a finger to his lips "We already talked about this at the house. I told you it was dangerous. I wasn't thinking; let's go," he said softly.

"But we have nothing to eat at the house!"

"I'll drive you back home and I'll go to the store near the house and get some food there."

"And wait in line for how long again? Are you kidding me?"

"You can't go into the store with me and you can't stay out here by yourself. It's too dangerous."

She had to admit, he had a point. She didn't much like the idea of being alone out here. Scanning around, she spied a bench with a sign that read 'Bus Stop' across from the market. "I can wait for you at the bench over there."

"No way. An agent might come and start questioning you. It's too risky."

"Eric, I'm not laughing anymore. I wanted to come out and see things, not stand in a stupid line to get some food."

"Well, it's too late to do anything now," he sighed. "Let's just go home and I'll have to stand in line again."

"There are only three people ahead of us. I'll wait at the bench and you go get the food."

"Look, I don't like you being out here alone. Why don't you go back to the car and wait for me there?" He held out the car key for her.

"I don't want to go to the car. Plus, there is no one here. It's just the people standing in line waiting to go in the store."

"And if an agent comes?" he asked.

"Then hurry up so we can get out of here." She kissed him then walked across the street and sat on the cool metal bench, before he could argue further.

It wasn't long before Eric had gotten to the front of the line. Holding out his hand, they scanned it and the light on the device turned green.

She waited for what felt like hours while Eric was in the store. The shadows from the building across the street hid the sun. The day was nice even though it felt cooler here than in her world, or even in 1776.

A man with a black coat and a black book sat down next to her.

"Hello," he said with a grin.

"Hello."

"Can I ask you a question?"

He already asked a question, but today she was in a good mood and decided to be polite and let him ask another one. "Yes?"

"Why didn't you go inside the store with your friend?"

Did he know that she was with Eric? "Who are you?"

"I was watching you and your friend standing in line. Why didn't you go inside?"

She had to be careful. Eric still hadn't come out of the store. "Who are you?"

"I'm an Immigration officer. You have an unusual accent. Where are you from?"

The man frightened her. Eric still hadn't come out of the store. Where was he? She silently willed him to hear her, to come rescue her. She fought to stay calm, digging her nails into the bench. "I'm from Milestown."

The man gave her an inscrutable look. "I've never heard of that place. Do you have any ID?"

He was definitely one of those agents Eric had warned her about. *Why didn't I listen and go to the car?* She began to stand. Where was Eric?

The man put his hand gently on her arm to stop her. "Please don't. I'm authorized to use deadly force to stop you. I really don't want to do that. But I will if I have to." He opened his jacket and moved it back, revealing a gun. If she ran, he would shoot her dead. If she stayed, she had no idea where he would take her.

The man asked her name and where she lived. Audrey told him her name but couldn't tell him where she lived. What would she say? Just as the panic was starting to bubble over, she caught sight of Eric finally, exiting the store.

Catching sight of her and the man, he ran across the street. "What's going on?"

"Who are you?" the man asked.

"Who are *you*?"

"I'm with Immigration. And you are?"

"I'm her boyfriend," Eric slowly turned his face to her while the man writing in his little black book and mouthed for Audrey to get up.

She slowly stood.

He turned to look at Eric. "Audrey here has no form of identification. And like I told her, I'm prepared to use deadly force to stop her." He pulled back his jacket again for Eric's benefit.

Eric's face turned red. "Since when does a person need identification to walk the streets?"

"I noticed she was with you when you were in line."

"And I remembered that she didn't have any ID with her. That's why she came over here and sat on this bench. I still don't know what the problem is," Eric said defiantly.

"I know she's not from around here. Listen to her talk. I haven't figured out where she's from. She's a foreigner and probably illegal." He looked between them. "Audrey, you're coming with me."

*No!* She wasn't going to just let them take her. She looked to Eric. As the agent turned around and called another agent to come and help, Eric grabbed Audrey's hand and they ran.

"Hey!" the agent yelled after them.

Audrey ran fast. She didn't want to get shot. It would be even worse if Eric got shot trying to help her. It was like being chased by the Feds in New Scranton or the dogs when she ran away from the plantation. They were running for their lives. How did she keep getting into these messes?

Eric steered her into a side street lined with large green containers that overflowed with black shiny bags. Eric pulled Audrey onto another side street that was wider. Looking both ways they darted off down the street, running through a park and found themselves among a large group of people.

There were hundreds of tents all around them. People strolled, or sat in chairs, or lay on the ground wrapped in some sort of thick, shiny silver cloth. Audrey looked at the people as she ran past them, their eyes devoid of any enthusiasm. She risked a glance back and saw several agents running into the park. The people round them suddenly reanimated. As if coming back to life, they all bunched together, causing the agents to slow down, giving her and Eric time to sneak away unseen.

As they exited the park on the other side, they didn't slow their pace. But several blocks down, she spied another park just ahead; then she realized, it was the same park. They were running in circles! Was Eric lost?

"The agents left, but they'll be back soon," said a rough voice. A black woman with a sunken face and grey, lank hair sat on a blanket in the long grass near them. She looked at Eric and then at Audrey. "Are you an illegal alien?"

"No, she's not," Eric said, trying to catch his breath. "Can you help us?"

"How can *I* help you?"

"If you have something for us to wear, we can give you the clothes we're wearing in exchange."

Audrey glanced at Eric in confusion.

The woman nodded and called out, "Bill! Get me a pair of your pants and a shirt. Then get my green sweats."

A scruffy man emerged from a tent. His shirt barely fit, ripping at the shoulders and exposing his stomach.

"I got you some new clothes," she said to Bill then turned to Eric. "You two can change in the tent."

"Thank you." Eric took the clothes.

"Why are we changing clothes?" she whispered, as they entered the tent.

"It will make it easier for us to hide here without being noticed. They're looking for a girl with blue jeans and a white blouse. They're not going to be looking for someone wearing dirty green sweats."

It was incredible how Eric thought fast.

"Those are the agents you said would send me away, right?" Audrey asked, taking off her clothes.

"Yes. They're with the government. They look for and arrest illegal aliens."

"Illegal aliens?"

"People who are here without the proper papers," he explained.

She knew about not having the proper papers. It was because of her not having the proper papers that she had found herself being taken into slavery. It allowed Isaac to give her up to the slave traders. Freedom was a word that had no meaning in this world.

The green clothes didn't feel right. A fierce itch spread over the upper half of her body. Eric was also scratching himself.

"What did they put in these clothes?"

"I think they have fleas."

"Fleas?"

"Yeah. We better hurry." Eric didn't elaborate. "I'm going to get the car and bring it around the side of the park. You stay here until I get back," he said.

"Can't I come with you?" she begged.

"Listen," he said, grabbing her arms, "if we were a black couple or a white couple, we could blend into the city easily. By being black *and* white, it will be easy for them to spot us."

"How would it be easy?"

"Audrey, you're black and for all intents and purposes I'm white and that is a problem right now."

So many years had passed, and nothing had changed. "Blacks are still slaves?" she asked.

"No, blacks aren't slaves anymore. It has nothing to do specifically with being black."

"Then what is it?" she asked, now becoming agitated that her skin color was a problem once more.

"I don't know if you've noticed, but there aren't that many couples out there that are a white man and a black woman." Eric stopped for a few moments as if waiting for his words to sink in and then continued. "Even though it's acceptable, it's still noticeable... and since there are so few couples like us, it will be easy for them to find us. We stand out, Audrey."

She couldn't understand why the people in this time noticed couples of different skin color. They weren't a rarity in her world and nobody cared. She nodded her head. "How long will it take you to get the car?"

"I'll be back in about ten minutes, fifteen at the most." He held her face between his palms. With a peck on the lips, and a smile of reassurance, he grabbed the bag of food and disappeared out of the tent. She followed him outside and watched him leave, her heart twisting, gut wrenching, as she fretted that something might go wrong.

Outside of the tent people came and went. They all looked the same—hungry.

"Your boyfriend there really cares about you," said the woman who'd given them the clothes. "I think he's more worried about what happens to you than you are."

"I was the one who suggested we come here," she explained, feeling guilty.

"Why'd you want to come here?" the woman asked. "Nothing here but misery. No food except for the ones that can wait in long lines and have money to pay for it. People living on the streets fight for what little crumbs they can find."

"I didn't know that. I just wanted to find out what this place was like." Audrey flopped down next to the woman.

"So you *are* an illegal alien." Audrey winced and the woman added, "You can trust me. I won't tell anyone."

"They think I'm an illegal alien. There's no way I can prove who I am."

"Where are you from?"

"It's kind of hard to explain," Audrey said, but before she could think of what to say, Government agents swarmed the park. They were walking in her direction.

They approached a black woman wearing something similar to her old jeans and white top. Their scanner turned green and they moved on. Audrey started to get up but the old lady grabbed her arm and hissed, "Don't make yourself obvious to them. Sit." And then she turned her head and said, "Dwayne, Shanika, come and sit next to this pretty young woman."

Dwayne was a short black man with balding hair. Shanika was a young black woman, about her age, a little on the heavy side, but pretty.

"This way you won't stand out in the crowd," the woman continued to explain, "they'll just pass us by. Don't look worried. These types are taught to spot people who look worried. If you look nervous, they'll come over and start talking to you." She gently rubbed Audrey's hand to calm her down. "What's your boyfriend's name?"

"Eric." She wondered if he had gotten to the car by now.

"How long you two been together?"

Cold sweat gathered on Audrey's brow as she saw the agents approaching. The woman squeezed Audrey's hand and repeated her question.

"About a month now," Audrey replied, taking deep, calming breaths.

"He seems like a nice young man. How did you meet?"

Audrey explained how they met at Eric's house without going into the details. She talked about the things she learned and about Eric helping her get through the seat belt problem and about the agent at the bus stop. Once she started, it came pouring out.

The woman smiled, "Sounds like someone's in love."

Audrey's heart made a flip. The answer was obvious, but she had never really thought about it. She smiled at the woman. "Yes, I am in love with him."

"Do you think he loves you?"

She didn't know how to respond. Did Eric love her? What was she to him? He did say he was her boyfriend to the agent.

The agents walked along the footpath and passed them by without so much as a glance.

"I hope he does," Audrey said, meaning every word.

"You hope he does what?" said a deep voice. Eric stood right in front of her.

The sun was behind him and she could only see his silhouette. She put her hand to her eyes to block out the light. She looked around and noticed that the agents had gone.

"You hope he does what?" Eric repeated.

"I was hoping that you'd come and get me," Audrey said, feeling her face flush.

"Well, here I am." He smiled.

Audrey stood up and turned to everyone around her and thanked them. She gave the old woman a hug, kissing her on the cheek. "Thank you so much for your help."

"Don't think about it." The old lady waved her hand in dismissal.

"By the way, I'm Audrey and this is Eric. What's your name?"

"My name is Lilly."

Audrey's jaw dropped as she stared at the woman astounded. "I once knew someone else named Lilly who helped me." She turned to Eric and said, "This is so amazing! What are the chances that the two women that helped me are named Lilly?"

"We need to go." He pulled her away from the group. "Thanks for all your help."

Lilly waved goodbye and shouted out to them, "God has plans for you two."

Eric held Audrey's hand and led her to the car. There were no agents around. He took the nearest street that would take them out of the city.

"This world is amazing. There are so many places to go and so many things to see and you can see them all just by sitting in this thing," Audrey said with excitement. As they got off the express way heading back toward the house Audrey noticed there were many people with makeshift houses along the street. She thought of those people going hungry and not being able to purchase food if they didn't have the mark. It wasn't safe to be anywhere. There was no freedom here. It was a miracle that all these people could live in one place. She turned to Eric, who was concentrating on the road ahead. "Why don't these people grow their own food?"

"Most of it is brought in from other places. Less and less food comes into the city each day. There are a whole lot of problems right now and feeding the people is one of the biggest problems."

# Chapter 32

Audrey needed to get back to 1776 and give Tom the other timepiece to be able to return back here to this time. He had been wrong. They weren't going to meet.

Audrey showered and slipped into the T-shirt she had been using to sleep in. Eric took her clothes to the basement to wash. She waited for him on the sofa.

"Today was crazy, wasn't it?" she said when he returned.

"Is this place anything like you imagined it would be?"

"Everything here is so different from what I've seen in 1776, not to mention my world." A stream of tears marked their way down her cheeks.

He put his arm around her and brought her head to his chest. His fingers brushed through her hair. "Don't cry. Things will get better."

"That's not what I'm crying about," she said. "All of this is underwater in my time. It's all gone. And you're..."

"Dead?" Eric gave her a squeeze.

She put her head on his chest because she didn't want to look in his eyes. He said the truth. In her world he was dead. He would only be a memory: her memory. "I've decided I'm going back tomorrow." Eric looked at her in shock. "I can't stay in this house forever." She pulled her back up from his chest and looked at him; she could see the disappointment in Eric's eyes. "You were right. If I go outside without that stupid mark on my hand, I'm going to wind up in jail or be sent to some faraway place."

Eric looked at the floor. "I understand."

"I've also decided something else." She paused, knowing what she wanted to say but not knowing how to say it. She reached out and touched his hand. Her breathing became shallow. She moistened her lower lip with her tongue. "I want you to be... my... my first man."

Eric's mouth fell open. He sat there staring at her, not saying a word. Was she wrong to offer herself to him? She so desperately needed him to say something—anything. Was he interested in her in that way? She had thought he was... what if she'd got it wrong? Now she wasn't sure.

He leaned toward her and kissed her on the cheek. She tensed up, not quite sure how to interpret what he had just done. Then he brought her hand up and kissed it with a slight tremble. He turned it over and kissed her palm, then inched toward her, bringing his lips a hair's breadth from hers. His warm breath caressed her, and his scent aroused her. She closed the distance between them and pressed her lips against his.

"I'm afraid," she whispered pulling back just a little.

"Don't be." He kissed her again. "I won't hurt you. I promise."

She had heard those words before, but she knew this man wouldn't hurt her. Her head fell back, giving him access to her neck, which he promptly kissed and lightly nibbled. His hand moved up to her breast and gently cupped it. She covered his hand with hers.

After another deep kiss, he stood and took off his shirt. His ripped muscles made her tremble with longing. She felt hot, perspiration rolled down her lower back. This was really going to happen.

"Here?" she said, trying to grasp the full ramification of what was going on. Was this the right thing for her to be doing? After all, she was leaving the next day and would never see him again. Then she banished all hesitation. *Yes. This is what I want. What we want.*

"Yes, here," he said and then started to unbutton his pants.

"No!" she responded and got up. She took his hand and led him up the stairs into the bedroom. This night would be special. Tonight, she would become a woman. It was overwhelming and exhilarating.

When they reached the room, she turned toward him and moved her hands across his chest, pressing into his strong muscles. He grabbed her by the waist and pulled her close to kiss her. Reaching down, he pulled her T-shirt up over her body. Bare from the waist up, she surrendered to his touch as he bent down to take a nipple in his mouth.

His mouth traced a path on her skin back up to her lips. Pulling back, he started to say something when she pressed her fingers against his lips. She leaned in and kissed him. His tongue followed the outline of her lips before finding its way inside her mouth.

Things were going as she had fantasized they would. She held his hand and walked with him inside the bedroom. They both lay on the bed and Eric reached for the light.

"No!" she stopped him, overcome by shyness. "You don't need to see with your eyes. Please, just let me feel your hands on me."

---

Eric woke up to someone gently rubbing his cheeks and then kissing him. He opened his eyes and smiled at Audrey. "Morning. Why are you awake so early?"

"Couldn't sleep." She smiled and kissed him again. She stared at him for a long time and then with tears in her eyes said, "I'm going to miss you."

"Don't go" he pleaded. "You have the timepiece. You can leave any time you want."

"I promised you I would stay with you two days, and look, it's over a month!" She started to laugh and cry at the same time. Her body brushed up against his. "Plus, if I stay any longer, I won't want to go back." She kissed him once more.

"I don't have a problem with that." He kissed her back.

"But I do." She pulled back, got out of bed, found her clothes. She dressed quickly and without another word, walked out of the bedroom.

He came into the office as Audrey was just turning on the timepiece. Why did she have to go? Why couldn't she just stay here with him? He came over and put his hands around her waist and kissed the back of her neck. She sighed and turned around, putting her arms over his shoulders. He pulled her closer, but she shook her head and pushed away.

"What?" he said.

"I shouldn't have stayed for as long as I did."

"Why not?"

"Because I'm confused and you're not helping me make the right choices!" she sobbed.

"We haven't made any wrong choices. We're made for each other. I think you know that too. What am I going to do when you're gone? Stay with me, please."

He buried his face in her hair. She surrendered to the embrace, reveling in it. She didn't really need to go back. For what? To keep some silly promise?

"Let me come with you," he pleaded.

"No," she sniffled. "Only one person can use the timepiece and there are only two: one for me and one for your father." She broke down. "You can't come!"

She buried her head in his chest. They both stood still, comforting each other. There was no solution. She'd go back to her time and he'd stay here in his.

A short while later, she lifted her head and he kissed her tears. She moved back and looked down at the timepiece.

"Damn it!" she cried in frustration. "I've been changing the calendar and now I don't know what date to go back to."

Eric took the timepiece, set it, then handed it back to her.

"August 4, 1776? How do you know what day to send me to?" she asked.

"My dad is a history buff. I always teased him about signing the Declaration of Independence and if he is in 1776, he actually does sign it. I've set the timepiece to the day after the delegates are supposed to sign the document."

He wrapped his arms around her squeezing her tight. They kissed for what felt like an eternity then she stepped back and took the other timepiece off the desk and placed it in the bag.

"Wish me luck!" she said as her beautiful lips trembled.

"Don't go," Eric whispered. His heart squeezed tight in his chest.

Her smile faded as she pressed the blue button.

He was alone. Pain shot through him. He would never see her again. His thoughts were on the timepiece. Some part of him wanted the damn thing to fail.

"Wow," he said in sad amazement. "It really does work."

His cell phone began to ring. It was his sister.

# Chapter 33

**Philadelphia, August 4, 1776**

Audrey appeared in midair and fell to the ground heavily, landing on her butt. It was quite amusing to her and probably to the horses in the field that had seen her materialize. How she wished Eric was here to laugh with her about it.

She got up and turned off the timepiece, placing it in the bag, then wiped the grass and dirt off her green sweatpants. Wiping the tears from her face on her sleeve, she continued her journey back to Mr. Franklin's house. There was a chance that someone might stop her on the street and with no papers, anyone could claim her as their own. The thought of being owned made her feel ashamed; she was more determined than ever to free the slaves in her city.

She took Ridge Avenue south. From her recollection, it was the street that would take her to Mr. Franklin's house. The people standing around the farmer's market stared as she passed by, making her nervous. Remembering where she was, she was careful to look down at the ground and avoid eye contact. It was hard to remember how to act here since she'd been away. She chastised herself again for staying with Eric so long.

Entering the city proper, the streets became more crowded with yet more stares. Some whispered among themselves, never taking their eyes from her. The thought of running came to mind, but she quickly dismissed that idea—any suspicious movement would give them an excuse to chase her. It was better to walk and keep calm. She took a deep breath and did her best to put them out of her mind.

At the corner of Seventh and Arch, she decided to risk a quick glance back to see if anyone had followed her. No one had. Sighing in relief, she turned around and made the corner when she abruptly walked straight into a man.

"Excuse me." She stepped back to move out of his way, then looked up and met his widening gaze, her heart sank.

"You're—" he started.

"Isaac!" she blurted out.

Isaac's eyes narrowed and his lips puckered. "Where did you come from? I thought you were dead." He looked her up and down and his lips curled. "What's this that you have on? Why are you wearing men's clothes?"

Audrey was surprised to see him here. She didn't know what to do and couldn't move.

"Did you come here to meet Joseph?" He stared her down. "I don't understand why he'd want to be with a nigger instead of my daughter."

Fear crept up inside her. She tried to bolt, but he was faster and managed to grab her arm. "I have you now, you black whore!"

With lightning speed, she turned and hit him square in the mouth then kicked him in the groin. He buckled, taken completely by surprise. He cupped his flesh and crumbled to the ground.

Noticing two men were watching from the other side of the street, she took off running.

"Stop her!" She could hear Isaac shouting. "She's stolen my bag!" When the men didn't move, he screamed, "It's a woman. She's wearing men's clothes! Stop her!"

One of the men began the chase and ran after her. She ran faster, turning back only to see Isaac getting up and starting the chase with them.

Several men congregated down the street to see what the commotion was about. He shouted at them, "Stop her! She's impersonating a man. She has my bag!"

Audrey continued to run as fast as her legs would carry her. The hot sun was beating down, and she felt the sweat forming on her body. At least the streets weren't too crowded this time of day. Isaac was yelling and screaming for people to stop her. A few people tried to get in front of her, but she managed to dodge them. Some young boys found the whole thing amusing and joined in the chase. But the heat was taking its toll.

The corner of Arch and Fifth meant just three more blocks to Benjamin Franklin's house. She willed herself to keep going and pumped her legs harder.

On Fifth Street vendors sold fruits and vegetables. Animals were hanging on hooks. It reminded her of New Scranton. Weaving her way through the stalls, a soldier pulled out his pistol and aimed it at her, but she was too close and ran straight into him, sending them both flying into a fruit stand. Hitting the ground hard, she managed to keep the bag and its contents from being damaged. The vendor started to yell obscenities at her. The soldier appeared dazed but made to get up as the furious vendor tried to grab at her but she lashed out, scratching his arm. He let go with a growl.

She continued to run. Several people moved out of the way.

*Bang!*

The swooshing sound of a bullet flew by her ear and ricocheted off a tree; she didn't stop running.

*Bang!*

She ducked. A bullet came from another direction, missing her. The same sound that day when she'd left Lilly to die in the forest.

*They're trying to kill me!*

"Do not shoot!" a soldier cried out. "Do not shoot! You might hit a bystander. Do not shoot!"

Audrey turned the corner on Chestnut Street leaving the market behind. One more street and she would be there, she would be safe.

On Fourth Street she turned another corner. Mr. Franklin's house was halfway down the street. A mob of about six to eight people came down Fifth Street. Breathless, she reached Mr. Franklin's house and banged on the door. A servant boy she didn't recognize answered the door. "I'm here for Mr. Franklin," she said between gasps.

The boy squinted his eyes and said, "He doesn't live here."

At that moment, someone in the group spotted her. "There she is!"

"Where is his house?" she asked the boy. "Tell me now!" She was worn out but couldn't think of stopping now.

The boy pointed toward the back of the house. "He lives behind this house."

She was aghast. She hadn't run far enough. The mob had grown and they were coming after her. She had come this far and wasn't about to give up. Not yet.

"Thank you," she said to the boy and ran down the street.

"You can just go through..." the boy started.

There was no time to linger. She bolted, needing to get to Mr. Franklin's house as fast as possible. Her body was tired and there were only a few more meters to go and now it felt like she might not make it. They were getting closer. Isaac wasn't with them. These people had taken up the chase without even knowing the reason for it.

The last corner was Market Street. A rock hit her on the leg and she tripped. Her hands stopped her fall. She straightened up and got a second wind. As she reached the house, the group was seconds behind her. She banged on the door with all her might. It felt like an eternity. She turned to see the mob drawing closer and saw something flying through the air toward her.

# Chapter 34

Tom entered the room as quietly as he could so as not to disturb her, with a glass of tea, and a plate with eggs and bread, placing them on the table next to the bed. Audrey hadn't woken up since her ordeal the day before. A servant girl was starting to take the bandages off from around her forehead where the stone had made contact.

Slowly, Audrey's eyes opened. They were sunken and purple. She went to touch her forehead and winced. "What happened?"

"Mr. Franklin. He saves you!" The servant spoke excitedly before Tom could speak. "They was about to stomp on you and he tells them to stop. They say you stole that bag there. Mr. Lynch, he asks them to tell them what be in the bag if you stole it. Nobody be able to answer him. Soon they all be gone, and they brought ya into the house. But that be yesterday."

"How are you feeling?" Tom asked.

"Not so well." She rubbed on the new bandages. "I made it back. I brought the other timepiece," she said, trying to get up, looking around the room.

"I know," Tom said gently, forcing her back down to rest. "I grabbed the bag before anyone else could." He took her hand and smiled at her. "What happened that brought you back today?"

Ben entered the room and stood at the foot of the bed.

"I met your son," she said to Tom.

He nodded, perching on the side of the bed. "Go on."

"I was playing with the timepiece and I forgot the day I left and didn't know what to set it to, to get back here. Eric figured out that you sign some document either today or yesterday?"

"Your son helped her get back here?" Ben asked Tom.

"It seems that way."

Ben's brows creased. "Where were *you* then, Tom?"

"We couldn't find you," Audrey said. "Eric tried calling you. Audrey turned to where the timepieces lay on the table. "I figured you weren't there because you were here."

"Well, that would make sense," Mr. Franklin chimed in. "How can you be two places at once?"

"Being here and being there is not being in two places at once. There are over two hundred years separating the same place," Tom said and then shook his head. "It doesn't make sense that you wouldn't find me there. Unless of course I came back farther into the future because I had forgotten the date I left as well."

He smiled at her.

Audrey smiled back then sniffed the air. "You smell different. Like burnt trash."

"Oh, it's not that bad." he sniffed, wishing he had some lemon-scented air freshener to spray in the room.

The food was next to her. She looked at it, and then at Tom. "You didn't know I was going to be awake. Why did you bring me the food?"

"To be honest, I was hoping you wouldn't be awake so I could eat it." Tom smiled, eyeing the eggs. "This means I need to get something to eat. I'm famished."

"This seems to be a predictable pattern with you, Tom." Ben sighed.

---

Audrey watched Tom leave the room. Mr. Franklin stayed behind and approached her, positioning a chair next to her bed. "It was brave of you to come back with the second timepiece." He shuffled nervously on his seat. "Uh, I wanted to ask..." He paused. "In your world, is everyone a negro?"

It was amazing that he had even asked such a question. What would it matter? He would be long dead by her time. Mr. Franklin was smart, yet he allowed himself to be guided by his prejudices. She could see that with most everyone now, especially herself.

She grabbed the fork and the plate and started eating before she answered, giving herself a few seconds to compose her thoughts. "My father is mayor in my world, and he is a negro." Audrey felt repulsed by the word alone, but that was probably the only word he understood in his time.

Mr. Franklin seemed surprised by her answer, his eyebrows raised.

"Not everyone in my world is a negro," she added. "My best friend has the same skin color as you. What color would that be?"

"White," he said as if he had not expected the conversation to go this way.

Audrey took hold of the cup of tea by the handle. "My servant had slanted eyes and straight black hair. I guess in your world you would call her... an Indian? Even though her skin is as light as yours. In my world there are slaves that are negro, slaves that are white, and slaves that are... Indian." She shrugged. "Mr. Franklin, it doesn't matter what you look like to be a slave. It matters where you're from."

Mr. Franklin cleared his throat. "In this world, there are only a handful of educated negroes. None talk the way you do. When I hear you speak, I instinctively expect you to be white but then I look at you and..." His voice faltered. "You are a very beautiful young woman. That, along with your intelligence, makes you very desirable indeed. I can understand Joseph's attraction to you." He smiled at her and continued, "But that accent of yours, young lady..." He guffawed.

Audrey joined him in a round of laughter. He had changed. He finally understood that it was who she was that mattered. That God spoke to *her*—Audrey—not just to a negro girl.

Audrey enjoyed talking with Mr. Franklin, or Ben as he insisted she call him, about her world. He had so many questions and she didn't have all the answers. And even though he couldn't imagine living in a world like hers, it was her home and she missed it more than ever.

---

Audrey took a breath, closed her eyes, and felt a sense of relief that she was finally going home. Looking out into the valley from the landing on the cliff that would be the cove in her time, she could see the plantation off in the distance and trembled.

"Are you okay?" Tom asked.

She exhaled, her eyes filled with tears, looking at Tom for a moment. "I'm so glad we're getting out of this place."

Tom took the timepieces out of the bag and handed one to Audrey. "What was the date on the timepiece that you told me about at Ben's house?" he asked.

She closed her eyes then turned on her timepiece to set it. "August 29, 2276."

Tom set his own timepiece. "Put in August 30, 2276."

"Why that date?" Audrey asked.

"To be sure that the you that has left for 1776 is not still there when we arrive."

She pressed the blue button on the disc and found herself on the beach with Tom on the ground and Logan pounding his fists into him.

# Chapter 35

**August 30, 2276**

Logan sat in the cave to stay cool as the hot sun shone down on the cove. He was grateful for the ocean breeze. Out of nowhere a man appeared by the shore. He was obese and wearing the strangest clothes. The man's pants and socks looked tight and uncomfortable, like nothing he had ever seen before. But his shoes looked like the leather shoes the people of New Scranton wore. He got up and ran toward the man, screaming, tackling him to the ground, pummeling his face. The man held his hands up trying to block the punches.

There was a noise in the background. Logan paid no attention. His fists kept pounding, one after the other into the man. All of a sudden someone pushed him into the sand. He quickly jumped back on his feet.

"I said, Stop it!" Audrey snarled at Logan as she got up. "He's with me."

"I didn't see you," Logan growled. "I thought he was a Fed." He began wiping the sand off. "When did you show up?" He looked her over. She was different, cleaner, and prettier. "Why are you wearing that?"

"He's not a Fed. He's the one I was supposed to find." The man didn't have any noticeable injuries. She knelt next to him. "Tom, are you all right?"

"I think so," Tom said, checking for broken bones and bruises.

Logan felt guilty for what he'd done and leaned over the man, holding out his hand. Taking the offer, Tom scrambled off the ground and then brushed the sand off his clothes, looking around.

Audrey hugged Logan. "It's been such a long time. I missed you so much."

"What do you mean? It's only been a day."

"Logan, it's been over two months for me!"

"What are you talking about?"

"I'll explain everything later."

Logan came in for a kiss on the lips and got a cheek instead. What happened over there that made her not want to kiss him on the lips? She held his arm and quickly turned to Tom who was scanning the cove. "Tom, this is my best friend Logan."

"Yes." Tom rubbed his sore arms. "We've met."

Logan inhaled deeply.

"This," she waved her hand out toward the ocean, "is what used to be Pennsylvania."

"I wasn't sure what to expect... certainly not this." He looked up into the orange sky. "Look at that..." he whispered, then louder, he said, "To be honest, I really didn't believe you when you told me about this." He turned and approached the metal cave.

"Is it the same metal cave?" Audrey asked.

"Yes, it is." He nodded, moving toward the panel. "You spent the night in there?" he asked not expecting an answer. "Did you get the electricity working?"

"What's electricity?" Logan asked, then turned his attention to Audrey. "Why are you wearing those clothes?" The clothes appeared to be very comfortable and made her look distinguished, like she was royalty from another city.

"A woman gave me these clothes when we ran away from immigration."

"Immigration? What's immigration and why were they chasing you?"

"I didn't have the mark on my hand and no other identification. Eric and I ran from them and we ended up in a park with a lot of homeless people. We exchanged our clothes with someone named Lilly, so immigration wouldn't find us."

"Oh yeah, the stupid mark." Tom showed them his hand. "I don't have the mark either and I don't plan on getting one."

"Who's Eric?" Logan asked, confused by all this new information. Is this Eric the reason she gave him her cheek instead of a kiss on the lips?

"It's a long story, Logan." She blew out a puff of air. "My timepiece was taken away from me and the people there tried to make me a slave."

Logan threw a furious look at Tom. "Is he—"

Audrey ran and stopped him. "No, not him, Logan!" She tapped Logan on his chest, calming him down a bit. "He's the one that I was supposed to find, the one in the letter. There were other people there that did this to me. He helped me and gave me his timepiece to go to his world and get another one." She held up the timepiece. "This one."

Logan inspected the device. "It looks just like the one you had when you left."

"By getting this timepiece, I ended up in these clothes."

"Your hair looks different though. It's fluffy." He reached out and touched her hair. "Wow! It's so soft. It really makes you look so... beautiful."

He put his hands on her waist and pulled her in closer. Audrey grabbed his hands and pulled them off.

"What's wrong?" Something was definitely different about her; he wasn't at all sure he liked it.

"Oh, Logan," she said walking toward the metal cave. "You should see 1776. It's so beautiful. And all the buildings in 2052 are so unbelievable. The buildings are bigger and taller than the ancient buildings at home."

"Are they really?" Logan said, noticing how she dodged the question. "Who's Eric?"

"And they have these machines that make water and ice and others that can wash and dry your clothes. It's amazing!" she hedged.

"Who's Eric?" he repeated.

"My son," Tom said.

"His son," Audrey replied at the same time.

Logan's cheeks were a bright red and he noticed his lips twitching. He loved her and thought she loved him. But now... she wouldn't look him in the eye. Was there someone else? Was it Eric? They had been friends since they were kids. This seemed to be the natural course for them to go—to become lovers. Wasn't she supposed find Thomas Lynch and then come back? She wasn't supposed to fall for someone in another time!

He tried putting his hands on her waist and pulling her in closer to kiss her. Audrey put her hands on his shoulders and lightly pushed him away and ran to Tom, who was now looking at the panel with the symbols. His stomach started to ache.

"We didn't know what those symbols were," she said pointing to the panel, as Logan approached. Audrey continued, "We pushed on them, but nothing happened at first. Then eventually, the door opened."

Tom knelt in front of the tiles. "There are five tiles that open the door. If you press the correct one, a small current is created. When all five tiles are pressed correctly, the door opens. If you press the wrong tile or the same tile twice, the current is removed and the door doesn't open."

"So which tiles should be pressed for the door to open?"

"The tiles with the numbers two, five, ten, six and twelve," Tom said as he pressed them.

"Those are numbers?" Logan said in disbelief as he stared at Audrey.

"Yes," Tom nodded. "They're called roman numerals."

The bolt inside the door slid. The door unlocked.

Audrey disappeared into the cave, while Tom sat on the sand by the door and looked out into the water. Logan came and sat next to him. Neither said a word to each other.

Tom broke the silence. "What do you have to eat around here?"

"I haven't eaten in two days." Logan grimaced.

Audrey joined them and Tom asked her the same question. "We didn't find any food here, but here is the—" she raised her hand with a piece of paper in it.

Tom stood up, raised a palm. "Hold that thought!"

He disappeared into one of the passageways and was gone. Logan was alone with Audrey. She just smiled saying nothing. He was still deciding what to say when Tom reappeared with two cans and a large container that had 'RICE' written on it.

Audrey took a can and frowned at it. "How do we open these?"

"If I know my brother, he would have put a can opener inside with the rice."

Audrey mumbled, "I can't believe we missed all this food."

There was some metal object, like tongs, inside the container of rice. Tom took it and opened a can. Inside was a thick solid piece of blob. It looked like the Jello in New Scranton. The smell of it made everyone gag. Logan covered his nose. Audrey turned green and started to retch.

"The soup is bad. We'll just make rice," Tom shrugged, and opened the other can. "Take these and rinse them out and fill them with water."

Logan took the cans from Tom and dumped their contents in the ocean, washed them out, and filled them with water as instructed; he was too hungry to protest. When he returned with the water-filled cans, he saw what Audrey was doing and started to dig into the sand. Tom stared wide-eyed in amazement.

It was quite a bit of effort, but eventually they found a branch. Logan gathered some rocks and formed a sharp edge on one of them by chipping away at it with one of the blunt rocks, cutting the branch into smaller pieces.

"Wow!" Tom said, watching them dig. "That is really... who would have thought... Wow."

"In 1776 there were many trees here," Audrey said. "Something must have happened to make them end up underground."

Tom started a fire and cooked the rice in the cans. Once they finished cooking Audrey got one can and Logan the other; Logan wasted no time eating.

"My god! You remind me of Eric," Audrey giggled and smiled. Tom burst into laughter.

Logan didn't like this Eric person. Was this the man she had feelings for? He glared at Audrey. "You must have spent a lot of time with him to make that kind of observation."

"His dad eats the same way. Look."

Logan turned to look at Tom who was not eating anything at all. "Is Eric as fat as him?"

"No," she chuckled. "He's as thin as you."

"Yeah, right," he said, looking away.

"I didn't spend that much time with him," she said. Her voice cracked nervously. "I just went to get the other timepiece."

Logan picked up on the lie. So many things ran through his mind. *Why not just tell me the truth? Just tell me you like someone else because I'm just not good enough for you. Break my heart why don't you?* He didn't know how to handle this rage of jealousy he felt inside.

"Do you have rice in your village?" Tom asked.

"In our city," Audrey corrected him. "Yes, we do. We grow a lot of it on the west side."

"A quarter of my father's farm," Logan said and then got lost in thought thinking about his parents and reliving the images of how they died.

"That's a lot of rice I suppose, assuming of course that your father's farm is big."

Logan could feel the tears welling in his eyes. He missed his parents; this had to be a dream, a really bad dream, that he wanted to wake up from. He rubbed his eyes with his fists and stared out into the ocean.

"What's wrong?" Tom looked to Audrey, when Logan didn't reply.

"His dad was the ambassador to the Feds." Audrey leaned over and squeezed Logan's hand. He clutched hers, raising it to kiss. She didn't resist this time.

"Oh. I remember you telling me about that," Tom said, then looked to Logan, "I'm so sorry."

They spent most of the time in the cave away from the sun and the fire. Tom had taken off most of his clothes. Logan dug up more wood for the fire and Tom cooked more rice.

The day had been warm with a cool breeze coming in from the ocean. The cliffs now started casting a shadow over the beach and the breeze was much colder. Audrey stood up and looked out into the dark blue ocean as the orange sky got darker.

*She is so beautiful.*

"The nights here are cold and last longer," she explained to Tom.

"No need to worry about that. I bet the generator still works,"

"Generator?" Her face twisted in confusion.

"It's what keeps the lights on."

"But those don't work anymore." Logan went over to the emergency switch and pressed the red button a few times and nothing happened.

"Those are the emergency lights. To be honest, I'm surprised they worked at all. I would have thought that the batteries would have died a long time ago."

Tom removed a panel from the floor in the center of the main room. Laying on the ground with his hand in the opening, Logan heard a click and a green light on the wall in front of them turned on. Then another click followed by some humming, which intensified into a soft whine. Another click and another green light appeared on the wall. When the third green light appeared, a white flicker came from the ceiling. It wasn't long before the flickering light became steady and bright.

The door remained opened and the wind could be felt blowing in cold air. Tom went to close it.

"It gets cold in here," Logan argued.

Tom moved to the wall where a switch was. "Oh, it's already on." He turned a knob and warm air started coming out of the vent instantly.

Logan rubbed his hands together and sighed. "I wish I'd known." He turned to Audrey and asked her to tell him everything that had happened since she'd left.

Audrey told Logan what happened when she arrived in 1776 up to how she'd been chased to Benjamin Franklin's house. He could tell she had grazed over her encounters with Eric; she still couldn't look him in the eye when she said his name.

Tom stifled a yawn.

"So much has happened." She took in a deep breath. "When I went back to 1776, their world was so different from ours. They captured me and tried to make me a slave: *twice*. The first time I escaped, I made a promise with God to free the slaves when I got back."

"God?" Logan asked.

She talked about someone named Lilly and a promise she made to help end slavery here in this time.

"This god helped you find Tom?" Logan asked, noticing that Tom was now snoring softly, sprawled out on the floor.

"Yes, and then Tom sent me to his time, where he lives, to get another timepiece."

"Where you met Eric," he stated flatly.

"Where I met Eric," she said, squirming a little.

He stared at her, trying to get into her mind and find out who this Eric person was; and more importantly, how much she liked him. "After listening to your story, it doesn't sound like you made a promise to any god. You made a promise to a slave that helped you escape."

"I promised her, originally," Audrey conceded. "And then I promised God."

"What happens if you don't keep the promise?"

"Why wouldn't I keep it?"

"You're here already. The slave girl is dead." Logan shrugged his shoulders.

"You think I'm making this all up? You don't think I spoke with God," she scoffed irritably. "I never once thought about breaking my promise."

---

When Tom woke up, he found both Audrey and Logan fast asleep on the cement floor. He went and opened the door; he'd let the morning light and the sound of the ocean wake them. It didn't take long.

"Good morning!" Tom said. The salty smell of the ocean and cool breeze reminded him of the New Jersey beaches. "Are you all ready to leave this place?"

"How can we leave?" Logan asked.

Tom threw the giant orange raft on the floor in front of Audrey and Logan. It looked like a large cinder block by the way it had been compressed.

"Where did you find this?" Audrey asked, placing her hands on it. "What is it?"

"It's a raft. And I found it here," he said, pointing to the back.

"We're all supposed to fit in that?" Logan asked.

"It's inflatable. Come on outside and I'll show you."

Tom picked up the raft and walked out of the cave. He unfolded the raft and found one the blow tubes and started blowing on it and motioned for Audrey and Logan to blow through the other ones. Hesitantly they began to do the same. Within a few minutes, the raft had fully unfolded. Half an hour later everyone was exhausted, but the raft wasn't anywhere near inflated.

"I think we're done," Audrey said, collapsing onto the sand.

Tom shook his head. "Not yet. It's almost halfway there. We'll rest for a few minutes and then continue."

By midmorning, they had the raft fully inflated. Tom found the paddles stashed in the cabin.

"This thing will float?" Logan asked.

"Yes, it will," Tom said. He grabbed the raft by the ropes and dragged it out into the water, past the crashing waves. *Woah!* The water was freezing cold. It felt like the energy in his body was being sucked out. He started shivering, calling for them to come out and climb into the raft.

Audrey and Logan waddled through the cold water and climbed into the inflated raft. The center sank down and he worried for a second that it wouldn't support them. Both of them hung onto the sides as if their lives depended on it.

"Don't worry. We won't sink." He said, more confidently than he felt.

"Are you sure?" Logan asked.

"Well, unless someone punches a hole in it, yes, I'm sure."

Tom and Logan used the paddles to move the boat in the direction of the city.

"We left the door open to the cave!" Audrey said, looking back at the cove.

"No, I closed it when I got the paddles," Tom assured her and noticed her hanging on, afraid. "Don't worry. This will be fun!"

They continued paddling.

"By the way, I wanted to show you the letter I found that told me to come and find you." She reached into her pocket and sighed. "I must have dropped it in the cave," she said wistfully.

"It's all right. I believe you." Tom smiled.

"That's not why I wanted to show it to you. I was hoping that you would recognize the writing. Maybe someone from your time... maybe Eric..." Audrey was close to tears but somehow found a way not to cry. She looked out to the water, drifting in thought.

They paddled for almost an hour. No signs of the city, only cliffs along the coast.

"I don't see the city," Audrey said.

"Are we going the right way?" Tom asked.

"Yes, we are," Logan roared defensively.

## Timepieces

Thirty more minutes went by and the cliffs towered on their left while the expanse of the ocean was on their right. As they reached the edge of the cliffs they came into the view of a bay. Logan pointed and shouted, "There it is!"

One building stood in the distance. It wasn't very tall. A thin layer of black smoke blanketed the city—they had smog.

Two fishing boats approached the raft and greeted Audrey. The boats were about the size of the raft, allowing two to three people to fit inside. The fishermen escorted the group to the shore where they were met by two soldiers.

Audrey waved at the soldiers who looked surprised to see her.

"What are you doing here?" she asked them.

"The mayor told us to capture whoever came off the boat." The soldier looked at everyone and said, "I don't think he was expecting you to be on it."

Audrey jumped out of the boat first. "We need to see my father immediately!" she said, walking ahead of the soldiers toward the city. Logan followed with Tom right behind him.

The soldiers wore a robe and belt that went around their waist and across their chest. They looked more like policemen than soldiers.

They all entered the mayor's office and found him talking with another man. Immediately he stopped. His face turned to surprise as he saw them entering.

"What is this?" he said, noticing the clothes she had on. "Are they dressing this way in New Scranton?"

"Daddy!" Audrey cried out. She went around the desk and hugged her father. "Daddy! It was awful."

He returned her hug and looked quizzically at Tom. He held her at a distance. "What was awful?"

"Everyone at the embassy is dead!"

"What?" He stood up, almost knocking her down. "Is this a joke?"

"They killed my father and mother." Logan was trying his best not to show any emotions. "They killed them, cutting them up and putting the pieces in boxes. They eat people, sir!"

"What?" he said in disbelief. "Why... Are you sure this is what happened?"

"We saw it with our own eyes, Daddy!"

"I don't understand," he said. "Why would they eat people? What about the animals they raise?"

"I don't know, Daddy. Logan and I barely escaped."

"And they dressed you this way? Why?"

"A lot has happened to me since then. But right now, we have more important things to worry about."

"How did you two get away?"

"We managed to escape by hiding on top of the water tower." Logan sat down on one of the chairs facing the desk, as Tom hovered at the door, feeling uncomfortable. "We almost got caught. Audrey's slave shouted for the guards. We escaped down the river. When we got to the ocean, there were Fed soldiers along the cliffs. We fell into the water and found a cove with a metal cave."

The mayor listened and stared at Tom. "And who is this?"

"This is Thomas Lynch," Audrey said. "Tom, this is my dad, Mayor Oberon of

Milestown."

Tom saw the resemblances between Audrey and her father. They had the same eyes and lips. His hair was not as curly as he somehow thought it should be. The mayor spoke in a way that made others know that he was the authority here. Tom extended his hand to the mayor. The mayor just raised his hand.

"I'm Oberon Bushnell. Welcome to my city," the mayor said. "You helped my daughter escape?"

"Actually, I did," Tom said somewhat flippant. "But not from the Feds."

"If you're not a Fed, then who are you?"

"No, Daddy!" Audrey said. "He's from... He's not a Fed."

"I see." He paused. "We have a guest. Let's get back to the house so we can be more at ease. I'll have the servants prepare something for you to eat."

Tom's face lit at the mention of food. "That sounds like a great idea."

# Chapter 36

Tom noticed the houses in the city were made of stone. The mayor's house was large, possibly having a dozen rooms. It looked like Frankenstein's version of a mansion with some parts made of stone and other parts from the houses of 2052. They attached the different pieces with something that looked like tar. Audrey's mother greeted everyone. The resemblance between Audrey and her mother was remarkable.

Mrs. Bushnell squinted, staring at Tom in confusion. "Have we met?" she asked.

"I don't think we have."

"I'm sure we have," she said, looking him over. "It'll come to me."

"I'm pretty sure we haven't." Tom smiled at her, sensing that she disliked him.

The servants were given commands to prepare food for everyone as they gathered outside on the patio and sat on plastic chairs. Moments later servants came out with drinks and food.

"Oh, Daddy!" Audrey said. "In their world, they have running water in their houses to bathe in, and machines that can make ice. They have buildings ten times taller than the ancient one here in Milestown."

Milestown? The name made him think of his brother whom he missed dearly, then chuckled in thought that a city would be named after someone named Miles. *Hey brother, they named a city after you.*

"Their world?" The mayor listened to Audrey with an intrigued expression. "Where are you from?" the mayor asked, interrupting her descriptions.

"He is from another time," Audrey said matter-of-factly.

Mr. Bushnell almost choked on his drink. "What do you mean 'from another time?'"

"It's true, sir," Logan interjected. "We found this device addressed to Audrey."

Audrey took the device and handed it to her father. He examined it.

"When Audrey activated it, she disappeared," Logan explained.

"It's a time machine," Tom said. "I built them. You can travel to any time you like."

The mayor listened as Tom explained how the device worked and it didn't take long for his face to register understanding.

"Then we can use these to change events," the mayor said. "We can save the ambassador and the entire staff!"

"Well…" Tom rubbed his neck, "Yes, but one device works for one person. Your daughter is the one that found out about that. We only have two and I need mine to get back home."

"If all we need to do is warn the ambassador a week before it happens, then we'll be fine!" Audrey said.

Something was gnawing at Tom. The plan made sense, yet somehow, he knew it wouldn't work.

"I don't think it will work," Tom echoed his thoughts to the group. "I think that because we are here now with the events as they have already happened, we cannot go back and change them."

"We should at least try," Logan said as his eyes filled with hope. "Audrey and I can go back and warn the others."

Tom shook his head. "That could pose a problem. If you see yourself in the past and alter the course of events, then you will never find the timepiece and Audrey will never find me and we won't be here having this conversation."

"And that is what we want!" the mayor said. "We want them to succeed so that you won't be here."

"Thank you," Tom scowled. "But that's the problem. There will be two of them from that point onward—the ones that will be in that city prior to the events before they happen and the ones that go and tell them of the events that are going to happen."

"But won't we disappear once we change the future?" Audrey asked. "Since I won't find the timepiece afterward?"

"Time doesn't change the events that are happening. If you go back, then you are there regardless of where you came from." He saw the glazed look in everyone's eyes.

"This all sounds like guesswork and we won't know the answers, or the problems, until we try saving my parents," Logan insisted. He snatched the timepiece out of Audrey's hands. "How do I set the time?"

Audrey looked at Tom, who kept mum. She took the timepiece back, turned it on, and set the date to a week before the Feds attacked the embassy.

"I'll go with you. I can help." Audrey said holding out her hand for Tom to give her his timepiece.

Tom stared at her, not quite ready to give up his only way home. Yet, he wouldn't be the one to stop them from trying to save their own people. Reluctantly, he handed her the timepiece.

Audrey turned it on and set the date and then said to Logan, "Now!"

They pressed their blue button simultaneously. Nothing happened. Audrey tried pressing the button again. Still nothing happened.

"It's not working!" Audrey cried. "Let me try 1776," she said and pressed the blue button on her timepiece. Tom noticed her twitch.

"It does work when I go to 1776. Why won't it work when I go to a week ago? When I set the date, I just stay here in this time."

They all looked at Tom.

"I think there is a law that we cannot break no matter how much we try," Tom said.

"A law?" Mr. Bushnell asked.

Tom grabbed a slice of bread from the table. "Yes, like the law of gravity. If I let go of this piece of bread in my hand, the law of gravity dictates that it will fall to the ground." At that point, Tom opened his hand and let the bread fall to the ground. "The same thing might be happening with the timepieces. There's a constraint that prevents someone from going somewhere they already exist."

"But how does this thing know we already exist in that time?" Logan asked.

"It's not that this device that's preventing you from traveling to that time, it's time itself that's preventing you from traveling to that time."

Audrey handed Tom back his timepiece and stared at him expectantly. Tom raised his brow. "You want me to try it?"

"If you're right, it'll work because you were never here before."

Tom took the timepiece and pressed the button and found himself on the patio. Three women were sitting. One of them looked up at Tom. It was Mrs. Bushnell.

"What are you doing here? Who are you?" she shrieked. "Guards! Guards!"

Two uniformed men rushed through the patio doors, surprising Tom. For a moment, it felt like the wolves were chasing him again. He pressed the blue button and was back with Audrey and everyone else in the present. No one had noticed he had left. He turned to Mrs. Bushnell and said, "Mrs. Bushnell, I was wrong. We have met before." She tilted her head and stared with glazed eyes not comprehending. "Think about what happened last week on this patio."

She shook her head once, twice thinking and then her eyes almost popped out of her head. "So that was you?" Tom smiled and nodded. "Oh my! It does work." She seemed surprised and pressed her fingers to her lips. "Oberon, we need to save our people!"

"Is it possible? Can we send you to save our people?" the mayor asked.

"No, we can't." Tom turned off the timepiece. "Anywhere we go in time is where we are meant to be. For us, it may seem like we chose to be there, but it isn't a choice. We are destined to be at that place. I know that now."

He received blank stares. People shuffled in their chairs. No-one grasped what he was saying.

"If I go back and tell the ambassador to leave, then you'll never go to the vault, or the metal cave as Audrey calls it, and you'll never meet me and I won't be here to do what it is you want me to do, and that's to warn the ambassador that he'll be dead in a week." He let it sink in before he spoke again. "Everything that has happened or is happening is supposed to happen that way and there's nothing we can do to change the outcome, regardless of how awful it may be."

"Then this timepiece is worthless," the mayor sighed.

"If you want to change the effects of time," Tom explained, "then yes, it is worthless."

"Why would I want to use this then?" the mayor asked in abhorrence.

"To observe," Tom said, moving his hands up. "To see why things happened the way they did."

"I can read about that in a history book."

"But history is usually written from one point of view," Tom argued. "Almost always. It's very subjective."

"What does that mean?"

"It means that you don't get the point of view of everyone involved."

"We must at least try!" the mayor cried, clenching his fists.

Tom looked at the stricken mayor and his wife. He needed to give them a rational reason that this course of action would go nowhere. He addressed Audrey's mother. "When I went back last week and appeared in this room, Mrs. Bushnell, how did you react?"

"I thought you were an intruder. I didn't know what you wanted."

"So, you called the guards."

He then turned to the mayor, "And what would you have done once the guards captured me?"

"I would have tried to determine what your intentions were, of course."

"And if I told you that I was from the future, how would you have answered, not knowing what you know now?"

The mayor thought for a moment. "I wouldn't have believed your story. I would've thought you were a spy from another city and had you killed."

"And nothing would've changed except *my* timeline. I would be dead. So, can you see now why this won't work?"

---

Tom Listened to Audrey explain that the black objects on the walls found in the dug-up homes were for watching moving pictures. She entertained them with accounts of how Eric would cook whole meals in just a few seconds in a small, magical box. How they cleaned their dishes in a machine right there in the kitchen. Tom suppressed a chuckled—when had Eric suddenly become so house-proud? The thought of Eric made his heart ache; he longed to be back home with his family, but knew his place was here in this time. He had unfinished work to do—he just didn't know yet what it was.

After a few hours of her stories, the mayor stood up, and smiled warmly at his daughter. "As interesting as this is my dear, it's getting late. Let's talk more about your adventures in the morning." He turned to Tom and Logan. "We have prepared rooms for you to sleep. The servants will show you where they are." He squeezed Logan's shoulder, "Logan, I will avenge your father. We'll make sure the Feds pay for what they've done."

---

After a good night's sleep, Tom found himself at the dining room again waiting for breakfast; he was the first one there. The bed had been surprisingly comfortable, made from a sackcloth filled with leaves and sand; it must have been all that time spent in 1776 at Ben's house, he mused.

It wasn't long before the rest of the household began to file into the dining room. Tom greeted them as they entered.

"Don't tell me," said the Mayor, "you were the first one here?"

"Yes, I'm afraid I was," Tom said apologetically and then leaned toward Audrey who sat next to him. "Was that wrong?" he whispered. "Should I have waited for your father to come in first?"

"No," she chuckled. "He's just being silly. Did you sleep well?"

"Actually, yes!"

Breakfast looked like oatmeal served with a cube of cornbread and a drink that tasted like carrot juice with lime. The oatmeal was spicy hot. Tom started to choke.

"Is everything all right?" the mayor asked.

"It's spicy." Tom gulped down the rest of his juice.

"Really? I don't think so." The mayor reached over and dipped his spoon in Tom's bowl, scooping up some oatmeal.

Audrey was surprised at what her father had done. "Dad, that's so rude!"

Her father shrugged. "It's not like he's going to eat the rest of it." He ate the spoonful of oatmeal and then said, "This is not spicy at all."

The servants brought Tom some other foods to eat; he waited for the throbbing sensation of the hot spices to settle in his mouth before attempting to eat anything else.

"Perhaps, since history can't be changed," Mr. Bushnell said, tucking into his own plate, "we can visit these places you mentioned and see for ourselves what it's like."

"Daddy, just because history doesn't change, doesn't mean you can't get hurt. They tried to make me a slave and when I ran away, they whipped me." She pulled her dress down off her shoulder far enough so that her father could view the scars.

"They did this to you?" he said with an appalled expression. He turned to Tom ready to rip his face off. "*Your* people did this to her?"

The scars surprised Tom. This was the first time he had seen them.

"No, Daddy. It wasn't his people. It wasn't his time," she said. "It was 1776, the year the letter told me to go and find him."

"And why that year? What was so important about that year that you needed to go there to find this man and get hurt in the process?" He leaned in toward Tom. His face was filled with anger.

Audrey came between Tom and her father. "Daddy chillax! I don't know why they sent me to that time. Maybe it was to learn things and to keep a promise."

"A promise? What promise?"

A messenger entered the room and interrupted them before she could explain. "Excuse me, Mr. Mayor." The messenger bowed his head. "There are ten soldiers outside the city on the beach and their commander wishes to speak with you. They say they are from a city called Williamsport."

The mayor's face filled with rage. "Why are they at the beach?"

"They came in two boats that looked similar to the craft your daughter arrived in, sir," the messenger responded.

Tom became curious. Someone had found two rafts and figured out how to inflate them. Not altogether a difficult thing to do, but where would they have found them in this time and why would they come here to talk with the mayor?

"Take them to my office," the mayor ordered, "and send the sheriff to kill everyone at the Fed embassy!"

"No!" Tom interrupted. "I'm sorry. But right now, the Feds don't know that Audrey and Logan are here. Why not keep a close eye on them? Invite the ambassador over and find out as much as you can before... killing them. This way, you can prepare for whatever they are about to do."

He turned to the messenger. "Bring the commander to my office." To Tom, he looked at him with a slight disgust, "You speak wisely... even though you don't look it."

The mayor left to meet this commander from Williamsport. Mrs. Bushnell's face lined with concern. She scurried off after her husband with a polite apology to Tom.

Audrey called a servant over and kindly asked him to clean the table and bring water for everyone. After the servant did as she asked, she thanked him.

Logan looked as surprised as the servant. "You've never treated any of your servants like that before."

"The world in 1776 has made me see things in a different light," she said.

"What else is there to do around here?" Asked Tom, "Are there any places to go, sights to see? It's kind of boring just sitting around. Plus, there's nothing for me to eat."

"How about I show you around a little later?" Audrey said. "I have a few things I need to take care of. Afterward, I can show you around the city." Throwing Tom a bright smile, she upped and left without another word.

Logan watched her go.

Tom nudged him with his leg, and whispered, "Tell her how you feel."

"I did." Logan sighed, still gazing at the empty doorway she'd not long ago exited, as if waiting for her to reappear.

"Oh?" Tom raised a brow. "And she rejected you?"

"I thought things were going well, but since she came back from *your* world she seems to be pushing me away."

"You need to give her the one thing she's missing: romance," Tom said raising a hand and waiting for Logan to slap it.

Logan grimaced. "Romance?"

Tom looked at Logan a little puzzled. "I'm sure that word still exists today. *Romance? Romantic?*"

Logan stared at him.

"Try surprising her by doing things she likes, before she asks you to do it."

"Like what?"

Tom waved a hand in the air. "I don't know…. like a picnic at the beach! A boat ride through the Great Bay! Write her a love letter. You can wash the dishes after dinner! Now that would surprise *any* woman."

"Are you married?"

"Not anymore."

"Your wife is dead?"

"No." Tom was a little taken aback that Logan would jump to that conclusion. "She left me."

"For another man?"

"No. She just left."

"Oh. That's even worse."

"What do you mean 'that's even worse'?"

"I mean, maybe you shouldn't be the one giving advice." Logan raised a brow and snickered.

Tom's mouth dropped open, then he muttered. "Fair enough, fair enough."

---

Tom was excited, as he set off with Audrey and Logan, for a private tour around their city. Many similarities existed between the past and the present. Some of the buildings that existed back in 2052 were still being used in Audrey's time. They had patched up with whatever material they could find, it seemed. There were some new structures, but they looked more like primitive dwellings by comparison and certainly not as durable as the older buildings from Tom's time.

A soldier approached them. "The mayor wants to see Mr. Tolbert."

"I have no idea why your father would want to see me," Logan shrugged, then followed the soldier.

Tom walked to a granite monolith that stood a little over six feet.

"This was dedicated to the founder of Milestown and our first Mayor, Miles Lynch," she said standing behind him.

"Yeah." Tom nodded in astonishment. "Miles is my brother." *So, this place is named after you, brother. But why?*

Audrey put her hands to her head and closed her eyes. "Of course. Miles Lynch. Thomas Lynch. I didn't make the connection in the letter."

Tom read the inscription aloud.

*This monument, built in the year 23, is dedicated to the founder of the city of Milestown for his wisdom and leadership that kept us all together through the good and bad times. We start a new life and commemorate 2060, the last year of a dead civilization, and year 0, the first year of a new way of life.*

*To Miles Lynch, for whom this city carries the name: First Mayor (2052-2059).*

*Alexis Lynch-Ireland: (niece of Miles Lynch, Commissioned this statue)*

Tom put his hand on the tablet, touching the inscription of the name at the bottom.

"Who is she?" Audrey asked.

"My daughter," Tom said.

"There's nothing in the history books about you or Eric." Her voice quivered.

"Maybe we never made it to the cave, or maybe we died somewhere else," Tom whispered in a croaky voice, thick with emotion. "Maybe we escaped to another time. Perhaps we used the timepieces to escape." He paced back and forth, clearly worried. "Why wasn't she with us? But... She lived farther away from the vault. It would have made more sense for her to have gone to her uncle," he muttered.

"How could Eric have escaped with you to another time?" Audrey asked, a nervous twitch in her voice. "He didn't have a timepiece!"

Tom looked at Audrey and her timepiece. "I made one for him. I was going to make another for everyone else when I got back," Tom revealed.

"But we only found the one you made for me. We didn't see another!" she cried, the back of her palm pressed against her lips and her eyes opened wider in shock. "If we had found that one, he could have come with me and he would be here right now."

Tom's face flooded with guilt. "I put it in his backpack. He probably never looked in it. It has so many pockets," Tom studied the monolith. Suddenly, his face lit up. "Aha!" He snapped his fingers and smiled. "I'm going back to 2060."

"Why that year?"

"Because that's when things changed. That's when your calendar started."

"Why don't you go back to the year you came from? That makes more sense."

"No! I'm here now and going home would take too long, plus Alexis lives in D.C. By the time I find her, it might already be too late. But we know she's here in 2060. She holds the answers to what happened here."

"I'm coming with you," she said, turning her timepiece on and setting the date.

"No! I need your timepiece. In case I need to bring her back with me."

Audrey nodded in understanding and handed over her timepiece. Tom set it to 2060, clicked on the blue button, and disappeared.

# Chapter 37

**Milestown, September 15, 2060**

Tom found himself in a town that had been destroyed. It looked as though a volcano had erupted close by and spewed ash everywhere; But Pennsylvania had no volcanoes. The black ash felt rough like hard dirt, as he massaged it between his fingers. *What happened here?*

The early morning sun hid behind dull, grey clouds, set against an orange sky. No noise could be heard, no wind, just a gloomy day. The ocean water was already here, the smell of salt in the air distinct. In the distance, the building that Audrey called the Ancient Tower already had the large, gaping holes on one side just like in her time, over two hundred years from now. Other buildings were buried under a layer of ash; only the rooftops remained above ground.

The monolith dedicated to his brother wasn't here.

There was a pit that had been dug up to expose a building, which looked as if it had been blown up from the inside. Debris was scattered away from the base of the building.

Tom followed the river to the bay where he found people on small wooden boats in the water. Others stood along the shore—three adults and six kids. These people might know about Alexis! He called out and ran toward them. The children and two of the adults ran toward the city immediately; the third adult pulled out a rifle and pointed it at Tom.

"Whoa!" Tom said, holding his hands up.

"Leave us alone!" the man shouted. "We don't have any food."

"I don't want food. I'm looking for my daughter."

"We don't have her either," the man said. "Keep your hands up!"

Tom did as he was told. "Her name is Alexis Lynch. Have you heard of her?"

"If you're her father, where the hell have you been and why are you wearing that costume?"

As Tom was about to speak, noises erupted in the distance. He turned to look towards the source of the sound. The man holding the gun kept his eyes on Tom. Four adults ran toward them bearing weapons, some children tailing behind at a distance. As they got closer, Tom recognized two of the adults and an overwhelming sense of relief washed over him. Tom made to put his hands down.

"Keep them up!" the man with the gun shouted.

"It's all right, Paul," one of the men said running up to join them. "It's Alexis' dad."

"Patrick!" Tom said as tears filled his eyes. "Where are Alexis and Eric?"

"Alexis is at the house taking care of the kids. We don't know anything about Eric."

# Timepieces

A young black man came forward and nodded. "I'm Marcus." He was handsome. A long face, round eyes, and a flared nose, he towered above most of the other men.

Marcus shifted on the spot, like he wanted to say more. Tom nodded back, confused. "Hi."

"I'm Alexis' husband. We've been married for over six years now."

Tom remembered Alexis mentioning him.

"Can you take me to her?"

They walked further inland with Marcus and Patrick in the lead, Tom close behind. The kids followed, their excited banter a welcome distraction from the destruction all around them. Most of the houses they walked by had huge, gaping holes in their walls, roofs blown away, yet several looked like they'd been recently repaired. Turning a corner, the path opened up to a field carpeted by tall cornstalks. He saw cabbage, carrots, and broccoli growing in other fields surrounding them. It was a miracle how all of this bounty could exist and flourish when everything else around them looked dead.

They eventually came to a dug-up building and descended into it. Marcus ran into the house ahead of the group.

---

Alexis was reading to Monica in her bedroom and heard someone coming into the house, racing up the stairs. She smiled as Marcus hurried into the room.

"What's the rush?" She asked accepting Marcus' kiss. He looked at her somberly. She frowned. "What's wrong?"

Marcus stood there not saying a word. The storm door opened downstairs. "Your dad is here."

"What?"

"Your dad. He's here. Downstairs."

Alexis went downstairs and couldn't believe her father was standing in the living room. Their eyes met, then his gaze fell on the little girl standing next to her. She stood holding her daughter's hand and approached her father.

"Daddy!" she cried, embracing him. She pulled herself away from his embrace, wiping her eyes, and turned to Monica standing next to her with a smile. "This is your granddaughter Monica."

"Hello, Monica." Tom bent down and put out his hand.

Alexis nudged her daughter. "Say hello to your grandfather."

Monica took Tom's hand and he shook hers very lightly. Everyone laughed.

"We thought you were dead," Alexis wiped away more tears, as they rolled down her face uncontrollably now. "Where have you been? And why are you wearing that?"

"It's a long story," Tom said, putting his hand on her arm gently. "It'll take some time to explain." He looked around the room. Did he recognize any of these people? Some of them he'd last seen when they were kids. "Just tell me what happened here?"

Alexis put her hand on her forehead and pushed back her hair and gave her dad an odd look. "What do you mean? We left the city in chaos and came here."

"I mean what happened after 2052?"

Everyone gasped.

"How do you not know what's happened since then?" Patrick asked. "My father died trying to keep us alive. We've fought other people wanting to take over this place."

Alexis stared at her dad as if he were a ghost. He put his hand on hers. "I know I've been missing for a long time. Please, just tell me what happened."

Alexis sat on the floor and let her daughter sit on her lap. The pain of remembering things that had happened such a long time ago brought back a rush of grief. Her father stood in the middle of the room oblivious to what had happened in the last eight years. Marcus gently squeezed her shoulder. She put her hand on top of his. Alexis looked up at her father. "It all started in September… of 2052…"

## Washington D.C., September 8, 2052

Alexis put away next Wednesday's court briefings and headed over to the living room to relax. Lounging on the cold beige leather sofa, she flicked through the TV channels, landing on the news. The stories never seemed to change about the Middle East. The Moslem Jihad was already inside Israeli territory; they had taken Haifa and Nazareth, and in a few days, the reporter speculated, they would take Tel Aviv.

There was some good news. Unemployment had decreased, falling from 37 to 35 percent as the military acquired more resources for the war effort. A two percent drop was good, but the stock market had spiraled down out of control. Alexis remembered her dad telling her that he had sold several high-priced stocks and converted U.S. dollars into Chinese Yuan and Euros. They would be financially secure—at least for a while.

As the segment ended, the time was announced by the newsreader: 7:47AM. *Time to get ready for the day.* Today was sunny, but the trees in the yard were starting to turn; summer was winding down. Glancing at the giant sun-shaped thermostat on the balcony, it showed the outside temperature was seventy-two degrees. Still warm enough. She rifled through her closet, eyeing Marcus' favorite summer dress, plucking out a pair of high-heeled sandals to complete the ensemble.

From the bedroom she could hear a news reporter on the television speaking excitedly. The words *Los Angeles* caught her attention. *Mom.* She walked back into the living room and searched for the remote, turning up the volume.

"We're hearing reports that a major earthquake has just hit two of the largest cities in California. I repeat, Los Angeles and San Francisco have just been hit by twin earthquakes. We're getting reports that both areas have been struck by an earthquake with a magnitude of 8.5. We have not been able to confirm that as of yet. When we get—"

The phone rang. She snatched up the phone. "Oh my god, Marcus, did you hear? There's been a huge earthquake in California! My mom lives in California!"

"No, I didn't hear a thing. I was calling to—"

"My mom, Marcus! She might be hurt! I need to call her now."

"Alexis… Alexis," Marcus spoke calmly through the phone, "if there was a major earthquake in California, everyone will be calling, you won't get through. The phone lines might even be dead." Neither said a word, and then Marcus spoke. "I'm coming over. I'll be there soon."

"Okay," she said, weakly. She wandered in a daze into the bedroom and slipped under the sheets. Her stomach was tied in a thousand knots. She knew Marcus was right, but she couldn't help herself; Not knowing was the worst. She dialed her mom's number, waiting for it to ring. It went to voicemail. "Mom? Mom, call me when you get this."

She dialed Eric and the phone just rang and went to voicemail. She yelled into the phone crying, "Eric, there was an earthquake in California. Mom might be in trouble. Call me the minute you get this."

Tears fell onto the phone as she dialed her dad. He wasn't answering. *Where could he be?* She didn't leave a message.

She tried her mom again. "All circuits are down. Please try your call again later."

"Damn it!" she swore aloud, throwing the phone angrily onto the comforter. A lump of anxiety lodged in her throat.

When Alexis woke up, the afternoon was almost over. The sun had shifted to the west side of the house, no longer shining directly into the room. She hadn't even realized she'd fallen asleep. Rubbing sore eyes, she realized she must have been crying. A banging sounded; the front door. Scuttling out of bed and making her way across the apartment, she could hear Marcus yelling at the top of his lungs.

"Alexis are you in there? Open the damn door!"

She unlocked the door and Marcus barged into the apartment.

"Did you hear what happened?" His voice crackled with dread.

"What?" she closed her eyes not wanting to hear more dreadful news.

"No!" Marcus hollered, waving his arms in the air, "Two tsunamis hit California about half an hour ago! The entire Pacific coastline from Mexico to Alaska was hit hard. The water went about five miles inland, all along the coast. It destroyed everything in its path."

Alexis dropped to the floor. She wanted to throw up. "My mom..." she choked.

Marcus immediately dropped and enveloped her in his strong warm arms. A voice was speaking quietly in the background; she must have left the TV on. Marcus guided her to the couch and lowered her beside him, keeping her close. On the television, a woman came on air with a special report. Alexis rested her head on his chest, and they watched the grim news unfold. Images from store cameras and amateur videos showed the devastation.

"At around 8:30am Pacific Standard Time, twin earthquakes of magnitude 8.5 hit Los Angeles and San Francisco. This seems to have been a direct result of an earlier 10.2 magnitude earthquake that hit about five hundred and fifty miles off the coast of Central California. There has never been an earthquake of this magnitude in recorded history. The quake off the coast caused a huge swell. Scientists say that the earthquakes on land resonated in sync with the swells in the ocean, causing the tsunami to increase in size by an additional 20 percent. At around 8:32am, the tsunami reached the coast of California, hitting Santa Barbara. The tsunami went inland approximately three and a half miles. It's uncertain how the second tsunami formed, but scientists speculate that an aftershock occurred in the ocean at the same time the earthquakes in Los Angeles and San Francisco occurred. The second tsunami hit California at approximately 8:55am, reaching inland almost six miles."

Footage of a convenience store, in Los Angeles, showed people getting struck by boxes of food falling off the shelves. The timer on the video showed the time to the nearest millisecond. People got up and moved the debris, and others were helping the injured. Just a few short minutes later, out of nowhere, a flash of water rushed into the store. The flood water rose quickly. The camera flickered and then stopped working.

The reporter continued, "That footage was found by a news crew skimming through debris looking for survivors. The entire West Coast has been devastated. Hawaii was severely hit about an hour ago. Japan, China, and the Pacific Islands have all been warned of the double tsunamis that are headed their way; tsunamis will reach them sometime in the next few hours."

As the day progressed into evening, tales of devastation that had happened along the western coast of the United States kept spewing in from the news media via satellite. Stories of families being lost under falling buildings or washed away by water, along with the reports of heroic efforts made by some in the rescue of strangers. The Coast Guard was overwhelmed.

"The cities are gone," said a man in torn shorts, face streaked with what appeared to be blood, "the water has taken away what the earthquake has torn apart. It's like a huge beach here."

The reporter was shaking her head when she appeared on the screen. "We'll return with more breaking news right after we hear a few words from our sponsors."

As the commercials came on, Marcus brought her a glass of water. She took it with trembling hands.

"Are you hungry?" he asked softly.

She shook her head no.

Ignoring her, Marcus brought salsa and chips and placed it on the coffee table. After a few minutes, the reporter was back on the air.

"A special report will follow in a few minutes about the devastation along the West Coast of the United States. But now for something a little bit more cheerful. I don't know if many of you remember a few months ago when astronomers discovered a new comet, they named Tonatiuh, named after the Aztec sun god. The comet is due to pass by the earth as it makes its orbit around the sun. Recent reports suggest the comet is passing closer to the earth this fall as it leaves our solar system not to return for another six thousand years. Astronomers say it will pass within one million miles of earth, allowing a closer glimpse at its colorful tail."

---

Alexis woke in her bed, alone, to loud noises outside her window. She got up to see what the commotion was about. People rioted the streets fighting among themselves and the police. *What's going on?*

Marcus walked in, eyes wide. "The Pope, Peter the Roman, was assassinated today," he said. "And Iran launched nuclear missiles against Israel."

"Oh my god!" Alexis said.

"Tel Aviv was sacked today. Israel nuked Jerusalem."

Alexis looked back out the window. The rioting had stopped. Now she saw immigration agents lining up Hispanic men, women, and children and putting them on buses. Mobs threw things at the people as they lined up to enter the bus. She watched the police doing nothing as rocks landed on the faces of little kids. Off in the distance a mosque was on fire.

"We need to get out of here." Her voice heavy in desperation. "We need to get to my uncle's place in Pennsylvania," she said to Marcus

# Chapter 38

**Milestown, September 15, 2060**

Alexis stared at her dad. By the end of the summer of 2052, he had been missing for nearly two months. Her brother kept reassuring her that dad was okay. When she'd asked how he knew, his response was dad was just doing what dad does. What did that even mean? And here he was standing right in front of her—alive. How had Eric known he was okay?

Alexis moved Monica off her knee and sat on a box with a dirty blanket. There had been so many events that led up to the end of civilization. Tears began to well up in her tired green eyes as she remembered that time. She pushed her hair back and looked around the room, imagining what it once looked like when things had been normal.

The astronomers had claimed the comet, Tonatiuh, would pass within a million miles of earth in a few weeks. There was nothing to worry about, they had said...

**October 4, 2052**

Alexis had finally convinced Marcus and two of her closest friends, Jennifer and John, to journey out into Pennsylvania with her, to stay at her uncle's place at the cove. Had she listened to her instinct, and not her pig-headed boyfriend, and left a few weeks earlier, they could have traveled by car. Now, they only had enough power to take them to Harrisburg. There were no power stations with charged batteries—their sole means of transportation was on foot.

Food was getting harder to find. Scores of trucks had been hijacked on the streets, making it harder for the food shipments to get into the city.

As they made their way out of Harrisburg, they soon found that they were not alone in their exodus. Most of the people had no real plan, no real purpose as to where they were going. They just walked, hoping they would find food. Her own group was carrying sleeping bags and as much food as their backpacks could carry, and each of them carried one gallon of water.

As they walked along the highway, she decided to try Eric, fishing her phone from her backpack.

"Hey, Sis."

"Eric! Where are you?" she asked.

"I'm still at home."

"Why are you there? You're supposed to be with us. We've been walking for three days now. We're almost at Uncle Miles' cabin. You haven't been picking up your phone. I've left a ton of messages; I was worried sick—"

"I know. I heard them all." Eric said, matter of fact. "The power went out for the last few days and I couldn't charge my phone or the car. It just came on this morning. So far, most of the rioting has been in the downtown area. Nothing's been happening over here."

"Has dad come home?"

"No. I'm still by myself."

"Oh my God!"

"Sis, I think dad is alright. Maybe wherever he was when the riots began he thought it was too dangerous to get home. Maybe he went to Uncle Miles cabin and is waiting for us. Maybe *he's* worried because we aren't there. We should have gone a month ago. This is all real crazy. I haven't left yet because I wanted to have some clean clothes, so I'm washing some underwear and shirts."

"Are you crazy?" she screamed. "There's no time for that. You need to be here with us!"

"I'm almost done. I'll catch up with you. Don't worry, I'll be there."

"Oh, Eric! I've already lost Mom and possibly Dad. I don't want to lose you too."

"Yeah, I wish mom had stayed on this side of the country with us. Let's pray that she was able to survive."

"You need to get over here!"

"I promise. I'll be there. I love you."

"Love you too." She disconnected.

Alexis got bored after a few miles of walking and turned on her portable radio.

"Where did you get that thing?" Marcus asked.

"My dad gave it to me when I was a little girl." She couldn't bring herself to part with it.

Finding a radio station was difficult. Most had gone out of business. Of the stations she could find only the emergency broadcast announcements were being aired, saying that water would be turned off most of the day and that it would only be on during the morning hours and again briefly in the evening. Any water used for drinking needed to be boiled before consumption. They warned people not to drink water from the rivers and creeks because of pollutants. Rationed food would be distributed at the local high schools. They reminded everyone that they would only sell things to people who had a valid ID. Anyone who didn't have a valid ID was to report to the nearest immigration office immediately.

The ID tag system was idiotic. Senator Williamson of Arizona was the one who'd come up with the idea to help get rid of illegal aliens. It didn't happen. The illegals stayed and an underground market developed.

Alexis kept switching stations. "A new study has revealed that there are signs the magnetic orientation of the sun will be changing soon. Scientists say this occurs during a major solar storm and it will have little effect on the earth."

She tried to find a station playing music. She caught one of her favorite songs near the end. "That was Upside Down's cover of *'Viva La Vida.'* It's another hot day here in Pennsylvania. There's been a lot of bad news out there. A lot of things are going on, none of it all that good. At least we get to see a comet close up as Tonatiuh passes by very close to the earth. People used to think of a comet passing by the earth as an omen of bad things to come. Well, with the Gulf of Mexico a dead ocean and now the West

Coast pretty much all f'd up and electricity and food shortages everywhere, it looks like they were right. Another interesting—"

She tuned the radio to another station. "There have been reports that D.C. government officials are being sent with their families somewhere out in Pennsylvania. Officials are not giving any reason for this. At least three hundred families are being transported from Washington D.C. to Pennsylvania. President Coburn's family is among them.

"The weather today is going to be hot and balmy, with temperatures reaching into the high nineties. Another record for October here in Pennsylvania—"

Alexis turned off the radio.

"Why did you do that?" Marcus asked.

"I got tired of listening to bad news."

They wiggled their way through the street of abandoned cars and tried to keep a low profile. Gangs had cropped up and would kill anyone for a candy bar. People roamed the highway hopelessly, as though they had lost the will to live. Their thin bodies and sullen faces gave them a zombie-like appearance.

"Why don't they do something?" Jennifer asked. "Why do they just give up?"

John winced. "What do you want them to do?"

"I don't know. But they shouldn't just give up."

"Then let them worry about it and not you," Marcus said, his face an inscrutable mask. "I don't want to sound insensitive, but at this point, each person has to defend their own. We must keep going and try to stay alive."

It was a hard pill to swallow, but he was right.

They made their way up to the cabin, exhausted and disillusioned.

"I'll be glad when someone invents transporters that beam you to specific locations. We could have been up here four days ago," Jennifer said.

The cabin was enormous, much bigger than Alexis remembered. It was clean and filled with supplies, enough to sustain them for a very long time. There were several books on the table: one titled *Keeping the Cabin Going* and another one titled *Sun Storms*. Uncle Miles was there with his wife Elizabeth and son, Patrick, as well as Patrick's girlfriend, Britney.

"I wasn't sure you would make it. Where's Eric?" Uncle Miles said, hugging Alexis.

"He said he would catch up," she replied, then turned on her phone and tried connecting with him.

Uncle Miles shook his head. "There's no signal up here. But I'm sure Eric can take care of himself."

Alexis began to cry. Her Aunt Elizabeth rushed to her and put her arms around her shoulders. "I'm sure he's all right. I'm sure he'll show up soon." She didn't sound too convinced. Alexis tried to calm down. Things were hard for everyone.

They went inside to listen to the monitors that Uncle Miles had set up to access live news broadcasts. One of them picked up the local station which continuously displayed The Emergency Broadcast System. Captions showed the addresses where shelter was being provided. Another monitor showed satellite images of earth.

She changed the channels on one of the monitors and there was a broadcast with a scientist talking about the latest sun storm.

"A major solar flare has been detected on the sun. The storm is southbound. All electrical devices need to be turned off for a period of twenty-four hours."

"A sun storm can destroy our electrical devices if they are left on," Uncle Miles said, then headed to the cabin. "Let's make sure everything electronic is turned off." Alexis followed her uncle into the cabin and watched as he opened the floor panel and reached in. All the lights in the cabin went out.

After dinner, they relaxed in their chairs and told stories of events now long past and ghost stories that would make a five-year-old laugh. The last light of the sun had just disappeared, it was a beautiful night. A full moon was up in the sky. Tonatiuh, with its magnificent tail, could be seen flying close to the moon.

Uncle Miles pointed out the aurora borealis. "It's a strong one, this solar storm."

The talking subsided as they stared in awe at the stars. The comet was beautiful.

"It looks larger in the sky tonight, being at its closest point to earth before it makes its trek back out into deep space." Miles explain, as they all stared up in wonderment at the night sky.

Alexis was amazed. She had never seen a comet pass this close to the earth. She looked on in admiration at the beautiful show of colors that the comet displayed.

"Dad? What's that?" asked Patrick.

"Is that supposed to happen?" asked Marcus, at the same time.

Within a matter of seconds, the comet had broken into several large pieces. "Whoa! Did you see that!?" Patrick yelled, pointing to the comet, eyes wide in awe, mouth open.

Everyone pointed and shouted excitedly as they saw a stray piece of the comet slam with great force into the side of the moon. Flashes of light emanated from the impact and there was a spectacular explosion. The size of what was left of it had increased significantly; now a bright orange-red like a raging bonfire, it became clearer as the comet slowly grew in size. Alexis looked to her uncle; Miles peered up at the other parts of the comet. His face paled, in the moonlight.

"Oh shit!"

"What's happening?" Alexis asked.

"The comet's trajectory is all wrong. The solar storm must have changed its course and now it's going to crash into the earth! Everyone get inside the cabin. Now!"

At that exact moment the winds picked up almost instantaneously. Loose dirt swirled around and breathing became difficult. The currents of air were fierce and the ground shook violently. Alexis felt as if she were floating, even though her feet were planted on the ground. As they all struggled toward the cabin, the light from the full moon disappeared. Stars began falling out of the sky. Alexis crawled into the cabin along with the others. Miles helped pull them all in as fast as he could, and slammed the door closed, before collapsing in exhaustion on the concrete floor.

For hours the door kept banging from debris as it smashed into it. Then, finally, there was silence. As miles slowly, tentatively opened the door, Alexis could see that it was no longer night but day. It was as bright as mid-afternoon. The sky had changed color. The blue was disappearing from the sky and the stars could be seen while the sun still shone. In the distance, a white cloud formed across the horizon, approaching very fast. Miles yelled for everyone to get back into the cabin. Everyone started to scream. He slammed the door closed once again, turned on the battery-powered lamps.

Alexis didn't understand; how could it have been evening, and within two hours, day? But not morning; it was clearly afternoon. What on earth had happened?

They waited. She heard hissing air at the door. It became harder to breathe.

*Boom!*

The sound was so powerful it felt as if an eighteen-wheeler had slammed into the face of the cabin. The hissing started again, air began blowing in from the door.

*Boom!*

Tension filled the room. Aunt Elizabeth prayed as Jennifer broke into sobs, everyone else held hands and stood perfectly still, only shaking when something hit the door.

*Boom! Boom!*

The earth moved beneath them. They all screamed in unison. Alexis held on to Marcus and buried her face in his shirt.

The eerie banging continued. It was like a giant hand trying to scratch its way through the metal door.

"Please God," Alexis prayed out loud. "Please help us."

The earth shook again. They all huddled together.

More tremors followed; none diminished in intensity. It felt as if the earth would rip apart at any moment. Each tremor lasted for minutes at a time though it felt like an eternity, only stopping for a few short seconds between each occurrence.

By the end of the day the tremors had reduced in frequency and duration. The next day, after a fitful night, they could still feel aftershocks. But this time, the quakes were tolerable. The monitor showed the wind speed outside to be 183 kilometers per hour—the same speed as a category 3 hurricane, Miles told them. It still wasn't safe to venture outside.

By the third day the monitors showed that the winds had finally died down to around 70 kilometers per hour. The earthquakes had virtually stopped, only occurring once during the day. Yet, they could still hear a loud dull thud outside.

On the fourth day the winds had died down considerably. Alexis opened the door, welcoming the rush of fresh air into the humid cabin. But when she looked out, she stepped back in shock. Trees were sprawled all over, piled high. Thick white ash littered the ground. The valley below was flooded with water. The clouds were black with light coming through in very few places.

On the fifth day the earth shook in the morning, at midday, and again in the evening. It felt like a ship running aground. She could make out rocks and debris bouncing off the entrance to the cabin.

On the sixth day a large aftershock made everyone fall to the ground. Uncle Miles looked to his instruments. The winds had died down even more, blowing at thirty kilometers per hour.

It was afternoon before he dared open the door. Crowing round to peer out as, they saw the landscape was arid, different, like they'd landed on the moon. White ash covered black rock.

On the seventh day everything was calm. There were no winds, and the earth had stopped shaking. The faint sound of thunder off in the distance.

Miles opened the door to the cabin and peered outside. Everyone else followed. It was cold. Dark clouds wisped through the upper atmosphere at tremendous speed. Off in the distance, lightning shot across the sky. The valley below had filled with water. The cliff ledge was now a beach cove.

Uncle Miles turned on the monitors that showed images from the satellites orbiting the planet. Only one satellite was sending signals—a weather satellite that had a high-altitude orbit around the earth.

Patrick commented at the images, "Look at the continents. They look so different. Is this still earth?"

Where the satellite outlined North America, it showed only several large islands. Only the eastern half of South America existed.

Marcus turned on the radio and managed to tune in to a station. The Emergency Broadcast System was telling everyone to find shelter. The message kept repeating:

This is a message from the Emergency Broadcast Agency. If you are outside, find shelter immediately. Take as much food and water as you can. If you cannot get clean water, you can boil the water before drinking it or you can add two drops of chlorine to each gallon of water to kill most biological contaminants. Take plenty of blankets. You will need masks to cover your face. The comet Tonatiuh is heading toward earth. It will hit the eastern shores of the United States. Take cover! There is a 30 percent chance that the comet will hit the moon instead.

"That comet was huge. Did you see the one part that hit the moon?" Patrick asked. "The parts that hit the earth should have done more damage than this."

"I think the earth turned upside down," Marcus said, not sounding totally convinced. "That's why we saw the moon disappear and what seemed like the stars falling. Which means that the comet hit somewhere between here and the other side of the world: probably closer to Australia."

---

Alexis was overwhelmed with emotion recounting those times, dad held her hand gently, tears streaming down his face. How was it that he wasn't with them dealing with this ordeal? And what kind of clothes was he wearing? Was he at a costume party while the world was ending? Could her dad be this selfish that he didn't care about his children or his family? Eric tried to tell her that maybe dad was at the cabin, but he wasn't.

"How did you find this place?" Tom asked.

What did it matter? How could he be gone all this time? "Where were—"

"My father and I found it," her cousin Patrick spoke out. He was Uncle Miles' only child. He was supposed to start college this year. He learned a lot more being with his dad than college could ever teach him.

# Chapter 39

Tom sat listening to Patrick tell his story about the events that happened from the time they decided to leave the vault. How they found this town; how they met a group of people, led by someone named John Torkton, that occupied some of the houses; how the two groups got together and how his brother managed to keep them alive.

"My dad became the go to person since he had knowledge of almost everything. Eventually the adults decided to create a city counsel with dad being mayor," Patrick said, his mother crying on his shoulder. That would mean that something happened to Miles. *Oh please, say he's still alive.*

"By the fourth year, the weather stabilized, dad had mapped out the growing season and determined what times to grow the crops. Everything was meticulously written in journals. He told me that he didn't want to miss anything in case something should happen to him.

"As the years passed and the food supply became stable, people would come wandering in from out of nowhere and tell of their plight. Dad would always welcome them. But that changed during the seventh year when a cold snap decimated the harvest. We lost over half of our crop that year. As we rationed what little we had, people kept wandering into the city only to have dad send them away. He explained to them that there wasn't enough food to feed them. Those people were only concerned about their own needs. It was hard but necessary if we were to live out the year.

"One day I saw dad standing on a boulder looking out into the fields. The crops weren't growing as well as they did the previous years, many of the plants were dead. Dad turned to me as if he were afraid, shaking at times and said, 'you need to take care of the journals now. *You* need to make observations of all the plants, just like I showed you.' I told him I was already doing it, but he continued saying I needed to be the one heading it up. I asked him what was going on and he just said 'I want us to be safe.'"

Patrick started sobbing uncontrollably. Tom stood and put his hand on his shoulder, trying to calm him. "It's alright, Patrick. It's okay."

Patrick swat Tom's hand off his shoulder and started yelling. "No! It's not okay. You don't know what happened. They killed my dad!"

Tom took a step back surprised. "What? When? How?" Patrick stood, shaking and crying. Not saying anything.

"A small group of people started stealing the food we planted," Alexis started speaking. "We started guarding the areas so we could defend our crops. But the Harvesters, that's what we started calling them, came with weapons. We weren't prepared since we didn't have any weapons except for the rocks we could find on the ground. They shot him in the chest."

"Miles…" Tom choked up saying his brother's name. "He's… he's… dead?"

Audrey shook her head acknowledging what her father had said. She continued, "we retaliated by sneaking up on a small division of their group, stealing their guns and ammunition. Without mercy we killed as many of them as we could. Men, and woman. We left the children to fend for themselves. We didn't care. We were mad."

"So, you killed them all?"

"No. This last year has been a back and forth battle between them and us." Alexis put her hands to her face and said nothing.

Tom sat on the floor and listened, amazed that they had survived and were able to rebuild. He was glad his brother was here helping everyone. If only he could have been here to help them fight the Harvesters or made them the timepieces to help them escape this hell.

"I'm so sorry that you and my brother had to go through all that," Tom said as tears dripped down his face. He went over to hug Elizabeth, Miles wife. She stepped back, not letting him touch her, crying out. "Where were you all this time, Tom? Why weren't you here helping your family get through all this?"

Tom didn't have any answers. He felt as if he were a selfish child who had been too lazy to do his part for the family. Alexis and everyone else seemed to have that same questioning look in their eyes. His heart sank with grief.

Everyone waited. He had nothing to tell them to help them understand what was happening. If only he had come from some faraway place with some good news, but Tom had no news to give them. Only questions to ask.

He looked around the room and noticed that Eric hadn't come to greet him. Something must have happened. His heart sank even deeper. He looked into Alexis' eyes. "What happened to your brother?" he asked, bracing himself. "What happened to Eric?"

Alexis looked at her father with tears streaming down her cheeks, dripping onto her dress. Shaking her head, she whispered, "I don't know."

# Chapter 40

Philadelphia, October 4, 2052

Eric put away his phone after talking with Alexis. She was upset that he wasn't already on his way to their uncle's cabin. grabbing the sleeping bag and backpack from the basement, he packed the clothes he just finished washing. The excitement that Uncle Miles was right from his conspiracy theories and the hope that he wasn't filled Eric with an anxiety he hadn't felt before. Was the world coming to an end? Audrey was proof that it hadn't. Something happened that would make life harder in the future. But it didn't completely end.

Nothing seemed to be worth taking. Only the clothes and the food made the cut. On the shelf in the office was the handprint he gave dad for Father's Day when he was five; the ashtray his sister made in second grade; the trophies they had accumulated over the years. They were things that reminded him of better days, but they would have to stay. There were so many things that brought back memories of life in this house. On a side table in the office was a picture of mom, dad, him, and Alexis in D.C. by the Potomac River waiting for the Fourth of July fireworks to begin. He slipped it in the backpack.

Several weeks had gone by since he'd seen his dad. What could he be doing? Eric knew about the timepiece. He disappeared on occasion, but not this long. Hopefully, he was safe and just got caught up doing something enjoyable that prevented him from coming home. Or, like he told Alexis; he was with Uncle Miles at the cabin.

Eric found a piece of paper in the office and wrote down that everyone was going to Uncle Miles' cabin, or the vault, as his dad liked to call it. He stuck it on the inside of the door just above the knob. Somehow, he knew it would never be read.

Interstate 476 north was littered with cars left abandoned on the highway, he was barely able to find a path through. The car got him all the way to Harleysville Pike, to a town called Souderton near a deserted strip mall, before the batteries finally died. The windows to all the stores were broken, the stores themselves just shells of what once was civilization. It made sense to walk toward the middle of town; a food center might be there. A group of people attacked a man carrying several bags, running off with them. Another group were fighting. Running into and out of a house. He didn't know what was happening and saw no need to get involved. walking around here didn't feel safe. He picked up his pace.

People loitered by a corner doing nothing. Their malnourished bodies and hopeless attitude made them appear like the living dead. Eric remembered years before the fuel shortages, the government making announcements telling everyone to start growing their own food. Not much land was available to do that in the cities—in the last half century, all the good farmland had been converted into residential homes and commercial buildings. The hard surface of the road that just yesterday everyone took for granted as paths connecting one part of the city with another, were now just a curse that prevented them from growing food.

He spotted the food center up ahead. The price of food had been going up since Audrey left, and even then, it was expensive. It was ridiculous, but what could you do? If you wanted to eat, you paid the price.

Eric looked up into the clear sky, trying to catch some of the sun's rays. He was almost at the front of the line; it had taken three hours to get this far, not much longer— he hoped. His feet were aching in the heat. Why the woman standing next to him decided to have the ID on her forehead was baffling. It looked so awful. She was probably a full supporter of the senator, who made the law that required these stupid things be put on people. He read her label surreptitiously: PA 420 510 222 KL. *Huh. Interesting.* The first two letters and the first set of numbers were the same as his—she was more than likely from his neighborhood. Bored, Eric added each of the three sets of numbers:

*Four plus two plus zero.*
*Five plus one plus zero.*
*Two plus two plus two.*

His logic kicked in, and he counted them again. He thought it was odd that each set totaled six. The ID on his arm read PA 420 312 114 PH and even though the numbers were different, each set on his arm also totaled six. Was this Satan's mark? He remembered his Uncle Miles saying that congress would be the one that put Satan's mark on people. *That's a lot of Uncle Miles theories that seem to be coming true all of a sudden.* Did everyone's mark total 666? The other people standing around were too far away for him to see their numbers.

As he stood looking around trying to figure out the mystery with the IDs, the man in front of him dropped to the floor, limp and lifeless. It happened so fast. He was sure the man fell before the gunshot blasted his eardrums. Several more shots were fired. The sound could be heard coming from several directions all at once. Joining everyone else, he ducked. Police ran into the streets and gunned down the cyclist who'd shot into the crowd from a distance.

Dead and wounded were sprawled along the line. Those who needed major medical help received a bullet in the head from the police as relief from the gunman's bullets. Even with the fear of being shot, no-one moved. The line remained. Eric knew, as did the others, that if he broke line now, he may as well starve to death, and that wasn't an option. Other than the occasional stepping over dead bodies, four hours of standing in line did not register on the blank faces and distant eyes that greeted Eric's arrival at the food counter.

A woman with a long, tired face took a small, blue light and passed it over his mark to validate its authenticity. She swabbed his mouth and put it into a machine that beeped and eventually, a green light shone. That was a good sign. His DNA matched what they had in their database. The woman gave him two bags of food; there was no choosing what you wanted to buy. There hadn't been for a long time. Food was food, and if you wanted to eat, you bought what they sold.

# Timepieces

Eric had a feeling that as soon as he was out of sight of the police, someone was sure to steal his food. At the end of the counter he spied several cartons of sand. He quickly unpacked the food from the bag and placed it in his backpack. He scanned around to check no one was watching and placed the containers of sand in the bag.

He walked away from the line and into the street. Scrawny children ran around begging for food, while their parents just sat in the streets sitting, doing nothing. No one lived here anymore. They just existed. Their dirty and wrinkled faces showed the hell they endured.

Eric clutched his bags tighter as he walked, not bothering to stop and offer help, averting his eyes from their stares. Nothing could be done for them now, anyway. The food he had was only enough for one person.

As he rounded a corner, three men huddled across the other side of the street turned in unison to face him. They didn't have the same lifeless look as everyone else. These men were hunters. Closing the distance, they crossed the street at a trot and positioned themselves in his direct path. Their long, drawn faces stared hard as he passed. He could almost feel their pangs of hunger; hunger that would make any man kill just for a piece of bread.

One of the men approached and grabbed for his backpack, as another threw a brick. It skimmed his arm, not quite quick enough to pull away. He tossed the bag on the ground and ran. All three of them lunged for the bag, fighting amongst themselves for the loot. Sand littered the ground as the cartons fell to the floor. Taking the opportunity to make an escape, Eric quickly ducked into an abandoned warehouse before any of the men noticed. *Too late.* The echo of footsteps chasing him reverberated on the concrete.

One of the men yelled, "It's in his backpack!"

Eric ran for his life.

# Chapter 41

Stacks and stacks of crates, taller than himself, took up most of the space in the warehouse. Eric felt like a rat in a maze. He climbed on top of one of the stacks of crates, trying to find a place to hide. He noticed an opening among the stacks, a small narrow space that might just do the trick. Climbing down carefully, he slid between the crates that now surrounded him, lodging two small crates in the gaps about to hide him from view. He sat still, waiting for the men to pass by and leave.

The men walked around the warehouse, banging on the crates as they passed to scare him out. Two of the men got up onto the stacks and rattled them. Another jumped on the stack just above him with a loud thump. In a fit of rage, the man roared, and crates clattered to the floor. Eric flinched and held his breath. It wasn't long before the men were apparently satisfied that Eric had escaped and continued their search elsewhere.

After an hour or two of waiting—just to be safe—he was confident the men weren't coming back. Eric decided to stay the night and continue his journey in the morning. He took out the food from his backpack and ate a small amount, saving the rest for later. Thinking it might be better to just finish it off, he devoured the remainder.

The sound of a barking dog woke him up. There was a yelp, and the barking stopped.

The crates from above were easy to move, and it didn't take long to climb on top. From outside of his hiding spot, he heard voices coming his way and panicked. Losing his balance, his foot got caught in one of the crates while several other crates fell on top, trapping him. He clenched his jaw hard to keep from screaming. The ruckus would have been loud enough for anyone near the warehouse to hear. Muffled voices and steady footsteps approached. Three shadows filled the back wall and then disappeared just as quickly.

After what felt like an eternity, but what must have been only a few minutes, shadows appeared on the back wall, followed by a girl with long, black hair tied back in a ponytail. Another girl, smaller but with the same dark hair, appeared behind her, followed by a man—bald, black beard, about the same age as Eric. They all had the same lifeless look on their faces: hollow cheeks, deep-set eyes, and thin frames that suggested they hadn't eaten for days.

He tried to free his leg to no avail. With a sigh, he said, "Do you think you can help me?"

The small group didn't answer. They stood, looking around, as if searching for the source of the voice.

"I was trying to get away from these three guys and I got stuck trying to get out."

"We saw those three guys leave here yesterday," the girl with the ponytail said as she approached, finally spotting him. She pushed her thick framed glasses back up the bridge of her nose. "I'm Lakisha."

The other two introduced themselves as John and Gina.

"I'm Eric. Any chance you could help me get out of here?"

The trio moved the crates, letting them fall to the floor, until Eric could free his leg.

"Thanks." Eric climbed down from the crates and then squatted as he rubbed his ankle. "Are you guys from around here?"

"We're not from here. We're trying to get out of this city," John said, peering suspiciously at Eric.

"What's been keeping you?".

"We just thought of leaving today," Gina revealed.

Gina was pretty, even though she looked malnourished. By the way she stood next to John, Eric could see they were together.

"Why aren't you guys with your families?" Eric asked.

"We could ask you the same thing," Lakisha said, giving him a skeletal smile.

"My family's waiting for me. I got sidetracked and ended up here instead."

"We're from Virginia," Gina said.

Eric told them about his uncle's cabin and how they should come join him.

"What would we do there?" Lakisha asked.

"We'd hang out, I suppose. My uncle has everything. We can even grow our own food if we need to. As a large group, we have a better chance of fighting off thieves that try and take anything."

"I don't know if we want to do that," said Gina, glancing at John.

"What the hell!" John said. "If we don't like it, we can always leave and go somewhere else. I'm in, man!"

"Fine, Okay." Gina rolled her eyes. "Where are we going?"

"It's about ten miles northwest of Allentown," Eric said, suppressing a smile.

"That's far, man! That's, like, over fifty miles away!" John said.

"We have nowhere else to go," Lakisha shrugged. "Even if we try to get to one of our folks, we're going to be walking over sixty miles. We can go as a group. Like Eric said, if we're a bigger group, we can fight off thieves. Right now, we have four people in our group: two men and two women. I like that ratio."

"You're making so much sense, man!" John said.

"Let's do it!" Gina grinned.

"Okay, we need to go back to Interstate 476 and go north. About ten miles past Allentown, we go west and get to the cliffs," Eric directed.

"Man, how are we going to walk up cliffs?" John asked.

"You don't," Eric said, reaching for his backpack. "A little way to the west, we can climb a slope going to the top of the hill. We can only get to the cabin from the top."

---

There were fewer abandoned cars on the interstate than on the streets. A loud crashing sounded in the distance. Approaching from the south came a caravan of vehicles. In the lead was a large truck that had two huge slabs of metal that formed a triangle at its front. It slammed into the abandoned cars, shoving them out of the way.

The crashing grew louder as the caravan came closer. Several dozen Humvees roared past accompanied by a dozen trucks with military personnel. Following these were several commercial buses filled with civilians. A dozen additional trucks carried tanks. Several helicopters flew over following the caravan.

"I wonder where they're going?" John said.

"Where did they come from?" Gina asked.

Eric stared at the procession and then mumbled, "I have no idea"

They all stood watching the caravan pass.

---

Every abandoned car they came across was searched. They hit the jackpot when the trunk of a grey sedan was full of canned food.

"Why would anyone leave this here?" Lakisha asked, surprised.

"They probably couldn't take it, and they weren't going to stay here," John said.

"Whatever the reason, we now have food." Eric flashed them a grin and loaded his backpack with cans. "Put as many cans as you can fit in your backpack," he commanded them, and then noticed that none of them carried any kind of bag. "If you don't have backpacks, find a bag in one of these cars, fill it with cans. Anything we can't take. We'll eat here tonight and move on tomorrow."

Lakisha didn't hesitate and started searching the other cars for bags to put the cans into.

It was getting dark and this was as good a place as any to spend the night. The men took seats out of one of the cars, while the girls collected magazines and random papers from the cars to start a fire. The canned food was much better than the rations he'd waited hours for in line the day before. To help pass the time, they told stories of their childhoods and discussed what classes they had been taking in college. After a while, they started getting tired and one by one fell asleep.

---

Eric was the first to wake up the next day. Lakisha was bundled up next to him, trying to keep warm. It took all day to reach the base of the hill; the sun had already settled under the horizon when he told them to stop and rest for a minute while he got his bearings. It had been a while since he'd been there, and he'd never done the entire journey on foot before—there had never been any need. Scanning the landscape, he wasn't sure this was the correct route to the cabin, he didn't recognize any of the landmarks, and saw none he was expecting to see. But night was approaching fast; he had to make a decision.

"Hey look, man!" John said pointing to the top of the hill. "I think that's a cave."

They all looked up. Luck was with them.

"Let's try and get to it." The moment Eric spoke, the wind suddenly picked up.

# Chapter 42

With loose dirt and the wind blowing so hard, Eric had a hard time walking up the mountain slope. Lakisha tried to get her footing on the loose rubble, but for every step she took, she'd lose two. The cave opening loomed above. The wind bore down on them from the mountaintop, as if the gods themselves were against them.

Eric kept an eye on Lakisha, who seemed to be on the verge of giving up. It was hard trying to motivate her to catch up with the others, especially with the strong winds making it difficult to be heard. They had to shield their faces with their arms just to be able to breathe, making it hard to keep their balance on the steep, slippery incline.

Eric got down closer to the ground and started to crawl up the slope. John grabbed onto a rock which came loose and suddenly he flew backwards, toward Lakisha, and hit the ground hard, the rock flew out of his hand. It happened so fast Eric didn't even have a chance to move. Lakisha ducked away from the flying stone, but the wind threw her off balance, and then she was gone, flying through the air, in front of Eric's eyes, all the way back down the slope. All thoughts of getting to the cave above now abandoned, Eric ran down to help.

As he reached her, the wind started to die down. The sky grew darker. The stars began falling out of the sky as the moon disappeared. The earth began to quake, and the ground below them split apart.

Eric reached over and grabbed Lakisha, hauling her back up the mountain slope in desperation. As the earth cracked and crumbled around them, they fell to the ground, before righting themselves and ploughing on once more, climbing as quickly as they could to reach the others. Eric was grateful that his backpack helped cushion the fall; Lakisha was not so lucky, and was getting up slower, wincing. Eric paused to peer ahead; the winds kicked up again, and the ground shook again violently, but they were almost there. Lakisha stopped and stared into the darkness. Eric tugged on her hand; they had to keep moving. Feeling out with his hands, they moved on. Just as his night vision was settling in, a huge dislodged tree toppled toward them from above. Lakisha held on tight as the tree collided, knocking Eric off his feet once more. He fell back to the ground, hard, on top of the backpack.

He was underwater; instinctively, he held his breath remaining motionless. It was freezing. He allowed the water to guide his body toward the surface. What felt like an eternity finally ended in relief as his head came up out of the water and he gasped for air, glad to be alive.

Blinking the water out of his eyes, he saw where he was; a large body of water surrounded him—a lake perhaps, that he'd not noticed before. He swam towards the shore with difficulty, shivering all the way. Nothing around him looked familiar; nothing hinted as to where he was. Scanning around he noticed a cave set into a hill further inland. Was this the cave they were trying to walk up the mountain to get to? What had happened to the storm?

The cave entrance appeared to be littered with rocks. He didn't understand; just moments before, it had been dark as night, and now it was as bright as day. Lakisha had held onto him as a tree fell on top of them. Where were his friends now?

An orange sky loomed above. What was going on that would make the sky orange?

It was dark as he ventured further inside the cave. He hollered for the others but was greeted with silence. He turned on the flashlight from his backpack, illuminating the area. Evidence of human presence lingered, beer bottles lay around black ash, but no one came to greet him.

"Lakisha!" he shouted. "Gina, John!"

No answer.

Eric decided to spend the night inside the cave. The cold crept in as the winds from outside found their way into the far reaches of the cavern. Eric put up the tent deep inside the cave and unfolded the sleeping bag. It was a little wet, but it was better than sleeping on the dirt floor.

He had no idea if wild animals ventured into the cave, or for that matter, lived in the cave. With no weapon, he searched for a stone heavy enough to do some damage, but not too heavy that it couldn't be used. A few feet over to the side was the perfect rock.

Morning came with the light of the sun creeping into the cave. The light penetrated farther inside than it had when he had arrived, giving him an excuse to explore. He came upon a pristine human skeleton. A large groove from the forehead went all the way to the back. The only clothes it had was a shirt. A shiny object caught his attention off to the side near the skeleton. It looked like a broken circle; in fact, it looked very much like... the disc! The one his dad made for Audrey.

Grabbing his backpack, he emptied out its contents onto the ground at his feet. There was nothing there. Dad had to have placed one in this backpack, how else did he get here, wherever here was? Searching each of the pockets in turn, he finally found it—the timepiece! The same one that he'd found left on the desk left for Audrey; the same one next to the dead man. He raised his hands and smiled. "Thank you, Dad."

A tear rolled down his cheek as he thought about Audrey. *I could have left with you after all.*

The date on the timepiece showed October 8, 2052. That didn't make sense. It was the same day they were trying to get up to the cave. He pressed the blue button on the disc. Suddenly there was howling wind. The ground shook with great force yet felt as if it was floating. Two figures struggled to enter the cave—Gina and John.

"How the hell did you get in here before us?" John yelled.

Both stared at him and held each other, afraid. The air began to get sucked out of the cave. It was getting harder to breathe. The timepiece displayed February 12, 2268. Looking at his newly found friends pain coursed through him. He wanted to help them to save them, but he knew he was helpless. Nothing could be done for them now. He couldn't take them with him. Only one person could use the device, that's what Audrey had said. Pressing the blue button, the noise disappeared, the shaking ceased. Once again, it was daylight and there was calm.

Gina and John were gone.

# Timepieces

Poking around, he thought of Lakisha. She hadn't been in the cave. She hadn't made it. But John and Gina had been there. Why weren't their bodies here now? What happened to them? They may have died that night. Hopefully, they survived.

The cave was enormous, and he found nothing of interest. There was no reason to stay. Eric packed his gear and started walking east. The flat terrain quickly turned into a cliff with land on the left and water splashing against the rocks below to the right.

After walking for most of the day he came to a waterfall that cut through the cliffs. The width of the river at this point made crossing impossible. There was no choice but to turn around and spend another night in the cave. The next morning, he re-packed his backpack and set off once more; this time, he went west.

Barren land was all he could see in every direction. Few plants existed here. More importantly, he hadn't spotted a single animal, nor a single person. After a long day of walking, no caves in sight or any form of natural shelter, it seemed as good a place as any to stop. Eric dropped his gear and made camp where he stood. Taking out his notebook, he began writing the day's events until it got too dark to see. The sleeping bag couldn't keep the cold winds away and it was a struggle to keep warm. He wanted to build a fire, but there was no wood—and even if there were, he had nothing to light it. He laid there shivering and mused about his current circumstance. The sky was filled with many stars compared to the nights when the city lights blocked all but a few. The Milky Way was clear as day in the night sky.

*How ironic. Another night in hell and there's no fire.*

He started to laugh. How was he going to survive in this barren world?

# Chapter 43

The next day revealed the same empty, rocky expanse, encountering nothing. He was alone. Walking was difficult during the day with the heat, his energy was being drained—he needed to find shelter soon. He opened a can of soup, its contents cold, but better than nothing. Seven cans remained—enough to last a week. Surely that would be plenty of time to find food, he hoped.

On the third day, a path emerged that at one time could have been a highway. He followed it for the entire day; again, not one person, not one animal crossed his path. Being here felt much like he imagined it would on the moon—desolate and quiet. Rummaging in the backpack among his rapidly dwindling supplies, he found the timepiece. What would happen if he went back in time before any of this occurred?

Setting the calendar to a date three years earlier—February 16, 2049—he pressed the blue button; nothing happened. It didn't change anything, yet the date on the timepiece showed February 16, 2268. Pressing the blue button again showed the date he had just set. In his frustration, he set the calendar to the date he was born: March 3, 2031. The landscape changed. The dirt path became a two-lane road. It was morning. The date on the timepiece again showed February 16, 2268.

Eric smiled. The timepiece *did* work.

The road sloped down and veered to the right a quarter mile up ahead. Hopefully, it would lead to a nearby town. Walking without a jacket was not ideal in this kind of weather. If only a car would come along and give him a ride somewhere, anywhere, it didn't matter. Just seeing another person would be a godsend. By midday, a light snow began to fall.

His spirits were high as he strolled along the asphalt road. He could see a gas station up ahead. A car was approaching from behind the bend in the road. But something was happening. The scene changed again and suddenly he found himself back in the future—back in hell.

He pressed the timepiece again and again, but nothing changed around him. Several times he tried, still nothing. It didn't make sense. The timepiece was broken. If only he had used it to go find Audrey. But he didn't know what year she was from. Instead, he should have gone to 1776 and tracked her down in Pennsylvania. With the timepiece not working the trip seemed futile.

After walking seven days in the heat, he decided today he wouldn't eat the last can of soup, instead save it for a few more days. The walk today was much slower; trying not to expend too much energy. He took his time, walking on simply for the sake of walking. He had no destination. The hunger pangs grew stronger and by the middle of the ninth day he was suffering. The scorching rays of the sun forced him to hide and seek shelter; finding food would have to wait.

# Timepieces

He continued toward the east. Patches of grass and weeds grew around a few dead trees. A well-traveled path on the ground seemed to point north. He hadn't followed it for long before he realized that the path led nowhere, except to another road that used to be a highway. The road came to an abrupt end, with water flowing through a deep ravine below. He ran down the hill as fast as he dared without falling over, and threw himself to the water's edge, drinking the cold water greedily. After taking his fill, he noticed what used to be a bridge; he was standing on the remnants of an off-ramp. Tonight, camp would be here at the cliff bridge.

He finally ate the last can of soup. Ripping the wrapper off, he turned the can upside down in the dirt, found a pen in the backpack and wrapped the wrapper around it then jammed it through the top of the can and yelled out loud, "I hereby name this place Ericsville."

Huddled up in his sleeping back, he gazed up into the dark. This many stars never appeared in the night skies of Philly. The streetlights had erased most of the star light in the city. It was a beautiful sigh; but the more he stared, the more it felt wrong—none of the constellations were where they should be. The North Star, Polaris, was nowhere to be seen. On the horizon, many large orange stars shone against the black sky.

Eric sat up. Those lights weren't stars. They were fires. Seven of them on the other side of the river.

Morning couldn't come quick enough. He packed his sleeping bag, walked to the river, and down the ramp. Based on the speed of the current, he figured that crossing here would end up taking him half-a-mile downstream. The ramp appeared to be the easiest way to get up on the other side.

He began his crossing half a mile upstream. The water wasn't too deep making the swim awkward only because of the icy cold water. The current brought him to the ramp on the other side as expected.

Shivering from the cold, a voice came from further up the ramp. "Will you just stay here all day?" Startled, Eric looked up at two men clad in potato sack type outfits. One of the men was standing on the edge of the cliff, probably the man who had spoken. His accent had been heavy. He couldn't compare it to anything he had heard before.

"I just crossed the river. I'm cold and tired." His voice trembled with both cold and excitement at finally finding civilization.

"Yes, we watched you."

Eric stood and staggered to the top of the ramp. "My name is Eric." He extended his hand out to the man closest to him, but he didn't seem to understand the gesture and kept his hand to the side.

"I'm Random, and this is my brother, Spinner," said the man.

"We will walk with you into the city," Spinner added with a nod.

Eric studied their strange clothes that appeared to be made from older pieces of clothes stitched together; they had flimsy shoes. He questioned them about their community. They told him that they roamed around in search of new shelter when the food in the area ran out; they had made it a rule not to interact with other people.

"We don't share with others and they don't share with us," Random explained.

"What if you want something that they have?" Eric asked.

"We learn not to want it."

They lived in makeshift houses made of pieces of wood and stone. Next to one of the houses was a pit. Some of the houses were dug out of the earth, which was not unusual considering how he'd found a streetlamp in the dirt on the road. The older structures were stripped to make new houses. People passed by with baskets filled with wheat and berries, from an area outside the village.

Most of the villagers came out to see him. One man stood out wearing an outfit that was thicker and seemed to be made from a single fabric. He walked up to Eric.

"Hello," he said. "I'm Motts, mayor of this city,"

"I'm Eric. I'm from across the river. I've been wandering around for a while and found a trail that led here."

"That's an old trail. The bridge fell away a long time ago. About the time that Jury here was born," the mayor said, tapping the boy next to him on his head. The boy couldn't have been more than three years old.

The mayor's accent was different from Random or Spinner. It was more guttural and drawn out. Eric talked, trying to understand what had happened to the world. The mayor didn't have any answers—or, perhaps he just didn't know anything. Time wasn't important to these people, at least not in the way they expressed it. They didn't seem to have a calendar system, or even to care about what day it was. They were very relaxed and nonchalant about everything.

Eric was tired and hungry. "I haven't eaten in two days," he said, rubbing his stomach. "I was hoping that I could work for food." He didn't want handouts.

The mayor looked at him and smiled, "I'm sorry, but we don't have any food to give you."

Eric couldn't believe what the man had just told him was true. As he spoke, a line of people were carrying baskets of food.

"Please," Eric begged. "I can do anything. Don't you have work that needs to be done?"

"I'm sorry, we don't," the mayor said pointing. "I'll ask you to leave now."

Confused and angry, Eric didn't know what to do. He didn't have enough energy to fight and there were too many of them to risk taking whatever food he could get.

"Where is the nearest city?" Eric asked, staring at the mayor.

"We don't know."

Eric looked toward where the people brought baskets of berries and decided to walk in that direction.

"Please! Go back the way you came," the mayor called out pointing in the direction Eric had come.

Eric looked in that direction and said, "But there's no way to cross the river."

"You already crossed it once. You can cross it again." The mayor said, still pointing. This was unbelievable. Several men took out their knives.

"Please." The mayor continued pointing away from his so-called city.

Eric turned and went back to the river, defeated and dejected. The men who greeted him earlier followed, watching his every step.

He walked down the ramp and let the freezing water take him farther downstream and out of sight of Random and Spinner. The numbness of the cold water was unbearable. Instead of crossing the river back to the side he came from, he spotted an area where the cliff slope was easier to climb. At the top he could see people from the town picking the berries and wheat that grew wild.

# Timepieces

He moved behind a small boulder and tried not to be conspicuous as he began picking berries. Dry beans grew amongst berries, but they were too hard to eat. A pot would make them well worth picking—if he had one. He stuck with the berries and on occasion put some bean pods in his backpack, just in case something could be found to soak them in.

He picked and ate, ate and picked, trying to keep out of sight.

He paused as the sound of gurgling voices approached. The voices grew louder. There was nowhere to hide. A group of girls passed the boulder and when their gaze met his they ran away screaming. His hands were stained blue, and probably, so was his face. But he was too tired to chase them, and if it were possible to catch them, how would you get screaming girls to shut up?

One of the girls in the group stopped, slowly coming to him, helping fill his backpack with bean pods, wheat, and berries. After filling the backpack, she told him which way to go.

"Thank you," Eric said, turning to run.

She got in front of him. "I'm coming with you!"

There was no time to waste asking questions. He turned and ran, and the girl trailed behind. It wasn't long before he came to an area with small sharp rocks. The girl tripped and fell, cutting herself on her arms and legs. Eric's decision to come back and help was costly. Men from the town had now closed the distance, and he found himself surrounded. There was no choice but to surrender.

Some rushed ahead to prepare for his arrival. He was taken to the largest of the makeshift houses and presented to the mayor alongside the girl.

"I told you to leave!" the mayor said to Eric. "But instead you steal our food and rape our women."

"I didn't rape this woman!"

"If you didn't rape this girl, then why is she bruised and bleeding?"

"She—"

"Silence!" the mayor ordered with one hand raised. He turned to the girl standing next to Eric and asked, "Did he rape you and then force you to run with him so that he could do it again?"

"He didn't rape me," she cried, as blood came down one of her arms that had been cut by the rocks. "I hel—"

"Silence!" The mayor repositioned himself on his chair and looked into her eyes, then took a deep breath. "If he was never going to rape you and you helped him, then you will die with him for betraying your people."

"You would do that to me?" she asked. She clearly had some kind of relationship with the mayor. Perhaps the mayor had always wanted to get rid of her—It would explain why she wanted to run away.

"As an example to the people." He sat back in his chair. "No one escapes punishment."

Eric could see her anger as her cheeks turned pink with rage; he liked her conviction.

"This man did nothing to me. I fell on the rocks as we ran," she said, defiantly.

"Don't think your mother can save you from this," the mayor hissed. "I will have you killed!"

Eric didn't know how high in the hierarchy her mother stood. Perhaps these were idle threats. Perhaps not; the mayor seemed more upset with the girl than with him.

"Did he rape you and then force you to run with him?" the mayor said, nodding his head as he said it.

The girl said nothing.

"I won't ask again..."

Again, she said nothing. The mayor turned to Eric, then back to the girls and grinned. "Very well. For helping this stranger steal our food and helping him escape, I sentence—"

"He did," she blurted out, avoiding Eric's stunned gaze. "Yes, he did. He raped me and then beat me when I tried to leave." Tears filled her eyes and she looked away from him.

The mayor persisted, his face now wearing a smug expression. "Did this man rape you?"

"Yes, he did." She started to cry now.

"And did he beat you and force you to run away with him?"

"Yes!"

The mayor motioned for the soldier to take her outside and turned his attention to Eric. "Stealing food is not punishable by death, but raping our women is."

"I didn't rape anyone." Eric understood why this girl wanted to run away. The mayor was a cruel dictator.

"We have witnesses that saw you on top of her and she herself admits that you raped her and forced her to run with you."

"I didn't rape anyone. You forced her to confess a lie!"

The mayor smiled. "You are like all other outsiders, always wanting to take things as if they were free for the taking, never honoring the customs of the people you've intruded upon."

"I just met you today. How am I supposed to know your customs? As for the berries and other foods, they grow *wild* here. How can you claim them to be yours alone?"

The mayor ignored him. "The sentence is death. In the morning, you will be tied to a post at the center of the city and stoned to death." He addressed one of the men. "Take him to the pit."

Had Eric's hands been free at that moment, he would have lunged for the mayor and broken his neck. The guards walked him through the city. People gathered around watching the spectacle. They hissed and jeered. One even spat on him. At last, they came upon an area where there were many holes in the ground. Some had people in them—prisoners.

"You shouldn't have taken *that* girl," one of the guards said as they walked Eric toward the pit.

"Who is she?" Eric asked.

"She's the mayor's daughter." The soldier laughed.

"Or more specifically," the other soldier said, "she's the mayor's wife's daughter."

They both guffawed as they untied his hands from behind his back and retied them in front, before throwing him into the pit. It appeared to be an old swimming pool. The guards rolled slabs of what looked like plastic tied together with loose rope over the top. At the four corners and the center of each side, they placed a heavy stone to keep the cover in place. There would be no way to escape, at least not with his hands tied.

Night came and shadows flickered against the trees from the light of a fire blazing nearby. There were footsteps and then one of the heavy stones was moved. A soldier, using a rope, lowered down food in a bowl. The food was spicy, what appeared to be a mixture with beans and wheat. It didn't taste all that great.

The soldier asked Eric if he wanted more. Eric said yes and also asked for some water. Moments later, he came back and let down more food and water. Eric drank the water first. Out of nowhere someone grabbed the soldier with such a force that they both fell into the pool, breaking the plastic beams on the way down. The assailant wore some kind of leather jacket and started beating the soldier. Eric stood immobile, helpless to do anything, and watched.

The man jabbed his knife deep inside the soldier, killing him, then turned and saw Eric, held up his knife and charged with a yell. Eric ran around the pool trying to avoid the attacker. "I'm on your side!" he screamed.

The assailant didn't let up. The pool wasn't big enough to escape the man. Eric ducked out of the way when the man made a swing at him. A stone connected with the man's face, knocking him unconscious. At the edge of the pool stood the girl who sacrificed him to save herself. Eric found a piece of the broken plastic about two feet long and swung it hard on top of the man's head, making sure he was dead.

"We must go!" the girl whispered.

"Who are these people?" Eric asked pointing to the one he had killed.

"We need to leave now!" she said moving another stone on one side of the pool. "Don't ask questions."

Eric didn't need to be convinced that this was not a normal situation. "My hands are tied!" he shouted.

She hung over the top and dropped herself into the pool and cut the rope. She turned and extended her hands reaching for the edge. Eric understood and grabbed her by the waist pushing her up. He took a few steps back and jumped, pulling himself up and out of the pool.

*Bang!*

Eric ducked at the sound of gunshots. Chaos seemed to have erupted throughout the village. The girl grabbed his hand and led him away. People ran in different directions and houses were on fire. Not several meters in front of them, a dozen people were being beaten to death by a group of attackers sporting police batons. Others were forced against the walls of buildings and shot with rifles. A select few had their hands tied with rope and were led toward a larger group of captured people.

"What's going on here?" he asked.

Without saying a word, the girl led Eric into the dark of night: away from the village; away from the burning; away from the fighting.

They walked north at a fast pace for what felt like several hours and then stopped to rest. He had no idea what time it was. The moon was not out tonight, but for all practical reasons, it didn't matter. The girl didn't look too unhappy and seemed to be content with the situation. Grabbing some berries, she offered some to Eric who took them gladly. She asked, "Can you build a fire?"

Her accent was not like the mayor's. It was more like Random and Spinner.

Eric shook his head. "I don't have anything to do that with. I wish I had my bag. There are things in there that I need."

To his surprise, she threw his bag in front of him.

"There's nothing in there except the beans we collected, a blanket, a jug for water, and a thick plate with numbers that light up." She pointed with her face at the backpack. "What does the plate do?"

"It's just a toy," Eric said avoiding eye contact.

"How does it work?"

"Why did those people invade your city?" he asked, ignoring her question.

"They're Feds. They invaded our home once before and took many people," she said, putting some dry beans into Eric's water bottle. "We've seen them invade other cities as well. They take the people as slaves."

"You have a home city?" Eric inquired.

"We're wanderers. We don't stay in one place for very long. We find cities that have buried buildings and they become our new city."

"Why do you leave those cities?"

"We leave when there's nothing to eat," she said.

Eric was impressed that these people could just get up and move to another place after the resources had been exploited and build a new settlement. "You called the other people Feds. Why are they called Feds?"

She shrugged. "That's what they're called."

"The Fed city must be big if they need slaves."

"I don't know. I've never been there," she shrugged. She put the cap back on the water bottle before placing it in Eric's backpack. The pebbles and debris were brushed away from the flat dirt surface leaving a clearing wide enough for them to lie down. "We'll sleep on the dirt and cover ourselves with your blanket," she explained.

Eric lay on the dirt with her next to him and put the sleeping bag over the two of them. Her warm body touched his.

*If anything is going to happen, I should at least know her name.*

"My name is Eric," he said turning over his shoulder to look at her.

"I am Camila," she said closing her eyes. "Sleep now. The Feds will be out early in the morning looking for people who have run away. We'll need to wake up early and continue walking."

Eric turned facing her warm body and pushed up against it. He was too tired to do anything, but still, when he put his hands on her waist, he became aroused. His heart raced. She turned her head to look at him and said, "Can you turn the other way?"

If anything was going to happen tonight, it would be nothing more or less than a good night's sleep. Eric turned as she got comfortable. After a few minutes, her rhythmic breathing relaxed Eric enough to fall asleep.

# Chapter 44

Eric slept well last night and turned to see his partner in crime. Camila stared at him with big dark eyes. "Good morning, Camila." Eric stared approvingly at her hispanic features; long black hair and dark, round eyes. "Did you sleep well?"

"I woke up a few times during the night. I heard some scary noises," she said, then smiled. "But I soon realized it was only you."

He liked her sense of humor.

Camila rolled up the sleeping bag. She fished some of the soaked beans out of the water bottle and ate them, before handing the bottle to Eric. He wasn't too excited about eating plain beans, but his stomach rumbled, reminding him he was starving. He reached out, but hesitated.

Camila shook the bottle, "You must eat. We have a long walk."

Reluctantly, he grabbed a handful and put them in his mouth. The beans were still hard and he swallowed them whole as if they were pills. When they were finished eating, she put more beans into the bottle to replace them.

"You didn't add water," he noted when she put the cap back on.

"We don't have water. We need to find some without getting caught."

They walked for several kilometers over the barren land. An occasional plant would sprout up out of the sand, barely surviving. Up ahead they could hear water flowing. They approached cautiously. Camila motioned for Eric to stay and went on ahead alone. She signaled for him to come over to the river; all was clear.

Eric looked up the river and decided they should follow it until they found another city. Camila agreed.

They spent another night sleeping on the dirt. Camila took no time falling asleep. Something always kept Eric awake, but finally her rhythmic breathing calmed him down.

In the morning they ate the beans. They were better this time around—softer. They found a few berries and ate those too.

By the afternoon they had walked a good distance. Camila started dragging her feet. "Can we rest a little? I'm so tired."

The geology of the area had changed. There were more rocks and boulders scattered on either side of the river, some twice the height of a person. They rested briefly, then continued to move, as soon as they were able. But the rocks and boulders were hard to navigate, and eventually, they gave up and waded through the shallow water's edge. The cold water soaking in his shoes was soothing to his sore feet.

Camila didn't talk much. Every time Eric would ask a question, he would get a yes or no answer. It was like pulling teeth. "You're not the mayor's daughter, but your mom's his wife?" Eric asked, trying to start a conversation.

"How do you know this?" she turned toward him with eyebrows raised.

"The guards were talking when they took me to the pit."

She stared out along the river and continued to walk. "My dad was mayor when I was a little girl. He was killed in a Fed raid many years ago. When my father was mayor, we didn't run strangers out of the city. We welcomed them. When Motts took over, he wanted to isolate himself and his city from everyone. He convinced my mother to be his wife."

"How did he become mayor?"

"He was in love with my mother and wanted to marry her long before she met my father. He became my father's advisor. When my father died, he became the new mayor. He liked me even less when my mother became his wife."

They walked along in silence.

As they passed a boulder, a boy and a girl were making out up ahead. Their light blue clothes hung loosely on their bodies—they looked much better than the outfits Camila's people wore. The boy had light brown curly hair, and from this distance, Eric couldn't tell if he was hispanic. The girl was of asian descent with straight black hair.

Eric started to approach them, but Camila pulled him back behind the boulder.

"Wait until they're finished," she whispered.

"Why?" he asked.

"If you go there now, they will be afraid of you."

They waited, and waited, and waited.

Across the river three men wearing leather vests pointed at the couple. Eric was filled with apprehension. "Aren't those people across the river the ones that invaded your village?" he asked.

Camila peeked around the boulder and looked across the river toward them. She quickly returned to hiding, breathing heavily, and nodded.

Somehow, they had made it to Fed territory.

His heart raced as they leaned back against the boulder. Camila squeezed his hand. They peered over the boulder and watched as the Feds waded across the shallow water and approached the couple. The men appeared to be friends by the way they interacted at first, but two of the men grabbed the boy and girl, while a third tied their hands. Eric was surprised that they didn't scream or shout. Then he saw the knife the man held. He turned to Camila and told her to find some rocks the size of her fist. She made sure to lay low and out of sight by the other men. When she came back, Eric told her to take off her clothes.

"Why?" she asked.

"I have a plan," he said and then turned to see what the three men were doing.

"I'm not so sure—"

"Come on!" he whispered. "We don't have much time. Trust me!"

She pursed her lips and took off her dress.

Eric wrapped the rocks in the dress. "Now go out into the river and get those men to come over. I promise I'll protect you." She pressed her lips together as she looked at Eric, as if trying to decide whether to trust him. "Go, please!"

Reluctantly, she went into the water and shouted at the men. They turned around in surprise. Predictably, lust filled their eyes. One of the men came toward Camila. The others waited. Eric spotted the gun and knife the man carried.

Camila's face turned to horror and she screamed, "Oh no! You're Feds!"

She ran back behind the boulder where Eric was waiting. The man came chasing Camila. By the time he realized what was happening, a sack of rocks landed on his head. He was out cold. Eric took the man's knife and gun.

"Jetral!" one of the other men cried out. "What are you doing?"

Eric motioned Camila to scream.

"Oh no! Don't do that to me! No!" she cried out, standing next to Eric. "No! Please stop."

Another man approached the boulder with a smug smile.

"Jetral?" the man called out.

Eric saw that the man was far enough away from the couple. He aimed the gun and fired.

*Click!*

The Fed realized what was happening and the smile on his face disappeared. He pulled out his gun and came toward Eric and Camila. Eric fired again.

*Click!*

As the Fed got closer Eric started getting nervous. The Fed pointed his gun at Eric and fired.

*Bang!*

Eric ducked and heard the bullet ricochet against the bolder. He tried firing the gun one last time.

*Bang!*

The Fed's body twisted in the air, and he fell back, landing face-first in the water, turning it red. The third Fed was already running across the river. Eric walked out from behind the boulder, aimed, and fired.

*Bang!*

It hit the Fed in the leg; he lurched forward into the shallow water. He got up and limped across the river. Eric bent over the Fed he had just killed and pulled out his revolver. Checking the cylinder and saw that there were only two bullets. He took the bullets and put them into the first gun.

The Fed was almost all the way across the river. Eric walked across the shallow water and fired his gun once more. The bullet found its mark and hit the Fed in the shoulder. The fleeing soldier stopped in his tracks and fell in the water bleeding and screaming in pain.

"Put your hands in the air!" Eric pointed the pistol at the man.

"I can't!" the Fed yelled from the pain. "You shot me in the shoulder."

Eric came above him and cocked the revolver.

"Put your hands in the air!"

Wincing in pain, the Fed did as he was told.

"How many of you are there?" Eric asked.

"There are only the three of us."

"How many of you are there?" he asked again, kicking the man in his bleeding shoulder.

The man shrieked from the pain, but still held up his hands. "There's no one else here! I swear!"

Eric turned to Camila. "Go to that one," he said, pointing to the dead man in the water, "and get the rope hanging off of his belt."

Camila waded across the river and took the rope from the corpse, handing it to Eric.

He handed her the gun.

"If this man tries to run away, shoot him," he said.

Eric went to the Fed and grabbed his good arm. "Stand up!"

The Fed stood, and Eric yanked the man's arms down behind him tied the rope around both hands. The Fed screeched in pain, but Eric didn't care. When the knot was secure, he turned him around.

*Bang!*

Eric ducked instinctively and looked over at Camila. The man whom Eric had hit with the sack of rocks was lying in the river, dead. The barrel of the gun in her hands was smoking.

Her body shook, as she stared at the corpse.

"I'll take the gun now," Eric slowly pried the gun from Camila's hands.

They cut the bindings off the couple, who had stood gawping from the water's edge as the events unfolded, clearly not sure whether to run or stay. Close up, Eric could see that they both had Native American features, but the boy had African features as well. They clung to each other, clearly afraid.

"I'm Eric and this is Camila," he said, motioning toward Camila who was now, once again, dressed. Despite the friendliness in his tone, they kept staring at the ground and wouldn't look up at him. "We mean you no harm."

The boy finally looked up at Eric. "I'm Latte and this is Uma."

"Latte?" Eric's eyes narrowed in confusion.

The girl stared at Eric. "It means warm and wonderful."

Eric could feel the tension. He had to make them understand he wasn't the enemy. "Where I come from, *latte* means—" Eric started and then decided that the meaning he knew wouldn't be as funny to them as it was to him. "Never mind. Where are we?"

"We're in Williamsport," Latte said, seeming to calm down a bit.

"This is Williamsport?" Eric looked around for other signs of life.

"The main city is about two miles inland," Uma said.

"Do you think it would be possible to work for food in your city?"

"I'm sure the mayor would allow you," Latte and Uma said in unison. They smiled at each other. The tension was gone.

Eric was hopeful that this city would be friendlier than the one he and Camila had just run away from.

# Chapter 45

Eric, Camila, and their prisoner followed Latte and Uma to Williamsport. The city reminded Eric of the suburbs in Philadelphia—quiet and peaceful. The buildings here were more exposed than Camila's village. Some of the roads still had asphalt, and most of the buildings were intact. It looked as if Williamsport had survived whatever catastrophe had happened in 2052.

They had been able to remove the cars from the streets. People walked the roads wearing coarse-looking shirts and loose pants made of linen woven in brown, tan, or light yellow. The shoes were soft sandals. It was hard to tell the men from the women based on their clothing alone. Every so often someone wore a rust-colored shirt making them stand out in the crowd. Vendors set up shop along the old asphalt, selling their wares. Groups of people dug up the dirt to where asphalt had not been exposed and some of them dismantle the cars they found.

Eric's little group started to attract attention. Two men in rust-colored shirts approached, carrying batons. From the way they behaved it was apparent they were policemen of sorts. One of the officers frowned at their prisoner, "Who is this?"

"We captured him by the river. There were three of them. The other two are dead," Latte told the policeman. "This man killed them and caught this one."

The officers eyed Eric. Camila shifted uncomfortably on her feet.

"Where are you from?" one officer asked Eric.

"We walked up the river and saw that these men had captured this couple and tied them up," Eric said, pointing to Latte and Uma.

"You dress almost like a Fed. Where are you from?" he asked again.

"I'm not a Fed. *He's* a Fed." Eric motioned to his captive.

"The mayor will want to talk with these two," another officer said.

The captured Fed was taken away, and another officer led the group in a different direction. The buildings on the street had been deliberately destroyed. Whole sections of wall were gone. They turned a corner and faced a structure that looked very much like a castle. Most of the windows had been replaced with a primitive form of glass that didn't allow a clear view. A dirt road descended toward the building and leveled off at the entrance where a lamppost flanked the door.

Camila went over to Uma, "Are these your soldiers?"

"No," she said. "They are the guards of Williamsport. They protect the people. The soldiers wear a different outfit and protect our borders."

The marble entryway led into a huge hall. Several doors lined the walls. At the end of the marble passage were two large doors. Two guards stood on either side of the doors. The guard escorted Eric's group through the large doors.

The room was long with a passage that led up to an elevated desk. In front of it were two smaller desks and behind them were benches on either side with a door at the very back. The guards motioned for the group to be seated and told them that the mayor would talk with them after hearing the petition of a citizen.

Eric's jaw dropped when the mayor entered through the back door wearing a flowing blue robe with gold lining draped over a dark purple shirt. A large emerald ring sparkled on his right hand. He projected a confidence that Eric had never seen before. His olive-skinned face framed large penetrating black eyes. Camila appeared to be just as mesmerized by his appearance.

The mayor focused his attention on the man who was standing in front of him and listened to his petition. Within a few minutes, he made a decision about his case. The citizen thanked the mayor and left the room. Another man then entered from a side door and went to the mayor to whisper something in his ear. The man was thin with small sharp eyes and nappy black hair. His bony fingers motioned the guards to bring Eric and his group in front of the mayor.

"Who is the one who captured the Fed?" the man asked.

Eric stepped forward raising his hand. "I am."

"You're not from this city. Where are you from?" the man asked with a smirk.

"I'm from the south," Eric said since he didn't belong to any city in this time. And technically he wasn't lying.

"From the south? What's the name of your city?" the man probed.

Eric was unsure of what to say. Perhaps he should tell them he was from Philadelphia. They wouldn't know of the place and it really wouldn't matter.

"We're from Nanticoke," Camila spoke up and then came to where Eric stood.

"Nanticoke?" the man said in disbelief. "That city doesn't exist anymore."

Camila insisted, "We are from that city."

"And where were you when the Feds approached?" the man asked Latte, ignoring Camila.

"We were by the river."

"Just the two of you?" the man asked. "You know it is forbidden to go to the river without a guard present. What were you doing there?"

Latte held one wrist in his hand behind his back. "We walked and didn't realize how far we had gone. We ended up at the river."

The man didn't believe him and it showed on his face. He returned his gaze to Eric. "And why were you at the river with these two?" he asked.

"The Feds attacked our city two nights ago," Camila said. "We escaped."

"But Nanticoke doesn't exist. Why do you lie?"

"We are a wandering group. We find abandoned cities and stay until we decide to move to another city," Camila explained.

Eric already didn't like this man.

"Do you expect us to believe that? Look at the way this one dresses," he said, pointing to Eric.

Everyone turned to look at Eric who had on a pair of jeans, a polo shirt, and running shoes. It was different enough that there was no simple explanation for it. No need to offer one until they asked about it.

"So you wandered around with the Feds until you found these two?" the man said, looking at Eric and trying to create a version of the story that suited him.

"We aren't with the Feds."

This man had many of the same attributes as the despicable mayor in the first city.

"We followed the river looking for any city," Camila said. "It was just the two of us. We knew we had come to one when we found Latte and Uma."

"How do you explain your clothing?" the man asked Eric.

"In the last city we were at, we found an ancient building that contained these clothes. There was only enough for some of the people," Camila offered.

"Does she always talk for you?" the man asked Eric.

Eric looked at Camila, smiled and turned to the man. "Yes. She's my advisor."

The mayor laughed. "Ha! She's like you, Kratz."

Kratz' face contorted with anger and his eyes narrowed.

"So how did you take on three men?" the mayor asked. "The Feds have guns."

"We hid behind some rocks when the Feds captured and tied up Latte and Uma. I lured one over to our hiding place and hit him with a sack of rocks," Eric said and noticed that Camila had begun to blush. "I took his gun. Then I shot the others."

"Bravo!" the mayor praised, clapping his hands. "One man killing two men, then capturing another singlehandedly. You'll be a hero in this city. Don't you agree, Kratz?"

"Indeed, a hero," Kratz muttered.

"We would like to stay in your city for a while, possibly permanently. We could work for food and shelter," Eric said.

"Perhaps he could be useful in the military," the mayor said. "What do you think, Kratz? He can join the army."

"I think they would both serve Williamsport better in the fields, Mayor Frazier."

"No. He's a hero, Kratz. Let him try out for the army, and if that doesn't work out, he can always be a guard of Williamsport."

"As you wish, Mayor Frazier."

Eric realized in some way he had made an enemy in Kratz, but the mayor liked him. Hopefully that would be all he needed while he lived in this city.

The mayor gave orders for him and Camila to be placed in an apartment. Eric was to report to Commander Oshkosh in the morning. The four of them were escorted out of the room. Eric and Camila said goodbye to Latte and Uma; on their way out, he heard Latte asked the officers where they would be staying.

"The eastside apartments," the officer replied. Their grinning expressions made it obvious they didn't like that part of town.

---

They entered a dilapidated apartment complex, jumping over broken steps, handrails missing, they held on to one another for balance. The guard didn't seem phased, striding over the gaps with ease. Both Eric and Camila were panting when they reach the third floor.

White scuffed walls that were crumbling in places and floorboards that were broken with a clear view of the apartment underneath, invited them inside. Eric now understood the expressions on his newly found friend's faces. Could anyone actually live in this place? They had some furniture; a beige sofa in the living room and a pair of chairs in the dining room all made of wicker. There was no table to eat on. Two window frames with no panes of glass looked out into the street below. His foot hit a bucket next to the window; it suddenly became apparent why the people always walked in the middle of the street and not on the sidewalk.

"There's a cafeteria downstairs," the officer said while reaching into his pocket, handing Eric what must have been money but looked more like metal buttons of various sizes. "They're only open until sunset."

The front door had no knob and the bucket seemed to be the only thing that would keep it closed. Eric joined Camila in the bedroom. The bed was a cot with sackcloth filled with dried-out leaves, a chair next to it. Camila seemed to be pleased with this place, she lay on the bed stretching her arms and legs. At least this room had a set of glass windows. These were the same primitive windows where light came into the room but couldn't be seen through. Eric looked around some more. The plumbing didn't work. The toilet had no seat and looked like it hadn't been used in over a century.

*How can these people live like this?*

Making his way back to the bedroom, Camila was already asleep, breathing gently and evenly. Eric sat in the chair and stared at her restful face. He thought about the events that had taken place in the last few days, how Camila had been so helpful. He wouldn't have been able to take on those three men without her help. Would any other woman have done what she did? Maybe Audrey would have. Thinking of Audrey made his heart ache; he missed her. He missed home. The time machine had failed. This *was* home now. *Better get used to it.*

They would need to get to the cafeteria soon if they wanted to eat—Camila had slept for a long time. Gently rubbing her arm, Eric woke her and she groggily followed him downstairs, clutching onto his arm and moving mechanically, still half asleep.

A line had already formed at the cafeteria when they arrived. It was like being back in high school. More people gathered behind them.

"I haven't seen you around here before. Are you new?" a man standing behind him asked. The man's beard was filthy, like the homeless people that filled the streets of Philadelphia. The man was in desperate need of a bath.

"Yes," Eric said. "We live upstairs."

"I live across the street over there." The man pointed behind him. "My name is Guinness."

"I'm Eric and this is Camila."

"Oh, a married couple," Guinness smiled. "You have a beautiful wife," he said to Eric and then turned to Camila. "You have a beautiful husband."

Eric and Camila laughed together.

"Are you both working the fields or the mines?" he asked.

"Neither," Eric said. "I'm in the military."

"The military?" Guinness said, his face knotted in confusion. "And they let you live in this dump? The military live in better houses on the west side." Guinness put his hands on his waist and snickered. "Someone doesn't like you."

Eric had a good idea who that someone could be—Kratz. He didn't like that some aspect of his life was being manipulated. He needed to and would work on changing that.

Guards stood around the lines and inside where the people were eating.

Eric and Camila found an empty bench. the spiced mashed potatoes and eggplant were decent, better than berries and raw beans. Guinness joined them. He didn't eat much of his food, moving it around his plate absently, nothing actually touched his lips. Camila finished everything on her plate and sat with a satisfied smile.

"Guinness," Eric said, getting the man's attention. "How do things work in this city?"

"Well, let's see." Guinness said, twisting his fork in the potatoes. "Everything is controlled by the mayor. All the food is prepared in places like this; you can have food in your apartment, but only a small amount. The farms are owned by the mayor. The mayor assigns jobs and you keep that job for the rest of your life. You get paid with money that barely lets you eat and buy clothes—not that there is anything else in this city that you would want to buy. Some people save their money so they can eat a little more on special occasions like birthdays and anniversaries."

"But in the city not everyone wears the same thing," Eric said.

"In the city? You mean the west side? They actually have something called fashion over there. The military and the politicians live on that side."

"Politicians?" Eric asked.

"Yeah, there are these people we vote for that are supposed to represent us. They're supposed to be able to make laws with our interests in mind. The mayor can veto any law that the representatives come up with. And most of the time he does. The representatives can override his veto, but that has never happened. The representatives are supposed to live in the district they represent, but when they get voted into office, they move to the west side."

"Interesting… tell me about the jobs. You said your job is for life?"

"Pretty much," Guinness sighed. "As a child, the schools determine what you're capable of doing. Then, you're taught those things that have to do with your capability. You start working in those areas, and if it doesn't work out, they try and find something else. If you can't do anything, you work in the fields or the mines."

Eric didn't like what he was hearing. These people were forced to work for the city. Williamsport had become a fascist society and the mayor was their dictator. It would be impossible to live here like this, not being able to make choices. Then again, this was how these people had survived all these years. How could he judge them on standards from a time that no longer existed?

"We had similar ways," Camila said. "Everyone has a position in life. You could not choose." She paused then asked Eric, "Is it like that where you are from?"

"Where I come from, you could choose your position in life. You could do whatever you wanted to do. Do nothing, if that's what you prefer. The mayor was not as powerful as here."

"Where is this place?" Guinness asked. "I would like to live there."

"It no longer exists. It was destroyed," Eric said.

"This is why he showed up in my city," Camila said.

"So why aren't you still in your city?" Guinness asked.

"Her city was destroyed too," Eric told him.

Guinness frowned at Eric. "You bring bad luck wherever you go." He got up, bent over and whispered into Camila's ear, then he left the table.

Eric and Camila went back to their apartment. It was almost dark and cold; empty window frames in the other parts of the apartment offered little protection. Eric took his sleeping bag and laid it over the bed. Camila slipped inside as Eric took off his shoes and pants.

"You'll be cold without your clothes on," Camila said.

"I'm fine." In just his under-shirt and shorts on, Eric laid down in the bed next to her, and they snuggled up for warmth. Lost in thought, he lay on his back wondering what would happen to them in this regimented city. how they would survive? Would they be allowed to freely leave if they wanted to go?

Camila reached over and ran her fingers over his arm, up to his shoulders. "You're tense. Let me relax you."

She got up and told him to lie on his stomach, while she rubbed her hands to get them warmed up. Eric turned over and enjoyed the touch of her soft, warm hands on his back, shoulders and neck. Her hands knew how to work him. She had the skill to weed out the knots of tension in his muscles.

"Better?" she asked when she was done.

Eric looked into her beaming face. "Oh yeah. That was great. You were great."

He opened his arm for her to come lie next to him. She cuddled, resting her head on his shoulder, pulling his hand to her waist. Were they a couple now? He kissed her on the forehead. She moaned and then said, "me too."

# Chapter 46

A knock rattled the door early in the morning, the sound of the bucket sliding on the floor had him on instant alert. Looking over, Camila was still asleep. He nimbly slid out from under her hand and leg which were draped over him, and shivering, quickly pulled on his clothes. Entering the main living area, a soldier stood across the threshold.

"I am supposed to escort you to Commander Oshkosh," the soldier said. A light foggy mist left his mouth.

"Let me put on my shoes. I'll be with you in a few minutes."

The soldier cleared his throat. "This is your uniform." He handed Eric a small pile of clothes that had been neatly folded.

Eric took the clothes into the bedroom. The shirt and pants were brown and tan: the same color that he wore back in the days when he was in the Reserve Officers' Training Corps. He sat at the edge of the bed thinking about his days in college, about home. *Why did that all have to disappear?* He thought about his sister and wondered what happened to her. They were supposed to meet up at Uncle Miles cabin. And what about Mom?

The soldier peered into the bedroom and coughed. "We're already late."

Camila woke and sat upright. "What's going on?" She looked at the soldier and then at Eric, a mixture of confusion and fright on her face.

Eric finished putting on his shoes and gave her his best smile. "I guess I'm going to work today." He kissed her on the lips. "I'll be back later."

---

One week later, Eric walked back to the dilapidated apartment. It was empty. His clothes were folded in a corner of the living room. Camila was nowhere to be found. The apartment actually looked cleaner than when they'd first moved in. He lay on the leafy bed and soon fell asleep.

It was still light outside when he woke. From the street below lots of people walked about, most of them in groups of three or four.

"Eric!" a woman shouted. The sound ricocheted between the buildings, making it hard to tell where it was coming from. "Eric!"

Camila stood in front of the building waving her hands.

"You're a sight for sore eyes," he said, with a big smile.

She left the group of women she was chatting with and ran into the building. Footsteps echoed throughout the stairwell. Eric had barely taken his head out of the window when the door swung open and she ran up to hug and kiss him.

"I didn't know if you were coming back!" she wailed and then hugged him again.

"I didn't know they would keep me there for so long," Eric said wrapping his arms around her.

"I'm going downstairs to eat. Are you hungry?" she said grabbing his hand.

"I can come with you," he said letting her guide him to the door.

Camila held on to Eric's arm as they walked into the cafeteria. They sat down next to her new friends, Brianna and Janis, who were already eating.

"Isn't he going to eat?" Janis asked.

"I'm fine. I ate before I came here."

"Tell me everything that happened," Camila said with a smile that went from ear to ear.

Eric told her about meeting the commander and other high-ranking officers; how they saw his natural leadership abilities and made him a corporal of a squadron.

"I've made quite a few new friends there," he added.

"He's a leader," Janis said, and then making sure Eric could hear, "I like men that are leaders."

Camila gave her friend a cold look. "He's already taken," she snapped, then bit her lip nervously. Her smile faded. She got quiet and looked down at the table.

Eric smiled, neither confirming nor denying her remark.

"So when do you have to go back?" Janis asked.

"I have two days off."

"It's harvest time. I only get tomorrow off." Her tone revealed disappointment.

"That's fine. We'll manage," he said, grabbing her hand and squeezing it.

Camila's smile came back.

An hour went by before Eric and Camila bid farewell to her friends and went upstairs to their apartment. He watched her enter the apartment ahead of him. Even though Camila wasn't gorgeous, she had a way about her that was attractive. They wasted little time with words.

---

The water at the creek was cold. Bathing was something that didn't happen very often; now he understood why. Eric was in a playful mood and started to throw mud on Camila. She retaliated. Soon they had mud all over their bodies and in their hair. They lay on the ground and kissed while the mud started to dry on their skin. Camila was the first to get up. Taking Eric by the hand they walked into the deep end of the creek. She washed the mud off of his body, then he did the same for her.

Afterward, they sat by the shore while their clothes dried in the sun.

"It would be so nice right now to go to grill a nice juicy steak with a baked potato filled with sour cream, butter, and chives, and then top it off with a cold beer," he said, sitting next to her and gently rubbing her side as she lay on the ground. "And then have some ice cream and apple pie."

Camila laughed at him. "What are all of these things you speak of? Sour cream, and butter, and why would you put it on a potato? Why not mix it all up?" Camila asked, looking at him confused. "I've had pies, but what are apples? And ice cream?" She leaned in and kissed him on the lips. "How do you make these things you talk about?"

He kissed her. "I wish I could show you my world," Eric said leaning back on his elbows as the rays of the sun dried him.

"Is it that much different from this place?"

"Oh yeah! It's a *lot* different than this place."

"How far away is your world?"

Eric sat up and captured her face between his hands and gave her a lingering kiss. As he looked into her eyes, he realized how beautiful she was. But thoughts of Audrey surfaced again. In some strange way, he had been hoping to find her here in this world.

"My world doesn't exist anymore," he said, still staring at Camila and realizing that he'd never see Audrey again. He needed to stop thinking about her. They'd had their moment—it was time to move on.

"How did it get destroyed?" she asked while squeezing his arms.

"I don't know," he said. "One day I was walking up a mountain and then the next thing I know, I'm swimming in water."

"It happened that fast?" She frowned, lips pursed. "So, your world, the place you come from, is underwater?"

"Yeah. It's all underwater."

"Your entire family is dead?"

His mom and dad were dead, he was sure. He didn't know about his sister or his uncle and cousins.

"My sister may have survived," he said.

"Why don't you go find her?"

"Oh, she's probably dead by now," Eric said. "That was a long time ago."

"How old is your sister."

"She's two years older than I am."

"Then how can you say that she is probably dead by now?"

"You wouldn't understand. Can we talk about something else?" Eric moved his hand from her waist and caressed her cheek. His thumb played with her lower lip.

She stared out into the creek.

"Explain it to me," she insisted. "I'll decide what I can and cannot understand."

"It would take all day to explain."

"Do you want to do something else?" she asked, running a finger up his stomach and over his chest.

"Actually, I would." He smiled and pulled her close for a kiss. She returned his embrace, grabbed his hand, and put it on her body.

"Is this what you want?" she said in her most sultry voice.

"Oh yeah." Eric pulled her body closer.

She backed away from him and curled her fingers around his erection. "The faster you talk, the faster you can get what you want." She winked.

"If I tell you, you won't believe me."

"Let *me* decide that," she said, looking into his eyes. "Tell me."

Eric did exactly that. He told her everything about his world, how he got to this time and what happened to the world just before he came here. He was lucky that his father had put the timepiece in his backpack. "My dad sent a girl to my time to get another timepiece," he reminisced. "Had I known that the object was in my backpack, I would have gone with her. I tried to convince her to stay with me."

It took a long time to tell her everything. She had many questions and needed the definitions of many words he used. Her expression turned from serious to chagrin.

When he finished, she said flatly, "You're right, I don't believe you."

Eric laughed.

"You told me that thing was a toy," she said upset.

"I said that so you wouldn't try and use it—it's a machine that lets you travel through time!"

"And the world you come from has a blue sky, not orange?" She said, casting a skeptical eye at him.

"The time I come from, yes, the sky is blue."

"Hmm." She stared into the distance, then turned to him. "This girl, the way you talk about her..." she paused. "Was she your woman?"

"Yes she was." Eric held his emotions in check.

"Where is she now?" she asked, jealousy tinging her tone.

"I don't know. I don't know what year she was from. She never told me or I just don't remember. Plus, even if I did know the year, I don't know where she lives."

Camila's lips pursed. Her eyes narrowed, a wrinkle appeared on her nose.

"Are you jealous?"

"No. I'm not," she snapped looking away stolid.

"If you say so." He laughed. Audrey had done the same thing when she thought that Freddy was a girl.

"Why are you laughing at me?" She slapped his thigh.

"You look so cute when you lie."

Her teeth clenched in a veiled smile as she grabbed his nipple with her hand twisting it.

"Ouch!" he snapped swiping her hand away.

They spent the entire day together and every now and then Camila did things that reminded him of Audrey. For an insane moment, he thought of trying to find her; but the more he got to know Camila, the more he knew that this was where he wanted to be. Over time, Audrey faded from his thoughts and memory.

# Chapter 47

Being an officer meant they had to assign Eric quarters on the west side with an apartment that had glass windows. The place didn't compare to 2052, but it was way better than the east side had been. It bugged Eric that the people on that side of the city didn't have some of these simple luxuries, but what could he do?

Two years passed and Eric moved up in the military. Commander Oshkosh let him know how pleased he was with his performance and leadership ability by promoting him to Lieutenant. The mayor also congratulated Eric, saying his hero was working out.

Eric walked home to be with Camila and their first son, Thomas. He thought about the world he grew up in and how Tommy would never experience that. This world was so different. There were no longer seasons in this part of Pennsylvania—it never once snowed here. The nights were colder than usual and the days were always hot. The days were just as long as the nights, never getting longer or shorter at any time during the year. He wished Tommy and Camila could experience the different seasons.

Camila met him at the door holding Tommy in her hand. Eric took his son as Camila prepared dinner for them. They both played with Tommy after eating.

"He needs a brother or a sister," Camila said.

"Tommy needs a sister?" Eric said rubbing his nose against Tommy's nose. "Mommy is saying this needs to be done *now!*" He set Tommy on the floor. "Hey buddy, can you wait here while me and mommy go make a baby?"

"Let's just wait 'till he falls asleep?" she said bouncing Tommy on her lap.

---

Kratz sat in his office, after coming back from a diplomatic mission with the feds, preparing documents for the mayor to sign. He had been the mayor's advisor for over six years now. Lieutenant Eric Lynch seemed to be befriending the mayor. It wouldn't be long before the mayor would be listening to his hero, as he liked to call him, over his advisor.

Kratz made a feeble attempt at befriending Lynch, but they both disliked each other and Kratz treated him more as his nemesis than a colleague. He even saw Lynch meeting with city councilmen, obviously trying to build close bonds with many of them. If this continued Kratz would lose all influence with the mayor. No way was that going to happen while he was still the mayor's advisor. He devised a cunning plan to keep the lieutenant away from the council and more importantly away from the mayor.

Frequent skirmishes occurred on the eastern frontier. The Appalachians constantly invaded and pillaged the bordering towns along the eastern frontier of Williamsport. The mayor tried unsuccessfully to negotiate a peace treaty with the Appalachian mayor to no avail, the raids continued.

Kratz quickly entered city hall to meet with the council leaders and proposed that Lynch be sent to subdue the Appalachians, since he was the mayor's Hero. The city council agreed and sent the lieutenant with the men he requested to join him on this mission.

Kratz visited the mail room daily, eagerly waiting for correspondence about the Lieutenant. Instead, the lieutenant sent correspondence that the negotiations with the mayor of Appalachia were not working and that a war might be eminent. Yes, this is what he wanted. Soon Lynch would have to fight and hopefully he would be killed. More correspondence came in discussing the raids. *Yes, yes, yes. What about the lieutenant? When will they fight?*

Kratz' jaw dropped when a letter came into the mail room written by Lynch himself that the Appalachian Mayor was impressed with the lieutenant, so much so, that he made a truce and agreed to stay on his side of the border. Kratz found it difficult to contain his rage, yelling out as loud as he could. Everything Lieutenant Lynch touched turned to gold. The young man had gone out to prove himself and was coming back an even bigger hero, especially in the eyes of the mayor.

He needed to be stopped.

After eight years of Lynch having a spotless career in the military, Kratz was convinced that now, more than ever, was the right time to get rid of both the mayor and the colonel.

---

The mayor hosted a party for the city council every year and always invited the military officers. Eric and Camila arrived at the party fashionably late, which to Eric meant being there on time. The aristocrats dressed elegantly compared to the common people of the city. The men wore brightly colored shirts and pants. Most of the women wore togas the color of red strawberries or green leaves, a few wore yellow; but only Camila wore orange, Eric in his officer's uniform hanging on her arm.

Eric and Camila arrived and entered the building, it was apparent from the rafters that this was once a warehouse. They had replaced the fluorescent lighting with large chandeliers filled with candles.

Eric walked slowly, allowing Camila to walk ahead of him. She turned around and their eyes met.

"Why are you walking so slow?" She smiled.

"Just checking you out." He winked.

She grabbed his arm and tugged on it. "After eight years and two kids, I'm glad you still find me attractive."

"So am I." Eric grinned, teasing.

Camila's eyes narrowed. He clasped her hands and then kissed her.

A few officers saluted Eric as they approached.

"We don't salute at parties, gentlemen. Military protocol is not obligatory at social gatherings"

"Sorry, sir!" the men said, placing their hands to their sides quickly.

Camila appeared relaxed, while Eric's stomach twisted.

"You're comfortable with these parties, aren't you?" he said, his hand on her back.

"When my father was alive, he had parties like these. Everyone wanted my father's attention and because of that, they wanted mine." Camila picked an appetizer off a platter as the waiter offered it to them. "I knew how to influence my dad, but Motts... He was ready to kill me for helping you."

The mayor spotted Eric and waved for them to join his circle. Kratz, as usual, stood out in his blue uniform beside the mayor.

"Colonel Lynch," the mayor nodded. "Congratulations on your promotion."

"Mr. Mayor." Eric bowed. "Thank you for inviting us to your party."

"I always want my military officers to enjoy some time away from the barracks," the mayor said. "You remember my wife, Lazzat?" After the introductions were made, Mayor Frazier turned his attention to Camila. "Mrs. Lynch. You are looking lovely as usual. The colonel definitely has good taste in his women."

"Oh really?" Camila said, turning to face Eric. "I can't wait to meet them."

Eric's eyes crinkled at the corners and he could feel his face heat up with embarrassment.

"Trust me," Lazzat said, smiling. "He's only talking about you."

"Of course I was," the mayor muttered, looking a little embarrassed. He threw a thankful look at his wife.

"Camila," Lazzat said, "I love the color of your toga. I don't think anyone here has that color. Where can I get one?"

"I made it myself. I took some carrots and crushed them up to a pulp, added a little berry juice, and I was able to make this dark orange dye."

"It's lovely. It looks like the evening sky. You might want to think about creating your own line of clothing and selling them." Lazzat took Camila by the arm and steered her away from the men, flicking a glance back at the men as she spoke. "Let me introduce you to some of the ladies you haven't already met."

Eric turned his gaze from his wife to Kratz who grabbed a bite-size portion from a tray of hors d'oeuvres, sniffed it, before putting it in his mouth. Apparently Kratz didn't find it very appetizing, going by the sour look on his face as he chewed.

"Mr. Mayor," Kratz said around a mouthful of food, "Councilman Boyle from Coalstown and Councilman Patronose from Highland want to talk with you about the budget for next year."

"It's a party, Kratz. We don't talk about budgets at parties," the mayor said, sounding annoyed.

"They are heading this way."

As soon as the mayor looked up, two distinguished men came strolling toward them.

"Hello, Homer. Hello, Mark," the mayor said, with obvious forced enthusiasm.

"Mr. Mayor. Perfect time for a party," Homer said. "The food is excellent."

"We are enjoying ourselves, to say the least." Mark nodded in agreement.

"Let me introduce you two to one of my top officers." Mayor Frazier pulled Eric into the center of the group. "This is Colonel Eric Lynch. He is one of the newest, fastest rising officers Williamsport has ever had the privilege to have serving in its military."

"Is he the one who singlehandedly fought a dozen Fed soldiers, killing all but one?" Homer asked.

"He's the one."

Eric was amazed at how politicians could spin a story and make it bigger than life itself. "That was eight years ago."

"And it's still fresh in the mayor's mind," Homer pointed out.

"Maybe we should commission a statue to be built in your honor," Mark suggested. Everyone laughed. Kratz just rolled his eyes.

"Mr. Mayor, we need to discuss this budget," Mark said becoming more serious.

"We're at a party, can't this wait until tomorrow?"

"We've tried getting your attention during the council meetings and you ignore us. We need to discuss this today or we will have a big problem on our hands," Homer insisted.

"Very well," the mayor said. "Kratz, Colonel Lynch, please excuse us and enjoy the rest of the party. I'm afraid I won't."

As the mayor left, Kratz and Eric found themselves alone together.

"So how are you doing, Kratz?" Eric asked awkwardly.

"Be careful, Colonel," Kratz said with a sneer. "Just because the mayor finds favor with you doesn't mean I still can't make your life miserable."

"So far, you've been doing a great job," Eric drawled. "I don't think I could have made colonel without you." With that, he turned his back on Kratz and made his way to the table to get some food. He managed to turn around just in time to catch Kratz fuming.

Commander Oshkosh came up behind him. "Are you enjoying yourself, Colonel?"

"As much as anyone can when everyone here has an agenda."

The commander smiled and started talking about military matters. Eric could see Kratz across the room, nervously watching the door the mayor had gone through with the other councilmen. Probably wanting to be there advising the mayor on anything and everything.

Eric enjoyed the food and really didn't want to talk about military matters with the commander, but every time he changed the subject, the commander came back to it. Looking across the room, Eric's gaze landed on Camila. She turned to meet his eyes, as if feeling his gaze. Someone started talking, she looked away. After a brief spat of conversation, she excused herself.

*Bang!*

Camila twitched in surprise and stopped dead in her tracks. Everyone looked around trying to identify where the noise had come from. The door Mayor Frazier had gone into had opened, and a voice shouted, "Come quick! The mayor has been stabbed!"

Homer stumbled out, blood staining his clothes. The mayor's security blocked the entrance and wouldn't allow anyone in. Eric ran to the door. Kratz had already gone inside.

As Eric got to the door and tried to go in, he was stopped. "I can help."

"I'm sorry, but my orders are not to let anyone in."

Peering around the guard, Eric could see Kratz, Homer, and Commander Oshkosh looking over the scene.

"Commander, permission to enter," Eric shouted to Commander Oshkosh.

The commander looked over to Kratz who shook his head and then he addressed Eric, "Permission denied. We have this under control, colonel."

Eric went over to Camila who was consoling Lazzat. A few other women gathered around her. Security began escorting people out of the building. Eric motioned for her to join him. She whispered something in Lazzat's ear and came over to Eric.

"Are you all right?" he asked.

"Who shot Mayor Frazier?" she asked, not fully believing that it had happened. "Is he dead?"

"I think Mark did it. I mean, Councilman Patronose," Eric said, looking back at the room. "Yes, Frazier's dead."

"I don't know if Lazzat knows. I'm going to stay with her," she said. "Can you handle the kids tonight?"

Eric nodded and kissed her. "I'll see you in the morning."

The next day, the commander announced that the mayor was dead and that Councilman Patronose had stabbed him multiple times with a knife. Councilman Boyle, in an attempt to defend the mayor, had shot and killed Councilman Patronose. Councilman Boyle was deemed a hero.

Something didn't sit right with Eric. He approached the commander and told him his thoughts, "Commander, I think that the real killer is not Patronose, but Councilman Boyle."

"And why do you think that Colonel?"

"Because Boyle had the gun. Why didn't he shoot Patronose before he had a chance to use the knife?"

"Maybe, Patronose was too fast for Boyle to stop him."

"For the first stabbing yes, But the mayor was stabbed multiple times. Boyle could have stopped him, since he had the gun.

"I've heard some of the other councilmembers telling me a different story, colonel."

"But sir, why would either of them bring a weapon to the mayor's party? Even if Patronose was the real killer, which I don't believe. Why would Boyle have a gun?"

"Maybe he knew something like this was going to happen."

"Sir I think Boyle killed both the mayor and Patronose."

"We have the evidence and it points to Patronose being the killer. I don't think you know what you're talking about Colonel. The matter is closed, let's just leave it alone."

It didn't sit well with Eric that the commander was fine the way things turned out. Boyle was the murderer. Why wouldn't the commander look further into it? Eric didn't want to believe that Oshkosh somehow might be involved in the mayor's murder.

---

Three days later, Kratz entered the council chambers to help decide who would be the next mayor of Williamsport. Since the mayor had no children to ascend to the throne, Councilman Boyle proposed that Kratz become the next mayor. But Councilman Rahama stood up and proposed that Colonel Lynch become the next mayor. Kratz knew Rahama was good friends with Mayor Frazier and knew that the mayor had a fondness for Colonel Lynch.

Kratz didn't expect Colonel Lynch to be someone who would be nominated to take the place of the mayor.

"Colonel Lynch is not from Williamsport!" Kratz cried out. He was pissed off. *Eric*

*Lynch is a nobody. What is he to them?* Kratz had been the mayor's right-hand man. He deserved the position more than anyone else.

"You are not from Williamsport either," Councilman Rahama retorted. "Perhaps we should remove you from consideration as well?"

Kratz showed a cool exterior but inside he was burning with aggravation. He grinned. "Very well then, let Colonel Lynch be considered for the position of mayor," Kratz scoffed, taking his seat.

Eric was asked to enter the council chambers before the vote. He came in looking politically ignorant of anything that was happening in this city. How could anyone want him to be mayor?

They voted and to Kratz' surprise, the city council came to a tie. Now it was obvious that at least half of the councilmen didn't like him. Once he did become mayor, they would be dealt with severely. As the role of advisor to the late mayor, it was obvious what he had to do.

He stood up and announced, "I will cast the tie-breaking vote."

The council quarreled among themselves. The noise level grew. Councilman Rahama stood up and raised his hands until everyone quieted down. "Kratz can't cast the tie-breaking vote. He is one of the men being chosen to become the new mayor," he argued. The council agreed and decided that the choice should be made by the mayor's wife.

Mayor Frazier's wife, Lazzat, was led into the council chamber and asked to cast the tie-breaking vote. Kratz glanced over to her as she smiled at him. The colonel was watching them. She glanced over to the colonel and offered him a smile as well, which he returned.

"I choose... Kratz," she declared.

Kratz stood with his hands raised in the air. Victory was his. He would now become the new mayor of Williamsport.

The news spread throughout the city like wildfire.

It was only a week after Mayor Frazier had been buried and an elaborate ceremony took place to coronate the new mayor. Everyone in Williamsport came to witness this momentous event. Cheers rang throughout the crowd as they put the mayoral robe on Kratz' shoulders and gave him the keys to the city.

Kratz sat down in the mayor's chair and closed his eyes. It was done. He was the mayor. This was the happiest moment of his life. All the people cheered as the procession went down the street. Many promises had been made to those who supported him. He had no intention of fulfilling any of them. The only promise that would be kept was the one to make Williamsport another city for the Feds.

After the ceremonies, he sent for Commander Oshkosh.

Within an hour, the commander stood at the front of his desk.

"We need to dispose of Councilman Boyle," Kratz ordered.

"Homer is good. He'll keep his mouth shut."

"He might." Kratz cut off a small piece of paper from a document, rolling it between his fingers. "And he might not. I don't want to take any chances."

"I understand," Oshkosh said and turned to walk out of the room.

"And, commander," Kratz stopped him, "make it look like an accident. I don't want anyone wondering if my ascension was planned."

The commander nodded and walked out of the room.

After all this mess was sorted out, the commander would have to be dealt with too. Kratz would miss him. After all, he was a good friend.

Five days later, Councilman Boyle was dead. The commander had made it look so real. No one suspected Kratz for having the commander arrested and killed for the murder of the councilman.

The next day, Kratz came into his office and found Lazzat sitting at his desk. His lips curled into a slow smile.

"You've gotten rid of everyone involved?" she said in a sultry voice.

"Almost everyone," Kratz said as he approached his desk.

"And what are you going to do about that?"

"I'll have to find a way to neutralize the problem." Kratz stood next to his chair.

Lazzat got out of the chair and put her arms around his neck. He pulled her closer and circled his hands around her waist.

"We make a good team, don't we?" she whispered as she kissed his chin.

# Chapter 48

Eric had trained his men to the point that they acted as a single body. A command could be given and hundreds of men acted to make that directive happen. The men respected and feared him. The approach used to discipline and reward the men shaped them into the military machine he had envisioned.

Eric liked Williamsport and had no intentions of leaving. He became political, not because he wanted to, but because he needed to in order to survive Kratz, who feared the loyalty his men had for him. When the decision of selecting a new commander presented itself, the position was given to a man named Elroy Skype.

The mayor loved Skype who was a shooting star and the perfect puppet to do as Kratz' wished. The new commander was aware of the relationship between the colonel and the mayor. Nonetheless, the day came when Skype made a decision to make Eric his right-hand man.

It filled Eric with so much satisfaction to know how furious Kratz would be.

Eric brought his men out to the field to perform military maneuvers when the commander sent for him.

He entered his superior's office and saluted. "Commander."

"At ease, colonel," Skype said, shuffling through the reports on the table. "I have a task for you." He found the report he was looking for and read through it. "I need you to go on a scouting mission for Williamsport. We've never tried to explore the frontier to the north. We've always assumed it was Fed territory, but now we want to make sure. You are needed to assess the surrounding cities in that area and determine their military strength."

"Sir," Eric started, "you can get Lieutenant Saggar to do that. Why send someone like me?"

"We need you to represent Williamsport diplomatically. You can speak on behalf of this city and the mayor will give you the authority to make treaties with those cities if you feel it benefits Williamsport."

"But I'm not a diplomat," Eric argued. "Why not send the lieutenant with a council member?"

"The mayor doesn't trust the councilmen," Skype said.

"And he trusts me?" Eric immediately knew something was awry. This made no sense because the mayor had the city council in his pocket. Eric could do nothing to challenge this order. The decision had to be Kratz' way of getting him to resign and possibly leave Williamsport.

"I understand," Eric said. "I'll need at least twenty men, sir."

Skype took a piece of paper and handed it to Eric. "You can take these ten."

All the men on the list were privates and new to the army.

Eric was dumbfounded. "I'll need at least two officers."

"This is all you're getting," Skype said with an inscrutable gaze.

Eric saw that his work was going to be cut out for him. "May I take my wife and children with me?"

Skype shook his head. "This is a military mission. No wives allowed."

"You just said it was a diplomatic mission."

"No wives or children allowed," Skype repeated, his tone brooking no argument.

Eric got home later that night and told Camila about the mission.

"For how long?" she asked. The news distressed her, but Eric assured her it wasn't dangerous and she needn't worry. There was no mention that part of being safe and out of danger meant not encountering the Feds.

"I'm guessing a year. Maybe less if I don't find anything," he said.

"I don't like the idea of you leaving for so long. Why are they sending you?"

He didn't want to burden Camila with the twisted politics of Williamsport. There had never been any worry that his family wasn't safe from reprisals from the mayor; but now he wasn't so sure. But where could they go? This was home.

Eric stood alone in his room packing. Tucked away in his backpack was the timepiece. Was there any reason to take this? After all, this would be an expedition to find new cities. What were the possibilities that by some strange set of circumstances they would stumble upon the vault? And if he found it, what were the odds of finding his family alive or seeing Audrey once more? Images of her filled his mind. Was she the reason, and not his family, why he took on this assignment with such little resistance? Camila stayed in the living room with the kids, helping pack the rest of his gear. When their voices flowed into the bedroom, guilt rode through him. Still, the need to bring the timepiece was stronger than his common sense. The timepiece was packed along with the clothes he had on when he was first transported to this time period. Thoughts of Audrey resurfaced in his mind as he saw her standing by the stairway at his house wearing her ragged clothes.

*Damn, she was beautiful.*

It had all happened so long ago. Barely a thought had been spared to her in over ten years. If they were meant to be together, it would have happened already. The chances of finding Audrey were slim. Was she from the past? Was she from the future? Was she here now? A sharp pain shot through him as he pondered the idea that she could be here in the present. If anything, she was probably in the future and his purpose, if he did find the vault, would be to leave the timepiece for her to find. That made so much more sense. After all, who else knew how she found it besides dad?

Thoughts of dad and Alexis filled him with sadness and nostalgia. He took out the photo of his family from the past and wanted to cry but had no time for that. He needed to be strong and didn't want his wife and kids seeing him like this.

Too soon, everything was packed and ready. He took a few moments to say goodbye to his family. Tommy was the oldest at eight and his little sister, Mariam, was three years younger. He could see Camila in Tommy's face.

"Daddy, why can't we come with you?" Mariam asked, climbing onto his lap and looking at him with her big puppy-dog eyes.

"It's part of my job and I can't take any of you with me." He paused and then added, "I asked and they said no."

"Aw, Daddy!" She hugged him tight, and her soft wavy brown hair brushed against his face. "How long will you be gone?"

"Maybe a year. I'm not quite sure," he said, hating having to give such news to them.

"A year! So, you're going to miss my birthday?" she pouted. She knew which buttons to press to make him feel guilty.

"And mine too," Tommy mumbled.

"I'm sorry." Eric held his children close to him. "I'll get each of you a present."

"Really?" they both said. Their faces lit up with excitement.

"I promise." Eric said as he stood up and then turned to Tommy and said, "Thomas, you are now the man of the house. You are responsible for protecting your mom and your sister. Okay?"

"I will," Tommy said somberly saluting.

Eric returned the salute and then kissed the kids goodbye and turned to hug Camila. They kissed for a long time.

"What's that about?" she asked.

"I'm going to be gone a long time and I just wanted to remember your kiss."

Camila ran her hands over his shoulders and arms. "Want to stay longer and make another baby before you go?"

The offer was tempting, but his men were waiting. He hugged the kids once more and kissed his wife one last time before leaving to join his team.

# Chapter 49

Eric and his men followed a dead river north. There was no indication of where it went. A map would have been a godsend. Unfortunately, all of the maps in 2052 were electronic. It made sense why Uncle Miles printed all the essential manuals on paper. It was something real that you could hold in your hands and didn't rely on electricity.

Three days they walked through unknown terrain. They stumbled upon a small deserted town that had been occupied recently. The buildings had been dug up, yet there were no people here. Two men were sent ahead to see what they could find. They came back reporting that there was a river farther to the north.

They picked a small building to camp in and busied themselves preparing a meal. Eric took Dwayne with him and they found a building that had its walls broken into. It was perfect. They broke the timber used to support the wall for a fire.

The afternoon was quiet as the fire burned nicely. The men ate in silence. Satish kept staring toward the town.

"What's wrong, private?" Eric asked.

"I don't know, sir," Satish answered. "But it feels like someone is watching us."

"I feel it too, sir." Dwayne nodded.

Eric looked around—nothing caught his eye. But if his men sensed that someone was there, he would look into it.

"Dwayne and Satish, you're with me," Eric ordered. "The rest of you stay here."

They walked out into the town. Eric asked Satish what his instincts told him and which area was of most concern to him.

"I can't really say, sir. It was more the sensation of being observed."

"Okay then. What direction did this sensation of yours come from?" Eric asked, trying to at least get a feel for a building they could investigate.

Satish pointed off to the right. There were two buildings, one taller than the other, both with no windows. They would look into the shorter building first. Dwayne was told to go to the back of the house and yell for anything unusual. Satish and Eric approached and entered the front door. It was dark inside. Everything had been reduced to rubble. Black dirt was all over the floor. There were signs of a fire, but nothing else.

Farther down the street, they came to the taller building, two stories higher than the first. They all stayed together. The inside looked pretty much the same—black rubble on the ground, burned debris. A stairway took them up to the second floor. It was an open space with rooms off to the sides. One of the rooms had a window that looked out to the camp where the men were sitting around the fire. An elevator shaft was at the center with light coming through from the floor below.

A noise came from upstairs—light footsteps, then nothing. Eric motioned Dwayne and Satish to be quiet, then pointed toward the stairs and climbed. Satish was a few steps back. Dwayne followed closely behind. They each pulled out their weapons and walked up, maneuvering the gaping holes in the concrete. On the third floor, they entered the first room to their right. It was then that hurried footsteps echoed from the stairs behind them. They turned and saw a little girl fleeing.

"Hey! Come back here!" Satish yelled and chased the girl. As he started toward the stairs, a man came from behind and grabbed him.

"Leave her alone!" the man screamed pummeling Satish's head with his fist.

Satish fell to the ground with the man on top. They both rolled down the stairs, falling through the cracked concrete and landing on the second floor. Dwayne and Eric ran down the stairs.

Satish had the disadvantage and couldn't defend himself except by attempting to block the punches. Dwayne came over and kicked the man off Satish.

"Leave my daddy alone!" the girl cried, punching Dwayne in the groin with the precision of a three-and-a-half-foot-tall little girl.

Dwayne lifted his hand to swing at the girl.

"Stop!" Eric bellowed.

Everybody froze. The man lunged after Dwayne. Dwayne stepped to the side, catching the man's hand and flipping him over on his back. He sat on the man, holding his hands out on the floor.

"Daddy!" the girl cried out. She lunged at Dwayne and pulled at his hair.

Eric managed to get close enough to get the girl off Dwayne.

"Let my daddy go!" the girl shrieked as Eric pulled her away.

"Don't touch her!" the man screamed, struggling with Dwayne on top of him.

"Stop this!" Eric shouted. "All of you, stop!"

The room got quiet.

"We would rather die than become your slaves," the man stated. His eyes filled with hatred and fear.

"Who do you think we are?" Eric asked.

"You're Feds!"

"No, we're not!"

The man looked at Eric and then at Dwayne who was still sitting on him. "Then why are you here?"

"Who are you?" Eric asked, motioning Dwayne to get off the man. "And where are we?"

Dwayne released the man, who rolled to his side and lifted himself up. Eric put the little girl down. She ran to her dad.

"I'm Troy and this is my daughter, Valerie," the man said.

"Are there others?" Eric asked.

"Everyone is gone. The Feds took them all."

"Where are we?"

"This place was called New America, until the Feds came over and took all of the people."

Eric needed to be extremely cautious. If the Feds were close, ten men wouldn't stand a chance against them.

It was getting dark outside and they needed to get back with the others.

"Let's go back to camp. Please, follow us," Eric said.

Troy looked cautiously at them then squeezed his daughter's hand lightly and walked alongside Eric.

The other men at camp looked surprised to see two new people.

"We have guests." Eric said, then came over to one of his men named Jerome. "Give these two something to eat."

"We have enough rations for twenty days. If these people stay with us, the rations will last us thirteen days, sir."

"Fine," he said, sitting down. "Feed these people. I'm sure we'll find another city where we can trade for food."

"How do you know that, sir?" Jerome asked. His face gave away the fact that he didn't agree with Eric's decision.

"I don't," Eric told him. "We'll manage."

"But, sir!"

"I gave you an order, private!"

Jerome grabbed some rations and handed Troy and Valerie the food. Eric had never seen anyone eat that fast. Not even his dad.

"When did the Feds attack your city?" Eric asked as Troy finished his last bite.

"Three days ago. We hid inside the building you found us in."

"Are you the only ones who got away?" Eric asked in disbelief.

"They had already taken my wife and two sons. I needed to find a place to hide where they wouldn't find us," Troy said, picking at the crumbs that had fallen on the ground with his fingers.

"But there are no doors in any of the rooms. How could you hide from anyone?"

"Inside the building there's a metal closet with a door in the ceiling. It has cables that connect to it. When the hole is closed, it's hard to detect."

"What's he talking about?" one of the men asked.

"He's talking about an elevator," Eric said.

"A what?" his men asked in confusion. Troy also sported a blank look.

Eric continued questioning the man. "How did you know how long to stay in there?"

"We stayed for an entire day in the darkness. When we got out, no one was here. The Feds took everyone," Troy said. "We tried to look for food, but the Feds burned our crops." He sighed then added, "Why are you here?"

"I was sent by my city to find other cities to establish relations," Eric said. "Unfortunately, your city is gone."

"Where will you go now?"

"We'll continue following the river north," Eric said.

Early morning the next day they all packed their gear and prepared for travel.

"We will not follow you along the river," Troy said.

"Very well. If you follow the dead river south for several days, you will come to another city, larger than this one. That is where we are from. Tell anyone in a red uniform that Colonel Eric Lynch sent you and they will help you."

"Thank you," Troy said.

Jerome gave Troy and his daughter Valerie enough rations for two days.

Eric and his men started walking south and continued for another three days along the river until they found a new river that flowed north. A steel truss spanned the river, a vestige of the bridge which existed here with no walkway to cross over it. Eric assessed that it was passable and grabbed on to the rusted steel beams and slowly made his way across. He gripped the beams tighter as he watched the water cascade against the rocks below. It took all of fifteen minutes to make it to the other side without incident. The other men came over the bridge one by one. Every one of them paused in the middle when they saw the rocks and how fast the water was going. Eric shouted at them not to look down and to continue. It was midday by the time everyone had finally crossed.

They continued following the river until it came to a cliff overlooking a huge body of water. The river fell off the cliff down into the ocean. It was a spectacular-looking waterfall. Eric had been here before; except he had been on the other side.

"Someone's been here," Satish shouted as he stood next to a dismantled, makeshift hut made of rocks.

Eric went over and looked at it. The area had wood debris on the ground. The people who were here had built a fire and hid it, maybe a day or two earlier. Probably refugees from New America.

Eric sent two men, Fred and Kramer, to scout ahead.

"If you see anyone, especially Feds, don't try and contact them," Eric instructed. "Gather as much information as you can and report back here."

Kramer took the lead with Fred following behind.

It was late afternoon when the two men returned and reported to Eric. "We found Feds off to the southeast," Kramer said.

"We also found a cove in between the cliffs," Fred added.

Eric's heart leapt. Could they have found the cove that Audrey talked about?

"How far away are the Feds from the cove?" Eric asked.

"About five kilometers," Fred said.

"Take me to the cove."

Kramer again took the lead. They came to a point where the cliffs continued with a small path heading north. The cliffs were not one solid piece of rock; the men had to jump from one rock formation to the next. If anyone slipped and fell it would be impossible to get back up. Kramer led onward through the path, regardless.

"What made you decide to come this way?" Eric asked as he jumped from one rock formation to the next.

"We didn't come this way," Fred said. "We walked along the upper cliffs and saw the cove from there."

"So why didn't we go that way?" Eric asked, jumping over to another rock formation and almost losing his equilibrium.

"Because there was no way down from up there," Kramer explained, catching Eric's arm and helping him regain his balance.

They came to a clearing where the cliff was wide enough for at least four of them to stand side by side. It narrowed toward the west and curved as it went back up to the main cliffs. Eric saw nothing that reminded him of his uncle's metal cave. At the bottom was the cove that Fred described. The area was covered in sand.

"How do we get down?" Dwayne asked.

Everyone started searching for a path leading down.

"I've found a way down," Kramer yelled. "It doesn't look like a trail at all."

# Timepieces

The men made their way cautiously down the cliff. At the bottom, Eric turned and saw the vault. With the exception of a few rusted spots, it looked the same as it did when he was younger. Off to the side, he noticed that someone had recently built a fire.

"What the hell is that?" Kramer and Dwayne said staring at the vault.

The other men got close and touched it.

"Move away from it," Eric ordered as he approached the metal door.

His men backed up as he stepped forward and put his hands on the door. He looked in the direction of the waterfall as he thought about Audrey.

*I was so close.*

His attention moved to the panel as his fingers passed over the numbers. He knelt down on the sand and tried to remember the combination. After a brief deliberation, he pressed the numbers two, ten, five, eight, twelve. Nothing happened.

*I forgot the combination.*

It had been so long ago. He tried again: two, seven, four, eight, twelve. Nothing. There was a riddle Uncle Miles had taught them to remember the combination. He concentrated.

*Two brothers divided ten pieces of candy. They each got one extra and multiplied it among themselves.*

"Two," Eric said aloud, pressing the tile marked II. The men grouped together and stared at him. "Ten divided by two is five." He pressed the tile marked X and the tile marked V. "Add one extra," he pressed the tile marked VI, "multiplied among themselves." He pressed the tile marked XII. The latch on the door slid. He got up and pushed the door open.

His men looked at each other and then at Eric.

"Who are you?" Dwayne asked.

# Chapter 50

The metal cave door pivoted open. Eric looked inside remembering a time when he would come here with his family. Now it was an empty shell; nothing on the walls, except a clock. An object on the floor caught his attention. He bent down and picked up a crinkled piece of weathered paper and read it.

*Dear Audrey,*

*I know you've never been here before and I know that you would never expect to find something addressed to you. I cannot explain anything to you at this time. But soon all your questions will be answered. Inside the box you will find a timepiece. The display on the timepiece can be set to take you anywhere in time. More importantly, it cannot take you to any place except where you are standing. The reason I'm leaving you with this timepiece is because you must go back in time to a place called Philadelphia and find Thomas Lynch. I've already fixed the settings on the timepiece to send you back to May 4, 1776. When you're ready, go outside and press the black button on top to turn it on and then the blue button to transport you back in time.*

*Your friend*

The handwriting looked familiar. *Dad?*

Audrey had already been here. She never told him what year she lived in. The paper was old and parched and torn in several places. She may have been here decades ago. He continued down the hallway to the closet that had a hidden wall; his uncle had told him this was where he stashed things for emergencies. The closet door was already open and so was the hidden wall. Whoever was here had already taken everything. Maybe it was Audrey. Some writing scrawled on the door made no sense. Whoever had been here last took everything.

His men remained silent but watchful as he knelt in the main room, lifting a floor panel, reaching down, turning on a switch. There was a click followed by some humming, and another click. Three green lights, on the wall, came on.

The men stared at him questioningly as he positioned the plate back. "We'll eat in here tonight," Eric said.

"Sir, how do you know these things about this place?" Satish asked, his voice a little shaky.

All the men locked their eyes on him, jaws dropped. Eric prided himself on being honest with his men but knew they wouldn't believe him. Nonetheless, he reasoned that this was not his problem and decided to tell the truth. "I used to come here as a boy. This place belonged to my uncle." He looked out onto the cove; it brought back memories of family and friends. What happened to them? Where did everyone go? Where was Audrey?

"Sir, we've never been here before," Satish said, closing his mouth.

The other men were getting nervous.

"I'm not originally from Williamsport," Eric revealed.

"Where are you from?" Dwayne asked raising his hand.

"I'm from very far away. The city I'm from doesn't exist anymore. To be honest with you, I never expected to find this place."

He told the men to close the door and they sat around eating their rations as he told them stories of places and things that none of them would ever believe were real. But that was all right. Nothing could be proven, and nothing needed to be proven. He was just happy to tell his stories.

The heater kept the cold out, but Eric couldn't sleep that night. Kramer had mentioned spotting the Feds along the cliffs. Were the Feds getting ready to attack a nearby city? With only ten men, he wouldn't be able to help those people and wouldn't risk the lives of his men in a battle that they didn't have a chance of winning.

When morning came, he was still pondering what they should do next if they couldn't get past the Feds. They'd have to go back the way they came and inform Kratz that this was as far north as they could go. If they could leave by way of the ocean, that would be ideal. The raft his uncle had was gone. Then an idea struck him. He grabbed his backpack and told the men to stay and wait for him. He cautioned them about the Feds and to stay in the cave out of sight from anyone on the cliffs.

"Where are you going?" Satish asked.

"Don't worry, I'll be back," Eric said. "Stay here and try not to be too loud. Being in the cove gives us a disadvantage."

"Good luck, sir!" Satish and the other men saluted him.

Eric saluted back and turned toward the loose rock that had brought them down into the cove. At the top, a boulder hid him out of sight from his men below. He brought out the timepiece. It hadn't worked correctly the last time. Hopefully, this time it would.

The letter addressed to Audrey mentioned May 4, 1776. Eric set the timepiece and pressed the blue button. The landscape changed; the sky was blue once more. There were trees here, lots of them. His heart almost stopped as he stepped closer to the edge and saw a figure below—Audrey. A crow swooped into the cove causing her to jump back. He almost laughed out loud but caught himself in time; she might hear even from this far away.

He sat on a boulder, looking out at the sky, breathing in fresh air, and waited for Audrey to venture up the hill. Several minutes later, a deer came up out of the cove. It fixed its big round eyes on him, then darted off in the opposite direction. A little later Audrey came up and looked across the valley walking away from Eric, still not sensing his presence.

"Hello there, little girl," he said.

She stepped back almost losing balance. "Hello," she said in a surprised tone, catching her breath. "You scared me!"

She was still the same girl that Eric had met twelve years ago. His feelings for her started to resurface and he had to remind himself that he was married.

*She's eighteen and I'm thirty-two. It's not quite the same anymore.*

"You seem lost," he said.

"Actually, I am," she said coming closer and smiling. "I'm trying to get to Philadelphia. Would you know how to get there?"

"You're far away from Philadelphia." He chuckled. "Why are you going there?"

"I'm supposed to find someone named Thomas Lynch."

"Who is he?"

He knew everything that was going to happen to her. Eric wanted so badly to hug and squeeze her and tell her who he was, but Audrey didn't know him at this time, and it would probably scare her.

"I don't know, really. I was told to find him."

She held the timepiece in her hand. If she loses it, she won't get home. But that was how they met. She needed to lose it.

"What's that thing you're carrying?" he asked.

"It's a plaything," she said, closing her hand around it.

He didn't want to frighten her, but he also didn't know when she would lose the timepiece. "You should put that away," he said. "Something like that must be very valuable. Someone's bound to steal it."

She took a step back. He shouldn't have said anything about stealing the timepiece. He looked toward the valley below where people worked in the fields. "I'm sure those people in the valley down there can help you get to Philadelphia," he said, pointing to the farm below. As he held out his right hand, he noticed his identification and immediately put his arm down and covered it with the other hand. He didn't think she'd notice it.

"Maybe they can. Do you know them?"

"Afraid not. What's your name?"

She stared at him. Did she recognize him? But that was impossible.

"Why do you look at me that way?" She peered at him through narrowed eyes.

"What way is that?"

"I'm not sure," she said staring back at him.

He was losing her trust, asking questions he already knew the answers to. Somehow, she could sense that.

"It was nice meeting you," she said walking away from him.

"You know Aud—" he said, stopping in mid-sentence. She hadn't mentioned her name and hopefully she didn't notice that he almost said it. She turned around. "If you want to get to the valley," he continued, "it's an easier walk this way." He pointed to the path behind him. "Be careful. I know you're not from around here and this place is not easy to navigate."

"Thank you for the suggestion, but I think I'm going to go the other way," she told him and headed in the opposite direction.

"It's your choice. You're going to find that there is no way down from there."

"I'm sure I'll manage," she said, continuing in her original direction.

Even in those ragged clothes she was beautiful. Eric watched as she walked away, wishing he could change time and be with her, but after thinking more about his wife and children, he was glad that things had turned out the way they did.

It would be a while before she would reach the valley below going in that direction.

# Timepieces

He stood up and walked farther away from the cove behind another boulder and opened his pack. Footsteps sounded. He craned his neck to see that Audrey had come back. She'd decided that his way was the better way after all.

"You should have listened to me the first time," he whispered to himself, smiling as she disappeared down the path.

He turned back to his backpack and took out the clothes he originally came with to this new world. When he set the timepiece to his birthday in 2031, nothing happened. It was strange he couldn't go to the day he was born but he could go to ancient times and the future. So, this thing wasn't completely broken. The term 'ancient times' reminded Eric of when he was a child and called his grandfather ancient, teasing him for being born in a different century. It would inevitably end up with Eric in his grandfather's lap as the old man recounted his adventures of being a teenager in the 1990s. If only his grandfather could see him now! *That's it!* He set the timepiece to a much earlier date—to when his grandfather was fifteen—July 8, 1989. He pressed the blue button and the landscape changed—but only slightly. There were still trees; the sky was still blue; squirrels scurried about. He laughed out loud at the wild thought that perhaps some of them could have been alive in 1776.

This wasn't home, but he was happy to see a world that resembled something close to home.

# Chapter 51

Eric walked east for half an hour and came to a road called Lizard Creek where he tried to hitch a ride. Almost thirty minutes passed before a man in an old ragged pickup truck pulled over.

"Where you going?"

"I just need to get to the nearest town," Eric said.

"That would be Lehighton. I'm heading there myself. Hop in the back. We'll get there in about ten minutes."

When they arrived, the man stopped on a street called Blakeslee in front of a K-mart. Eric thanked the man for the ride and found out that today was Saturday. There was a McDonald's across the street. His mouth started to water, and his stomach growled. The one thing needed in order to eat was the one thing he didn't have—money. How was he going to get that? With no ID to get a job and no way of getting an ID it would be impossible.

His grandfather told him stories of getting cash by cutting lawns. The residential area across the street had several houses with un-kept lawns. Thinking it was a good idea, he walked up to one of the houses and rang the doorbell.

"Excuse me," Eric said to an old man who opened the door. "I'm trying to make a little extra money and I was wondering if you would let me cut your lawn."

"No, thank you," the man said, closing the door. The same results happened at the next three houses.

On the fourth house, an old lady with short salt and pepper hair came to the door.

Eric smiled. "Hi, I'm trying to make a little extra money and I was hoping that you would let me cut your lawn." He subconsciously slumped expecting her to say no.

"Oh... well... yes, I would," she said. "My husband passed away a few years ago and the boy down the street is not that reliable. How much you gonna charge me?"

Eric hadn't thought about how much to charge for cutting someone's lawn. A hundred dollars would be cheap in his time, but if he charged too much, she might not want the grass cut.

Eric shook his head in thought, then opened his hands. "I tell you what. Let me cut the grass and after I'm done, you decide how much you want to pay me. Fair?"

"Okay. The lawn mower is in the shed in the back. Let me go get the key."

At first, Eric had no idea how to start the machine. The lawn mowers in his time were electric and automatically cut the grass using GPS. This machine had no GPS. He walked around the mower and found some instructions at the top of the handle. It didn't take long for him to start the mower.

An hour later, the lawn in front and back were done. The mower was placed back in the shed. The old woman sat on the stairs outside admiring his work.

"Wow!" she said. "You've done a great job. I was gonna give you ten dollars, but this is wonderful. I'll give you twenty."

Eric looked at what she handed him; this would barely buy him a candy bar. "Thank you so much."

"Are you thirsty? Want some water?" the woman asked and stood to go inside.

"That would be wonderful," Eric said.

She came back with a glass of water with ice in it. Eric hadn't seen ice in many years and put the glass up to his face to cool it off and then drank. Its taste was like nectar from the gods.

"What's your name?" she asked as he downed the last sips.

"I'm Eric," he said handing her back the glass.

"I'm Mrs. Porter. Nancy Porter. Where you from, Eric?"

"Williamsport," he said, realizing too late that Williamsport probably had a different name in this time.

"I have a sister who lives there. It's too big of a city for me. I like the quiet rural areas like this one."

The name hadn't changed. He thanked the old woman, and with a renewed vigor at his small amount of success, he went on to the next house. Most of the people didn't want a stranger cutting their lawn. This endeavor was going to be more difficult than he first thought.

Finally, after the sixth house he tried, a man took him up on his offer. "If you have equipment, I'll pay you to cut the grass."

Eric had to think of something fast. At last, an idea dawned on him. "Let me go and get my equipment."

The man looked at him oddly. "Okay. Come back when you have a mower."

He ran back to Mrs. Porter's house and knocked on the door.

She opened it. "What is it?"

"I was wondering if I could borrow your mower to cut your neighbor's lawn." Eric smiled with pressed lips afraid she'd say no. "I promise to bring it back." The mower wasn't electric. His grandfather told stories about how mowers used gas. "And I'll fill the mower back up with gas," he told her.

"I don't know," she said.

"I tell you what," he handed her back the twenty dollar bill, "I'll leave my money with you. When I return with your mower, I get my money back."

"How much money you trying to make?"

"As much as I can, ma'am."

"Okay, I'll go get the key."

Eric went back to the man's house to cut the lawn and made ten dollars. He went to the gas station to refill it with gas. There weren't that many in his time. Most everything was electric. It was amazing how cheap everything was in these times. Gas was only $1.29 a gallon. He returned the mower to Mrs. Porter who was sitting outside on the porch.

"I brought your mower back," Eric told her. "The tank is filled with gas like I promised."

"You need to go to Selma's house. She lives around the corner—the blue house on the right. And then you need to do another house. It's the yellow house next door.

That's Betty's house."

"Why are you helping me?" he asked, surprised that anyone would do this for a stranger.

"Because you seem like a nice young man and I want to help," she said. "Now go before it gets dark."

Mrs. Porter had arranged for Eric to cut the grass at six more houses. Most of the houses were close enough together that he could do them at the same time. By the end of the day he had made one hundred and thirty dollars and was exhausted.

He made the third and final trip to the gas station, filled up the tank, and dragged the mower back in Mrs. Porter's shed. She had already opened the door before he could ring the doorbell.

"You finished so fast?" she said.

"I mowed so many houses today," Eric said. "I'm surprised I finished them all."

Something in the air smelled good. His stomach rumbled from hunger. He wanted to get out of there fast and get something to eat.

"Would you like to stay for dinner?" she asked. "I cooked a roast while you worked."

"If that's not a problem," he said filling his lungs with the sweet aroma.

"None at all," she said and let him in. "You probably want to take a shower after working so hard."

Eric was grateful. He hadn't taken a shower in over ten years. He took a long one, enjoying the warm water as it fell on his body. This was so much better than bathing in the river. Afterward, he joined Mrs. Porter at the dinner table and tackled the roast. It was the best thing he'd eaten in a long time, perhaps ever.

She let him sleep in the guest bedroom and arranged for him to do another three houses on Sunday.

He put the mower back in the shed after finishing and thanked Mrs. Porter and left. This town, the houses, the street, the sidewalks—they didn't exist anymore in the future. It wasn't home, but it was very close to it. Did he really need to go back to the future? Things were so much better here. He was tempted to forget all that and not to go back. Almost, were it not for Camila and the children.

He entered the K-mart where he bought two eight-foot inflatable boats. Buying a gun required an ID. Instead, he bought a flare gun.

Eric walked past a theater. The price of a movie was only $5.25. They were playing *Indiana Jones and the Last Crusade*. He had seen every Indiana Jones movie, and this was his favorite. To the side, a poster of an upcoming movie caught his eye: *Back to the Future Part II*.

*How ironic,* he mused. *Too bad the real future didn't turn out to be the way it was in the movie.*

Eric hitched a ride off the highway back to the area he had come from. They passed a farm with people working the field, which somehow made him think about Audrey. He sat up in his chair suddenly realizing where he had sent her—the plantation.

"I am so stupid!" he said out loud.

If she didn't show proof she was free they would make her a slave.

"Are you okay?" the man asked.

"Yeah, I'm fine," Eric said readjusting in his seat. There was a writing pad on the dashboard. "Do you think I can take a few sheets of paper?"

"Take what you need. There's a pen in the box. I think it still works."

Eric fished out the pen and scribbled something on a piece of paper. When they got to his stop, he gave the man the rest of his money—thirty-three dollars and sixty-one cents.

"I only drove you less than ten miles," the man said.

"Where I'm going, I won't need that."

A worried frown creased the man's face. "Are you going to kill yourself?"

Eric laughed. "Not after buying all this stuff."

He got out of the car and made his way back to the cove. Everything he'd bought was dropped on the ground. Hanging on to the piece of paper, he then found the timepiece and set the date a day before Audrey arrived in 1776. She would eventually get captured although he wasn't quite sure when. If she ended up going to that plantation it might be the next day. From the story she told, someone had tricked her, causing her enslavement. Hopefully, this letter claiming her to be free would help. At the bottom of the path, the paper was placed on the ground. A small rock held it down to prevent it from being blown away. Hopefully, she would see it and these people would help her get to Philadelphia.

Back at the top, he returned to 1989 and took the flare gun out of the packaging and noticed that there were only two flares in it.

*I should have bought more flares.*

He removed and discarded the packaging from the rafts and held them both, then pressed the button on the timepiece and was back in the future. The backpack and one of the rafts weren't with him.

*How does this thing know what to take?*

After retrieving the rest of the objects in 1989 and returning to 2276, Eric changed into his army duds and headed down into the cove to meet his men, who flocked around him.

"What happened to you?" Satish said, looking him up and down in shock.

"What do you mean?"

"You just left and now you look so…"

"Clean, sir," Kramer finished.

"What have you got there, sir?" Jerome asked looking at the assortment of goodies.

"I brought back two boats and a flare gun."

"A what gun?" they all said in unison.

"It's a gun that…" Eric looked at them. "You'll see when we use it. For now, we need to inflate these boats so we can cross the bay."

"Those don't look like boats. How did you get them, sir?" Satish asked.

"I told you," Eric said. "My uncle brought me up here a lot."

"But I've never seen anything like this before," Satish said.

"Satish," Eric put his hand up, "right now you need to trust me, and we need to get these things out in the water!"

Satish understood the order and got five other men to help with the task.

An hour passed before the men had inflated the boats and were almost done. He went back to the vault to turn off the generator. At the moment the generator switched off, Kramer screamed out loudly, "We're being attacked!"

Eric came out to see what was happening. Rocks came falling around them like rain. It was a miracle that no one was shooting.

"Get everyone in those rafts and out in the water," Eric commanded.

"But the rafts are not fully inflated, sir!" Satish protested.

Eric could sense the fear in Satish's voice.

"You can continue to inflate them in the water," Eric said, pointing toward the ocean. "Get everyone out in the water!"

*Bang!*

They did have guns. Eric took his handgun out and shot blindly in the direction of the hailing rocks. Kramer and the other men followed suit.

*Bang! Bang! Bang!*

More rocks hailed down on them.

"Stop shooting!" Eric shouted. "We have limited ammunition. Just get to the rafts and get out into the water."

The rocks were small and thankfully didn't do all that much damage. The occasional bullet was what worried him the most. If they hit either raft, they would render them useless. The men did as commanded and pushed the rafts out into the water. Some of them had to swim to the rafts just to get in. They waited for him to join them.

"I gave you an order!" he screamed. "Get those rafts out of here!"

As he spoke, a rock hit him square on his back, causing him to fall to the ground. Kramer jumped out of the boat and came to his side.

"Damn it, Kramer! What are you doing here?"

"I'm not going to let my commander go down without a fight, sir."

The enemy was starting to swarm down toward the cove. The raft was still near the shore.

"Get those rafts away from here! Now!" Eric shouted as loud as he could.

"But what about you two?" Satish cried out.

"Do what I say and get out of here."

The men did as ordered. They took out the paddles and went farther out into the water, leaving Eric and Kramer behind.

The leather jackets confirmed that these attackers were indeed Feds. Several of them had reached the sand and headed toward them.

"You are outmanned," a soldier shouted. "Surrender now and we will make your death painless."

Eric pulled out his flare gun and aimed it at the soldier. Bullets rang out and Kramer went down. He pressed the trigger and the flare went into the soldier; his chest radiated a bright red light. As the other soldiers stopped and looked at their wounded commander, Eric used their distraction to escape, and ran into the water, diving under the waves.

*Whoosh! Whoosh!* Bullets passed thru the water, but none hit. He swam for as long as he could hold his breath before coming up for air. The raft was out farther in the water than expected. The men had done well; they were too far away for the Feds to go after them.

The cold water was having an effect on his ability to swim fast. He stayed above water as he inched toward the rafts, breathing in short, quick gasps. But he was losing strength with each stroke.

Then came a welcome sound—the voice of one of the men.

"He's alive!"

They paddled toward him. Dwayne and Satish pulled him into the raft.

"I didn't know you could swim, sir." Dwayne smiled.

"You'd be surprised of all the things I can do," Eric quipped between the panting as he tried to catch his breath.

"Which way, sir?" Dwayne asked.

Eric pointed toward the west and closed his eyes.

# Chapter 52

Eric had no idea how long he'd been unconscious. He could hear the gentle sound of the ocean. The ground moved beneath him; He was still on the boat. Tall cliffs loomed to one side. Eric rubbed his eyes and propped himself up, Catching sight of a few small boats nearby. Peering past his men there was a bay dead ahead, with a city at its shore. One building taller than the rest, seemed out of place.

"Are they Feds?" Eric asked, sitting up.

"No, they're not, sir," Dwayne assured.

By the time they reached the shore soldiers were waiting for them. This was a good sign. This city was on alert to defend itself. Not like the first mayor who, as Camila explained to him on previous occasions, tried to move away from the problem instead of confronting it.

"I am Colonel Lynch of Williamsport," he said to the soldiers of the city as the rafts came to rest at the shore. His men disembarked, standing with the water splashing against their feet. Eric continued to speak, "We come in peace. There are Fed soldiers camped outside your city. It's important that I speak with your mayor."

"And you've come to save the day?" one of the soldiers said, laughing at Eric's convoy.

"I've come to warn your mayor."

"By threatening us?" the soldier said outstretching his arms.

"What's the name of this city?"

"I ask the questions here. Not you!" The soldier gave Eric an intense gaze as he pointed his finger at him.

It was always hard dealing with men who needed to show authority and had no clue about what was really going on. The other soldiers had taken out their swords. Eric motioned his soldiers to stand down. This soldier's attitude needed to be nipped in the bud.

"Listen to me," he addressed all the soldiers. "We are evenly paired. If you engage us, we will still be standing." He stared into the eyes of the defiant soldier. Eric was bluffing and hoped the pompous ass would take it. "Your first mistake was to let us come onshore. You lost your advantage."

The soldier stood stoic, without saying a word. His jaw twitched irritably. Eric had hit a nerve. Now, to ram the nail into place and show this soldier who was boss. "Send two of your men to your mayor and tell him Colonel Lynch of Williamsport needs to speak with him." The soldier didn't move. "Now, soldier!"

Two of the men were dispatched to tell the mayor about the men from Williamsport. Barely ten minutes later, the soldiers escorted Eric through the city while his men remained with the rafts.

# Timepieces

The city was smaller than Williamsport but had many similarities: the excavated streets for one; the use of coal for another.

The soldiers led him into a brick building. The place looked very much like 2052. The reception desk had been rebuilt. The walls and marble flooring were old, cracked, and coming apart in places. They passed through a hallway with offices on either side. One of the rooms was closed off by a set of heavy double doors made of wood. They looked old and in desperate need of repair. His escort opened the doors and gestured for him to go through.

As he entered, a man sat behind an old wooden desk, wearing a simple cloak with no embellishments. In addition, two men stood behind the man, dressed the same as the soldiers, an older woman stood to the side of the desk, her dress matched the grey colored drapes. She was pretty, her lips and the shape of her nose, the way her eyes gleamed, reminded him of Audrey.

Eric extended his hand to greet him. "I am Colonel Lynch of Williamsport."

The mayor raised his hand in greeting but did not shake Eric's hand. "I am Mayor Oberon. My men tell me that you have soldiers camped outside our borders."

"That's not true." Eric studied the mayor. The man sat back in his chair, projecting authority. "All my men are in your city and there are only nine of them." Mayor Oberon's gaze was sharp.

"The soldiers camped outside your city are Feds."

"What do you know about the Feds?" The mayor motioned to one of his soldiers, "Go and find Logan Tolbert."

The soldier turned and quickly left the chamber.

"I've encountered them several times before," Eric said, "their agenda is to invade cities and destroy them."

"They claim to be our friends. If they invade us, we are ready for them."

"No, you're not. Your men are ill prepared to deal with this threat."

The mayor narrowed his eyes. "Tell me again, why you are here?"

The mayor stared at Eric, tapping the table. Eric needed to show him that he was not the threat. It was as if they were in a poker game and Oberon had just checked his hand. This city was not in a position to fight and its mayor didn't know that. He needed to fold gracefully.

"I assure you I am not here on behalf of the Feds," Eric said calmly.

"And why should I believe you?" the mayor leaned over his desk, both hands on the table. His tone became ever more hostile.

"I can understand your mistrust. But if I were a Fed, there would have been no reason for me to give away my position."

"There would, if your intention was to get my army to attack you on the eastern front while the majority of your army attacked from the south."

At this point, the soldier returned with another man. His thin build and orange hair made him stand out. He looked to be about 18 years old.

Oberon looked at the young man. "Have you ever seen him anywhere while in New Scranton?"

The young man looked at Eric and shook his head. "I've never seen him before."

Oberon turned to the soldier and told him to get the ambassador.

"Do you think that is wise, Oberon?" the older woman interjected.

The mayor took a few moments to ponder.

Eric couldn't stop noticing the resemblance this woman had to Audrey. Could she be her daughter or grand-daughter? He addressed the woman, "Excuse me, but—"

The mayor held his hand up to stop Eric and then looked to the woman and the orange haired young man. "Why don't you two prepare quarters for our guests?"

The young man and the woman walked out of the room.

"While we wait, tell me about your city. Who is the mayor there?"

It was too easy. The mayor didn't care about his city or his mission. He was just biding his time until the ambassador arrived. For what? Eric told him about Williamsport and his mission.

"Oberon," the ambassador said peeking behind the door before coming in. He sauntered into the room as if *he* were the mayor. His eyes scanned Eric as he took a seat next to him.

"Bartlett," the mayor greeted. "Do you two know each other?"

Bartlett smiled. "I don't think we've met."

"This is Colonel Lynch of Williamsport." The ambassador's brow raised before narrowing in suspicion. "So, you know him then?" Oberon asked.

"I don't know him, but I've heard of him," Bartlett said cautiously. "Williamsport is one of our biggest trading partners. The colonel used to be a hero there, but he is now wanted for treason."

"That is a lie!" Eric tried to keep his emotions in check. "Sir, I was sent on a mission to befriend new cities for Williamsport. Williamsport does not have relations with the Feds. They're our enemy."

He sounded like a babbling idiot. Letting his emotions control him was a mistake. What was Bartlett trying to do? He needed to do something; say something.

Oberon stood. "Thank you, Bartlett. We will see you again on Friday, yes?"

"Of course." Bartlett rose and, as he left, nodded to Eric. "Colonel."

"You believe him?" Eric asked after the ambassador was out of the room.

"I know him. I don't know you."

Eric had no idea what was going on. It made no sense. Williamsport was trading with the Feds? But then again, he wouldn't put anything past Kratz.

"Sir, the reason I'm a hero in Williamsport is—"

"I really don't care," Oberon said raising his hand and then paused in thought. "I've heard several stories about the Feds in the last two days and I need to find out if they are true. You, I don't trust at the moment, and if I find that you haven't been honest with me, I'll have you killed. You and your men will be placed under arrest." The mayor stood up and called the two guards and then looked back at Eric. "I'll need you to hand over your weapons."

Hesitating for just a moment, Eric stood, placing his weapons on the mayor's desk.

# Chapter 53

Audrey recognized the girl that appeared in front of her. She looked nothing like her brother but was a spitting image of Tom.

"You're Eric's sister," Audrey said, then put her hands to her chest. "I'm Audrey."

"You know my brother?" Alexis asked looking around confused. "I don't understand. Where am I?"

Audrey smiled. "You're in Milestown."

"Wait. This is Milestown?" she said an octave higher.

A noise came from behind the monument. Tom appeared, smiled at both of them.

"Audrey, this is my daughter Alexis," he said approaching them. "Alexis, this is Audrey."

Alexis dipped her head giving her father a worried look. "What just happened? You said you were going to take me someplace. I didn't expect to just appear here. Where are we?"

Tom grabbed Alexis by the hand. "We're in the same place we were just a moment ago. But now we're in the future. We just travelled through time."

"Dad, that doesn't make sense," Alexis said.

"I know I didn't understand it either at first, but that's what is happening." He turned Alexis around and pointed at the monument. "Take a look at this."

Alexis approached the monument and touched it, then scanned the plaque reading the names. "This is fantastic. Am I really in the future?"

Tom smiled and nodded.

Audrey remembered the books in the library that contained historical documents about the settlement of the city. There had to be something about Alexis, especially since her name was on the monument. "We have history books. I'm sure there is something about you," Audrey said. "Would you like to go and see what's there?"

"Lead the way."

They followed Audrey to the library which was on the opposite side of city hall. A commotion was going on around her dad's office. Logan and her mother came out and walked toward them.

"What's going on?"

"Your father is talking with a colonel from Williamsport. We're supposed to prepare quarters for him and his soldiers," Logan said curiously looking at Tom and Alexis.

"No, we are not," her mother said. "Whenever you hear the mayor say that, it means they are to be thrown in prison. Go to the barracks on the west side and tell the guards there will be new prisoners tonight."

She looked over at Tom and Alexis, "Oh my! Who is this?"

"This is Alexis. Tom's daughter," Audrey said.

Her mother studied Tom and Alexis for a second then pointed toward the office. "Oh, I must be thinking ridiculous thoughts." She faced the door to the mayor's office. "You look so much like..." She shook her head then asked, "Where are all of you going?"

"The library, to read some of the history books."

"Sounds like fun," she said in a huff, then walked away.

Alexis looked around in awe at the future Milestown. "In my time, excavating city hall had just started and creating a library wasn't on anyone's mind," she said.

The library was small and the books on the shelves were scarce. A good portion of them had recently been written. Audrey led them to the back. Alexis studied the shelves, scanning the books with her finger. She finally found a book about Alexis next to one of the old books about a mayor in 137, titled *The Biography of Alexis Lynch*. Alexis examined the book, but after just a few minutes she stopped and began to weep.

"Are you all right?" Audrey came putting a comforting hand on her shoulder.

"Yes," Alexis said with tears flowing down her face. "No. I have a son who dies and is buried next to Uncle Miles. They bury him and find a hardware store. If it weren't for finding the hardware store would they even have mentioned anything about him in the book?"

"Who wrote it?" Audrey asked.

"My daughter, Monica."

"Monica might not have written about your son, but the event about finding the hardware store was important enough and your son's death was significant to that end."

Alexis sniffled. "I don't really think I should be reading a book about myself in the future."

Tom came to her and held her hand. "Maybe you shouldn't read anything that has to do with you directly. You're going to find events that might be disturbing." Then he said, "You know, the comment you just made is similar to what Benjamin Franklin said in 1776?"

Alexis' jaw dropped. "You met Benjamin Franklin?"

"Yep," he said grabbing the colonial shirt he was wearing. "And I signed the Declaration of Independence."

"Are you serious?" she said in total amazement, wiping the tears from her eyes. "What you're wearing now makes sense."

"Actually, Eric was the one who showed me that I signed it," Tom said.

Alexis filled with sadness at the mention of his name. "I miss him."

"I do too," Tom and Audrey said simultaneously.

Tom pulled Alexis close and put his arms around her. "You're going to be just fine." He stayed with her for a while until she calmed down. Only then did he release her. "I'm going to see if I can find anything written about me."

He got up and walked down the hall. "I'm sure someone wrote about me. I had to be important to someone," he muttered, selecting a book seemingly at random.

Audrey watched as he sat on the floor and turned the pages. He seemed to be caught up in a book. After a while, tears began to fall from his eyes.

"What is it?" Audrey said, placing a gentle hand on his shoulder.

"My brother," he said almost whispering. "If not for Miles, none of this would be here now."

Audrey squeezed his shoulder. "He was a great man and we all celebrate him for the things he achieved for this city." Then in a louder voice so Alexis could hear, she added, "We celebrate all of you for making what we have here today possible."

"But I'm not there to make it possible. I'm here," Alexis countered. "So why hasn't anything changed?"

"Anywhere you go in time is where you're supposed to be," Tom said. "At some point, you'll go back and do all the things that are written in that book."

As Tom went back to reading about his brother, Audrey wandered over to sit near Alexis.

"How do you know Eric?" Alexis asked.

"Your father sent me to get another timepiece, but instead of finding him, I found Eric." Audrey's heart ached and she looked to the floor as she thought of him.

"What exactly happened between you two?" Alexis asked.

Audrey explained everything—how she met him at the house, how he gave her clothes to wear, and how they became lovers.

"That's not a very long time to get to know someone, is it?"

"I was there for almost a month; I just left him seven days ago." She paused. Alexis smiled at her. Audrey continued, "I have an idea of how we can bring Eric to this time. The same way your father brought you here."

"We can both go together and get him!" Alexis cried out excited that she would see her brother again.

At first Audrey agreed, but the more she thought about it the more she realized that couldn't happen. "No, you can't go because you already exist in that time." Alexis frowned. "It's true. We tried it. You can't go to any time in which you already exist. Your father calls it the law of time travel."

Alexis peered over at her dad who was deep into one of the books, then turned to Audrey, "When will you go?"

"I'll do it tomorrow," Audrey said. "I want to rest before taking that long walk. It would be nice if you could draw me a map of how to get there from here."

"If you have paper and a pencil, I could do that."

"I think they have some out front. I'll go get it."

It didn't take Alexis long to draw the map. Audrey took it and told Alexis that her father would be hungry soon.

Alexis looked toward her dad smiling. "So, you've gotten to know my dad pretty well."

She walked them back through city hall. As they were passing her father's office, they watched as a pair of soldiers went in, and just as quickly came back out followed by her father and a stranger. A man. When he looked up, she felt as though her heart had stopped. She was rooted to the spot.

"Eric!" Tom shouted and ran toward his son.

# Chapter 54

Audrey couldn't believe that it was Eric. He was older, but it was him and he was here, and he was alive! Alexis screamed and ran toward her brother. Eric turned toward the sound. The twisted look of confusion on his face turned to joy when he saw his family. Audrey walked up to stand quietly beside Alexis and watched as Eric hugged his sister and then his father.

As he let go of Tom, he turned toward her. Their eyes met. "Hello, Audrey," he said in a shaken voice.

"You know this man?" her father asked looking at Eric and then Audrey.

"Of course. He's my son," Tom interjected.

"He's my brother," Alexis said at the same time.

*He's my lover*, Audrey thought, standing there next to them all. She said nothing. She noticed her father looking at her in disbelief.

"What's going on here?" he demanded. "You are from the past," he said, pointing to Tom. "This man looks almost as old as you. How can he be your son?"

Tom pressed his lips in thought. "I'm guessing that you found the timepiece in your backpack," he said, looking over at Eric.

"Not before I got here." Eric smiled.

Audrey stared at him as if he were crazy. No way! No one could have traveled here without turning on the timepiece.

"I was on my way to the vault when a strong wind and earthquake rocked the ground, and then a tree fell on top of me. The next thing I knew, I found myself in water swimming toward the shore. It wasn't until I was in a cave that I realized I had one of your timepieces."

Alexis listened, eyes brimming with tears. She stepped closer to her brother and embraced him again. "I'm so glad you didn't die back there."

"How did the thing turn on in your backpack?" Tom asked.

"I don't know, Dad. All I know is that I'm here."

"Wow! What are the chances that we'd all meet here like this?" Tom said.

Mayor Oberon stared in shock, looking to everyone for some kind of explanation. "This is unbelievable. How could all of this be possible? And how is it that you know them all?" he said to his daughter.

Audrey explained quickly to her father how she knew Tom, Eric and Alexis.

After the newly reconnected group were being ushered to the mayor's house, servants were ordered to move Tom to a larger room where Alexis and Eric could stay with him and rest, and the mayor gave orders to prepare an area in the military barracks for Eric's soldiers.

Audrey decided to leave them alone for a while. She didn't want to interfere with their family reunion.

---

Alexis squeeze Eric's arm and smiled. "I'm so glad you didn't die that day when you didn't show up at the cabin. When the comet hit the earth, I lost all hope of ever seeing you again."

"What happened?" his dad asked, sitting on one of the beds.

Eric told them everything. When he had finished, Alexis couldn't stop crying.

"I saw the world being ripped apart, Dad. Thank you for putting that timepiece in my backpack," Eric said. "If not for that, I would be dead."

Next, Alexis told her story, the things that had happened to her up to this moment. She told them about Uncle Miles, and the things he did to keep them alive. Eric felt a pit in his stomach, sick with remorse. He should have been there. "Dad… why didn't you ever come back home?"

Tom sighed, Looking weary. "I came here from 1776. I thought that after I found out what happened here and why, I would return to 2052 and be with you guys. But it looks like that is not how things turned out."

Alexis noticed something catch Eric's attention at the door. Everyone stopped talking following his gaze. Audrey was leaning against the doorframe, silently. Listening. She smiled at them and then cleared her throat. "I just came by to check and see if you needed anything."

"Well, I guess there is one thing. Is there anything to eat?" asked Tom.

"Ben warned me about you," Audrey smiled, straightening up, as if to make off to fetch them some dinner.

"Oh, really? What did he say?" his dad asked, with a cynical grin.

"He said," she tried to imitate Ben's voice as best she could, "be careful, he will eat you out of house and home."

Everyone laughed.

"Well," Dad said, pouting, "I don't eat *that* much."

"Yes, you do," they all said together and laughed some more.

"Okay. You're right. Where's the food?"

"This way," Audrey spun, gesturing for them to follow her.

"This place is so similar and different than Williamsport," Eric said, as they sat at the table and Audrey left them to eat. They were served a stew that was all vegetables, with what looked like fish poured over rice. "Wow, they eat fish here. For some reason I thought they were all vegetarian."

"We caught fish in the early days too," Alexis told him.

The food here was good. A little spicier than what he was used to, but good. Today he was hungry and ate more than dad.

Dad was, as usual, caught up in his own world. Eric finished his meal and turned to his sister. "It makes sense why dad went to visit you to find out what happened to make all this." He gestured around the room. "But I'm trying to figure out why he brought you back here?"

"Why don't you ask him?" Alexis shrugged.

"Hey dad," Eric called out. When he didn't answer, he yelled again. "Dad!"

"What?"

"Dad, why did you bring Alexis to this time?"

Tom shrugged his shoulders. "I wanted to let her see what her future becomes."

"Even after what Benjamin Franklin said?" Alexis said.

"What did he say?"

"That you shouldn't be seeing anything about your own future?"

"Hmm." Dad went back to eating his food and just drifted off into his world again.

"That explains a whole lot," Eric said.

Alexis laughed. "He hasn't changed."

Eric looked around; Audrey hadn't joined them. He took a sip of water and sat back in his chair. Why didn't she join them? Even if she wasn't hungry, she could have sat and talked.

He stood, putting the glass down on the table. "I'm going to go outside to get some air."

"Do you want us to come with you?" his dad asked.

"No, I'm fine" Eric lied. Tucking in the chair, he went to leave.

Alexis grabbed his arm, pulling him closer. "She's outside, off to the side of the building," she whispered.

"Thanks, Sis," he smiled, patting her on the shoulder.

"Why is he looking for Audrey?" Tom asked inquisitively, as Eric headed for the doors.

"Audrey got romantically involved with Eric when she went to get the timepiece. Dad, aren't you following the story?"

"I didn't know there was a story to follow."

---

Audrey sat on one of the wicker chairs that encircled the patio. She was sitting alone, with arms folded and in deep thought. She caressed the timepiece which she held in one hand.

She turned to the creak of the door, Eric came out of the house, looking up into the orange sky and drifting clouds. He took in a deep breath; he seemed to like it here in Milestown.

She really didn't want to see him. She didn't want him to be an old man. But what could she do?

He approached, showing a half-smile. "I didn't see you at the table."

Audrey didn't move at first. She turned to look at him briefly, before calmly turning back around to stare down the street. "I wasn't hungry."

It felt awkward seeing him like this—*older*. She so desperately wanted to be able to go back to his house and fetch him; to save him. She wanted to be with his younger self. She reached into her pocket and took out another timepiece, holding one in each hand. "I didn't expect to see you with my father today… I told your sister that in the morning I would go back and bring you here."

"You won't need to do that now. I'm already here."

"Yes, you are." She took a deep breath and looked up, studying his face.

"Why are you holding two timepieces?"

"I got it out of your room," she said. "I don't know why I have them both with me." Tears brimmed in her eyes. She sniffled. "How long have you been here?" She placed the timepieces back in her pocket.

"I just got to Milestown this morning. I've been here over ten years already." He took a breath. "It's amazing how time goes by so quickly, isn't it?"

She asked how he found the city of Williamsport. He explained everything that had happened from the time he was supposed to meet Alexis at the vault, to how the timepiece brought him to the future, to the time spent trying to find her and not being able to. He told her about his first encounter with the Feds and how a girl saved him from death. He shared finding the vault and the note telling her to go to 1776.

Now she remembered that face. That old face. *It was him!* "It was you at the cove in 1776, wasn't it?" she asked standing, her face getting warmer and her fist clenching.

"Yes, it was," he said backing up with mouth open.

She flew at him, repeatedly hitting his chest with her fists. "How could you let me go down to those people?" she screamed hysterically.

"What do you mean? I didn't do anything." Eric tried to grab her arms, but she wouldn't let him hold her down. She backed up and kicked him in the stomach.

"They hurt me! You sent me to them, and they hurt me," she shouted. She felt the tears streaking down her face.

Eric's eyes opened wide as he tried to catch his breath. "I left you the slip of paper saying you were a free black woman. Didn't you find it?"

"No one believed what you wrote! They thought I wrote it. They claimed it was a forgery!"

Audrey began to cry and tried to slap him, but he caught her arm. She kneed him in the groin.

"Stop hitting me!" Eric said grabbing his groin. "I didn't know they would do that. I'm sorry."

She moved away from him. It was his fault. All this time and it was him. Could she ever forgive him for this?

Eric's eyes were wide, full of regret. He could only choke out, "I'm so sorry."

"Why did you send me to them?"

"I'm sorry. I wasn't thinking. I was just happy to see you again."

Audrey couldn't believe what she was hearing. She began pacing. "You were happy to see me? So why didn't you tell me who you were?"

"Audrey, please..." Eric had no excuses for not thinking about who those people were. He was the one who had sent her to become a slave.

"I told you about the old man," she cried out. "It was you the whole time!"

Eric stepped forward trying to hold her. She pushed him back. His hands went back down to the side.

"I couldn't tell you who I was because at that time we hadn't met yet. You still didn't know me."

She turned to him and cried out, "I wish I had never met you!"

Audrey's world was upside down. Everything was all wrong. The man she loved was not the same person. He changed. He was older now and stupid. But she still loved him.

"I'm sorry," Eric said. "I wasn't thinking about the time period. All I had on my mind was seeing you again. If I had thought it out, I wouldn't have let you go down there. I would have done something different."

Audrey wiped the tears from her eyes. How could he have sent her to those men knowing how blacks were treated in 1776! More tears pooled in her eyes. She used the hem of her dress to wipe them dry.

Neither said a word for a while. She sat on the chair looking down at the ground. Eric said nothing. She regained some of her composure and looked up. "So how old are you now?" she asked in between sniffles.

"I think I'm thirty-two," he responded with a half-smile.

"What happened to the girl that helped you escape?" she asked, knowing somewhere deep in her heart that she didn't really want to know the answer.

He cleared his throat. "That girl became my wife."

"Oh," Audrey gasped as her hand flew to her mouth. Her eyes squeezed shut as she couldn't bear the thought.

Eric put his hand on her shoulder. "Oh, Audrey, please, don't." She pushed his hand away. "It wasn't like I planned on it. I didn't know where I was. I didn't know what year you were from."

"I told you what year I was from," she said, not understanding why he couldn't remember even simple things like this.

"No, you never did."

"Yes, I did!"

"No, you didn't."

"I told you that I was from..." She stopped midsentence and then remembered what she'd said, "the future." He was right. There would have been no way to find her. They never expected to see each other again.

Audrey looked out into the horizon. "So, you're with her now."

"She and I had both gone through a lot together. I couldn't wait for you. I didn't have a clue where to look for you. A long time had passed."

"For me," she said, letting the tears stream freely down her face, "it's been a week since I last saw you." Audrey's eyes closed. She wanted to go back and get him when he was still in love with her. But deep down, she knew it wouldn't happen. She wished this moment wasn't real and closed her eyes. *Please be a dream! Please, let me go back and get you. God help me!*

She opened her eyes and he was still there—reality was there to stay.

"I'm still in love with you!" She blurted it out before she could stop herself. Would he tell her the same?

But Eric just stared without saying a word, watching her sob quietly.

She took one of the timepieces out of her pocket and set it back ten years then pressed the blue button. Nothing happened.

"You can't go back in time to where we met," Eric said.

"Oh really?"

She changed the time and set it to 1776. He grabbed the timepiece and said, "I'm already here, now, in this time. Nothing you try to do will change that. This is the way it turned out."

"Why?" she cried, trying to snatch the timepiece back.

"Because it's just the way it is. I'm happy with the way things turned out."

"But I'm not!" she wailed.

Eric put his arm around her and let her cry.

*God, why can't I have him?* her inner voice screamed. They stood motionless, locked in an embrace. At last, she withdrew from Eric, tasting the salt from the tears that had made their way down to her lips. "How long have we been like this?" she asked.

"It doesn't matter," he said wiping her face with his thumbs. "Are you feeling better now?"

She saw how different Eric was. "I can't blame you for the way things turned out. It's not your fault, it's not my fault. It's just the way things worked out." At that moment, she imagined being back at the house in Philadelphia, the two of them together as a couple. "I need time to deal with all of this. I need time by myself."

Eric nodded and left.

---

Logan had been standing at the corner of the building, listening. By her posture and listening to her tone of voice she was still in love with the other man. Even after their argument, after yelling about the things that upset her, he could see that she forgave him and still wanted him. It was in her voice; in the way she stood next to him. Logan laughed bitterly as his heart broke. He turned away from the scene and sat against the wall. It was true, after all. He wasn't just imagining someone else when she reappeared back at the cove. Jealousy was eating him up inside and there was nothing anyone could do to make her stop being in love with that old man.

As Eric left, Logan approached Audrey as she wiped the tears from her eyes. Logan heard some pebbles scraping under his shoes.

Audrey turned around surprised. "Logan! Where did you come from?"

"I guess you thought I would be him," he said, pain twisting his chest. "I heard everything."

"I didn't mean for it to happen," she sobbed. "It happened all so quickly." She paused for a moment and then started to laugh. "Believe it or not, part of the reason I liked him was because he reminded me of you."

"And that's supposed to make me feel better?"

"No, of course not. It was a stupid thing to say." Her hands shook nervously while she wiped her eyes.

Logan was upset, but he didn't want to lose her to another man. He didn't know what to do. "Are you going back with him to his city?"

"No."

"Why not?"

"Because he's married," she told him.

A mixture of emotions surged through him. It was great that Eric was already with someone else, but it was upsetting that he wasn't her first choice. He hated that she felt this way about someone else and not him. He gently took her hand. "Come with me to the beach."

"What for?" she asked giving a curious stare.

"To walk, to talk; let's take a boat out into the bay to see the stars. Let's just get away for a little while."

"But it's dark," she protested.

He pulled her toward him. "I know what it's like to be in love with someone and then to find out that they love someone else."

She stood motionless and looked up at him, then closed her eyes for a moment. "Logan, if I've learned anything, it's that you are so much better than I am. You knew that slavery was wrong, and I had to become a slave to know that. You're a good man, Logan. I'm so glad you're still my best friend."

He was her *best friend*. But what did that mean? This time he took the initiative and put his arm around her waist. She responded by putting her arm around him. Huddled together, she rested her head on his shoulder as they walked to the beach.

"I'm glad you're here with me now, Logan," she said.

"So am I," he said, feeling content.

They had a good conversation and talked about her adventures again. They laughed; they cried.

Audrey enjoyed the boat ride. They cuddled at the shore. He clasped Audrey's hand and kissed it. She smiled and kissed his hand.

He stared at her beautiful face as she lay asleep in his arms. *Things may just pan out, after all.*

# Chapter 55

Tom and Alexis decided to explore the city on their own. Eric was nowhere to be found.

"Shouldn't we let Audrey show us around?" Alexis asked.

"Oh, why bother? What better way to explore a city than to get lost in it?" Tom studied the house they came out of. "We just need to remember where we started our little adventure so we can get back."

They made their way to the center of town where the monolith was. Vendors had set up shops along the street. They had tables and canopies, selling everything from food to clothing to trinkets. Alexis stopped in front of a vendor who was selling polished black rocks. They were beautiful.

"They're twenty-five cents, miss," the vendor said.

Tom dug into his pocket and pulled out a coin.

"How much do you think this is worth?" Tom said, holding the coin up to the vendor.

"What is it?" Alexis asked.

"It's a Spanish silver dollar. Benjamin Franklin gave me a few. At the time he gave them to me, he was somewhat upset, saying something about his servants having other things better to do than to feed me." He turned back to the vendor. "So how much can you give me for it?"

"I'll give you five dollars for it."

"Five dollars?" Tom said in affront. He clasped the dollar in his hand and hid it from view. "You're joking. Come on, Alexis. Let's see if we can find a merchant who can appreciate the value of a Spanish silver dollar."

"Okay. I'll give you forty dollars," the vendor said.

"Sixty!" Tom insisted.

"Forty-five."

"Fifty-five!"

"Fifty."

"Sold!"

Tom put the coin down on the cart and whispered to Alexis, "See? You have to know how to haggle to get the best price!"

"But how do you know you got the best price? You didn't ask anyone else how much they would give you," she said.

"You're right! Maybe I should go around and find out how much it's really worth," Tom said, looking around for the coin.

"You already sold it to me," the vendor said, putting the coin in his pocket and counting the money.

"Well then," Tom said, "can you throw in some of those pretty rocks?"

"How many?"

Tom looked at Alexis.

"Four," she said, shrugging her shoulders.

The vendor grabbed four polished rocks and gave them to her, then gave the money for the coin to Tom.

"Thank you," Tom and Alexis said at the same time.

Tom walked away, counting his money. Alexis walked next to him, looking at the other wares being sold at the market.

"Hey! He didn't give us those rocks," Tom sputtered. He showed Alexis the money. "He sold them to me. Look, I only have forty-nine dollars!"

Alexis started to laugh. "Oh, Daddy. You really know how to wheel and deal, don't you?"

They spent the rest of the afternoon sampling food and buying clothes to wear. It was really amazing how much fifty dollars could actually buy.

---

Eric came back to the house to find that Dad and Alexis weren't there. The servants told him that they had gone into town to explore the city. He decided just to go back to the room, intent on relaxing and catching up on some sleep. He wasn't in the mood for sightseeing.

He woke to find a figure hovering over him. Blinking, his eyes came into focus, to find Audrey's young, beautiful face staring intently at him. How long had she been there, watching him sleep?

Sitting up on the bed, he noticed Audrey's change in clothes. "I like the green dress" he smiled. It looked like someone's first attempt at making clothes. He wasn't being unkind; this was one of the better items he'd seen on the people of this city. Once Williamsport and Milestown began trading, Williamsport would make a killing on selling clothes to these people.

Audrey looked prettier than ever. Eric had to remind himself that he was married. Why did life's events make things turn out the way they did? Why couldn't he have found the timepiece and been with her from the moment they met? But that was neither here nor there. This was the way things were and she wasn't going to be his.

"Thank you. We have a dinner party with my father and his guests. One of which is you."

"Oh. I see."

"They told me you were asleep, so I decided to come down and wake you."

"Is that why you stood over me like that?" Eric smiled and winked.

"I was standing over you," she said, lightly slapping his arm, "because you looked like you were having a bad dream."

"I was having a really weird dream," Eric admitted, yawning.

"Tell me about it."

"You know how to interpret dreams?" he asked sarcastically.

"Not I, but God."

"I forgot that you talk with God." Eric shook his head. "So, why doesn't God just talk with me?"

"He has. Where do you think the dream came from?" she said.

"Then why not give me the ability to interpret it?"

"God talks to people at different levels. The more you believe and follow him, the clearer his words become."

"Whoa! Wait! He talked with you when you didn't even know who he was," Eric said, finding a hole in her logic.

"That's because I'm special." She stuck her tongue out at him. "Seriously though, God has plans for me."

"Plans for what?"

"To interpret your dream for one thing; to convince my father and everyone else that God exists; and to free the slaves like I promised almost four months ago."

"That was the promise that kept you from staying with me back then?"

Audrey sighed. "A week ago. Yes. That was the promise."

Eric felt her excitement and conviction in her newly found belief. He didn't believe in God. It was his sister Alexis who had faith. But this god that Audrey believed in, was it the same god as the one that the Jews believed in? Or the Christians? Or the Muslims? Or was this a new god altogether?

Eric decided to tell her his dream. What harm could it do? "I woke up and found myself looking at a sky that was black, filled with stars, while the sun was still shining. I didn't recognize the landscape. It was open, looked like a desert, no signs of life. In the distance, I heard dogs barking; I was frightened. I wanted to run. But… something kept me rooted to the spot. Then a thousand vicious-looking dogs came over the horizon, gnashing their teeth and barking loudly. They were Great Danes with fur the color of snow. They were all on a leash and the leash was held by one man wearing a leather jacket and no shirt. He had on rough blue pants and black leather boots. The man's smile made me sick to my stomach.

"Then, on either side of me were more dogs; but these weren't barking. Both sets of dogs numbered in the thousands. Your father held on to one set of dogs and another man I couldn't recognize held on to the other set. For some reason, I felt like I had known the other man my entire life. Then your father let go of his dogs and they went after the Great Danes. As his dogs fought, the Great Danes would rip them in half, eat them, and become stronger. The Great Danes were too powerful, and I knew they would eventually destroy all of your father's dogs. He called the remaining dogs back and then a voice said, 'Those that believe in me shall not perish.'

"This time, your father and the other man both let the dogs loose and they attacked the Great Danes. It was their dogs that ripped the Great Danes in half and became stronger. The man with the leather jacket grew angry and fought with the man who was with your father. The man's dogs saw this and became enraged, utterly destroying the man in the leather jacket and the Great Danes. And then I woke up."

Eric wiped sweaty palms on the bed covers.

Audrey leaned over and squeezed his leg. "Interesting that you dreamt of dogs," she said. "This is an easy one: your dream is about a war. The dogs are soldiers. The two men, my father and the other man, represent the cities that the soldiers come from: Milestown and Williamsport. The man with the leather jacket represents the Feds. Their dogs are of a specific breed. This means that their soldiers are better than the soldiers of Milestown and Williamsport. My dad's dogs die because he doesn't believe in my god. And because of this, many of his soldiers are lost. In order to win your fight against the Fed army, you need to have faith in God."

"Interesting interpretation," Eric said. "But who is the other man, the one that I've known most of my life?"

"You are the other man," Audrey said. "*You* lead the city of Williamsport."

"But in order to win this war, we need to believe in God?" he questioned. His belief in God had stopped about the same time he stopped believing in Santa Claus.

"Yes," she said with determination. "The people need to know that He exists."

He wondered about her interpretation. Was it correct? He had no doubt that somehow these people would end up fighting the Feds. But in order to win a war, everyone was required to believe in God. This was something he couldn't quite understand. If any doubt filled his mind, that was it. If her dream was correct, a war was brewing, and he needed to help these people prepare for it.

# Chapter 56

Eric escorted Audrey to the dinner party. The red-haired man from the mayor's office stared hard at them as they entered. Audrey excused herself from Eric and went over to join the man. She took his hands and kissed him on the lips. The man kept his hostile gaze trained on Eric, intense jealousy emanating from him. She must have told him about the two of them.

*It was a long time ago. I don't feel the same way about her anymore.*

Eric sat across from his sister and dad. The tables were made of several different materials and sizes; some were wider than others, and none of them were the same color. There were two rows of tables with a combination of black, white, and brown tops. He knocked under one of the tables and could tell by the sound that it was made of plastic.

"What are you doing?" his father asked.

"The tables are all different. They must have found these when they excavated some of the houses around here."

Alexis nodded. "I noticed that too, I just didn't want to say anything." She giggled, pointing to the table adjoining theirs. "That one there is a conference table, or *was* a conference table, I guess."

"Recycle whatever you can, right?" Dad chuckled.

"So, what have you two been doing since you got here?" Eric asked.

"Just sightseeing, shopping and getting cheated," Alexis said smiling at Dad.

"When do you think we will get the chance to see your wife and kids?" Dad asked him.

"Come back with me," he said to his father, then added in a whisper, "You'll like Williamsport a lot more than Milestown."

"Hey! Don't be so cruel. They named this town after our uncle," Alexis protested.

They both smiled at her comment.

"What are the names of your wife and children?" Alexis asked, changing the subject.

"My wife's name is Camila. My son, who is the oldest, is named after you, Dad. We call him Tommy. My daughter is named Mariam, after Camila's grandmother."

"Those are good names," Alexis said approvingly.

The food was served. Both Eric and his father ate their portions. Dad wanted seconds, as usual.

"Dad, you shouldn't eat so much. You're the fattest one in this city," Alexis chided her father.

"Nonsense, these are all vegetables. By the end of the month, I'll be as skinny as everyone here. Regardless of how much I eat."

"Well, maybe you shouldn't act like a pig in front of everyone."

"They don't even know what a pig is."

"But I do!" she grumbled.

Ignoring their good-natured bickering, Eric looked over to Audrey. She was talking with the man who clearly liked her. He felt a little jealous watching them hold hands and forced himself to quell it. Averting his gaze in an effort to regain his composure, he spotted the mayor talking with someone in uniform. From the pins and sash that adorned his uniform, the man was a military leader. He excused himself and headed over.

The mayor smiled as Eric approached, but a soldier interrupted the mayor just as Eric joined the two men. "Sir, we've placed the Fed ambassador under house arrest."

"On whose order?" the man in military garb demanded to know.

"Lieutenant Poe, sir," the soldier said. "He intercepted a message the ambassador was trying to relay to the Fed troops at the border, sir."

"This message doesn't make any sense."

"What does it say?" Mayor Oberon asked.

"It says, 'Now!'"

"Now what?" the mayor asked, dumbfounded.

"It means the Feds are going to begin an attack as soon as they get that message," Eric interrupted.

"But *not* until they get this message," the mayor added. He introduced the man at his side. "Colonel Lynch, this is Commander Aruba who leads my military. Commander, this is Colonel Lynch from Williamsport."

Eric and the commander exchanged greetings. "I'm sure they don't have that big of a force along our border," Commander Aruba said. "Did Lieutenant Poe put the entire embassy staff under house arrest?"

"Yes sir," the soldier confirmed. "All of them."

"Commander Aruba, we need to defend ourselves," the mayor said. "dispatch our soldiers along the eastern border."

"There is one problem," Eric said. "Once the Feds see that your troops are building up at the border, they might engage."

"And if we do nothing, they might engage anyway," Commander Aruba argued the counter point.

"Sir," Eric told the mayor, "I suggest you bring the ambassador to your office and interrogate him."

The mayor nodded. Commander Aruba ordered the soldier to bring the ambassador to the mayor's office. It wasn't long before the ambassador was led in and strapped to a chair.

"What are you doing? Why are you doing this to me?" the ambassador demanded, red in face, disguising a hint of fear betrayed in his quivering voice. "I thought we were friends." He continued trying to get his hands out of the ropes.

"So did I," the mayor said sadly, with a shake of the head. "Why is your city doing this? Why are they planning on attacking us?"

"Attacking you? I don't understand," the ambassador said innocently.

"We've intercepted the note you were going to give your soldiers waiting at the border," the commander said, holding out the piece of paper in front of the ambassador's face.

After a moment of silence, the response was, "I didn't write that note."

"The staff member you gave it to says otherwise," Aruba countered. "We know you attacked our embassy in your territory. You killed everyone."

"I don't know what you're talking about."

"Come on now, Bartlett. We know what you do with your slaves. We know that you eat people," the mayor said in disgust. "Why would anyone eat other people?"

"We tried to get you to join with us," Bartlett shrugged, with a sigh, finally giving up the charade. "We brought meat to share with you. We felt that since you ate fish already your people wouldn't take long to get accustomed to the idea of eating meat. we hoped that eventually you would find it acceptable and join us." Bartlett laughed. "But your people found out too fast." He bared his teeth in an evil half-smile. "You can still join us now or your city will be destroyed."

"You're in no position to bargain," Oberon roared.

"Oh yes I am. Our forces are bigger and better than yours. Join us or be destroyed." He turned to Eric. "Williamsport is different," he added. "The new mayor, Kratz, was always a Fed."

Eric stared in shock. He had always hated Kratz and now there was a reason to hate him even more.

"Oh yes. The transition is going smoother than we thought. The city has already begun importing our meat. The people have started eating it and they love it!" Bartlett said with glee.

"Mayor, commander," Eric addressed them, "the Feds deal with cities in two ways. They either destroy the city and capture its people to eat, or they slowly get the people used to the taste of meat and assimilate them. The Feds are a threat to all the cities around them."

"I agree," said the commander pinching his chin with one hand. "But how do we get rid of them? We are too small a force to bring down the entire Fed army."

"Williamsport can help," Eric suggested. "Give me five hundred of your men and let me march back into Williamsport to win over the city."

"You're going to take over Williamsport with just five hundred men?" the commander asked.

"No, not with a force that small. I am second in command and I know which men in the Williamsport army I can trust. I know they will support me in this effort. Especially when they find out that Kratz is a Fed."

"Perhaps," said Bartlett, smiling. "But if the mayor is as smart as I know he is, he will have had all those men that are loyal to you executed. He couldn't kill you overnight because then he would have a mutiny on his hands within his own army." With a smug expression the ambassador continued, "So what to do?" He focused on Eric. "Send you away. Send you away on a futile mission to find other cities. And here you are." He began to laugh.

Overtaken by anger and revulsion, Eric submitted to impulse and hit the ambassador with his fist. Bartlett's mouth bled, but he did not lose his self-satisfied smirk. Eric had to try hard not to hit him again.

"You know, Commander Lynch," Bartlett said, "I've met your family. Your wife is... barely attractive, but your children are so adorable. What's the youngest one's name?

Mariam, I think."

Eric couldn't contain himself and started pounding his fist into Bartlett. Commander Aruba and two other soldiers held him back before he killed the vile man. "What have you done with my family?" Eric screamed.

Bartlett simply continued to laugh.

# Chapter 57

Camila heard a knock at the door, them Mariam yelling out to her, "Mommy, there's two soldiers at the door. They want to talk with you."

She quickly went to the door to find out what her daughter was shouting about. Two soldiers, dressed in their beige uniforms, stood at their door. Her heart started beating faster. She put her hand over Mariam's shoulder and squeezed. Tommy must have heard his sister; she felt his tiny hand grab hers, as she stared in anxiety at the soldiers standing before her. Thoughts of Eric flashed through her mind. Her husband lying there, covered in blood, killed by enemy soldiers. She pushed the images away and addressed the soldiers. "Yes?"

"Ms. Lynch, we have orders to move you and your children," said one of the two soldiers.

"Why? What's happen to my husband?" She spoke as calmly as she could so she wouldn't upset the children.

"We don't know. We were just told to move you."

"Move? Why would we move? We've been here for over eight years. We're not moving anywhere."

"Ms. Lynch, those were our orders."

"My husband is a colonel in the army! You have no right to treat his family this way. We're not going."

"Ms. Lynch if you don't come willingly, we will have to take you by force. These orders come directly from Mayor Kratz."

Camila had hated Kratz from the first day she'd met him as Mayor Frazier's advisor. Now she had a reason to hate him even more. It was unconscionable that these soldiers would take her by force. She packed a few clothes, the only things they allowed her to take. The rest, they said, would be delivered to their new location.

Camila and the children had been walking for most of the day. The children were tired. Mayor Frazier's wife, Lazzat, was among her group, limping and exhausted, staring at the ground. Camila tried talking with her, but Lazzat kept silent. Gazing into the distance, trying to work out where they were being taken, she could make out a large white building. She thought she could see two fences, one inside another, encircling the building, towers equally spaced around the perimeter. Squinting, she could see people, just standing around.

Men and women of all ages lined up, slumped over, dejected. None were chatting. None were smiling. *What is this place?* A man wearing a uniform she had never seen before told her which line to get into with her children. She didn't want to be here. Her line moved fast, and when she got to the front, a soldier handed her two blankets.

"Go through that door." The man pointed to the entrance to one side, mechanically, as though he'd said the same thing a thousand times. "Find two bunks, one for you and another for your children."

Why was she here? This looked more like a prison than another place to live. Or was that Kratz' plan after all? Incarcerate the wife of the Colonel and his children.

Lazzat stood waiting in one of the lines that was taking forever to move. "Lazzat," she called. The woman turned around but did not seem to recognize her. She tried anyway, "The line over there is faster."

"They told me to stay in this line," Lazzat muttered, her voice slurred, shoulders slumped.

"No talking!" Yelled one of the guards.

Camila looked at the soldier with indignation. "Sorry," she said through clenched teeth, and then whispered to Lazzat, "I'll save you a bed next to me."

Lazzat nodded.

Going in the direction the soldier had told her to find the bunks, Camila entered what looked like a warehouse with rows and rows of beds. Each row had about thirty, end to end, stacked three high. The beds were filled with what felt like beads. Camila took the beds closest to the door so Lazzat would spot them.

Even after Camila got the kids ready for bed later that evening, Lazzat never came. Worry snaked through her.

"Mommy, why are we here?" Tommy asked, rolling to one side of the bed.

"We're here to sleep," she said with forced reassurance. She wouldn't let the kids see her concern.

"Are we going to stay here for a long time?" Mariam asked, sitting on another bed cross-legged, fidgeting her hands and biting her lip.

"Half of these people will not be here tomorrow," a woman next to her spoke quietly.

"Where will they take them?" Tommy asked, sitting up and holding the bar that held the bunk beds together.

"To work the fields or live with some family as slaves."

Camila didn't expect this. She never thought that she would be taken away from her home to become a slave. Where was Eric? Did they kill him? She needed him now more than ever.

"The only good thing here is the food," the man across from them said. "The meat is very tasty, and spicy too."

"I didn't particularly like it," Camila said.

"Well, if you don't like it, when they serve you some, give it to me. I'll eat it."

Camila lay on her bed, staring at the ceiling. What if Eric had been killed and they would never see him again? She hugged Mariam closer, and worried herself to sleep that night.

The next day, Camila, Tommy, and Mariam set off in search of something to eat. Before they got too far, one of the workers, a woman, wearing powder blue pants and a shirt with a dark blue blazer stopped them. "The kids need to take their baths."

"Fine." Camila huffed, trying to keep her temper in check. "Where do we go to do that?" She guided the kids by the shoulder and moved toward the doors.

"I'll take them," the woman said her face blank. "They'll be fine with me. They'll be back shortly." The woman grabbed the kids' hands and left before Camila could protest.

Camila had never left her kids alone; this place didn't make her feel any more comfortable about it. But she could only watch as her kids were taken through the doors and out of sight. She tried to convince herself that everything would be fine and went to get food for herself and the children.

Much to her dismay, by the time she had returned with the same food they served the night before, the kids still hadn't come back to the bunks. Something was wrong. She could feel it. Without a second thought, abandoning all thoughts of food, she set off looking for her children.

---

Tommy held his sister's hand as they entered a room that was all-white from floor to ceiling. In the middle of the room was a small hole.

"In this room we go pee and poo," the woman told the kids.

"I already went pee and poo this morning," Mariam said.

"Me too," said Tommy.

"Well, try and go again. We need to make sure you get it all out because you won't be able to go pee and poo once you go outside and play."

"Okay," they both said innocently.

Tommy didn't like that he had to go potty in front of his sister and someone he didn't even know. The hole in the floor was as big as his butt. He squatted and nothing came out. After a few seconds he stood up. "I'm done."

"Me too," his sister said.

"Now, we're going to get all cleaned up before we go outside."

"Why don't we get cleaned up after we finish playing?" Mariam asked.

"Yeah, by then we'll be all dirty and need a bath anyway," Tommy said.

"You'll take a bath again after you play," the woman told them.

"We have to take two baths? Ugh!" Tommy grimaced.

They bathed and began walking naked to the next room.

"Don't we need clothes?" Mariam asked.

"Yes. That's where we're going next," the worker said as they approached a door. "Girls first. Mariam, you go through the door and get dressed."

Tommy watched his sister open the door and walk through. The door closed quicker than expected and he flinched. His sister screamed and he flinched again. He needed his mom and started to panic and cry.

"Don't cry," the woman began to console Tommy. "Your sister got scared by the people trying to help her. She's fine. You'll see."

The door from the opposite side of the room opened.

"Where are my kids?" It was mommy. Tommy was ecstatic and wanted her to take him back to the bunks. "Where is Mariam?" Her face strained with concern. Tommy pointed to the door and his mother ran toward it.

Tommy wanted to run into the room with his mom, but the woman wouldn't let go of his hand. The door slammed closed and Tommy was alone with this stranger who for now was his only comfort.

"Where is my daughter?" Tommy could hear his mother screaming. "What the... What have you... Tommy, run! Tom—"

Then silence.

Tommy didn't know what had just happened to his mom or his sister. He stared at the closed door then started to scream and managed to wiggle his hand free from the woman. He ran fast toward the door and turned the knob. The room was dark. Two men were tying his mother with a rope by her feet. Blood dripped on the floor from the slash in her neck. Mariam was nowhere to be seen.

"Mommy!" he cried.

The two men moved away from his mother and tried to grab him, but he was slippery and able to get away. Tommy ran back through the door dodging his way past the woman who had been holding his hand and ran out the door that his mother had come through.

"Tommy, come here!" the woman shouted running after him. He zigzagged through the lines. "Hey, stop that child!" she screamed at the people waiting in the lines. No one came after him. They just watched as he ran past them.

Tommy ran to the only place he knew—the bunks. He raced through the doors. There were no people here, just beds. Pretending to play hide-and-seek with his father, Tommy sought out a place to hide and not get caught. The beds were raised above the floor. Some of the beds were lined up against the wall and were not raised like the others. He jumped over the beds against the far wall and dug his way into one of the mattresses. The small white pebbles hid him. He lay motionless, his hand over his mouth to keep from breathing in the pebbles, he tried not to breathe too hard.

Tommy could hear the voice of the woman.

"Tommy?" she shouted. "Tommy, come on out. We aren't going to hurt you. Your mom and sister are fine."

Tommy knew better. He knew what he saw. Mom was dead. He wanted to cry but needed to be quiet.

After what felt like an eternity, their voices got closer.

"We can't find him," someone said. "He must be hiding in one of these beds."

Tommy's heart started to race. If they looked in each bed, they would eventually find him. Fear urged him to jump up and find a new hiding place. But if he learned anything from dad it was to never give up your position when you think someone has found you. Just wait. That's what he did.

"Shall we start tearing the beds open?"

"No. He's seven or eight years old. He'll come out on his own when he gets hungry." The footsteps retreated. "Tell everyone to keep an eye out for him."

They left. Tommy didn't know what to do now. Being hungry and tired didn't make things any better. Dad told him to be the man of the house and protect his mom and sister. He failed to do that. Tears filled his eyes as he tried getting comfortable.

His dad would be mad. Mom and Mariam were dead. He would be in serious trouble now.

# Chapter 58

Eric was not listening to the conversation between Oberon and Commander Aruba. He was anxious to get back home to his wife and kids. Could something have happened to them? If anything, Latte and Uma would be there to help them.

Getting into Williamsport without a plan would do him no good If the ambassador was telling the truth; a hostile mayor controlled the city with no way of getting in without being recognized as a traitor. He needed to find a solution, to enter the city and get his family to safety. After that, he would depose Kratz and establish one of the councilmen as the new mayor.

"We must prepare to fight the Feds," Aruba said.

"How many soldiers are along our eastern border?" Oberon asked.

"I would guess at least half of your total forces," Eric surmised, then thought about Audrey's interpretation of his dream. "The Feds' military is more advanced than yours."

The mayor looked over to Commander Aruba, who confirmed, "It's true, Mr. Mayor. Their military is superior to ours."

"So, what can we do?"

"We can delay them until I get troops from Williamsport to help fight them," Eric suggested.

"How can you do that? Your city is now occupied by the Feds." the mayor said.

"The mayor is a Fed, but the city is still not part of the Fed alliance."

"But you still need time to take over the city and put someone in charge and then bring troops," Commander Aruba said. "This all will take time. We don't have that much time here. If the soldiers are at our borders and they don't hear from the ambassador, they might decide to invade anyway."

"There is no way of knowing when or if the Feds will invade. But if you give me five hundred of your soldiers to take to Williamsport, and if I can bring the mayor down and convince the city council to elect a new mayor, I can bring thirty-five hundred soldiers here to help fight the Feds," Eric said trying to sell his idea.

Oberon shook his head. "I can't spare that many soldiers on speculation. I need guarantees. We need those soldiers here."

"How many can you spare?" Eric asked.

"None."

"Sir," Aruba interjected, "I can easily spare fifty men."

Eric knew that fifty men wouldn't be enough to remove Kratz, but he thought of another less forceful way this might be achieved. "I'll take the fifty men."

"How soon will you leave?" the mayor asked.

"Commander, can you have your men ready two hours before sunrise?"

"They can be ready by that time," the commander assured Eric.

"I came in by the sea. I don't know the terrain well enough to get back. Do you have someone who knows the area?"

"I have someone who might be able to help," the mayor said and asked for Logan to be brought to his office. The commander excused himself to get the soldiers ready. Ten minutes later Logan walked in. The mayor sat at his desk, Eric stood to one side.

The mayor spoke first. "Logan, I need you to escort Colonel Lynch back to Williamsport. I know you haven't been to Williamsport, but you know the terrain in that area better than anyone else."

"You would be a valuable resource," Eric added, trying not to be too patronizing. "We don't know the area and we need all the help we can get."

Logan nodded cautiously as he shot a surreptitious look at Eric. "Sure. I'd be willing to help."

"Then get your gear. We leave two hours before first light," Eric said.

The mayor and Eric walked back to the house discussing what to expect from the Fed army stationed at the border. When they entered the dining area everyone had gone except for Mrs. Bushnell, Audrey, Tom, and Alexis. They were in good spirits still sitting at the table talking.

"Is everything okay?" Mrs. Bushnell asked.

"Not everything," the mayor said solemnly. "We think the Fed army will attack Milestown soon."

"I'm going back to Williamsport to bring back reinforcements," Eric informed his dad and sister. He turned to Audrey. "Logan is coming with me."

"Why does he need to go with you?"

"He knows the area well," the mayor said.

"I know the area as well," Audrey said. "I'll come along."

Logan had just heard the last part of the conversation. He stood by the door.

"No!" said the mayor. "Right now, I only want Logan to go."

Eric sensed that the mayor didn't think this was going to help Williamsport in any way and didn't want his daughter caught up in someone else's civil war.

"I have an idea," Tom interrupted. "What if we went to some of the neighboring cities and tried to employ their help?"

"That probably wouldn't be a good idea," the mayor said. "As far as they are concerned, the Feds are their liberators. We've enslaved many of their people."

"But only after they attacked us," Audrey said, justifying the cause.

The mayor looked at his daughter. "They won't help us," he insisted.

Audrey saw the war as an opportunity to keep her promise.

"What if we free the slaves in Milestown and strike a deal with the mayors of the other cities never to enslave their people again?"

The Mayor seemed to muse on that for a second. "Well… that would be possible. If we win against the Feds, we *could* enslave them instead."

"No, Daddy! From this point on, no one is ever to be a slave!"

"What are you talking about?"

"I was a slave once and I made a promise to God to free the slaves in our city."

"God? Who is this God? There is no god!"

"Yes, Daddy. There is a god!"

"Stop! You're acting like an idiot! Your god is your imagination."

"No, that's not true!" she yelled.

"It's possible, Audrey," Eric interjected, "that it could have been the circumstance you were in that made you imagine you were talking with God."

Audrey stared at him with cold dark eyes. She pursed her lips. "What about the dream you had that I interpreted for you?"

"It was a dream and you came up with a convincing explanation for it. But it could just as well be a random set of events that were in my head."

"Why don't you just take a knife and jab it into my eye?" she said. Eric saw her teeth clench as she stared at him. He could feel her anger.

Logan walked into the room and passed Eric to face Audrey, "He's right, Audrey. You've gone through a lot and there's no reason why any of this couldn't be a way to cope with what has happened to you."

"You don't believe me either?"

"I believe what I see, and what I see is you putting events together in such a way to make it seem like there is a god helping you."

Audrey's eyes closed and she shuddered for a second. "Here's your proof!" she hissed as she looked at both Logan and Eric. "When you go back to your hometown of Williamsport, you will not encounter even one Fed soldier. On the third day you will set up camp. You will meet four soldiers that are from your city of Williamsport. You'll ask them why they are there and they'll tell you they are supposed to arrest you. But they won't because they're loyal to you. There won't be enough water for all your men. Then you," she glared at Logan, "you find a boulder, any boulder and touch it and say, 'God, please let water flow from this rock.' That's all you have to do, and water will come out from the rock. Do this so that you and all your men will believe that there is a god."

"And what if nothing comes out?" the mayor asked doubtfully.

"Daddy," Audrey started crying, "because of you, many soldiers are going to die."

"Oberon," Mrs. Bushnell said. "Maybe it would be a good idea to visit our neighboring cities and ask for their support. It wouldn't hurt to try. Audrey and I along with Alexis and..." she cleared her throat and glanced at Tom, "Mr. Lynch here, can go and try to convince these other cities that it is in their best interest to join us."

The mayor didn't look thoroughly convinced, but Eric saw his resolve waver. "Very well, go and try," he finally consented.

# Chapter 59

Eric and his men walked upfront with Logan. The other soldiers kept up with the quick pace. Not once did they encounter any Fed troops. Logan knew the terrain well, and by the evening of the second day, Eric had an idea of where he was. It wouldn't be long before they got to Williamsport. Audrey's prediction popped into his mind. He chalked it up to being really lucky.

Eric spent the night thinking about how different Williamsport would be with the Fed alliance. His wife and kids should be all right. Camila had made friends with many of the other officer's wives. If anything, they would help.

By the middle of the third day, the sun hid behind a thick blanket of clouds. Eric and his men arrived just outside the city. Two of his scouts returned with news that a small contingency of soldiers had been spotted by the road. Four of them. Eric ran up ahead with the scouts to where the soldiers were camped and slowly they came upon the group.

Eric stepped forward after recognizing the men. "Sergeant Jetson Sandalwood! What are you doing here?"

The men jumped up from the steps they sat on, clearly not expecting to be approached from behind the building.

"Colonel Lynch!" The sergeant smiled. "Are we glad to see you. We hoped you'd pass through here."

"Why were you hoping that I would pass this way?"

"Mayor Kratz says that you're a traitor and you went AWOL," the sergeant said. "We're supposed to arrest you and bring you back into the city."

"But I was sent on a mission that he…" Eric started, remembering what the ambassador alleged. He shook his head in dismay. "It makes sense now."

"After you left, sir, things got worse," Sergeant Sandalwood said. "The mayor has a mandatory curfew now. No one is allowed to walk the streets an hour after nightfall. Williamsport and the Feds established a new treaty. There are Fed troops in Williamsport."

"Mayor Kratz is a Fed. He had this planned all along," Eric said.

"Everyone suspected that he had ties to the Feds, but no one really knew how strong they were," the sergeant said. "Most of the other officers are supporting the mayor. Others have been sent away as criminals. They've been accused of helping you."

Eric clasped his hands behind the back of his head and let out a breath of air. "We need to come up with a plan to get Williamsport back."

"Sir, there are still officers in the army that secretly support you," the sergeant said. "At least, that's what they said two weeks ago."

Eric was happy that there were at least some people in the army who didn't believe the AWOL story. "Sergeant, do you know councilman Cauldron?"

The sergeant nodded. "He's one of the mayor's biggest supporters."

Eric didn't know what to make of it. Why would Latte support the mayor? Especially with the Fed soldiers being allowed free access to Williamsport. He would have to trust that the man had good reason to act this way. Saving his life, hopefully, was enough to get him to help in some way.

"Go back into Williamsport, find councilman Cauldron and tell him that his friend from the river wants to say hello," Eric said. "If anyone asks why you came back, tell them you came back for supplies."

"While you were gone, the mayor declared that all criminals would be sent to the Feds as slaves."

Eric's jaw dropped open at the sergeant's remark and thoughts of his family ran through his mind. "Do you know anything of my family?"

"We haven't heard anything," Sandalwood said.

The sergeant looked behind Eric. "I hope those men approaching are with you."

"Yes. They are. They're from another city and want to help." Eric turned and shouted to Dwayne, his second in command. "We'll camp here tonight."

"Sir," the sergeant said, "there's no water here. We go about half a day's walk to bring back as much as we can."

"Then why are you camped here?" Eric asked.

"Orders, sir," one of the other men said.

"Okay." Eric blew out a puff of air as he thought about the coincidences. He never fully believed in God and now he was getting nervous about the events that had happened so far. Had Audrey really talked with God after all?

Eric brought Logan up to speed. He also agreed that the coincidences were remarkable. The task now—find a boulder. The sun was still high above the horizon. It didn't take long to find the perfect boulder close to camp.

The men from Milestown had heard of Audrey's prediction and they gathered around to see if water would come out of the rock. The men from Williamsport also came to watch. Eric walked over to the boulder as Logan climbed it.

"What is he going to do?" Sergeant Sandalwood asked

"A very dear friend of mine says that there is a god. She told us that he would make water come out of the rock to prove that he exists."

"Where is this god?" the men asked.

"He is everywhere," Eric explained. "You just can't see him."

"And what will happen if we believe in him?"

"He will help us win our fight against the Feds."

Eric watched as Logan climbed one of the boulders. The clouds in the sky started forming and getting darker. If anything, it was going to rain.

Logan spoke so that everyone could hear him. "Let water flow from this rock!"

Nothing was happening. Eric moved closer to the boulder.

"Let water flow from this rock!" Logan yelled again.

But still, nothing happened. Logan's head sank. He stepped down from the boulder, not looking at anyone. "She was wrong," he muttered.

"I think you're saying it wrong," Eric said, and then climbed up on the rock himself. Looking down at the top of the rock he grinned at the bowl shape, with what looked like a spout.

Eric knelt, touched the rock, shouting out, "God, please let water flow from this rock."

Everyone looked at the rock and saw that a small area of it was wet. One of the men hollered, "I could've peed and gotten more water out of that rock."

Eric was about to break into laughter when a bolt of lightning shot down from the clouds and struck the man dead. The other men didn't even have a chance to react to his remark. Eric stood still not quite knowing what to do. Within seconds it started to rain. Moments later, water began to pour out of the rock. It wasn't quite the miracle that Audrey had convinced him it would be. Yes, water came forth, but it came from the sky. But the soldiers didn't see it that way. They seemed to see it as a miracle. Eric looked at Logan, and judging from his expression, he also seemed to have doubts.

Walking back towards the dilapidated buildings, Logan asked Eric, "Do you believe that this was a miracle?"

The men danced and sang and drank from the water that poured out of the boulder. Eric shrugged, then looked at Logan. "The Feds are stronger than we are and these men believe that a miracle happened. They believe that they are going to win the war because there is a god. Why would I tell them otherwise?"

"So, if the ends justify the means, let them believe a lie?" said Logan.

"Maybe there was a miracle. Water did gush forth from the rock and the man who made the snide remark was struck by lightning…"

"It rained, Eric. And the overflowing water poured out over the rock. That's not a miracle."

Eric shrugged his shoulders again.

Logan got up to leave. Eric grabbed his arm and stopped him. "Hey, I know you don't want to believe that this god exists. I mean I don't know if I want to admit it either. But Audrey said these things would happen and they pretty much did."

"It's alarming how obsessed Audrey is with her mystical god. But, it's not her belief that worries me. It's that she needs everyone else to believe it too."

"And from the looks of it," Eric said looking at the men dancing in the rain, "she's succeeding."

# Chapter 60

It had been five days since Eric and his small band of soldiers left Milestown. He wouldn't be surprised if the Feds had started their assault on the city. Hopefully, they hadn't.

While waiting at the river to meet councilman Cauldron, his mind went back in time to when Uma and Latte got captured by a group of Feds along another very similar river. A smile formed on his lips thinking about Camila's expression when asked to take her clothes off. A wave of longing hit him. He missed his wife and children.

"Isn't this the spot where we first met?" Latte said with a wide smile on his still handsome face. Eric hadn't even heard the man approach, so deep had he sunk in thought.

"It looks similar, but no, it isn't." Eric grabbed Latte's arm and gave him a hug.

"It looks like now I'll get the chance of returning the favor by helping you," Latte said getting serious.

"Well, you owe me two favors because I saved your wife too," Eric grinned.

"She wasn't my wife at the time."

"Well then, you owe me three favors because if it wasn't for me, you wouldn't be married."

"Wait, hold on!" Latte sputtered in mock indignation. "I'm married because of you? And you think I owe you a favor for that?"

They both laughed. They talked about the situation in the city. Eric told Latte about the Fed ambassador and how he came to find out that Kratz was a Fed. "How are my wife and children?" Eric asked, hoping they were safe.

Latte looked away. "Since you were tagged as a traitor, the mayor decided that your family should pay for your wrongdoing. He sent them to the Feds to be their slaves. He also sent a man and his daughter away for being spies, sent by you."

Eric's mind reeled. Kratz had sent his wife and children to those monsters. He wanted to run. To run to the Feds and take back his wife and kids. But what would that do? How could he save them? Knowing that his supposed friend stood before him had supported the mayor made his blood boil.

"Latte," he clenched his fist and relaxed over and over again, "you and Uma are our best friends. Please tell me that you helped Camila and the kids. Please tell me that they are in a safe place."

"I can't tell you that, Eric. You don't understand. Kratz had me watched more than any other councilman. He knew what kind of relationship we had." Latte looked distraught, gesturing wildly.

Eric didn't know if he could believe him.

"He was the one that questioned us the first day you came to Williamsport.

Remember?"

"So, you did nothing?" Eric was on top of him faster than a pack of dogs on a three-legged cat. Latte didn't have a chance to open his mouth—after all, Eric already knew what his answer would be.

It took two strong men to hold him back. Eric struggled to get free, but the men held him. They were Williamsport soldiers.

"Eric, you don't understand how powerful this man is. He can make people disappear," Latte cried, maneuvering out of his grasp, tying Eric's hands behind his back.

"What are you doing?" Eric cried out.

"I'm sorry my friend, but you're a traitor to Williamsport and I'm taking you back to face the mayor."

Eric was in shock. *Is my best friend really going to take me back to face Kratz? I will surely be killed.* "Latte, stop! What's going on? You don't have to do this."

Latte glanced uncomfortably at him. "You don't understand! Me and the mayor, we're friends now."

Pure rage ate Eric up inside. "How much did he buy you for, huh? You bastard!" He spat in Latte's face.

His erstwhile friend's jaw flinched, just a little. Latte's eyes flashed angrily, but he ignored Eric, turned around, and motioned for them to head toward Williamsport. Eric's words hadn't even dented his pride. Latte had no honor left.

Feeling a broken man, Eric let them drag him to his fate. He hung his head and wept silently, leaving behind a wet trail of misery and despair. What had Kratz done? What had he done to his family?

---

Logan witnessed the scene as it played out. Eric's friend had betrayed him. It was a trap and they would probably end up killing him. That's what he deserved. Audrey was never supposed to fall in love with him.

But the more he thought about it, the more he realized that whatever relationship Eric had with Audrey it was in the past. It was over. If not for the jealousy he felt, he wouldn't have been as bold to go after her. Yet he felt that he was always going to be second best.

As the soldiers marched Eric away, Logan tried to fight it. He wanted to look away and do nothing. But even though he was jealous of the man, Eric was their best hope of defeating the Feds.

Making his decision, he ran back to camp and told everyone what had happened.

---

Dwayne led Eric's men and caught up to where Logan told them they had taken their colonel. They moved so as not to attract attention, hiding behind large boulders and treading quietly. As the men took Eric down the crest of a hill, Dwayne ran behind a boulder to see how they could ambush the group.

His stomach roiled in fear at the site of over two hundred soldiers waiting to take his commander back. *Why so many men?* There was nothing his little group of men could do.

The men retreated back to camp.

"That many men are not here just to take the colonel back," Sergeant Sandalwood said. "I feel so stupid now. I should have come up to greet councilman Cauldron. Then I could have warned the colonel."

"And, why didn't you?" Dwayne asked. Perhaps Sergeant Sandalwood might just be a spy among them.

"Because the councilman ordered me to go ahead and tell the colonel that he was coming."

"Why didn't the colonel expect something like this?" one of the soldiers from Milestown asked.

"Councilman Cauldron is... *was*," he corrected, "his best friend. It was the colonel that saved the councilman from the Feds when they were younger," the sergeant explained.

Dwayne knew that sixty men was no match for two hundred. "So, what will we do?" he asked the sergeant.

"There is still one other person whom Eric can count on. I'll slip back into Williamsport and see if he can help."

---

Eric came into the courtroom and could see Kratz' eyes shine with delight. "what is this? A gift for me?" Kratz said, putting one hand on his chest. He turned to Latte. "Oh, Latte you shouldn't have. This morning I had a positive feeling that today would be a great day and what could be better than this?"

Kratz circled Eric.

"You've captured Colonel Lynch. How wonderful," he crooned. "Where on earth did you find him?"

"By the river where we first met," Latte responded.

"Well, this is a big surprise." He stared straight at Eric. "So, you came back to reminisce about how big a hero you've been to Williamsport. I really didn't think you were so stupid to come back."

Eric didn't respond.

"It doesn't matter. I think that we should make a public example of you and have you hanged right outside." Kratz went back to his chair, the smiled vanished from his face. "To show what it is that we do to traitors." Then with a dismissive wave of his hand, he finished, "Take him away. Lock him up until we can get a rope around his neck."

Eric still couldn't believe that Latte and Kratz had become good friends. It was surreal to watch the two of them laughing together as he was being taken away. What had happened while he was gone?

They put him in an old rusted cell. Kratz was probably rubbing his hands, relishing his execution and wanting to make sure he wouldn't be kept alive too much longer.

The guards brought in food and water—filthy, disgusting stuff. The other cells were full of reluctant residents. Were all these people political prisoners? And if they were, why would they be down here and not sent to the Feds? Unless that's what they did—rounded them up, and then when the prison got full, they would take them to the Feds. Was this what they'd done to his wife and kids? He swore to himself that if he ever got out, he would kill Kratz. Thinking about it, he would kill Latte as well, giving him a slow, torturous death.

"You have a visitor," said a guard, who came up to his cell and unlocked it.

Eric stood as Councilman Rahama entered. The guard closed the cell door behind him, leaving them alone to talk.

"How did you know I was here?" Eric asked.

"Sergeant Sandalwood told me last night." Rahama spoke quickly and quietly, in hushed tones. "I would have come sooner, but I decided to wait until Kratz informed the city council that they had captured you. There is to be a public hanging next week."

"I'm surprised that Kratz wants to wait that long."

"He wanted you to be hanged today, but the council was able to postpone it. Many of the council believe that you betrayed your city as Kratz had told them. What happened?"

Eric told Rahama the whole story about the mission he'd been sent on by Kratz. He also told him about the Feds and the horrors they were responsible for. Rahama's expression changed from disbelief to shock. From thoughtful, to being convinced.

"We need to remove Kratz as mayor of Williamsport," Eric finally said.

"That will be almost impossible. Kratz has removed everyone who was against him."

"And you? Are you with Kratz?" Eric wasn't sure why Rahama had come to visit him. Did he want to get information to give Kratz?

Rahama smiled. "I am a politician. I've been one most of my life, and if I've learned anything it is to keep your enemies closer than your friends." He frowned. "But Kratz is genuinely evil. I don't know how we can remove him."

"If we can get the people to rise against him, maybe, just *maybe*, we can achieve control of the city. Can you bring me paper and something to write with?"

"I don't know if it's allowed, officially. In any case, I will find a way to get that to you tonight." Rahama stood up. "I must leave before the guards start talking and it gets to Kratz that someone from the council has come down to visit you. It wouldn't take long for Kratz to find out." Rahama shook the bars of the cell, calling for the guard to let him out.

"Thank you," Eric said, hoping that there might be a way to turn things around and get out of this place.

# Chapter 61

Night came and the guards brought food for their prisoners. Eric was hungry, but not too excited about the bland concoction and murky water they provided. There was no possible way to escape. The bars were rusted, but not enough to make it easy to break them. The guards never opened the doors when they brought food, so there was no way to overpower them. Today's meal delivery was done by a new guard, who he did not recognize. Short, and sporting a beard, the guard slid the plate through the cell door, taking care not to spill anything.

"It seems you have friends in Williamsport. Kratz has allowed you to eat better," the guard said.

It didn't make any sense that Kratz would be this nice. Famished, he chanced a bite and emitted a sigh of relief. His stomach rumbled gratefully as he took another bite. Maybe Kratz wanted these last days to be pleasant.

The guard stood by the door, watching. "Don't forget to take the tray."

*Why would I want to do that?* He thanked the guard and got up to get it, then sat back down and waited for the guards to leave the area. At first there didn't seem to be anything unusual about the tray, but when the napkin was removed, it revealed a compartment. Inside were two pencils and several sheets of paper. Rahama had come through after all.

Eric spent the entire night trying to find the right words that would inspire the people to protest. Hopefully, they remembered who he was before leaving Williamsport, and not as the traitor that Kratz had made him out to be. He gave the sketchy writing one last read before copying it neatly on the last clean sheet of paper:

*In the course of human events it becomes necessary for the people to rid themselves of a tyrant who claims he is serving in the best interests of the citizens of his city. A long train of abuses, always afflicting the same groups, displays a clear design to reduce these individuals under an iron fist. It is therefore the duty and right of its citizens to throw off such a tyrant.*

*The present mayor of Williamsport has a history of repeated injuries he has inflicted upon us, all having a direct purpose in the establishment of an absolute dictatorship over the city. To prove this, let the facts be submitted to a candid world.*

*He has taken away the right of the city council to create laws or to veto laws that the mayor deems fit.*

*He has refused to acknowledge laws that are necessary for the public good.*

*He has constrained citizens from speaking out against him.*

*He has declared innocent people guilty of treason without a proper trial in the presence of a jury.*

*He has sent Williamsport citizens to be slaves in a foreign land.*

*He has introduced the concept of meat, yet no animal has ever been seen as the source of this meat.*

*The only land animals in existence today are humans. Is this the source of the meat that the people of Williamsport have been asked to eat? This begs the question: Is the mayor turning the people of Williamsport into cannibals?*

*Let the mayor produce the animals that are the source of the meat you eat. There is no need to keep this secret.*

*Because of these malicious acts, I, Colonel Eric Lynch, do hereby decree that Mayor Kratz is a traitor to this city and shall be placed under arrest and put on trial for his crimes against the people of Williamsport.*

Would this be enough to cause the people to protest and take away the hold that Kratz had on them? Rahama needed to make enough copies of these to pass out to the people in time for it to have an effect before his execution. If only the councilman could postpone that for another week.

The final document was placed inside the tray, then the remaining water in the cup was poured on the scrap sheets of paper, destroying them. The napkin hid the opening. The cup and bowl were placed back on top of the tray and set next to the cell door. The same guard came back, nodding as he picked up the tray.

"I need to speak with your master," Eric said in a low voice.

"I will speak with Kratz." He looked to his left. Eric guessed another guard was within earshot. "And see if he wants to speak with you."

Within an hour, Rahama was at his cell door, but didn't come in as before. "The mayor has become suspicious of my last visit here. I'm sure this time he will know that I've talked with you. I received the paper you wrote and it's very good, but I don't have any resources to reproduce it. One letter won't get around very fast."

These were all things that Eric had gone through in his mind as well. Hopefully, this wasn't a lost cause. "If you can get it to my men, they can reproduce it and circulate it among the people. But if the mayor is suspicious of you, I don't know how you can do that." Eric noticed that one of the guards was keeping a keen eye on them. "You need to leave," he said in hushed tones. "I'm sure you'll find a way."

---

Jetson knocked on the door to Councilman Rahama's house. It took longer than usual for the councilman to answer the door.

"What are you doing here, Seargent Sandalwood?" he frowned, pulling Jetson into the house. "The mayor is already suspicious of me and has spies watching my house. If anyone notices you, then everything we've done will be for nothing."

Jetson apologized as he let Rahama briefly discuss the situation. They came up with a strategy. Jetson would sneak to the back of the house later that evening and retrieve the sack with papers and pencils which Rahama had left lying in the trash. A few copies had already been made. One would be waiting at the council chambers to be read to the councilmen. Jetson had only one day to reproduce Lynch's document and return all copies so they could distribute them to the people.

Jetson left Rahama's home; as predicted, he was stopped.

Commander Skype interrogated him. "Sergeant, what are you doing here at Councilman Rahama's residence?"

"He's my uncle."

"With last names like Sandalwood and Rahama? How can he be your uncle?"

"Well, let's see. He's my father's sister's husband, he would be my uncle and we would have different last names. Is there something you want to accuse me of?"

"Sergeant, keep up that attitude and you'll find yourself dishonorably discharged from the military and in prison." With that the commander turned around and left.

Jetson had to move fast and get the sack out of the councilman's house. He had no idea how long it would take before Commander Skype found out that he wasn't in any way related to Rahama.

When Nightfall came, Jetson snuck to the back of the house and took the sack. The stench of the trash lying around made him gag. He stopped cold at the sound of footsteps. Someone knocked on the front door. He could hear the councilman open it. Probably soldiers. A few words were exchanged, but it was not possible to discern what they said from where Jetson stood. The conversation did not last long; Jetson heard the thud as the door closed. Peeking around the short passageway leading out front, He could see Rahama being taken away with his hands tied behind his back. The councilman was now an enemy of the state.

An hour passed before he dared make the trek back to camp. By the next day Jetson had dispatched thirty-five men to distribute the papers to all corners of Williamsport. A dozen were kept to distribute to the officers that used to be loyal to the colonel. The chance of getting caught was high, but this was too important.

Jetson saw an opportunity to save the colonel; by raiding the prison with the remaining men, it might be possible to overwhelm the guards and take control of the premises, thereby freeing Colonel Lynch. The idea was daring, and it just might work. The men were briefed about his plan. They all knew and accepted the risks involved. Every one of them was willing to sacrifice themselves to save the colonel.

Jetson didn't want them to be noticed as one large group and told them, all sixty-seven men, to walk in alone. The sixteen that would help free the colonel were to meet at the prison in the middle of the day. He drew a map on the ground to get everyone familiar with the streets of the city. When everyone was comfortable with the layout, they dispersed and walked into Williamsport individually.

# Chapter 62

Sergeant Sandalwood knew that sixteen men gathering at a prison would be a noticeable endeavor. They needed a distraction. Someone needed to draw attention away from the entrance.

Dwayne volunteered, and as the men came together nearer the prison, he walked to the closest open area and started shouting in the loudest voice possible. "Mayor Kratz is a traitor! Mayor Kratz is a traitor! And I can prove it!"

Citizens gathered to hear what Dwayne had to say. The fifteen men that swarmed in front of the prison was nothing compared to the number of men, women, and children who came to see what Dwayne was yelling about.

As Dwayne launched into the reasons why Kratz was a traitor, Sergeant Sandalwood and fourteen men crashed through the prison doors, overwhelming the unsuspecting guards. All of the prison guards were restrained except for three that escaped through the back. It wouldn't be long before they would come back with reinforcements. The sergeant stormed past cell after cell, yelling for the colonel.

"What are you guys doing here?" Eric called out, his hands wrapped around the bars, face pressing through.

"We came to liberate you." Sandalwood unlocked the cell door.

"Unlock this man's cell as well. He's coming with us," Colonel Lynch commanded, pointing to Councilman Rahama in the adjoining cell.

One of the men unlocked the cell and let him out. As they were leaving, the other men in the other prison cells began yelling to be freed. Eric stopped in his tracks.

"We don't have time for this, Colonel," the sergeant said. "We need to leave now!"

"Give that prisoner the keys," The colonel ordered looking at the man. "You need to unlock all the cell doors and free everyone here."

The man nodded.

When they reached the door, the colonel took control. "Sergeant, you're with me," he barked out. To one of the soldiers, he said, "You're with the councilman."

"No, sir!" Sergeant Sandalwood said. "This is my mission and I am in command until it's finished. Sir!"

Sandalwood wasn't about to let the colonel take over just because of his rank. *He started this mission; he would end it.*

"You," Sandalwood pointed at one of the soldiers from Milestown, "you're with the colonel." Then he pointed to one of his men. "You are with the councilman." Then he grabbed the nearest soldier to him by the arm, and said, "You are with me."

"Why that configuration, Sergeant?" Eric asked.

"They are already looking for me, sir! Logically, they would expect you to be with me."

"Understood."

They dispersed from the prison and one by one found their way back to camp. It was a slow process, but finally all of the men had arrived.

Sandalwood approached the colonel. "Sir, you are now back in command, sir!"

---

Eric was proud of the men under his command, especially the sergeant who showed extraordinary leadership and problem-solving ability.

All the papers had been distributed to the citizens. They would have to wait and hope that the people would stand up against Kratz. Eric decided to move camp. He didn't want Kratz' spies finding them or determining the size of his forces. He had no idea what he'd do from here on out. He found Rahama and talked to him about their situation.

"It does look bleak," Rahama confessed. "I don't know what we can do."

One of Eric's men addressed him. "Sir, there's a lieutenant from Williamsport who says he wants to talk with you."

Eric was surprised. They couldn't be here to arrest him. What would be the purpose of wanting to talk with him first? But then again, that's what Latte had done. He instructed his man to escort the lieutenant to his quarters. When the man came into the room, Eric recognized him immediately. "Rayes. It's been a while. What are you doing here?" He grabbed his arm and embraced him.

"My men and I read the paper you wrote about Kratz being a dictator and a traitor to Williamsport. We want to join your group and help you overthrow him."

Eric was delighted that at least one of the soldiers he trained was still loyal and would help fight Kratz. The number now totaled seventy-seven men he could command.

The next day, Eric sent scouts to find out what was happening in the city. Within an hour, they came back with news.

"Sir, you're not going to believe this," Satish said with excitement. "There are about five hundred civilians outside of the city waiting for you."

"Waiting for me?" Eric asked his faced filled with surprise.

"They want to join with us and fight."

Eric made sure Rahama and Sandalwood knew what was going on. "Now you have an army," said Rahama, with satisfaction.

"I can't fight with people that don't know how to fight," said Eric. "It would be a massacre. The soldiers would make minced meat out of these people." He didn't like the way things had developed. The victory belonged to Kratz. There was no clear way to remove him.

"This is all you have," Rahama said. "You must fight. If you don't, we'll all die for trying to save you."

The burden was on Eric to find a solution.

Eric went out to meet the citizens of Williamsport at the edge of the city limits. As soon as they caught sight of him approaching, there were smiles, waves, and cheers. The message on those papers had worked better than he had dared hope. They believed that he was the one who could save them from Kratz. Most of the people had guns, even the children. But it was one thing to have a gun; it was entirely different to know how to use one.

The next morning, Eric sent scouts to find out what was going on in the city. If the Williamsport army was occupied with civil unrest, this might be an opportunity to take the city. He spent the rest of the morning getting to know his new found troops of civilians and breaking them up into squadrons, with his soldiers heading up each unit. They needed to get closer to the city to be prepared for an invasion.

As they made their way to Williamsport, the scouts he had sent earlier intercepted them. A man approached. His face, sweaty and dirty, saluted. "Sir! The Feds and the rest of Kratz' troops are heading this way!"

Eric didn't expect there to be Fed soldiers in Williamsport. But Kratz was a Fed, it made sense that he would have those soldiers in his city. And it would make sense to use Fed soldiers to fight these people. They were outsiders; they had no relationship to these people. The killing of innocent women and children meant nothing to them.

"Assemble the men—civilians too. It's time to get organized!" Eric ordered.

The soldiers in each squadron organized themselves with the civilians taking the front lines of each. The men, women, and children with guns took up the middle with the rest placed in the rear with slings. The two opposing forces would need to get within twenty-five meters of one another in order for the guns to be effective. The slings, on the other hand, could be used at a much greater distance. Eric's instructions were simple—those with slings were to stay back at least fifty meters when the shooting started; everyone else was to disperse and hit the ground, take aim, and fire at the Feds.

Eric's forces charged toward the Feds, but to counter this move, the Feds lined up people in front and gave them no weapons. They used them as a human shield. When the civilians realized this, they halted their attack, refusing to fight against defenseless people. The Feds took this opportunity to come charging straight across the plains. Eric stood and watched as the Feds got closer.

*Bang!*

The sound of gunfire caused the people to disperse. If these had been soldiers, he would have shot them for desertion. He had no plan. Everything was in disarray.

*God, I really need your help now. I really, really need your help.*

Another group came up behind the Feds. Kratz had it planned well. The Feds did all the dirty work while the other soldiers cleaned up the mess. Eric watched as his whole army disintegrated in front of him. He wasn't going to win this battle; he wasn't going to win this war. Kratz would continue to be mayor for a long time. There was no way to help Milestown in their fight against the oppressor.

As the Feds came charging toward his army Eric noticed a second wave of soldiers coming in from behind the Feds. They were Williamsport soldiers. *What the hell?* The Williamsport soldiers were firing their weapons at the Fed Soldiers. The Feds suddenly stopped charging toward them. They were now exchanging gunfire with the mayor's own army. Eric led his men to continue the battle. Hopefully, some of the civilians would follow along. Now the Feds had two fronts they had to fight.

By the end of the day, Many of the Fed soldiers had been killed and many of his civilian forces had been decimated. There were fires in the city. Who knew how many were made by the Feds as they retreated? He spotted Commander Skype and raised his hand. The commander raised his hand as well.

"So, what made you come on our side?" Eric asked the Commander when he came withing earshot.

"When Kratz declared you a traitor for leaving Williamsport, I knew something was up since I was the one that sent you on that assignment. But I did nothing. And when that man and his daughter were killed because he said they were spies sent by you, I did nothing, even when I knew it was a lie. But when Kratz ordered me to march with the Fed Soldiers to fight you and that letter you wrote got to my desk; I knew that now was the time to disobey an order from my mayor."

"So how do you want to do this?"

"I'll go up and arrest him. Then he'll stand trial for his crimes against Williamsport."

---

Kratz watched everything from his window. His army was defecting to be with the colonel. He couldn't believe Commander Skype would do something like this, especially when he hand picked him as Commander of the Williamsport army over Colonel Lynch. Getting additional Fed troops here would take too long. After all, who would have expected this band of traitors and thugs to win? He watched as Commander Skype greeted Colonel Lynch and walked back to the capitol. What now? Was he really coming to arrest him? Kratz crossed back to his desk and sat behind it.

Skype came into Kratz' office with two other guards. Kratz smiled but said nothing. He knew what this was about. Before anything could come out of Commander Skype's mouth, Kratz opened a drawer in his desk, pulled out a gun, and shot Skype in the face. The two guards stood paralyzed with horrified expressions, not quite sure what to do. They each received a bullet for their hesitation. Kratz got up and exited the room.

---

Eric secured the city, then heard news that Skype had been killed—the weasel had managed to escape. Most likely running back to the Feds to tell them what was happening in Williamsport. He entered city hall and found Skype and two other soldiers lay dead on the floor. Someone was going to talk and give answers today. He pounded on the front door to the house of his good old ex-friend, Latte.

Uma answered; she seemed surprised to see him, her mouth hanging open in shock. "Eric, you're free! How did you manage to get out of prison?" she said, nervously.

"Where is your husband?" Eric demanded, stepping into the house uninvited. The dining table had two cups and two plates. One had remnants of food on it, the other unused.

"What do you mean?" she gasped. "I mean, I don't know. I thought he was trying to convince the mayor to let you go."

"What are you talking about? Your husband was the one that put me in jail!"

"That's not true!" she said. "He told me that you had been captured and he was going to beg the mayor to let you go. And if that didn't work, he was going to find a way to help you escape from prison. He promised me!"

Eric wasn't quite sure he believed her story, but there was no hint of a lie. "Did you know that Latte was friends with the mayor?"

"He told me last night, but I didn't believe it. It can't be true!"

Eric paced, mulling it over. Was it possible for Latte to keep such a secret from his wife? Or maybe she was the one pulling all the strings... What did she know? "Camila and the kids have been taken away."

"I know," she said, grabbing his arm, tears in her eyes. "I'm so sorry. I heard about it after they had taken her. I asked Latte if we could do anything, but he told me it was too late, that they were already in Fed territory. I'm so sorry."

Was she playing him? Did she even know what happened today? "So, you didn't know that there was a battle going on?"

She looked toward the window, eyes darting back and forth. "I heard the guns and I saw that some of the buildings were on fire, but I was too afraid to go out."

Eric shook his head and looked around the room, hoping he would see Latte expose himself. No such luck. She showed no sign of knowing what Latte had done. But what did that really mean? He tried again, more forcefully, "Tell me where Latte is."

"I don't know!" Tears welled in her eyes.

Was she really oblivious to what had been going on? "Where is your husband?" He stared her down. If she was lying… He pulled out his revolver.

Uma stared wide eyed in shock, hands out in front of her. "I told you, I don't know where he is. Why don't you believe me?"

"Because *he* allowed Kratz to kill my wife and kids! And, I think *you* know that!" Eric shouted so loud Uma recoiled, backing up until she hit the wall. She curled her body inwards.

"I don't know what happened to Camila and the kids until after it happened," she said, tears streaming down her cheeks. "Latte left this morning and I don't know where he is." She sniffed, and peered up at Eric through long, wet lashes. "I don't know if I can call Latte my husband anymore, if he really did all those things you said he did. I want to believe that he didn't know himself. I'm so sorry, Eric. I really am."

She showed no sign of knowing anything. Uma seemed to be one of those women who was oblivious; married to a councilman who kept her in the dark. It was probably for the best. If she had known anything or had done anything against his own family, Latte would be a widower right now.

Four favors is what Latte now owed him—four.

# Chapter 63

Eric walked into the chambers where the councilmen were waiting for him. They all stood and applauded as he entered. Once everyone had taken their seats, the head councilman stood up and addressed him. "Colonel Lynch, you are truly a genuine hero of Williamsport. Just like Mayor Frazier said you were, ten years ago. We owe you a debt of gratitude. Earlier in the day, all of us here in the council room decided to arrest Mayor Kratz. But the mayor has escaped, and his seat now sits empty. The city council has unanimously voted that you, Colonel Eric Lynch, should be the new mayor of Williamsport."

Eric accepted, and made himself the head of the army. But a second in command was needed; Lieutenant Rayes had initially joined with his forces and helped him, he hadn't so far shown any ability to act without orders. Sergeant Sandalwood, on the other hand, had proved that he was a true leader. Eric promptly promoted Sandalwood to the position of Commander of the military.

He quickly formed a group of soldiers with orders to find Kratz before he got to Fed territory or any other place he might manage to escape. He wanted him captured and tried in this city.

---

Kratz waited with Latte all night for Uma to meet them at the eastern side of the city. He spotted her before her husband and waved. A smile crossed her face. She came up to Latte and hugged him, turned to Kratz and hugged him as well.

"I'm guessing it worked," Latte said.

"He believed everything I told him, even the part about not knowing that Camila and the kids had been sent to the Feds."

They walked east away from Williamsport toward the next larger city. Each carrying what they could. It took four days to reach Appalachia. They were escorted to the capital and presented to the mayor. Kratz introduced himself, Uma, and Latte.

"You are the mayor of Williamsport and you show up here without an army?" the mayor of Appalachia laughed. His straight black hair, slanted eyes and large flared nose gave him an uncanny appearance. The thin band around his oval-shaped head was decorated with sparkling jewels.

"There was a coup by someone who is an enemy to both of us."

"And who is this enemy that you and I share?"

"Eric Lynch."

"Eric Lynch? Lieutenant Eric Lynch?"

"He is a colonel now," Kratz said.

The mayor laughed. "He was the one that convinced me to stop invading

Williamsport territory. Why would he be my enemy?"

Kratz had forgotten that it was this skirmish that made him colonel. He needed to convince this mayor that Eric was a threat and not a friend. Kratz smiled, pressing his lips tightly. "Back then the lieutenant followed orders. He has always tried to convince the mayors of Williamsport to invade and take Appalachia. He tried to convince me of this while I was mayor." Kratz bowed. "The colonel told me that I was weak and that one day he wouldn't have to take my orders. He said he would take Appalachia and make it part of Williamsport. He has become obsessed with this. It was the whole reason for the coup."

"So, you tried to keep the peace, he wants a war, and since you were overthrown you came to warn me?" the mayor said sitting back in his chair grinning at Kratz.

"It's as you say," Kratz said bowing to the mayor. "I can show you how to crush Williamsport," he said slamming his hands together.

"And return you as mayor of that city?" The mayor shook his head. "No."

"You don't understand," Kratz spluttered, "I only come here as an advisor to the mayor." He bowed once more. "You will be the new mayor of Williamsport."

"You hate this man so much you are willing to give up a city just to defeat him?" The mayor stared at Kratz wide-eyed.

"I am ready to give up the life of every citizen of Williamsport to defeat him," Kratz said with a crooked smile.

Latte and Uma took in a gasp of air and backed away after the statement he had just made. The mayor looked at him with contempt and then considered Kratz' two companions.

"Very well." He nodded. "You will be one of my advisors."

Kratz grinned and said, "As you wish, Mr. Mayor."

---

Weeks passed, Kratz grew tired as the mayor hesitated to invade Williamsport. He had told them everything they needed to know to take the city easily. So, why was the mayor hesitating?

The mayor requested his attendance at city hall. He didn't expect to see such a large audience in the court room. Had he done something that they mayor wanted to praise him about? What could it be? Uma and Latte sat up front and nodded as he approached the mayor. Perhaps they were getting ready to invade Williamsport and they wanted to praise him for all the help he'd given them. Yes, that must be it.

Kratz stood at the front of the desk where the mayor sat, then bowed. "Your Honor, I am pleased to come before you."

The mayor smiled, showing his teeth. "I wanted to thank you personally Kratz for helping build our forces in preparation for an invasion from Williamsport."

*I was right. They are going to honor me for helping them.*

"As you were divulging information to me and my military, we sent an envoy to find out what Williamsport's true intentions were. And do you know what they told us?"

*What's going on?* Kratz bowed again. He couldn't swallow, suddenly becoming parched. "Why would they tell you the truth, sir?"

"That is precisely what I thought. So, we're on the same page, you and I. But this is what Williamsport said. The mayor read a letter in his hands. 'We have a treaty with Appalachia and have no intention of dishonoring that treaty.'"

The mayor's eyes beamed like they were on fire. "We also asked about you. And they sent us another letter." The mayor waved the other letter in the air. "I'd read the whole thing, but I think the last part is the most important part. It says: 'Because of these malicious acts, I, Colonel Eric Lynch, do hereby decree that Mayor Kratz is a traitor to this city and shall be placed under arrest and put on trial for his crimes against the people of Williamsport.' And they asked, if we had you, to kindly return you to Williamsport so *you* could have a fair trial."

"How can you believe everything someone says?" Kratz smiled, playing with his fingers, sweat dripped down his back.

"I know Colonel Lynch! I don't know you, and I was naïve enough to believe you. But not anymore." The mayor came forward putting his elbows on the desk. "You have three choices." He raised up one finger. "First choice! We can hang you outside for lying to the mayor."

"But, your honor, I didn't lie."

"Second choice!" The mayor ignored his comment. Now two fingers were raised. "We send you back to Williamsport to stand trial.

"Third choice!" The mayor raised three, bejeweled fingers. "You can leave Appalachia and never return." The mayor sat back in his chair. "Now, I don't know if your companions want to leave with you."

"No! We…" Latte burst out with one hand reaching out toward the mayor.

"No! We don't," Uma said, holding latte's thigh. "We like it here and want to stay."

The mayor smiled grimly at Latte and Uma, then returned his gaze at Kratz. "The choice is yours."

Kratz gritted his teeth, trying to hold back his anger. He wasn't going to be able to convince this mayor to see things his way. Influencing people was so easy for him. Yet, this mayor was different. He stared into the man's eyes. They looked so much like… Eric Lynch's eyes. *Hmm*. Maybe this was why they got along so well those many years ago.

Kratz bowed and was about to speak when the mayor raised his hand. "On second thought, I've decided that I like the treaty we have with Williamsport and will return you to that city." He turned to look at Uma and Latte. "Your friends here can go with you."

"No!" cried Uma, falling on her knees. "This is our home. Why would you send us back to Williamsport? We didn't do anything."

"If you didn't do anything, why not go back to Williamsport?"

Uma cried as she held onto Latte. Her husband stared at the mayor, open mouthed. But Kratz wasn't about to go back to Williamsport.

"I'd rather be hanged outside than be returned to Williamsport."

The mayor looked at Kratz, brows raised. "Very well then. You shall *all* be hanged outside, for lying to the mayor."

"No! No! No!" Uma jumped up and yelled. Latte grabbed her waist, but she wriggled herself free. "We didn't do anything. Why would you have us put to death?" Uma stared at the mayor waiting for an answer.

The mayor leaned forward in his seat. "You two were Eric Lynch's best friends."

The mayor sat back, then pointed at Kratz. "I also inquired about you two just like I did your friend here? The reason you will be hanged is that you came into this city with this man."

Uma collapsed back down and buried her head in her hands, sobbing. "I am innocent!" She pointed to herself, then her husband. "*We* are innocent."

# Chapter 64

Alexis along with her dad, Audrey and her mother were on their way to the Poconos to try and get them to help fight the Feds. She thought about their encounters with this group in her time. They were not a pleasant people, always raiding their crops during harvest with many fights developing. She didn't have the heart to tell her father that this was the group that killed Uncle Miles.

"We've had problems with these people for over a year," Alexis said.

"Last year?" Mrs. Bushnell began to laugh. "My dear, the skirmishes you're talking about with Milestown and the Poconos happened over two hundred years ago."

Audrey looked over at Alexis and smiled.

They found a place to rest for the night. Alexis distributed the rations. Tom looked disappointed at what he was given. She could tell he was trying to eat slowly to make it last longer. Alexis knew her father would still be hungry. Regrettably, she couldn't help him.

Audrey sat in prayer before she ate her rations.

"I didn't see you do that at dinner last night," Alexis said.

"Starting today, I will always do this so that people can see my relationship with God," she said.

"Oh, Audrey, if you keep this up, people will think you're crazy," Mrs. Bushnell said.

"But I'm not. You believe in God, don't you, Tom?"

Tom was digging through his sack trying to find more food. "The concept of God is very tricky," he said, sounding philosophical and turning the bag upside down over the palm of his hand. "There's a lot of gobbledygook. People have used God to justify many bad things in this world. In a certain way, and well, for me personally, I'm not quite sure I want to just burst out and say that I believe in God."

"I believe in God," Alexis blurted out. She had no idea what her father was talking and more likely her father had no idea either. "I've never spoken to God directly, but I believe He exists."

"Well, the existence of God. That is a little different than the belief in God," Tom mumbled. "Those are different things. Does that make any kind of sense?"

"No!" both Audrey and Alexis exclaimed.

Over the next two weeks, the group visited five cities. Only the Poconos and the New American cities would help Milestown. Combined, the two cities had an army of three thousand soldiers. Just as Mayor Oberon had predicted, the other cities despised Milestown and saw the Feds as their liberators.

Audrey could see Milestown as they came up over a hill. There was fire and smoke spreading in the direction of the city.

"Oberon!" her mother cried out as she ran toward the city.

"Mom!" Audrey yelled, following her.

It was night before Audrey and her mom got into the city. The fires they had seen were south at the city borders. As Audrey had suspected, some of the crops had caught fire. The clouds made everything appear brighter as lightning flashed farther away.

Audrey and her mom entered city hall. Her father was talking with the city council and the army commanders. The mayor excused himself from the conversation when he spotted them.

"Tetra. Audrey. You've come back." He gave each of them a hug. "The Feds have begun their attack on Milestown. It doesn't look good. If we can't hold them, we may have to surrender."

"Was it the lightning that caused the crops to burn?" Audrey asked.

"No. The Feds started those fires."

"We mustn't surrender!" her mother insisted, her face lit up as if she had some secret weapon. "The Poconos and New America have decided to help us. They are here with three thousand soldiers. You can coordinate your efforts with their commanders. They'll be here soon."

"It might just be too late," the mayor said shaking nervously as he looked into her eyes.

A soldier walked into the room, handing a slip of paper to one of the officers, who scanned it quickly, before addressing his mayor. "Sir, we have less than one thousand troops left. The Feds are preparing a final assault on the city."

"Tell Commander Aruba to send two men to the Fed commander to discuss terms of surrender," the mayor said.

"No, Daddy! You can still win. You just need to believe!" Audrey screamed.

"In your god?" Oberon's face frowned as he shook his head at Audrey.

"Sir?" the officer waited for the mayor to confirm his last order.

Oberon grabbed Audrey by the arm and took her outside. He turned her around to face him and roared, "Why do you keep insisting that there is a god? You say that he can destroy the Feds. Then why doesn't he just do it?"

"Because you don't believe in him," she said tears filling her eyes.

"So, you're telling me if I don't believe in your god, the Feds will take over every city?"

"No. They will only take over Milestown." Audrey said wiping the tears as they fell down her face.

"Prove to me that there is a God! Make it destroy the monument. No! Make it destroy the ancient building over there. I want to see it happen." He stared at her with unbelieving eyes. He didn't think there was a god. But she knew that God would prove himself.

"The first thing you asked to be destroyed is the thing that will be destroyed. God will do this to prove that He exists," she said solemnly, wiping her nose. The monument meant something to Audrey, especially now after meeting Alexis. She turned to look at the monument one last time.

Seconds passed before a bolt of lightning hit the monument at its tip, causing it to crack and fall apart. The metal plaque flew off and hit the side of a building, dropping into the dirt below. The mayor looked on the scene in astonishment.

"The chances of lightning striking that monument while we are having this discussion are..." He shook his head. "But, darling, there is a storm above us, and it was just by chance that the lightning struck when it did."

Audrey looked at her father and couldn't believe that he still had doubt. She closed her eyes facing the sky.

Another bolt of lightning struck the same spot, causing the pieces that made up the monument to take flight toward them. Without a moment to spare, Oberon grabbed her and dove behind the building. She could feel him trembling beside her.

"The chances of that happening are even more remote." He sat up and looked around. "So where is your god?"

"He's everywhere!" she said kissing and hugging him.

When they returned to the others, her father addressed the soldier sent by Commander Aruba. "Delay that last command." He said in an excited voice. She knew that now that he believed Milestown would not be destroyed.

Audrey and her dad spent the next two hours trying to convince Audrey's mom about God. Her mom claimed that the only reason her father believed in this god was because her god would help Milestown win the war.

"And if this god wasn't going to help you win this war, would you still believe?" Tetra asked.

The mayor looked at Audrey and held her hand. "After what I've seen today, yes, I would believe even if Milestown would not be saved."

"Sir, Commander Aruba is waiting for your command," said the soldier the commander had sent.

"Any news from the Poconos and New America?" he asked.

"We are here, sir," said Commander Nikkor of the Poconos.

"Very well."

Logan entered the room. Audrey came over and hugged him. Logan kissed her and then went over to the mayor. "Colonel Lynch was successful in acquiring the troops from Williamsport," Logan told him. "He has over three thousand soldiers and is on the eastern border, sir. The colonel also knows about the next attack on Milestown and has given us instructions. When we see a red light in the sky, we are to advance our army and attack the Feds."

Audrey smiled as Logan came over. He kissed her on the lips as she wrapped her arms around him.

Audrey and Logan watched, waiting for the red light in the sky. Something that Eric had to have brought with him from his time. The storm had moved off and was now hovering over the Fed army. Lightning shot through the sky. She prayed that God was weakening the Fed army so that her city could win the fight against the Feds. She could see her dad clasping his hands, hopefully praying to God as well.

Two hours had gone by when a red glow filled the dark sky. It burst into a bright red light—the sign they had been waiting for from Eric. Audrey and her mother watched as Oberon gave the command and marched with the Milestown's troops and the troops from the neighboring cities toward the Fed territory.

# Chapter 65

Eric took his men, flanking west of the Feds while Oberon charged straight into them from the north. The Feds had no problem keeping Milestown from advancing, but as Williamsport pushed hard, the Feds couldn't hold two fronts, and their forces collapsed. When Milestown and Williamsport met up at the river, just outside New Scranton, not one Fed soldier could be found.

"Tomorrow we march into New Scranton and defeat the Feds!" Oberon yelled, raising his fist into the air. The soldiers raised their fists into the air, shouting and cheering.

"I agree with you Oberon. The smell of victory is in the air," said Mayor Roti of New America, his tall lanky appearance, along with his very short hair made him look young for a mayor.

Eric had reservations; this was too easy. The Milestown and Williamsport armies were within miles of New Scranton, the capital of the Feds. Not one Fed soldier had engaged them in battle for most of the day. The men were ordered to stay calm and not get too excited about what appeared to be a clear victory.

The next morning, they marched toward the city, a small group of men became overly enthusiastic and ran ahead. That's when it happened. At first Eric saw what looked like a rock flying through the air. Then it hit the ground and exploded, killing the men that had advanced ahead of everyone else. Nothing was left of the men except for a large crater. Rocks and debris flew high into the sky. No one had been prepared for the body parts that came raining down afterwards. Whole arms, legs, and torsos fell all around them. More explosions followed.

Eric yelled out the order to retreat.

"What the hell was that?" Sergeant Sandalwood yelled as they ran away.

Eric didn't respond. Once they had retreated far enough, the explosions stopped. The enemy had a distinct advantage.

"We can't fight them with those types of weapons," Sandalwood said. "How can they have such weapons of mass destruction?"

"But God is on our side. Won't he help us defeat them?" asked Oberon.

"I don't know," Eric said. "But I just saw a dozen of my men blown to pieces. I'm not letting that happen again. I'm betting they're tanks. Lucky for us, they're not moving."

"Those things can move?" Sandalwood shook his head in disbelief.

"If they're what I think they are, yes."

"Then why haven't they come after us?"

"Because those machines are probably too old to do anything but shoot."

# Timepieces

The day was long. Eric sat looking toward the Fed capital, thinking of a way to get past those tanks. Out into the distance only grey dirt and a few boulders scattered across the landscape. Five thousand men were at his command, and all it took was one machine to stop them. There had to be something to turn things in their favor and get those men through, but there was nothing in this time that could defeat a tank.

The men set up camp, pitching tents and building fires as night approached. A crescent moon appeared in the night sky. Faint glimmers of fires could be seen in the Fed camp. It reminded Eric of the first days in this time period when he'd found the town where Camila lived. Then, an idea struck him. He gathered Aruba and Oberon along with the mayors and commanding officers from the other cities.

"I have an idea that just might give us the advantage over the Feds." Eric said, scanning the orange faces listening intently around the fire. "First, we send a dozen men on a reconnaissance mission to find out how many tanks are operational."

"And if they're all operational?" asked Chatag, the paunchy mayor from the Poconos, brows furrowed in concentration.

Eric ignored the mayor's question. "Look, it's dark—the Feds can't see us, but they *can* see our campfires. We'll set up several fires and keep them burning as a distraction, while we'll actually be marching into New Scranton."

"You want us to march toward tanks?" gasped Oberon. "This is preposterous!"

"The cover of night will protect us. The Feds will think we are waiting before we make out next move." Aruba was about to say something, but Eric held up his hand. "Let me finish telling you my idea and then you can question me. It will be faster."

No one argued.

"We only need a dozen men to keep the fires going during the night. The rest will assemble away from camp, away from the fires. The Feds will only be aware of the fires as our men quietly march in and destroy them."

"Maybe…" Chatag said, rubbing his cheek. "It just might work."

"The downside is, if they see or hear us before we have a chance to do anything, we are dead. This would be a suicide mission."

"Let's discuss a strategy to get in and surprise the Feds, making the tanks useless."

The men from the reconnaissance mission returned. "We found men camped around these things that looked like huge boulders with long tubes sticking out of them. They were rusted in parts. They spaced them out very far apart. We split up and scanned the area, finding four," said one of the men—Sargent Jamal.

Based on the description his men gave, he was sure they were tanks; but how many did the Feds have in total? Would it be enough to just get rid of those four?

Eric assembled Five-hundred men to each scout that knew the location of a tank. They swiftly but silently marched to the outskirts of New Scranton, stopping when they were within a stone's throw of the 'rusted boulders' as Eric's scouts called them. Each group needed to attack simultaneously when the crescent moon fell on the horizon. If only he had another flare to shoot into the sky instead.

His group rushed the Fed soldiers that were camped around one of the tanks, taking them by surprise. The fires illuminated a rusted metal carcass. The tank was in complete disrepair. This one had missing tracks, with rusted holes in the armor. The other tanks hopefully were in similar shape.

The Feds fought bravely, but as the morning revealed what the darkness of night hid, it was plain that the Feds suffered heavy losses, and they began to retreat into New Scranton. The Fed army had dwindled to almost nothing.

Eric led the charge and surrounded the city.

# Chapter 66

President Lewis sat at his dining room table alone, eating what would probably be his final meal as the last ruler of this great empire. This was a gloomy day, both in its physical aspects as well as the depressing fact that his army was all but defeated. The army wouldn't be able to protect the city and its people. As he solemnly savored the steak on his plate, an officer came into the room.

"Sir! The enemy has surrounded New Scranton. Commander Ramses says that the army cannot hold them back. What are your orders, sir?"

"Tell Commander Ramses that he should ask for terms."

"Sir?" the lieutenant said, in surprise. "Aren't we fighting for freedom and democracy? We can't just give up!"

"We're surrendering, son. It's over," the president sighed.

Lewis admired the long wooden table, a magnificent piece built in a time when his government was at its peak. Now the government was coming to an end—a tragic end. How ironic that today was the 4th of July.

---

President Lewis expected that the terms of surrender would be simple. His primary concern was to keep the Fed citizens safe.

Colonel Lynch walked into the presidential compound. With striking grey eyes, the colonel moved with a natural grace that betrayed a quiet authority. A self-made man. This man clearly had the gift of leadership and couldn't possibly have learned everything he knew from Williamsport.

"Commander Lynch," the president said, approaching the colonel. "We finally meet."

"Mr. President."

Lewis was impressed that the colonel continued to show respect even though he was no longer the president of anything. "I'm to assume that Commander Ramses discussed terms with you?" Colonel Lynch's eyes held no expression. "My only concern is for my people. They are to be included in your franchise."

"Commander Ramses surrendered unconditionally," Colonel Lynch said, taking a seat next to him.

Lewis' smile faded. He hadn't expected the commander to give up this easily. His people had truly been defeated.

"But I will consider your request," the colonel added.

Would the colonel consider it or was he patronizing him? His expression was unreadable. The president mustered up a smile. "Thank you." After a brief pause he spoke again. "You know, a long time ago, these cities—your city and mine—used to be part of the same government?"

"Yes," Colonel Lynch nodded. "These cities here were all part of the state called Pennsylvania, which was one of the fifty states which made up the United States. It was the first of thirteen states that started it all."

He was impressed—the colonel knew his history. "I have the Constitution hanging in my office," the president said. "You might want to remember that at one time we were one people."

Colonel Lynch regarded him with narrowed eyes. "Doesn't the Bill of Rights apply to all men, Mr. President? Tell me, what part of your constitution provides for you to keep people as livestock and slaughter them for food?"

President Lewis looked at the man; how could he possibly answer that question? Politics had allowed his people to thrive. Anyone who was a citizen of the Feds could not be eaten. That was the law. This concept of being better than anyone else had kept them alive! "The Constitution applies only to the people that pledge their allegiance to it. Those people in the slaughterhouse would not pledge allegiance to anyone and they got what they deserved."

"Did you even bother asking them to pledge allegiance to the United States Constitution?" the colonel asked, appearing pensive, shrugging.

The president was well aware of the history of his people. Several turning points led them to become the aggressive group they were. Over two hundred years ago, the first Fed ate another human being—for survival. Senator Williamson said it was the only way they would be able to survive this new world. The senator had convinced the president to force anyone who did not have the mark to be slaughtered and consumed. The populace began to crave this perversion called meat. The government did provide an out for those who were captured by allowing them to pledge their allegiance to the Feds. They just never told them. By the next generation, most people outside the Fed territories had no mark and were rounded up and slaughtered. No longer were the Feds looking to expand their influence. They looked only to replenish their food supply. He had no regrets. "They did not pledge their allegiance to the United States Constitution," he repeated, firmly.

"Perhaps with a new constitution, the concept of liberty and freedom for all men and women will ring true again..." the colonel said.

Neither said anything more. The president looked around, shaking his leg nervously, waiting for the colonel. A mark on the colonel's arm, just under his sleeve caught his attention. The president moved in just enough to get a closer look. He had a mark, just like the one's he had seen in history books. He perked up in his chair. Now he was afraid. Was this man a god? "You have the mark on your arm. Where did you get it? Who are you?" No other person existed in this world with a mark like that—not anymore.

Colonel Lynch looked down at his arm, and smirked. "Where is this place you call the Harvest?"

The president wasn't at all surprised that the colonel knew of this place. But, if he was a god, he would already know of its location. The colonel was just a man. The president's fears subsided, just a little.

"One of your men will take my men there," the colonel said. He turned to one of his officers and told him to get several of his men ready to follow whoever the president assigned. The president in turn ordered one of his officers to be their guide.

The colonel's ability to keep his composure was impressive. Kratz had sent the man's wife and kids to the Harvest. Indeed, Kratz had sent many people there. He had no idea how many of them he might have known.

"Colonel Lynch, I want to express my deepest regret about your wife, son and daughter. Had I known, I wouldn't have allowed them to kill your children."

The moment the colonel moved was the moment Lewis realized that he should have kept his mouth shut. His heart beat faster and fear gripped him once more. He didn't even have time to utter a single word as Colonel Lynch lunged forward in his chair, and stabbed him repeatedly in the gut, letting his rage rule unconditionally. At first Lewis felt little pain, but soon his entire body felt as if it had caught fire. Unbearable pain enveloped him. He closed his eyes, and then something happened.

His heart stopped beating.

---

Eric ordered that the remaining Fed army be dismantled, and the officers thrown into a prison that had been built by the Feds, to await trial for their conduct in the war. Eric propped the Fed president's decapitated head on the end of a long stick and stuck it into the ground in front of the prison. If only killing every Fed for what they'd done to his wife and children would bring them back. Hanging onto a slim thread of hope that they may still be alive, he sent soldiers to try and find his family.

News quickly spread among the soldiers. The entire army wept with him. Eric spent several days secluded, shunning all company and state affairs. He wanted, no, *needed*, to be alone to mull over why all of this had happened to him. Somehow God was involved. Had he been more faithful at the time he'd left Williamsport, would that have changed things? Would he have been right with God then? Would his family still be alive now?

Not one soldier returned with any news of his family. And even though he didn't want to admit it, he knew deep down that they were gone. Butchered and consumed by monsters.

Eric soon discovered that the soldiers raided the prison, killing every man and woman incarcerated there for what the Feds had done to his family. Not one Fed officer survived. When his army started taking out their anger with the civilians, he knew it was time to overcome his grief and get back in charge of his command.

# Chapter 67

Satish, who was now a corporal in the army, listened to a group at the table next him in the mess-hall listening to the story about the miracle that God performed with water coming out of a rock. All the men were from the New American army. All except one—Dwayne, now a lieutenant.

Dwayne spotted Satish and raised his hand, calling him over.

"Hey guys, this is Satish. We both enlisted at the same time." Dwayne turned to Satish. "We're talking about how Commander Lynch's God led us to victory over the Feds."

"So, how do you know that the commander's god led us to victory?" a soldier named Fakri asked with a smirk.

"Haven't you noticed that we had very few casualties?" demanded Dwayne, slamming his hand against the table.

"Few casualties?" Fakri shrugged. "We lost over half of our men in Milestown."

"That was before the mayor of Milestown believed in his daughter's god," remarked an officer of the New American army—Colonel Kong.

"The mayor of Milestown's daughter? Audrey?" Satish said trying to figure out how she fit into this whole debate. "No! It's the commander's god that let us win this war."

"I know what I know," Colonel Kong said. "Once the mayor of Milestown accepted Audrey's god, we were able to push the Feds back and defeat them."

"Maybe it's both their gods that helped us," Fakri suggested. "Lynch's god and Audrey's god."

"Or maybe they're the same god," Kong proposed.

Satish and Dwayne argued for hours with the men from New America. They knew it was their commander's god that won the war. Who even heard of Audrey's god?

Dwayne raised his hand. "Okay, how about we do this. We'll each write the virtues of our gods."

When done, Kong came over with his list. Dwayne had just finished his. Both lists had the same number of attributes.

"Maybe, Audrey's god and Eric's god are the same god." Satish suggested.

"Oh, hell no!" Kong and Fakri shouted. Fakri snatched the list out of Dwayne's hand and everyone gathered round the table comparing the two lists.

A fight erupted around the table over which god was the more powerful god. Satish and Dwayne ran, barely making it out of the mess hall. Word got out and a rift developed between the Williamsport army and the armies of Milestown, the Poconos, and New America, becoming harder for orders to be followed.

# Timepieces

News of this debate about whether the commander's god or Audrey's god had saved them finally reached Eric's ears. He couldn't fathom how they came up with Lynch's god and Audrey's god. Who was coming up with this stuff? Is this how beliefs were made, with people arguing about things they didn't know? Each side forming an opinion and pushing that opinion until everyone believed it? It would be amusing to see which of the two gods would win, but this was serious, orders were not being followed because of who god was.

Eric sat at his desk and wrote a decree stating that there is no God, but God, explaining that the reason the water flowed from the rock was because Audrey told him to do it to prove that God really did exist. He explained how this god was not just the god of Eric, or the god of Audrey; it was everyone's god. He gave the letter and had it reproduced and circulated amongst the soldiers.

After a few days he got word that the arguments about God had subsided; but there were still a few who referred to God as Lynch's god or Audrey's god.

---

Now that the Fed cities were secured, Eric asked the commanders of the Poconos and New America to send a dispatch to their cities updating them on the situation. He also asked to have all the mayors meet in Milestown to decide the fate of the Feds. Because of the effort it took four cities to bring down the destructive power of one city, Eric wanted to keep all the cities together and keep them from fighting among themselves. A United Nations of sorts could be created, but ultimately it would have to become a single, central government.

He sent a dispatch to his father with a slightly encrypted message:

Dad,

*We won the war! The Feds are no longer a threat. I would like to ask you a favor. I need you to start writing a first draft to a document. Remember your trip to 1787? There are several documents that I am sending. Use them as a basis from which to start. Get Alexis to help you.*

Love,
Eric

Eric was pleased with the outcome of the war. Sandalwood was left in charge of the Williamsport army while Eric went to Milestown to bring all the mayors together to try and convince them to form a government.

Oberon and Eric left with a small contingency and headed back to Milestown. Aruba had gone ahead a day earlier with the Milestown army. On the way, Eric brought Oberon up to date on his plans with regards to the other cities that participated in the war effort.

"The biggest problem we have is how to deal with the Fed cities. I really don't want to break up the territories evenly into districts."

---

Oberon was cautious of Eric. In less than three months, Lynch had established himself as the ruler of a city. His army faithfully followed him because of the supposed miracle with the flowing water from the rock. And now, the other armies revered him because of that story. Oberon could see that Eric would become powerful and eventually take over all the cities.

"I agree that not every city should get an even share of territory," Oberon said. Why should they? It was Milestown that suffered the most losses, so it should be Milestown that receives a larger part of the city.

"I don't want to give any city any territory," Eric said as they walked.

Oberon smiled. *I was played the fool.* Eric had plans to keep the Fed territories all along. Milestown, along with the other cities, would be too far north for anyone to stop him. "You want the Fed cities to become part of Williamsport?" At this point, he wasn't sure if he could call Eric his friend any longer. He should have killed him when they first met.

"No." Eric said, turning to face him with a smile. "I want every city to be part of one government."

"With you being the head of that *one* government?" Was this really happening? This man didn't just want to take control of the Fed territories, he wanted to take control of the entire world.

The other mayors had been invited to come down to Milestown, innocently believing that they were going to be discussing what sections of the Fed territories they would take control of. Instead they would be meeting their new ruler. But God wouldn't let that happen. Didn't Oberon's belief in Audrey's god allow Milestown to keep the Feds from ruling them?

"Perhaps… Or, you could be the head, or one of the other mayors," said Eric. "It could even be a councilman or whoever the people want to lead them.

Oberon stopped mid-step. "What?" he roared. "You want all the cities to have a ruler that may not even know how to run a city? What kind of idiocy is this?"

"It wouldn't be that simple," Eric laughed, continuing to walk and explained to Oberon the concept of a democratic government in which the people ruled the cities. The foundation of this republic would allow every city to live peacefully and grow.

How did Eric think this was a much better concept than a monarchy? There were councilmen that met to create laws. How was this different? Eric explained that the main difference was that the mayor would have to be elected and not serve a life term.

Oberon hated Eric's idea; after all, his entire family had produced a line of mayors since Milestown was established. "Could Milestown still be a monarchy?"

"The people in Milestown would vote on it."

Oberon listened politely, but he wasn't totally convinced that it would work. There should not be one central government leading all the cities. If Milestown elected to keep him Mayor, it would still be possible for this central government to pass laws that would make Milestown bend to its knees. But if it was as Eric had described, provisions could be put into place that would prevent that from happening.

# Chapter 68

Tom got writer's cramp trying to keep up with all the changes, exclusions and inclusions. Even with the help of two assistants and Alexis making sure that the statements in the constitution didn't conflict and that the wording made sense, it was hard work. It took two months of writing before a document that everyone agreed to could be finalized. The mayors argued and quarreled and at times it didn't seem like anything was good enough for them. The smaller cities didn't want to see the Fed cities being a single, ruling area. They separated them into quarters, becoming the Northern and Southern Feds as well as the Eastern and Western Feds with New Scranton being its own city as well. Still, the smaller cities argued that they would have no real voting power in the government if each city would have representatives based on the population. Eric introduced a concept similar to the senate of the United States in which each state had a single vote which they could use to try and override the passing or veto of a law. Eric wanted to make sure that most of the power of the government rested in the hands of the representatives and not with the senate.

Audrey also had influence on the wording in the new constitution and introduced a proposal to free the slaves in every city. All the cities agreed to it—except for Milestown; Oberon couldn't seem to see his city functioning without slaves. The mayor from the Poconos introduced a compromise in which no city could have slaves with the exception of prisoners, which could be slaves for the duration of their sentences.

"There you are, Oberon," the mayor from the Poconos had said. "Now you still have a group of people you can treat like shit." He slapped his hand down on the table.

"We don't treat our slaves like shit," Oberon scoffed.

Everyone laughed.

"This is still not enough. The prison population is small. I can't run a city with such a small number of slaves. Surely you can understand, Chatag?" Oberon argued, trying to get sympathy from the mayor of New America.

"I will send you my prisoners, Oberon, the ones that have committed serious crimes. I'm sure my people will be more than happy to send them to you," Chatag jested.

"This is not acceptable. Milestown will not sign any document in which the slaves are freed."

Tom remembered a time when he had said something similar—it had been when the Declaration of Independence was being written. What would have happened had he done nothing and let the wording on slavery stand in the document? Unfortunately, it was too late to change that now.

The mayor of New America stood up and cleared his throat. "Oberon, there are several reasons why you will not have any slaves. Firstly, you promised us—my city and the Poconos—that you would free our people. Secondly, your daughter and the mayor of Williamsport, Mayor Lynch, have a powerful entity that is in their favor. Your daughter is the one who has come in here to this group and has asked us to do this for her. Why would you deny your daughter this simple request?"

Tom saw how Oberon was being pressured from the other mayors. After another half day debating, Oberon finally conceded and agreed to free the slaves. He made sure that the compromise of prisoners being used as free labor was left in. Audrey, with the help of Alexis, made sure the wording to use prisoners as free labor specified only public works. No prisoner could be used as a slave by any private institution or individual.

It was finally done! A new document was created whereby every mayor read and agreed with all the changes.

Tom watched as his son, the mayor of Williamsport and the head of the army, was the first to sign the document.

Eric raised his pen. "I know for myself that I would not be here if it weren't for my family. This is for my father and sister who helped bring this document together." He nodded at them as they stood behind the mayors. Tom put his hand on Alexis' shoulder. Eric continued, "And for my wife and children who are no longer with us. Today we sign this document. Today we become one people."

Eric put his signature upon the paper followed by Oberon and then Chatag, the mayor of the New America, followed by all the other mayors.

---

The people were still celebrating into the early hours of the morning. Alexis couldn't believe that this was happening, especially when in her time most of this was just arid dirt and less than a hundred people lived here. She wanted to get Audrey away from the steady flow of people that wanted to know more about her god. She had been talking for hours. It was amazing that she had any energy left. She tried to convince Logan to pull Audrey away from the crowd.

"I tried. Really, I did," Logan said, looking over at Audrey speaking animatedly with the people. "But she won't leave. She hasn't eaten since yesterday morning."

"I think she's talked with everyone on the planet," Alexis joked and excused herself to go over and talk with her brother.

Eric was all smiles as she approached. "You know, I wouldn't have ever imagined that the little kid with long wavy hair would become such an important person," she said, giving him a kiss on the cheek.

"Did you ever think you would see any of this?" Eric asked.

"That's what's so amazing, I thought civilization had ended. I never thought there would be enough people to actually create a new one! This is fantastic!"

Silence reigned between them, before Alexis finally broke it. "I've decided to go back home tomorrow," she said, as tears welled in her eyes.

"Why don't you stay until after the elections?"

"That will take another year. And even though no one will know that I've been gone for so long, I miss them. I miss my family."

"I understand," Eric nodded solemnly. He was probably thinking about Camila, Tommy, and Mariam. He darted his eyes away and bent his head staring at the ground.

"I'm sorry," Alexis reached over and took his hand. "I wish I had met your wife and kids. Knowing you, I know she was probably gorgeous."

Eric looked at her and nodded. He stayed quiet for a moment, then said, "well, if you can't meet mine, maybe I can come and meet yours."

"That would be wonderful," Alexis said. "We could do it tomorrow when I go back."

"It's a date," he said, and offered her a weak smile.

Just then, Tom came back from the buffet, food piled high on his plate. Yet, she couldn't help but noticed that he had gotten noticeably thinner.

"You know, I had to find someone to put more food out there," Tom said, sitting down. "They ran out! Can you believe it?"

Audrey finally managed to escape from the crowds and came over to the table to join them. "Oh! I'm so tired," she said, flopping down into a spare chair. "Where's Logan?"

"I think I saw him leaving," Tom said. "I think he went back to the house."

Eric smiled at Audrey. She didn't have any strength left to keep her eyes open. "I think you talked with everyone in the city," he teased her.

"I think so too," she said, resting her head on the table.

A slave came over to take the used plates off the table, her gaze fixed on Audrey.

"It's amazing how they all look at her like she's a hero for freeing the slaves. Did her god tell her to do that?" the slave mumbled, as she put the plates into the tub.

"Actually," Tom said, "*she* was a slave for a while. She originally made the promise to another slave. It was that slave who made her make the promise to God."

"You expect me to believe that *she* was a slave?" the servant mocked, looking at Audrey. She shook her head. "She's the princess of Milestown!"

"It doesn't matter what you believe," Tom said. "You're going to be free because of her."

She huffed but didn't respond as she continued to clear their table.

"Come on! Aren't you at all happy that you're going to be free? You can go and do whatever you want."

"I'm grateful for what she's done," she said to Tom, "but I would have been happier if this all happened five years ago. Then my boy wouldn't have died for wanting to be free," she said holding back her tears.

"Oh, I'm so sorry to hear that. Where did he die?"

"By the monument that her god destroyed," she said, nodding at Audrey again.

But Audrey wasn't participating in the conversation. She'd fallen asleep.

"What happened at the monument?" Tom asked curiously, helping himself to more food.

"My boy was trying to escape," she said in anger. "He died trying to be free."

Eric looked at their father, seemingly lost in his own thoughts. "What are you thinking, Dad?"

"You know, I think we can save him."

"What?" Eric said.

"What do you mean save him?" Alexis asked in confusion, almost speaking over her brother.

"I can go back in time and get him."

"First things first, Dad," Eric said, "I thought you said you can't go back in time and change things? Secondly, why would you want to go back and change things?"

"He dies!" Tom yelled, as if trying to drive the concept home with volume. "If I take him the split second before that happens and bring him here, he'll be dead there and alive here. Nothing changes." Tom stood up and spread out his arms. "I'm a genius!" He stood, taking out his timepiece and turning it on. He asked the servant to try and remember the exact day when her son died.

"You actually keep that with you?" Alexis said in surprise, looking at the timepiece.

"You never know when an emergency like this might pop up."

"Dad, this is not an emergency," Alexis said, looking worried. "You can get hurt. You don't even have the other timepiece. You need two if you're going to bring him back."

Eric frowned at his dad.

"Very well then," Tom said, setting the date on the timepiece. "I'll go scout out the area and figure out exactly how he dies so I can come up with a plan on how to bring him back."

The servant didn't understand. "You're going to bring my son back here?"

"If I can," Tom said.

He talked more with the servant to try and figure out the precise time of the day her son died. Alexis worried about what her father was trying to do. She had a bad feeling about this. He began to set the time on the timepiece to a day ahead of the servant's son's death.

"Dad, you're going to get hurt," she pleaded, trying to make him see reason.

"You won't even know I'm gone," Tom said and flashed her a reassuring smile, before pressing the blue button and disappeared almost instantly. Both Eric and Alexis looked at the entrance to the building, expecting him to enter.

Nothing. No sign of him. Eric embraced her tightly.

Audrey stirred, slowly opened one eye and turned to Eric. "What's going on?" she asked, shaking her head. Alexis told her what Tom had done.

"Eric, we need to get the other timepiece and find him!" Alexis urged.

Audrey turned and saw the slave standing next to her. She flung her hands to her face. "Oh my god!"

"What?" Eric asked,

Alexis wailed, "What's wrong?"

"Oh my god!" Audrey's bottom lip quivered. "Tom..." She bowed her head to Eric and Alexis. "Your father... he's dead!"

"What do you mean dead?" Alexis cried. She could understand finding out that he was hurt and needing help. She could go and help him. She could bring him back. But this?

"I was there," Audrey whispered. "On that day, Tom tried to stop the soldiers from killing her son."

"Oh my! That was him?" the servant said putting her hand to her mouth.

"You knew and you did nothing to stop it!" Alexis said, now feeling contempt for Audrey.

"I didn't know that it was your father. Not at that time."

"I need to get the timepiece," Alexis said and stood up. Her father was dead and this time it was for real.

"Alexis, you can't go back and help your father," Audrey tried to reason with her.

Alexis didn't want to hear it. She knew what she needed to do. She needed to go and find her dad.

"Where's the other timepiece?" she demanded. A small chance existed where she could reach her dad before he got killed.

"No!" Audrey stopped her. "Your father told us always that wherever we go in time that is where we were meant to be. The fate that was in store for your dad was, *is*, supposed to happen. You can't change that."

"I don't care. I'm going to get the timepiece and go look for my dad," Alexis said stubbornly. "Eric, please." She knew that Eric would want to save him. He would get her the other timepiece, and since there were two, he would probably go and help her find him.

"Sis," he said, holding Alexis by her shoulders, "we can't help Dad. He's gone."

"No!" Alexis shouted, pulling from his grasp. She couldn't believe that he would give up so easily. "No!"

She stared at Audrey and knew in her heart that somehow God was at fault for letting this happen. "I hate you for this!" she screamed out.

"It wasn't Audrey's fault," Eric said.

"I'm so sorry, Alexis. I really am," Audrey said.

Alexis wasn't screaming at Audrey, she was screaming at God. He was the one that let this happen. She couldn't stand the thought of staying here. She turned her back to them and wiped her eyes. "I need to go home," was all she said, before she ran out of the building.

As she ran to the house, she passed the destroyed monument and saw her dad's body laying on the ground. She ran over to him. "Daddy!" She screamed, turning him over. He was dead. "Daddy!" After the Great Catastrophe, dad's death was a thing of the past. No one knew what happened or how he died. Now she knew, and all those emotions came back. All the pain from 2052. She desperately wanted it all to go away.

Eric knelt down and held his sister, staring at his dead father who lay on the ground. Audrey came over, put her hand on Tom's body and started to cry.

Oberon had come out of the building smiling. The smile faded as he ran over to where his daughter sat on the ground. "What happened?"

Alexis looked up to her dad. "He tried to save a slave running away and one of your soldiers killed him."

Oberon looked around. "Just now? Where is the soldier? Where is the slave?"

"No daddy, this didn't happen just now. This happened a long time ago."

Alexis saw the timepiece in her father's lifeless hands and became furious. She grabbed it, yelling. "This thing is what killed my father!" She stood and threw it on the ground and took a large piece of the monument and smashed it against the timepiece. A bright light flashed. Everything went black.

---

Alexis woke up the next day getting out of a bed she didn't know how she got into. Eric slept in the other bed next to her. She rummaged through the counter trying to find the timepiece. She found it and turned it on. The display showed the wrong date.

She tossed the timepiece back down.

"I'm leaving now," she said, staring at her brother, who was just waking up. "Where's the other timepiece?"

"Isn't it there?" Eric said, not fully awake.

Audrey and Logan walked into the room. "I'm so sorry about your dad," Said Audrey

Alexis didn't feel like talking about it. She just wanted to go home. "Do you know where the other timepiece is?"

Audrey reached into her pocket, grabbing a timepiece, holding it out to Alexis.

Eric walked his sister to where the monument used to be, where their dad died. He gave her something to take home. It was a picture of the family during better times.

"I want to have a memorial service for Dad. Here, in this time. Will you come back?"

"I don't know," she said hugging him, then turned to see that Audrey had come. She embraced her too. She turned her gaze to the city that she would help shape in her time. Tears streamed down her face. Would this be the last time she would ever see her brother again?

Alexis pressed the blue button on the timepiece. Suddenly she was back in 2060. The devastation was so much more noticeable here. The rubble from the monument was gone. In a few years someone would suggest building a monument and she knew exactly how it should look.

Marcus was preparing the food when she walked into the house. "I missed you so much." She kissed him and put her head on his chest, holding on tight.

Marcus put his arms around her and frowned saying, "Um, didn't you just give me a hug and walk out that door a minute ago?"

Alexis couldn't answer. She kept her head buried in his chest as she sobbed.

"What happened?"

"My father died," she sobbed.

"How? When? Where?" he looked at her wide eyed, dumbfounded.

She sniffled and wiped the tears from her eyes. "It didn't happen here, Marcus." She sat down. "I've been gone for almost two years."

"What?" he said sitting in the seat next to her. "You've changed your clothes, that's all. How did you go away for two years?"

She showed him the timepiece and explained what happened. It was easy to read the expression on Marcus' face. A story about time travel would be hard for anyone to believe unless one experienced it in person. She held his hand and was grateful that he'd taken the time to sit and listen to her story. She was back home.

# Chapter 69

**August 22, 9 (2069 old calendar)**

Alexis hadn't thought about her dad, Eric, or Audrey in a long time. She'd purposefully kept busy, trying to keep the community going. The dream seemed to come from nowhere; and as soon as she woke, she knew what she needed to do. She recalled the conversation with Eric about Audrey finding the timepiece in the cabin—it had been her own handwriting on that paper, not his, as he had thought. It was suddenly so clear.

It was still dark outside. She turned on a flashlight and went looking for the timepiece that had been packed away long ago. Not once had she thought of looking for it or using it to visit her brother. The picture that Eric had given her lay flat on the rickety old desk; her mother and father's faces stared back at her. Only Eric was left. Turning it over revealed the date Eric had written on it that Audrey needed to travel back in time—May 4, 1776. With the last piece of modern paper in her world, she wrote the letter and put it in the box with the timepiece.

At the shore, many of the fishing boats were tied down on the rocks that made the pier. Scanning around, she was careful to make sure there was no-one there to see her and, taking the nearest boat, she hopped in and floated off into the bay. The sky was getting brighter even though the sun hadn't yet come up. Thoughts about the mornings of a world long gone surfaced in her mind. She began to feel nostalgic for those blue skies of her early years.

It had been two hours, and the rowing was hard. But the cliffs were spectacular. It was amazing how her family had found the town they now lived in. Uncle Miles had found it. He was the one who knew exactly what was going to happen before it happened and managed to keep them alive. She missed him now, in this moment.

As she approached the cove, the gentle waved carried the boat aground. The shallow water up to her ankles lapped at the metal walls of the cabin. Pressing the tiles in the proper order caused the metal to reverberate and unlock the door. She wiped the wet sand off her knees, pushed the door open and entered.

The cabin was dark inside. Light barely reached the hallway where she knew the closet door was hidden. With the only key, Alexis unlocked the closet door and placed the box on the shelf in full view, making sure Audrey's name was clear. The key needed to be put in a safe place. The rooms were empty.

*They've taken everything.*

The only things left were a red marker and the clock which hung in the main room. Curiously, it still kept time.

Exiting back into the cove, Alexis closed the door to the cabin, making sure it was locked. She'd had the timepiece all this time and never once thought of using it. Eric never came to meet her family, like they had planned before her father died. She missed them both. She pushed the boat back into the water and rowed back to the city—back home to her husband, her kids, her family, her future.

The sky was unusually bright today and there were no clouds. Suddenly, her stomach cramped. Something awful was about to happen. She knew it. The water became more resistant the faster she paddled to the point that the boat was not moving at all. It was a full three hours before the Milestown coast was near. Tired and out of breath, she managed to pull the boat on shore. She wanted to rest, but now was not the time.

Jumping out of the boat the minute it hit the rocky pier, Alexis ran.

When she arrived, exhausted and out of breath, no one was at home. The children had to be playing outside. Just as she was about to head out to find them, Marcus came in through the door.

"Where are the kids?" Her hands trembled as she spoke.

"They're all playing at the beach," he said. "Justin, I think, is throwing stones in the river." He looked down at her trembling hands, face full of concern. "What's wrong?"

She had just come from the beach—she didn't see them. She remembered the journal entries at the library of the future and the one her daughter Monica wrote about Justin. "I think Justin might be in trouble," she told Marcus, and without waiting for a response, ran out of the house toward the river.

"What makes you think that? Hey, wait!" Marcus shouted after her.

They found Justin at the river, perched on a large boulder in the middle of the flowing water.

"Justin," she said. "Come here! Right now!"

"Mom! I'm only throwing stones in the river," he said. "What's wrong with that?"

"What's going on?" Marcus asked.

"You didn't do anything wrong, honey," she shouted to Justin, ignoring Marcus. "I just need you to come here to me, right now."

People had crowded around nearby, watching the drama play out. Monica wandered over. "Mom, what's wrong?"

"Nothing, dearest. Stay with your dad," she told Monica, before swallowing her fear. She moved closer to Justin and raised her voice again. "Come here, Justin. Now!"

He threw one more stone into the river and turned to jump off the boulder. As he made his turn, he slipped and fell into the water with a splash. Alexis ran to the edge of the water, but Marcus was faster and dived into the water. The moment he started pulling Justin out of the water, the river swelled, and the current became stronger. Water crashed violently; unable to get a firm handhold onto the edge, they both slid back into the river. Alexis grabbed for Justin and managed to catch his clothes with her fingertips and somehow hauled him out.

Finally, Justin was out of the water and on dry land. The river swelled higher, enveloping onto Justin as if it were trying to suck him back in. Alexis started to sink into the mud as Marcus, who had now hauled himself onto dry land, fought furiously to pull them both away from the river. Finally, some of the gawking crowd came over to help and soon, Justin and Alexis were safe on dry land. As if it knew they were out of the water, the river almost instantly lowered, and the current became normal once again.

Alexis held her son tight; she was so glad she had read that little piece of information in the book. She hadn't wanted to know her future. Then it hit her; the events in time could be changed! Saving her father's life was possible—Eric needed to know.

Black clouds formed above them. Justin spotted a grey rock and ran over to get it. "Lemme throw just this one, Mommy."

"Justin!" Alexis screamed at him. "Come here right now!"

Justin turned to face his parents and out of nowhere, a bolt of lightning struck him, and he collapsed to the ground. Alexis screamed and ran to him. Marcus was right beside her as she lifted her son's lifeless body.

"No!" she cried, hugging her son tightly. "Not my boy! Justin! Not Justin!"

Marcus tried to pull her off their son, but she wouldn't let go. A crowd gathered around trying to console her. The clouds dissipated from the sky as quickly as they had formed. The sun began to shine again.

Alexis let herself be led back to the house and sat down on a chair, numb and frozen. She trembled. They had saved her son from drowning in the river. They had prevented his death… But he still died. She clenched her fists and pounded them against her thighs as she cried out, "Why did you kill my boy?"

"What are you talking about, dear?" one of the other women asked. "It was a horrible accident, there was no-one else there."

Alexis couldn't believe what this lady was saying. *Don't these people know what just happened?* "You didn't see the river try to take my boy?" she asked everyone in the room.

No one said a thing.

"Didn't you see the clouds forming right after we moved away from the river?" she screamed. She got up and went to the window. "Look! There are no clouds outside! God killed my boy!"

Patricia, Marcus' sister was in the room, her hands on Marcus' shoulder. He looked lost, unable to speak. He moved over to Alexis, sobbing into her hair.

She held him tight. "Marcus, God killed our boy."

"It was an accident," he said between sobs. "Just an awful accident."

"No, it wasn't an accident!" Why couldn't anyone see what she saw?

"I saw what happened, Alexis," he said, pulling back and brushing her hair away from her face. He kissed her gently on the forehead. "God didn't kill Justin. We lost our boy today to a horrible tragedy."

Alexis knew the truth. Anger filled her entire being. God had done this to her son. Why did Justin need to die? She would never forgive him for this.

She felt helpless. The journal entry her daughter wrote in the future came to mind. They discovered the hardware store when they buried Justin. Because of that miracle they were able to farm the land more efficiently. Was God so merciless that he would kill a boy for that?

Later in the day, Alexis overheard Marcus talking with Patrick and Patty about where to bury Justin. Alexis would pick someplace, any place that wasn't where they wanted to bury him. They wouldn't find that hardware store. Not now.

Marcus knelt beside her. "Honey, we've been talking, and we've decided to bury Justin next to your Uncle Miles on the cliffs that overlook the bay."

"No!" Alexis said in defiance. "I want to bury him next to the wheat fields. I want him there watching us all the time."

"But, honey," Marcus said, "we need that area to grow food."

"That's where I want him buried," she said.

"I think we can do that." Patty nodded. "We can bury him there."

"That's where I want my boy buried." She cried and cried, thinking about Justin, her firstborn son. God wasn't going to win this time.

It was agreed. Later that day the men of the city went out to dig the grave. By the afternoon, Marcus and the men returned to the house and entered through the kitchen door. They had strange expressions of shock on their faces.

"What's going on?" Alexis asked Marcus.

"Honey," he said, "we have some good news and some bad news."

"What's the bad news?" she said, afraid that one of her other children was hurt.

"We won't be able to bury Justin by the wheat fields."

A sense of devastation so strong almost made her keel over. She clutched the chair and sat on it and then whispered, "You found the hardware store."

"How in the hell did you know that?" Marcus roared.

Alexis said nothing and just cried. She had lost to God. She didn't understand why God would go to such effort to make something happen that didn't need to happen. There could have been another way to find that hardware store. It could have been done without killing her Justin.

From that moment on, she was at war with God.

---

Alexis prohibited her husband from mentioning God or heaven or anything religious at the service, and he kept that promise. The service was good. Marcus said many wonderful things about their son.

The other children and Marcus tried to comfort her by telling her that they loved her—but nothing eased her pain.

That night, Alexis thought about her conversations with Audrey about God. How God didn't meddle in the affairs of humans. People make decisions, good or bad, for themselves. Sometimes God intervenes when humans try to make changes without understanding the ramifications of those decisions.

Justin had to die. Just like her father. Because it was supposed to happen. If neither of them would have died, the future would have been changed. The change was big enough that God intervened. That didn't stop her from being angry. Never again would God be mentioned. God was the cause of all her problems. He should have kept her from reading the book about the future. It was his fault and she was determined to deny his existence and convince everyone that God was irrelevant in their lives. God needed to be wiped out from the memories of the people. This would be her way of getting back at God for all he'd done to her.

# Chapter 70

**New Scranton, June 15, 219 (2279 old calendar)**

It was the middle of June when Logan and Audrey helped Oberon campaign in New Scranton. Audrey felt quite uncomfortable returning, being back here where Logan's parents and her aunt and all the other embassy staff had been killed. If it weren't for Logan's fast thinking, they wouldn't be here listening to this speech. She smiled at him and saw her hero. She shook nervously in front of the old Milestown embassy that had been gutted during the war. Her father vowed to a cheering crowd never to let something like this happen again anywhere, to anyone.

After the speech, Oberon went off to talk with the people who came to hear him. Audrey was content staying with Logan, holding his hand. It was a while before he turned and kissed her. She liked the way he kissed. He wasn't as good a kisser as Eric, but not bad. She closed her eyes. *I need to stop thinking about him.*

Logan called her dad over to the building; some of the crowd followed and watched as Logan spoke. "This place reminds both of us of all of the horrific things that the Feds did to us: physically and emotionally."

Audrey nodded. It was true. This place was horrible and if she had her way, it would be torn down.

Logan reached for her hand and continued, "I want to change that and make it a place that reminds you and me of something wonderful." With that, he bent down on one knee. "Audrey Bushnell," he said, presenting her with a ring, "will you marry me?"

It was truly a surprise and totally unexpected. Why was she all of a sudden thinking about Eric? They weren't meant to be together. The last time she'd seen him was when he decided to run for president. Logan had loved her ever since they were children. They were destined to be together. Weren't they?

Logan held her hand as he waited for an answer.

"Yes!" she said and bent over to kiss him.

**Hazleton, January 2, 220 (2280 old calendar)**

Eric felt bad for Oberon who didn't stand a chance in the election against him. Every mayor of every city supported Eric. Oberon agreed that Eric was a better military leader certainly, but not a political leader? He tried to convince the people to see things his way and get other leaders to follow him. Yet, Oberon, in turn, couldn't convince the people that he had the experience himself that would make him a better president. Eric won by a landslide.

Having just given his inaugural address to the people, Eric was heading around town to attend the many big celebrations. All the people that helped him get elected came along to celebrate his victory at being the first president of the Community Alliance. He could hear music in the streets, wherever he went. People were in good spirits, waving and cheering at him as he passed by. His envoy escorted him to his first stop.

"Mr. President!" Someone called to him, louder than anyone else. The guards blocked the man's attempt to reach him. Ever since the people knew he would be the president, there were many who thought that they could have some time with him to say whatever was on their mind. "Let me through. I need to speak to the president," the man insisted.

Eric ignored the commotion and started to toward the building.

"Mr. President!" the man shouted as loud as he could. "Mr. President! I've found your son."

Over the last two years there had been many people who claimed to have found his family. These people would do anything and say anything just to be able to get near him. And when the lie was found out, they didn't expect to feel his wrath for not being able to deliver what they promised. His family was dead, and he knew how they died. They were merely a memory in perspective of the past and not in a hope of a future that would ever come true.

Eric turned around and looked at the man. The guards had grabbed both his arms and were taking him away.

"Mr. President! I've found your son," he repeated. "Your son, Mr. President! Tommy!"

Eric's heart flipped at hearing his son's name. Could it be?

"Stop!" Eric raised his hand yelling out to the guards. "Bring that man here!"

Eric descended the steps. "You've found my son?" He wanted so desperately for the man to be telling the truth.

"Yes. He says his name is Tommy Lynch. He says you were a colonel in the army of Williamsport. Once he told me that, I made the connection between you and him."

Eric had never publicly made known the names of his children. This had to be Tommy! What other way could this man know the name?

He paced back and forth, trying to decide if this man were telling the truth. "What about my daughter and my wife?"

"He was the only one with this family," the man said.

Eric told the man to go with the soldiers and prepare to travel. It had been two years—his biggest fear was that his son wouldn't recognize him.

"Oh, but your son is here and so is the family he's staying with," the man said.

Eric wasted little time and told everyone to continue with the celebrations. Two guards came along as the man led them to his son. They stopped at a house just outside of the city. The man knocked on the door while Eric and his guards stood outside waiting. A man, woman, and three boys came out and stood at the base of the house. They all looked alike—all but one.

Tommy had grown a lot taller since the last time he'd seen him at Williamsport with his mother and sister.

Eric approached, as the woman bent over to whisper something into Tommy's ear and pointed. With a gentle nudge, Tommy started to walk toward Eric. Eric knelt and looked at his son and saw Camila in Tommy's face. They embraced, but Tommy was unresponsive.

"I'm so glad that you're alive!" Eric said. He kissed Tommy over and over again. But why was he alone? Eric looked into Tommy's eyes and asked, "Where's your sister and your mom?"

"They're dead! I'm sorry, Dad," he blurted out. "There was nothing I could do. Please don't be mad at me. There was nothing I could do."

"Shh, shh. It's all right, Tommy." Eric held on to his son. "Why would you think I'd be mad at you?"

"Because you told me to be the man of the house and I didn't do what I was supposed to do," he cried. "Mommy and Mariam are dead because I didn't do what you told me to do."

Tears rolled down Eric's face. "Come here." Eric held Tommy close. "I'm not mad at you. There was nothing you could have done. I love you. I'll always love you."

After a long moment, Eric stood and thanked the people who'd helped his son. They were rewarded for the unselfish act of taking Tommy into their home and caring for him.

This celebration was far better than any of the other ones planned for today. Thoughts of Camila and Mariam resurfaced; he missed them so much. Here was his son, the only thing left that he had of his wife.

Holding hands, Eric and Tommy walked back to the President's House.

---

Even after two years into Eric's presidency, the days didn't get much easier. He sighed and stared out of the window as the breeze ruffled the leaves in the trees. He found that running a country was harder than running an army. In an army, everyone followed orders. If they didn't, they would suffer the consequences. In a government, it was totally different, and the politics at this level were not the same as they were at the city level. He was mayor of Williamsport, but he had never really ruled that city. That role was given up, to become the president. It may have been a better idea to have learned what it took to run a city before making the leap to lead a country, he mused.

The day had gone smoothly. No big issues to resolve; nothing that needed his immediate attention. But by the afternoon he'd done enough work for the day and decided to go see what Tommy was up to. The kitchen staff said they'd seen him playing out in the back of the palace. Heading outside, found him by the fence talking with a woman. She was black with long, wavy hair. It didn't take long to recognize who it was. The cream-colored dress she was wearing was not one made in Milestown; the cut was definitely a trademark of Williamsport. He liked the way It looked on her, accentuating her curves. She waved as he approached.

"Hey, Dad, look! This is Audrey. She says you two were really good friends." His voice fluctuated making him sound like he swallowed a frog. Tommy was growing up. Soon he would be a man; in a lot of ways, after all he'd been through, he already was.

"Yes," he said reaching the fence. "I thought we were *still* good friends." He took Audrey's hand and smiled. She still had that same glow about her that made anyone feel happy to be around her. "I'd give you a hug, but the fence is keeping me from doing that."

"That's okay. I just happened to be passing and I saw Tommy and decided to stop and chat. I suspected that he was your son." She smiled and they just looked at each other for a few long moments.

"Just passing by? All the way from Milestown?" Eric finally managed to say, his voice a little hoarse.

"Well, to be honest, I'm here to build a temple. What better place than the capital to have the people learn about God? Wouldn't you say?" Her short, shrill laugh clued him in to her nervousness.

"Why didn't you come and visit with us when you got here? You could have stayed with us while you did what you needed to do."

"I'm staying with a family not far from here. I was going to come and visit after I finished the temple." She winked at Tommy.

"You should come and visit when you get the chance," Eric said. "I hear you're engaged now. Congratulations. Tommy and I would love to come to the wedding whenever you decide to have it."

"Of course," she said curtly.

It was apparent from the response that she had no intention of inviting him. Why not? Weren't they still friends? Was it because he won the election against her dad?

A moment of uncomfortable silence followed.

"So where is your fiancé? I would have thought he'd be here to help you."

"He's still in Milestown planting the new crops before the month ends."

Eric stared into her almond-shaped eyes. "So, he left you all alone."

"Pretty much. But I always have someone to talk to. Look, I'm talking with you," she said with a strained laugh.

It seemed awkward to talk with her. It wasn't like old times—he had a new life here, and she was with Logan. An unwelcome wave of nostalgia washed over him at the thought of their first encounter.

"It's getting close to dinner and I came out here to find Tommy. If you don't have any plans, maybe you'd like to join us?"

Audrey smiled. "And I guess you expect me to wash the dishes afterward," she quipped. It seemed they were both thinking about times long past. Was she a mind reader? It elated him to no end that she even remembered a more carefree time. A time they'd shared. A time that was special. And more importantly, she hadn't lost her sense of humor.

"You know where I stand on that issue," Eric teased. "But you won't have to worry about that. I'm the president, remember? I have a kitchen staff that does things like that for me now. So, what do you say?"

"I need to do a few things at the temple, but yes, I'd love to join you two."

"Okay then," Eric said, his heart lighter than air. Then a thought came to mind. "Tommy, do you want to go and help Audrey finish whatever she's working on?"

Tommy shrugged his shoulders. "You want me to work? I can come and watch while you work."

Audrey's eyes opened wide. "Oh my god, Eric! He's so much like you."

"I think *you* were the one that wanted to watch *me* wash the dishes," he corrected her.

Audrey completed her tasks at the new temple, returning with Tommy to the Presidential Palace. A guard let them in, and Tommy led her to the dining area and told her to sit on the right side of the table.

"A guest, especially someone who was important, always sat on the right side of the president," he said.

She smiled and did as Tommy asked. A few minutes passed and then Eric came in and greeted them, kissing Audrey on the cheek. She didn't expect that. It felt good.

"What took you guys so long?" Eric asked as he sat at the head of the table.

"It just took me longer to finish than I thought. I did everything by myself while *someone* just watched." She winked at Tommy and then looked out at an empty table. "So, what are we eating?"

"Lo Mein," Eric said.

"My favorite!" Tommy said rubbing his hands together.

"I don't think I've ever eaten that."

"You've eaten something similar," Eric said.

A server emerged with a big bowl of noodles.

She stared at it. "Isn't that spaghetti?"

"Close," Eric said.

"It looks like spaghetti."

"Spaghetti uses tomato sauce," Eric explained. "Lo Mein is just noodles, cabbage, and onions."

The server scooped the food from the bowl and placed some on each of their plates. Audrey twirled some on her fork and popped it in her mouth. She wasn't quite sure which she liked better, the lo mein or the spaghetti. But it was close. She smiled through a mouthful of food.

Audrey took a sip of her wine.

"Good wine, isn't it?" Eric said, as Audrey drank the last of her glass.

"I've had better, actually," she replied.

"Oh!" Eric seemed shocked at the response. "Excuse me, Ms. World Traveler, or should I say, Mrs. World Traveler?"

She laughed. She was about to respond but resisted the urge and instead settled for a grin, studying his face.

"So, I guess you don't want any more of this inferior wine," he said holding up the bottle.

"I didn't say that." She giggled, holding out her glass.

He poured the wine. Her breathing became shallow and fast. A light perspiration was forming on her forehead. Was it getting warm in here? She brought the glass to her lips, taking another sip. He was handsome. But she needed to remember that he was the president and she was with Logan.

"So, tell me, Princess of Milestown," he teased, breaking the spell, "where did you have this glass of wine that was so much better than what you just drank here? And in case you didn't know, this wine comes from the Poconos."

She looked into his eyes, then brought them down to look at her glass as she twirled it between her fingers. She remembered the time she stayed with Eric and couldn't think of a time they had wine together. She brought the glass back up to her lips.

"Well?" Eric said.

"Hmm." She cleared her throat. "Benjamin Franklin had a wine that tasted so sweet. He said it came from the vineyards of a place called France. In a City named Champagne" She caressed the glass with her fingers. "Do you know this place?"

"Yes, I do, but I've never been there. I've heard claims that they make the best wine. But I don't know. The stuff here is pretty good."

"Can we do something else besides talk about boring stuff?" Tommy complained, sitting back in his seat, arms crossed. His voice sounded funny as it went from a high pitch like a woman's, to a low, manly, husky voice. Audrey started laughing. Tommy didn't seem to like being made fun of. He stuck out his bottom lip and shrugged his shoulders.

"Oh, Tommy, I'm not laughing at you. It's just that your voice sounds funny. Don't be sad. That happens to all the boys your age. To your dad too, I'm sure."

Tommy looked over to his dad who nodded.

"What would you like to do?" she asked him.

"We could play a game called crazy eights."

"Will you teach me how to play?" she asked.

"Sure." Tommy went to get the cards and came back so quick it was as if he hadn't left. "Are you going to play too, Dad?"

"Sure, I'll play, if you guys don't mind losing."

They played many games. Tommy won half of them and Eric won the other half. They were ruthless never letting Audrey win once.

"I think I'm finished playing," Audrey said after losing for the tenth time. "It's getting late and I need to be going."

"We have an extra room if you want to stay with us tonight," Eric suggested.

"Ooh! Stay! Please!" Tommy screamed. "If you stay, we can play more games tomorrow."

"I can't just play games all day. I have things to do," Audrey laughed.

"So, spend the night and tomorrow do whatever you need to do. And then come back for dinner. We can play games after," Tommy insisted.

"That does sound tempting, but—"

"Please!" Tommy cried. "Just tonight and tomorrow. Just two days. Please!"

"I think your father is teaching you how to be persistent." she said.

"What can I say? Being around a beautiful woman makes us go crazy," Eric said raising his glass of wine.

Audrey put her head in her hand as she rested her elbow on the table, staring at Tommy. Finally, she took her glass of wine and finished it off. "Okay," she gave in.

"Yay!" Tommy screamed out.

"But only tonight and tomorrow night. Just two days and no more."

Eric chuckled. "Didn't you say the same thing to me once?"

She shook her head and smiled. "I promise no more than two days."

Eric smiled. "We'll see."

# Chapter 71

Audrey stayed a week at the presidential palace. The plan was to stay in Hazleton several months to teach people about God, not to stay with Eric and Tommy. At night they all played a game or two. When it was time for Tommy to go to bed, she would give him a motherly hug, then talk with Eric late into the night about anything. It didn't matter what.

But now Logan was coming up from Milestown. He would be jealous knowing that she was spending her nights at the presidential palace. Her time with Eric and Tommy needed to come to an end. She would need to leave in the morning and return to her lodgings with the other family.

"Too bad you didn't save the last bottle of wine for today," she said, sipping her glass of water.

"I didn't know you would stay this long. I thought it was just going to be two days!" Eric grinned.

"Tommy is like a magnet. He's so easy to fall in love with."

The look Eric gave made her shiver from the top of her head to the tip of her toes. He wanted to say something, but in the end decided against it. She lowered her head, emotion eating her up inside. If he stared too much longer in her eyes, he'd see right through her and know that Tommy wasn't the only one she was in love with.

---

It felt like the first time she'd been with him. His presence was so overpowering. She wished it would never stop, but like all good things, it had to come to an end.

As she rolled off him and lay on one side of the bed, she turned on her side and started to caress his hairless chest. She tangled her legs with his.

Sunlight crept in through the parted curtains. They had been up all night. She kissed him and then stared into his grey eyes.

The thought of Logan shot through her and guilt overwhelmed her. Putting her face in her pillow she cried out, "What have I done?"

Yet even though she felt guilty being with Eric, the desire to be with him was even stronger. This was where she was supposed to be, but she was engaged to Logan. It wasn't right being here with Eric.

She turned on her back and lay next to him.

"Leave him," he said looking at her. "You don't love him. Staying with him is not fair to him. He needs to find someone who truly cares for him."

"But I do care for him! I'm engaged, aren't I?"

"You're in denial. If you loved him, why are you here with me? If you loved him, you should be married already, but you aren't."

His words struck hard. Every time Logan wanted to set a date she would postpone it because she wasn't ready. She turned over and looked up into the ceiling. "I don't know what to do. I don't want to hurt him."

"But it's okay to hurt me?"

"You're a stronger person than he is." She turned and saw his eyes shrink and teeth grit, making her want to back away. She didn't mean to say it that way.

"You really didn't mean to say something that stupid, did you?" Eric got up and out of the bed.

"Eric, you don't understand. Logan can't handle me leaving him. He would crumble. I'm his whole world."

"What are you talking about? What do his feelings have to do with you and me? You either want to be with him or you want to be with me." Audrey could see a dangerous pulse pounding beneath Eric's jaw—she'd never seen him so upset. "Go! Or stay. If you don't want to be with me then leave but do it because it's what you *want* to do and not because you feel obligated." His nostrils flared, and his mouth formed into a thin, cruel line. If it wasn't Eric, she'd be scared out of her wits right about now.

Audrey needed to leave and fulfill her promise to Logan. But leaving would be the hardest thing she'd ever had to do. Getting off the bed, she turned away from him. Without a word she picked up her clothes to get dressed in another room. No way could she speak right now and risk him noticing how devastated she really felt. A few glances at him revealed his anger. She gave him a departing kiss on the cheek.

Eric turned and grabbed her wrist. Her clothes fell to the floor.

She tried to free herself from his grip. "You're hurting me," she cried.

He stared deep into her eyes. "If you leave now, if you decide you want to be with him and not me, don't come back here thinking we're still friends. I don't ever want to see you!" He tossed her arm and turned his back to her.

Those words made something inside her crumble. She should never have come here to this city, to see him. It was a mistake.

With one last look at Eric, she picked up her clothes, and left the room.

# Chapter 72

Some members of Eric's cabinet expressed to him that they couldn't understand why he would be irritated at the smallest of issues. The country was running better than planned. Congress supported pretty much every decision his office proposed. Yet the meetings were stressful for everyone. It took so long just to calm him down and get the meetings back on track.

Eric was in his office reading a bill he had planned with one of the representatives from the Western Fed territory. The bill allowed the Community Alliance to impose a property tax on all citizens that owned land. It was long and boring, and unlike his sister, he didn't understand most of the legalese.

Tommy came into the room looking rather nervous. Eric stopped what he was doing to pay attention to his son. Something was wrong. Something happened and Tommy was afraid his father would get upset. Eric was proud that his son would confide in him and asked Tommy to tell him the problem.

"Just tell me what you did, and we'll deal with it," Eric encouraged.

"I didn't do anything," Tommy responded, his tone defensive. After a pause he said, "I know you've been mad at everyone. And I know it's because of Audrey."

"How do you know this?" *Since when did you grow up and become a wise man?*

"I saw her after she stopped coming here. She said she couldn't see me anymore."

He always looked at his relationship with Audrey as just between her and himself. He hadn't thought about how Tommy felt. Telling him what was happening was probably a better solution than just brushing it off and not explaining anything. Of course, Tommy wouldn't understand why Audrey wasn't coming back.

"I should've told you she wouldn't be coming back. Is this what's bothering you?"

"No," Tommy said. "I came in here to tell you that she's here. She's downstairs waiting to talk with you."

This was a shocker. She'd been with Logan as recently as yesterday. This wasn't about them. It was about politics, about some kind of favor. Not a problem. Listen to what she had to say and then tell her to discuss the issue with her representative. Tommy could go back and tell her that. But Eric thought it best to do it himself.

She was downstairs in the foyer, sitting on the butler bench fidgeting the dress with her hands. He stepped toward her noticing the tears on her face. When he approached, she stood. Her hands trembled slightly. Whatever she had to say would be hard.

"I explained why I couldn't be with him," she said, trying to stay calm. "That I was in love with you." She took in a deep breath and began to cry. Tears streamed down her cheeks and dripped onto the floor. "I'm not engaged anymore, Eric. I left Logan. I left him for you."

**February 12, 228 (2288 old calendar)**

The cities that made up the Community Alliance had expanded, and by the end of Eric's second term, several new cities had joined the union. As president of a new government, Eric created the Patent Office to give people the incentive to create new inventions. Metallurgy progressed, which brought back some form of indoor plumbing. A program was started which made sure every citizen was taught to read and write—not just the elite.

Eric had been president for two terms, and like the first president of the United States, George Washington, he decided not to go on after his second term in office. He retired and went back to his home in Williamsport. He talked with Audrey about using the timepiece to go back in time. She didn't have any aspirations of traveling and only wanted to stay in this time period. But Eric wanted to visit the years he knew as a child, but he couldn't go back to a time where he already existed. The thought of going back to visit his sister and his other relatives in Milestown kept coming back up in their conversations. Time traveling would require being in Milestown. Walking there from Williamsport in that time period would be extremely dangerous. 2060 was a hostile period for his family and he didn't want to take the chance that something awful might happen to him, especially now that Audrey was having their third child. This was where he wanted to be. This was home.

Eric had no aspirations of staying in politics or of returning to the military. Many tried to convince him to continue to stay in public life, but none were able to change his mind. He was tired of constantly trying to persuade people to his point of view. The military was easier, yet he was tired of waging war on others. Someone else would have to do that from now on. He just wanted to spend the rest of his days with his children and new wife.

He endorsed Audrey's father, Oberon, for president and campaigned for him in the southwestern cities. Unfortunately, the mayor of the Poconos, Mayor Chatag, was able to convince the people that he would be a better leader and won the presidential race.

After three failed attempts at becoming the president, Oberon remained home and continued to be the mayor of Milestown, which he ruled until his death in 246.

When news reached Audrey and Eric of Oberon's death, they came to Milestown with their family to participate in the ceremony which lasted several days. As they sat in the front, near the casket, one of the councilmen came over to the ex-president and his wife.

"Mrs. Lynch. I'm so sorry for your loss. We all thought he would be Mayor forever." He said with a smile. "I'm so sorry he didn't become president of the Community Alliance. We all voted for him here in Milestown."

"Thank you," Audrey said, tears coming down her cheeks.

"You know, the other council members and myself were thinking…" he paused looking at her.

"Thinking what?" she looked up at the councilman.

"We thought that maybe… maybe you would be the next mayor."

"Me?" she said, touching her chest with her hands, her voice an octave higher.

"You are legally the next successor in line to assume the role of Mayor. Plus, you're married to the former president, the first president of the Community Alliance. The people of this city would love you even more. You are the right person to be mayor of this great city."

"Thank you, councilman Harper. I may be the daughter of royalty, and now married to the ex-president of the Community Alliance, but I'm not the right person to lead Milestown."

We think you are, but if that's what you wish…"

"That's what I wish."

Eric, Audrey and their family were invited back to Milestown to participate in an historical event. Eric was proud to watch as his wife gave the keys of the city to the first elected mayor of Milestown.

# Chapter 73

Williamsport, April 23, 276

Audrey had been living in Williamsport for most of her adult life. She missed Milestown and the Great Bay. She missed the sheer cliffs that rose high into the sky along the coast and hid the cove with the metal cave. One day, if not already, someone would find the cove and the metal cave and figure out the code to get inside. Would the clock still be keeping time?

The moments she experienced in 1776 came to mind, making her smile. Philadelphia in 1776 was a wonderful and terrible place at the same time. There were so many conversations Ben and Tom had about the future.

Lilly emerged in her thoughts. She was sorry that those horrible people killed her. If not for Lily, she would never have been able to escape, and would never have made the promise to God, nor would she have been guided by God to be helped by Nathan and his family. It was a blessing that his family aided her. She wondered whatever had happened to him, his wife, Ruth, and his daughter? Did they have any more kids? She could almost see six-year-old Elsie standing right in front of her. What kind of woman had she grown up to be? And what became of Joseph? Did he eventually marry Sarah and have a family of his own? She never thought of going back after she had left. Now a twinkle of curiosity floated through her mind. She still had the papers Benjamin Franklin prepared claiming her to be free.

She had gone to find a man and ultimately ended up finding God.

Though no one else had talked with God directly, many claimed to have had visions from God. It was He who had saved them from the Feds. It was He who had given her people new commandments to follow, and these commandments were put into the new constitution of the Community Alliance.

She thought about her one-time best friend, Logan, and regretted how it had ended. That they had stopped being friends. But she could understand why that had to happen. She had left him for the same man, twice. The last she'd heard, he had traveled well past Williamsport and settled in Appalachia. She hoped that he had a wonderful life and wondered if he was still alive.

A paid servant brought her an ice-cold glass of water. She pushed down on the ice and watched it float back up. It reminded her of her husband, who she missed so much. She reminisced about all the adventures they'd had together and could still remember the first day they met, and how he wanted her to take off her clothes so he could see her naked. She loved his confidence and missed his wit. The night before he passed, he told her that he missed his hometown, driving a car, watching TV, and seeing ice floating in a glass of water. She wished he were here now so he could see how his presidency inspired the people to invent all over again some of the things that everyone used to take for granted; so he could see ice floating in water once again.

His country loved him, and they had built him a beautiful monument. Eric would never be forgotten.

The entire family came together at her request. She looked at her seven children and saw so much of Eric in all of them. Camila lived on in Tommy, even though she had never met his mother. Tommy had grown up to have the exact happy-go-lucky personality of Tom. She was happy that he'd been named after him.

The room filled to capacity with all of her children and grandchildren and great-grandchildren. She motioned to her grandson, Sadep, asking him to get some paper and pencils. The little boy nodded.

Her family waited for her to speak. "I want to tell you something," she finally said. All eyes were on her. Everyone in her family had great respect for her. "Sadep, I want you to be the scribe," she said.

"It would be an honor, Grandmother," he said, bowing his head.

She hadn't gotten used to being called grandmother. Why couldn't they just call her Audrey? It was a trivial dilemma and nothing she would put too much thought into.

"I grew up in Milestown," she started, "When I was younger, I used to play along the cliffs of the Great Bay. I had heard stories about a metal cabin, but never believed them to be true..."

Audrey was a good narrator. She held them all spellbound by recounting the adventures she had gone through. It took her all of two hours to tell the story. Not one grandchild or great-grandchild complained about being hungry or bored or needing to relieve themselves.

"God sent me to the past, to another world, to bring him back here to this world," she said. "God is with us again." Silence reigned and all eyes were on her. "This is important!" she continued. "This is what makes us who we are. This is part of our history."

She wondered as everyone sat listening to her: would these people remember her after she died? Would they even care about what she did?

She smiled as God spoke to her.

"Yes. They will."

# Epilogue

**Milestown, April 23, 378**

Ealdred sat on a cement bench in a large dining hall, eating his afternoon meal of cornbread with vegetable soup. Slits on the walls provided a small amount of light to enter the room, but it was the candles against the walls and on chandeliers that made it light enough to see. Spilling some soup, he wiped his grey robe surreptitiously. He always felt more haphazard, scruffier than the other Lynchian priests sitting with him at the table, despite wearing the exact same robes, the same bright orange belt.

Today the meal was better than most other days, especially the cornbread which tasted sweet. Several priests talked about time travel and how they didn't believe it could possibly be done.

"And why are you even bringing this up?" Ealdred joined in.

"It's in his journal," Oberon, one of the priests, said, holding the journal out.

Ealdred wiped his hands with a cloth napkin and moved his soup to the side. He took the book and read a paragraph:

*I don't know how many timepieces my father built: four maybe. Dad and I had one. Audrey had one too, but it got destroyed in 1776. I gave her another one at the house. I don't understand how she got the one that had originally been placed in the vault. Maybe Dad went to the future to put it in the vault for Audrey to find.*

Ealdred looked at the blank plain brown journal cover. "Where did you find this?"

"It was in the library," Oberon said. "It was hidden behind a bookshelf." Oberon watched as Ealdred looked through the journal. "Do you think it's genuine?"

"That book is all hype to make Eric Lynch more than he was," one of them said. "He performed miracles that God told him to do to show his people that God existed. Why make up a tale about time travel?"

"What if it is true?" Ealdred asked. "It might be possible to travel through time. God willing. There are stories that say his wife Audrey also traveled through time. That's how they met."

The other priests gave him disbelieving looks as they got up from the bench to go to the temple and say their prayers. The journal stayed with Ealdred. He wanted to believe that the book was indeed genuine, that Eric and Audrey Lynch had traveled through time and that eventually Eric Lynch travelled to 266 and made it his home.

What happened to the timepiece he had? What did he find in this world that made him want to stay here?

# Timepieces

Ealdred remembered the fables of how his second wife, Audrey Lynch, found the timepiece in the metal cave by the hidden cove, and the riddle that opened the door to a box where the timepiece was waiting for her. Glancing through the book didn't reveal any riddles that might hint at where Mr. Lynch had left the timepiece.

---

He decided to travel to Williamsport in hopes of finding something that would prove Eric Lynch had traveled through time. The city was modern and much bigger than Milestown. It was this city that made Eric Lynch who he was, and they decided long ago to make his home an historical landmark.

The house he lived in was a simple structure made of adobe. The furniture here had placards that mentioned what the items were and what they were used for. It was interesting to note that the only original items in the house were the beds that Mr. Lynch and his family slept on and the table they ate at. Everything else was imported from New America.

The eating table seemed out of place. It was made of wood, which even by today's standards was a scarce commodity. Another odd thing was that the base of the table was extraordinarily thick. He circled it and found a piece of wood on the side that looked odd in the way it was attached to the table; as if it were not meant to be there. The piece was secure and wouldn't budge. Ealdred applied his weight to try to loosen it.

*Snap!*

The sound resonated across the room and people turned and looked in his direction. He smiled and acted as if nothing had happened. There was an opening where the piece had come off large enough for his hand to fit. Without hesitation, he felt inside the opening and found nothing.

He pulled his arm back... but it wouldn't come out. Panic hit him as he yanked and yanked causing the table to tilt vigorously. A small object bounced against his arm.

"Ahem." The curator stood directly behind him.

Ealdred jumped, causing the table to lift up and fall back on the stone floor with a loud thud attracting unwanted attention.

"What are you doing?" the curator asked in an agitated tone.

Ealdred stared at the curator. *God, help me please!*

"This is a museum. No one is allowed to touch anything," he said sternly. "You know an Audrian priest wouldn't have done something like this."

Ealdred winced at the bigoted remark. He decided to play naïve and keep any comebacks to himself.

"I'm sorry," Ealdred said trying to free his arm. "I saw this piece of wood that looked like it was coming off and I tried to fix it. I saw a hole in the table and my curiosity got the better of me and my arm got stuck."

"That piece of wood came off the table?" the curator asked, inspecting the object. "It looks like it was broken off."

Ealdred had no intention of lying to the man, but at the same time wasn't going to admit that he broke it. He said nothing. Calming down he was able to slip his hand out of the opening and without anyone noticing, put the object into his pocket.

Fixing an apologetic look on his face, he took the piece of wood from the curator and put it back on the side of the table. The piece kept falling off and wouldn't stay in place. After several failed attempts, the piece was placed on top of the table. He stood up, smiled at the curator, and walked out, giving himself some distance from the museum before he took out the timepiece to examine it. The slick, grey object wasn't heavy. It was made from a material he had never seen before. Pressing the black button caused a display to light up showing July 8, 1989. He closed his eyes and imagined traveling through time and wondered what Eric's world must have looked like.

The only button not pressed was the blue button. He froze. Is this thing real? Just finding the device should have been enough excitement for one day. But curiosity outweighed his conservative senses. He pressed the blue button and found himself in a city alive with people and noises and things he had never seen before.

A loud noise blasted from behind which surprised him, and he spun around quickly. There was a shiny black object before him, with wheels and a window, with a person sitting inside looking at him.

The man stuck his head out the side and screamed, "Where the hell did you pop out of? Get off the street, idiot!"

The loud blasting sound roared again. *Honk!* Ealdred put his hands to his ears and stood there. The noise was deafening.

"Move already!" the man said and then made that awful sound once more.

Ealdred saw people walking on the white stones on either side of the street and stepped up onto them moving out of the machine's way. The angry man passed by, holding up his hand, curling his fingers in a peculiar way which Ealdred was sure was not a greeting.

Trees, distanced at regular intervals, lined both sides of the street. Other larger trees with small branches at the top and no leaves had ropes that were attached between them. There were many buildings along the street with large windows with letters on them. As he turned the corner, the smell of food drifted into his nose. Nothing revealed where the smell came from. Moments passed before it became more intense. Up ahead a man went into one of the buildings. Ealdred followed.

Inside people sat at tables, made of wood, eating foods he'd never seen before. Servants walked among those seated bringing them their meals. The smells were delicious and sparked a palatable curiosity to his senses. The temperature felt much cooler here than the warm air outside.

An attractive lady with slanted eyes stood next to a podium and greeted him, then said, "How many?"

"How many?" He didn't understand what she meant.

"Are you alone or with others?"

"I'm alone."

A man came up to the young woman and whispered something into her ear. She stopped smiling at Ealdred. The man turned to him and asked, "Excuse me, sir. Do you have money to pay for your meal?"

"Money?" Ealdred asked, thinking that this was probably the owner of the cafeteria. He reached into his pockets. "I have twenty dollars."

The owner looked at what Ealdred showed him and said. "That's not twenty dollars."

Ealdred looked at the money and said, "Yes, it is."

"I'm afraid I'm going to have to ask you to leave."

"Is this worth anything?" Ealdred asked. The food the people were eating at the tables made his stomach rumble.

"Not around here."

"I can work for food," Ealdred said. "I can clean the tables or wash the floors and windows."

"I'm afraid not." The man stepped to the door and opened it.

Ealdred walked away and smiled as he said, "God bless you."

"What a nutcase," the man said within earshot as Ealdred walked out the door. "You got to watch out for people like that. They pretend that they don't know anything."

Ealdred had no clue where Mr. Lynch might have gone when he came here. He probably wanted to remember a time that he knew as a youth. Ealdred walked around and finally got to the capitol building of Williamsport. It looked the same here as it did in his time. They had preserved it all these years.

He sat under the shade of a tree near the building and looked up to see small black creatures flying in and out of the trees. This place, this time, amazed him. It differed so much from the future. It was beautiful, although he had reservations about the noises.

People walked by and stared at him, while others ignored him. One woman in particular approached and gave him a piece of paper. Ealdred nodded as he took it. The paper was off white and had green and black markings on both sides. The number one was written on all four corners. Flipping it over showed a portrait of a man's face. On the bottom, it read "One Dollar." He understood why the man in the cafeteria didn't want to take his money. Did this dollar have any value? Probably not that much since the person who gave it to him had no problem relinquishing it to a stranger.

Reaching into his pocket, he took out the timepiece. How amazing that a single man could put together such a wondrous device. The display on the timepiece was different: March 23, 2478. He stood, then pressed the button and found himself back in Williamsport—the world that he knew. The capitol building was the only thing from these two times that had not changed all that much. The numbers now appeared as when he found the device. Passing his finger over the display changed the date. The different places in time that he could witness, the events that had happened long before the last three hundred and seventy-eight years in the history of the world he knew, called to him to come visit and stay for a while. As he fumbled through the dates on the disc, he remembered a part of Mr. Lynch's journal that said, "Wherever you are in time is where you're supposed to be."

"There are so many choices," he said to himself, changing the date on the timepiece. "God, help me make the right one."

He finally stopped, then stared at the display.

"Go," a voice said to him. He looked around and saw no one.

Today would be the first day of a new beginning. Wherever he went would be where he was meant to be.

"By the will of God!" he said aloud.

Then without another word, he pressed the blue button on the grey disc and found himself in a whole new world.

## Timepieces by Person
$TP_a$—Timepiece that Thomas used
$TP_b$—Timepiece that Alexis used
$TP_c$—Timepiece that Audrey got from Eric
$TP_d$—Timepiece that Eric used

### Thomas Lynch
$2052^{TPa}$→ $1^{TPa}$→ $2052^{TPa}$→ $1787^{TPa}$→ $2052^{TPa}$→ $1776^{TPa}$→ $2276^{TPa}$→ $2060^{TPa}$→ $2276^{TPa}$→ $2268^{TPa}$→ $TP_A$ Destroyed

### Audrey Bushnell
$2276^{TPb}$→ $1776^{TPb}$ → Plantation owner takes it and disappears. $TP_b$ is assumed destroyed. Tom gives Audrey his timepiece. $1776^{TPa}$→ $2052^{TPc\&a}$→ $1776^{TPc}$→ $2276^{TPc}$→ Gives $TP_C$ to Tom who gives it to Alexis

### Eric Lynch
$2052^{TPd}$→ $2268^{TPd}$→ $2031^{TPd}$→ 2268 →uses it again in $2276^{TPd}$ →$1776^{TPd}$ →$1989^{TPd}$→$1776^{TPd}$ → $2276^{TPd}$→ Left in Eric's table

### Alexis Lynch
$2060^{TPc}$→ $2276^{TPc}$→ $2060^{TPc}$→ Puts $TP_C$ in cabin

### Ealdred
$2478^{TPd}$→ $1989^{TPd}$→ $2478^{TPd}$→ unknown years$^{TPd}$→ destroyed in 1066

## Timepieces by Chronological Order
(Linear timeline based on first use)

### Timepiece A (Tom's Timepiece)
2052(Tom) → 1(Tom) → 2052(Tom) → 1787(Tom) → 2052(Tom) → 1776(Tom) → 2052(Audrey) → 1776(Audrey) → 2276(Tom) → 2060(Tom) → 2276(Tom) → 2268(Tom) → Destroyed by soldiers

### Timepiece C (Eric's and Ealdred's Timepiece)
2052(Eric) → 2268(Eric) → 2031(Eric) → 2268(Eric) uses it again in 2276 →1776(Eric) →1989 (Eric) → 1776(Eric) →2276(Eric) → Found by Ealdred → 2478(Ealdred) → 1989 (Ealdred) → 2478 (Ealdred) → unknown years (Ealdred) → destroyed by Ealdred in 1066

### Timepiece B and D (Audrey's and Alexis' Timepiece)
2052(Audrey) → 1776(Audrey) → 2276(Audrey) → 2060(Alexis) → 2276(Alexis) → 2060(Alexis) → Put in cabin to be found by Audrey → 2276(Audrey) → 1776(Audrey) → Unknown (Plantation owner disappeared)

Made in the USA
Middletown, DE
03 November 2020